I0647556

Murder in Montenegro

By the same author, the first three volumes of the tetralogy:

TO KILL A TSAR, by G. K. George

THE KIEV KILLINGS, by G. K. George

SIBERIAN SECRETS, by G. K. George

Murder in Montenegro

by G.K. George

Illustrations by
George O. Linabury

THESPRING

Washington, DC

Copyright © 2023 by Alfred J. Rieber

New Academia Publishing, 2023

All rights reserved. No part of this book may be reproduced or transmitted in any form or by any means, electronic or mechanical, including photocopying, recording, or by any information storage and retrieval system.

Printed in the United States of America

Library of Congress Control Number: 2023919852
ISBN 979-8-9875893-6-6 paperback (alk. paper)

THESPRING is an imprint of New Academia Publishing

New Academia Publishing
4401-A Connecticut Ave. NW #236, Washington DC 20008
info@newacademia.com - www.newacademia.com

In Memoriam
George O. Linabury

Contents

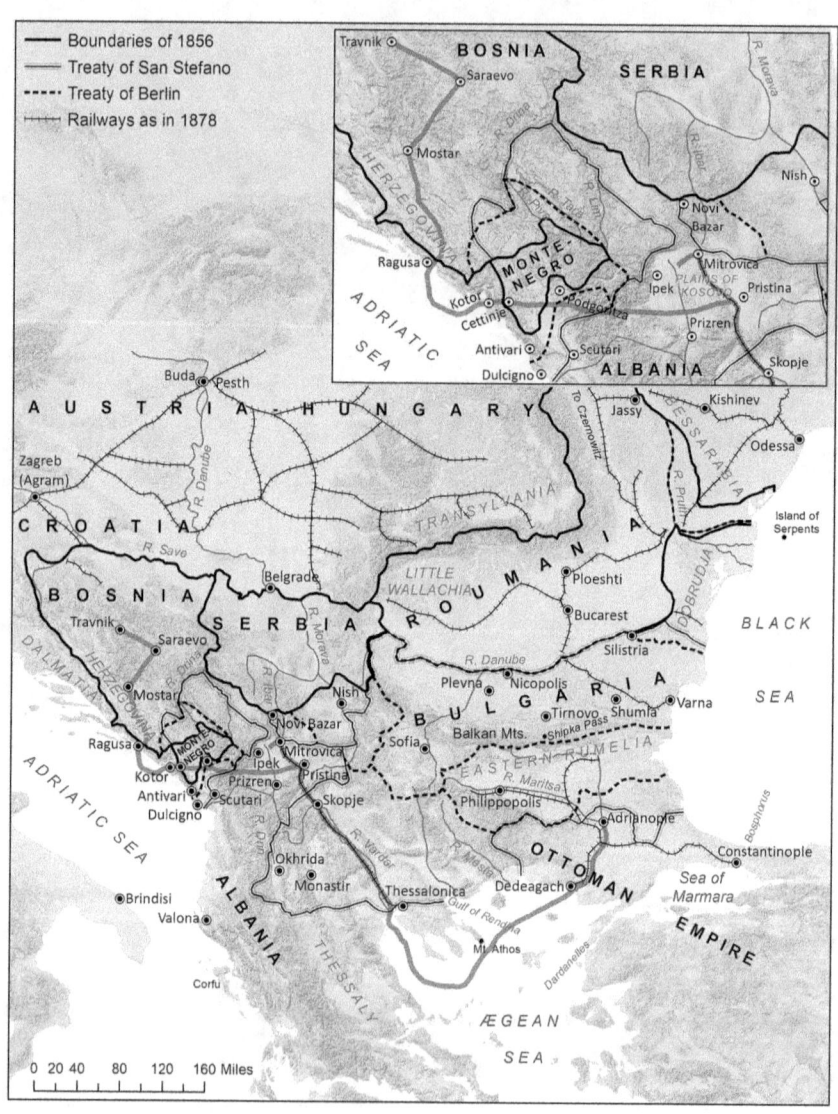

Legend

- Boundaries of 1856
- Treaty of San Stefano
- Treaty of Berlin
- Railways as in 1878

Inset map

Travnik · BOSNIA · SERBIA · Saraevo · R. Drina · R. Morava · R. Ibar · Mostar · Nish · HERZEGOVINA · Novi Bazar · Mitrovica · Ragusa · MONTE-NEGRO · PLAINS OF KOSOVO · Ipek · Pristina · ADRIATIC SEA · Kotor · Podgoritza · Cettinje · Prizren · Antivari · Scutari · Skopje · Dulcigno · ALBANIA

Main map

Buda · Pesth · AUSTRIA-HUNGARY · To Czernowitz · Jassy · Kishinev · BESSARABIA · Zagreb (Agram) · R. Danube · Odessa · CROATIA · TRANSYLVANIA · Island of Serpents · R. Save · BOSNIA · Belgrade · LITTLE WALLACHIA · ROUMANIA · Ploeshti · R. Pruth · Travnik · SERBIA · Bucarest · BLACK · Saraevo · R. Drina · R. Morava · R. Ibar · Nish · R. Danube · Nicopolis · Silistria · SEA · DALMATIA · Mostar · Plevna · BULGARIA · Varna · HERZEGOVINA · Novi Bazar · Mitrovica · Sofia · Tirnovo · Shumla · Ragusa · MONTE NEGRO · Ipek · Pristina · Balkan Mts. · Shipka Pass · Kotor · Prizren · Skopje · EASTERN RUMELIA · Antivari · Scutari · R. Maritsa · Dulcigno · Philippopolis · Adrianople · Bosphorus · Okhrida · ALBANIA · R. Vardar · Constantinople · Brindisi · Monastir · R. Mesta · OTTOMAN · Valona · Thessalonica · Dedeagach · Sea of Marmara · THESSALY · Gulf of Rendina · EMPIRE · Dardanelles · Mt. Athos · Corfu · ÆGEAN · SEA

0 20 40   80   120   160 Miles

Vasiliev's Travels in the Balkans

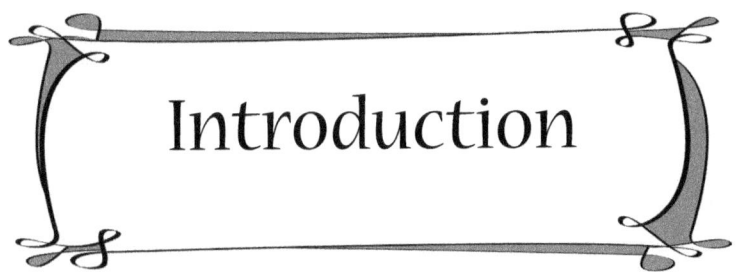

Introduction

Cetinje, Montenegro

"I can tell you frankly, Count, what I won't miss are the head-hunting stories." Alexander Ionin, the Russian minister at Cetinje, Montenegro, leaned forward from the ornately carved back of his Venetian chair and tipped the end of his cigarette into a small silver ashtray standing on the polished surface of a wooden table of the same Venetian design. His servants in the Russian consulate considered his Italianate tastes eccentric, but he was proud of the effect of his furnishings on his guest, the Italian ambassador in Constantinople. Count Luigi Corti nodded slowly in rhythm with the minister's mellifluous, Russian-accented French but his eyes were fixed on the ashtray, reminding him of the main reason for his presence in the Principality of Montenegro, the interest of certain highly placed individuals in Rome in the silver mines.

"Yes, deplorable, *caro mio*," he muttered softly, his own French sounding more like that of Marseilles than Paris. As he half-listened to his friend's familiar recounting of his recent experiences among the Northern Albanian highlanders, his mind wandered from silver mines to the more genial landscape of the great oaken forests where he and the Russian had spent a few pleasant hours hunting. Yes, he thought, glancing up at the menacing stuffed head of a brown bear looming over the entrance to the Baron's study. He would miss this moment of relaxation from the tense atmosphere in Constantinople and the even tenser negotiations at Berlin.

Ionin relished the prestige he would acquire by entertaining Italy's foremost diplomat. To be sure, the man looked more like a Milanese barber, at first glance, than an aristocrat who had been foreign minister in Rome. He was small in stature and rather ugly, Ionin had to admit. Now that he had a chance to study him he changed his mind, describing him to his wife as more Japanese-looking than Italian with his small, piercing eyes and flattened nose. But he was a wily sort and was involved in the most delicate negotiations that might avert war in the Balkans. They managed to get on well enough— their love of Voltaire and intense dislike of Victor Hugo— so long as they avoided politics. Beyond this, their views on their foreign colleagues dovetailed like the exquisitely wrought joints of the Venetian chairs. Their mutual dislike of the Austrian military expert, Lt. Colonel Thömmel, provided an especially rich source of spiteful anecdotes.

Ionin was frank, too, about the distaste with which he regarded his current residence.

"You know, Count that I much preferred Ragusa, although my rank was lower." Ionin had switched to Italian which he also spoke with a pronounced Russian accent.

A servant entered the room bearing a tray with two glasses of *slivovitz*. Ionin welcomed the interruption. It gave him an opportunity to temper his frankness, without abandoning his confidential tone.

Having emptied their glasses in honor of the King of Italy and the Tsar of All Russia, they paused to enjoy the effect. Then Ionin began to spin his embroidered tale.

"The capital of Montenegro is an overgrown village. Prince Nikola sits in his palace and plots to become the leader of all the Serbs. You know of course that the Montenegrins consider themselves more Serbian than the Serbs. No one can deny they are great warriors. But such arrogance! I do my best to restrain the Prince."

Did Corti detect the half truth? Ionin did not notice a change in his features. As he spoke his mind went back to the glorious summer of 1875 when the Serbs and Montenegrins had risen in rebellion. He had given his support to the Montenegrins. But much had changed since then. The Turks had beaten them badly. Ionin had been recalled to Russia. When the Russians finally entered the war, he returned to Montenegro, knowing that he had backed the wrong Slavic horse. Bulgaria had become the odds on favorite of the Petersburg Court.

Corti broke into his recollections. "Yes, but why then have you Russians proposed to hand over to these Montenegrins the Albanian tribes who despise them? They have been neighbors for centuries, and fighting one another most of the time. If it isn't over boundaries, it's over a blood feud."

Ionin sought to mask his disappointment. "I wish I could tell you, Count. But I am not privy to discussions at the highest level of our government. I only know that there are disagreements. Here we are, having won the war against the Turks, but undecided as to what to do with the peace. But you know all this better than I. You sit at the table with the masters of Europe in Berlin where, if I may use a colorful phrase, the fruits of our victory are being picked over by others."

"Not quite fair, *caro mio*. We are trying to save you from your own excesses. Prince Bismarck has assumed the role of honest broker. Your Count Shuvalov is a reasonable man. He is working hard with Lord Derby to prevent a war between you and the British. Yet, I understand that Disraeli and the Queen are all in favor of it. What a tragedy that would be!"

Ionin felt out of his depth. His Italian guest was the official representative of his government at the Congress of Berlin, rubbing shoulders with the great statesmen of the day. And he was stuck in this provincial backwater. What could he say?

"I cannot disagree with you on one thing. My colleague, Count Ignatiev, probably made a serious error at San Stefano."

"You mean by forcing the Turks to surrender so much territory."

"Yes, by creating a big Bulgaria he violated our promises not to create a large Slavic state. He antagonized the British, who see themselves as protector of the Ottoman Empire, frightened the Austrians who fear a big Slavic state and alienated our good Serb allies by ignoring their needs for a port on the Adriatic. Quite a performance."

"Indeed, an untrustworthy man. I agree. A Panslav, like you! But he favors the Bulgarians, while you support the Serbs. As for the Montenegrins, they are pawns in a big game. Perhaps your government has set a little trap for Prince Nikola? Hand over some fierce Albanians to tame— which is impossible—and keep him and his army occupied and more dependent on Russia for subsidies."

Ionin had never thought of it that way. His heart was on the Montenegrin side. But there was no reason to quarrel with Count Corti who seemed to know more about his government's intentions than he did. Or was there something else here, something for the Italians?

The minister decided to bring familiar litany of complaints to an end. "It's the one thing they have in common," he sighed, "the Montenegrins and the Albanians, the taking of heads of the hated Turk, or whoever falls under the curse of the blood feud, this taking of heads of the defeated enemy. It's almost a past-time of theirs."

"Ah, you go too far!" the Count murmured his reproach. "After all, as one of their clan elders said to our English friend Evans, "the French beheaded their king and queen, so who are you — well he meant a European of course —to talk."

The minister summoned up a deep rumble, recognized by all who knew him as the prelude to a burst of laughter. His ample paunch moved up and down in a rhythm of its own.

The Count was about to change the subject when an ear-splitting scream shattered the stillness of the night outside, coming from below the balcony through the parted curtains of the open French door. Both men came to their feet, but Ionin put a restraining hand on the Count's shoulder.

"No so fast, my friend, it could be a trick to lure us to the window. They are very good shots you know, even with their old flintlocks. And now they have Martini-Henry rifles!" The minister rushed into the hall calling on his orderly

"...and take your side arms," he shouted. "Now we'll see," he moved toward the open door and pressed against the wall peering into the darkness as he heard the commanding voice of his orderly ordering a woman who was down on her knees in the street, to remain calm. But his commands were not having much effect. She uttered another piercing scream that shook Ionin to the core.

"What is it?" the Count had joined him leaning out before the minister pulled him back.

"All I need is a scandal just before I leave."

"What is she doing now?" The woman had pushed aside the

restraining hand of the orderly and was fumbling with a large bag that she had placed in front of her, as she wrung her hands and threw back her head as if to scream again. The orderly struck her in the mouth and her head snapped back, then lowered like bull preparing to charge. She ripped open the bag and pulled out a misshapen object which she thrust in the face of the orderly. He recoiled as if he had been shot.

"*Mest'*," she screamed.

"My god, what is that?" exclaimed the Count.

"That, my friend is a head, and she is holding it up to us by the hair as if to accuse us or perhaps to summon our help." He stepped onto the balcony and shouted a few words to the orderly ordering him to bring her into the consulate. At the same time, he reached behind him and pulled down a hand telescope from the nearest bookshelf.

As the woman struggled to her feet, Ionin focused on her features. Distorted as they were, she still appeared to him as the most beautiful woman he had ever seen. Then he lowered his gaze to the horrible trophy which she held arm's length.

She repeated her cry, "*Mest'*!"

"My God," he exclaimed. "It's Grigoriev!"

"What is she screaming?"

"*Mest'*, Count, 'revenge'"

"The head, then, of one of your men?"

"Not mine, but a volunteer with General Chernaiev. A noble Panslav, but an extremist. Worst of all, a man with influential friends at court. This is for me not only a tragedy but a disaster."

Chapter One

Adrianople, Ottoman Empire

"Peace is declared, but the fighting continues." Major Vasili Vasilievich Vasiliev of the Moscow City Police seemed to be talking to himself. But his orderly, Sergeant Serov, fussing over the samovar, knew that this was the beginning of a monologue intended for his hearing as well. Nothing else was expected of him at this point. So he said nothing. He was well attuned to Vasiliev's moods, but this one was more complicated than he could ever remember. It had a great deal to do with the loss of his boyhood friend in the trenches of Plevna where, in the summer of 1877, the Russian army's advance against the Turks had unexpectedly stalled. That was before General Totleben had taken command and broken through the Shipka Pass, bringing the Turks to their knees. Serov may have been born a serf, but Vasiliev had taught him enough when they were boys to understand something of the political jumble that followed the Russian victory. Something was not everything to be sure. Serov knew that Vasiliev was upset about the way things had developed after that. So, a personal loss and disappointment in high politics, enough to feed anyone's bad mood. Even Vasiliev's own triumph in solving the murder of Colonel Firsov and restoring morale to the Danubian Corps in the winter of 1877-78 could not compensate. Serov kept listening for he wanted to know more. It was his best way to learn since his reading skills were not sharply honed, despite Vasiliev's instruction.

Vasiliev's mind had wandered farther and moved in a direction where Serov could not follow. A trick of memory had carried him back to Moscow on that unusually warm day in May 1877, when Ivan, the Iron Colonel had come down from Petersburg to pay an unexpected call. Perhaps it was a gust of wind outside his tent that snapped the canvas like a salute or summons. He often wondered at the way his mind worked. Most of the time he believed he had it under control until what seemed like a random notion interrupted his train of thought. Perhaps someday the scientists would discover how these flashes of insight happened. It mildly disturbed him that here was a mystery beyond his ability to solve. And now the sudden memory of Ivan emerging from his compartment of the overnight train from the capital, a gust of wind almost blowing off his forage cap. The last gasp of a Siberian winter? Or was the sudden tingling down his back a sensation he experienced whenever Ivan summoned him?

"Too early for our traditional dinner at the Slavianskii Bazaar," were the first words out of his mouth. "So let's find a nearby café. Secluded and quiet. I am in your capable hands."

As the cab made its way down Tverskaya Boulevard to Nikolskaya Street, Vasiliev wondered what this sudden descent from the rarified atmosphere of Petersburg might mean for him. Ivan, operating out of a non-descript office of the Ministry of Interior, did not pay social calls. Oh, there was a time, years ago, when their friendship was first cemented, that Vasiliev could look forward to their meetings, the dinners and then the theater, perhaps Shchepkin playing in Ostrovsky. But in the last few years something had changed. Ivan had become more secretive, the dinners rarer and more purposeful. He referred often to affairs of state. And his visits were a signal that he was about to involve Vasiliev in an affair that went beyond the normal duties of an inspector in the crime bureau of the Moscow police.

Over a breakfast of blini and sour cream with strong Turkish coffee, Ivan came to the point quickly. He apologized that "affairs of state" required his immediate return to the capital. He needed Vasiliev's help in a matter requiring great discretion.

"And when was 'great discretion' not required of me?"

"Ah, Vasili, please none of your sarcasm. You know I am obliged to make such official statements." Ivan drained his coffee and ordered another. When the waiter left, he took a deep breath. You may know much of what I am going to tell you, but not everything."

"I can hardly restrain my curiosity."

Ivan shook his head. "How do I tolerate you?" he laughed.

"So, to begin. It looks highly probable, which means almost certain that we will go to war with the Turks over the atrocities against the Bulgarians and in support of the Serbs and Montenegrins. Their revolt has, as you probably do know, has attracted Russian volunteers to fight shoulder to shoulder with their fellows Slavs. Some diplomats are scrambling to head off the disaster. Shuvalov is working in London with Lord Derby. Miliutin at the Ministry of War and Reutern at Finance are warning that we are not ready. But the pressure on the Tsar from the Panslavs among our 'enlightened' public aroused by the press and within the court, right up to the highest level, may prove irresistible. And the Turks will not compromise.

"Now what you do not know is that preparations are under way to strike the Turks on two fronts, across the Danube and in the Caucasus. There are disturbing rumors that the Caucasian Army is riddled with corruption. Unless this is rooted out, the campaign will suffer. Some of us do not trust the local authorities in Tbilisi or the Gendarmes from investigating."

"My antennae are vibrating, Ivan. I know where you are going, and I am not happy with this."

"Hear me out, Vasili."

"Of course, since you are paying for breakfast."

Ivan shook his head again but did not laugh.

"I have been given authority to recruit a trusted officer of the criminal police who can operate outside the normal lines to do the job. You would be fully supported by me. Your appointment to the staff of Grand Duke Nikolai Nikolaevich will be arranged with the approval of the Grand Duke. I need hardly add…that this is a matter of the greatest importance for Russia. Yes, a cliché. But in this case there is no better way of putting the matter."

"You know, Ivan, and I say this just to salve my conscience, once again, that I will do this under protest. I chose the criminal police precisely in order to avoid high politics. You, my friend, persist in frustrating that design. Well, I know it means you have great faith in me and all the rest. But you have to know Ivan that this does not make me a happy man. All right, I have said it. So, I will need Serov as my assistant. That is not negotiable."

Ivan smiled for the first time.

****

The flap of the tent fluttered and dropped. Vasiliev found himself back in Adrianople. Well, one thing had led to another. Success in the Caucasus had not given him his freedom but burdened him with another set of obligations, this one tied to the Danubian Army. And this, he feared would bring nothing but grief. He sensed a tragedy of vast proportions emerging from the great Russian victory over the Turks. Once again he would have to put aside his study of Pushkin. But that was not the worst of it.

"Men die and statesmen decide," Vasiliev was saying. "Now they're sitting in Berlin tearing up the treaty we won by blood." Serov was prepared for a history lesson, but Vasiliev fell silent. Perhaps a glass of tea would loosen his tongue. As an encouragement, Serov sipped his brew from a saucer and pronounced it fit. He had not been happy with the quality of water provided by the supply column. Luckily, he had discovered a source of pure spring water outside the camp on one of his foraging expeditions in search of fresh game. He chuckled as he imagined telling his fellow villagers back home that he had shot more wild fowl than Turks in the great war.

Vasiliev hardly acknowledged his efforts. This was not like him. Serov knew that he would have to wait for Vasiliev to reveal what was troubling him so deeply. He left the tent to survey the encampment. The troops were beginning to break it up; the first detachments were already on the march toward home, leaving Bulgaria and crossing the Danube. He had heard some grumbling among the ranks that they should have gone on to take Tsargrad, as they called Constantinople. Others cursed the English. One young officer who had some education sneered: "We Russians had fought our way to the outskirts of the city, only to see the masts of the English fleet riding at anchor in the Bosporus."

While Serov glanced about, trying to make sense of it all, a Cossack courier rode up demanding to know if this was Major Vasiliev's quarters. Serov acknowledged that it was. The Cossack leaned over the neck of his horse to hand over an envelope bearing the seal of the General Totleben's Headquarters.

Vasiliev tore it open, cursing like a peasant. It always amused Serov to hear the language of his native village spewing forth from the mouth of the bastard son of a nobleman whose mother was from the same peasant stock as his own. It was one of the many things that bound them together in a peculiar intimacy that was unique among an officer and his orderly. This time Serov did not have long to wait for enlightenment.

"A telegram from Ivan warning me that I might be summoned by the Grand Duke to investigate some outrage in Montenegro! Imagine, Serov, Montenegro. A wild country, like the Caucasus. By comparison Bulgaria is the Elysian Fields."

The reference escaped Serov, but he knew better than to interrupt. He felt out of his element since he had accompanied Vasiliev on special missions with the Russian Army. First it had been the Caucasus. Then the Balkans when Russo-Turkish War broke out the previous year. On loan, as he understood it, from the Moscow police force because someone in the high command thought Vasiliev's talents would be useful. And they were right.

"Can a man be too successful in his work? We Russians seem to reward success by piling on more work. Ah, Serov, I fear this war has turned me into a cynic." Vasiliev gulped down his tea. Then he noticed that Serov was waiting for a verdict. "All right, Sergeant, your tea is incomparable. I should have rendered it full honors. But I expect that Ivan's telegram will only have preceded the full bad news. We should be ready for it."

As if to confirm his prediction, a second courier appeared, a staff officer attached to the Grand Duke's entourage. The note was handwritten this time, signed by the Grand Duke himself. So the full treatment, thought Vasiliev. Now he was in for it. A summons to the presence of the tsar's younger brother. Up the social ladder, he thought, only to descend into the dark pool of politics.

The officer accompanied Vasiliev to the tent of the Commander-in-chief of the Russian Army of the Danube where he was ushered into the presence of Nikolai Nikolaevich. Serov stayed behind to pack and wonder at his fate. How many peasants from a village in Moscow Province could boast of becoming a world traveler?

The Grand Duke was gracious as always, standing up from his camp desk to greet Vasiliev. He repeated his appreciation for his service and, with a flourish, handed him a small box containing the Order of St. Anna second class.

"We regret there is not time to organize a formal presentation. You will understand that the Emperor himself would have attended." Vasiliev bowed. Whether this was true or not, he appreciated the sentiment. Still, what was a bit of brightly colored fabric attached to a silver medallion in comparison with what he had lost in this damnable war? At least he was prepared for the shock of his new assignment. Ivan, "the Iron Colonel" as he was known in St. Petersburg, an old friend, could always be counted on to watch Vasiliev's back and to send aloft warning signals when snow was about to fall on his head.

"The murder of Boris Andreevich Grigoriev has stirred some smoldering embers," the Grand Duke explained. "I'll be frank with you, Vasili Vasilich, the life of one man is often measured only by the importance he has assumed in the minds of those who have the ear of my brother, our revered emperor. In this case, the influence is rather weighty. How much do you know about Grigoriev?"

"Only that he was one of the first to volunteer to fight alongside General Chernaiev during the early days of the Bosnian uprising back in 1875. Then, I believe, he stayed on in some political capacity. I heard that it was to back up the claims of the Montenegrins for a port on the Adriatic. He stirred up the Austrians who did not want our friends to have access to the sea."

"Good! You are well-informed. What you may not know, is that he was a regular correspondent of Ivan Aksakov, our irrepressible advocate of liberating all the Slavs. You must know of Aksakov's journalistic, often inflammatory efforts to influence the more susceptible elements of our educated public. Aksakov is married to Anna Fedorovna Tiucheva, lady in waiting to our beloved sister-in-law, the Empress Maria Alexandrovna. I have known Anna Fedorovna for many years and appreciate her intelligence if not always her almost mystical view of Russia's destiny to free the Slavs. I do not know how closely she was acquainted with Grigoriev. Aksakov certainly was. They were both members of the Slavic Benevolent Committees in the 1860s. In any case, Anna Fedorovna was deeply moved by the brutal killing of Grigoriev. She has taken up his cause. For a long time, she has exercised a strong influence on the Empress. So it was no surprise to me when I received a letter from the Empress, requesting that I make a determined effort to have Grigoriev's murderer tracked down and suitably punished."

As he spoke, Nikolai Nikolaevich kept shifting back and forth between French and Russian. Vasiliev had trained himself to listen to speech patterns. It was his way of detecting when a person was dissembling or lying outright. He was also a mimic, instructed by his father's serf, Foma. When he assumed a disguise, as Foma had taught him, he also changed accents and intonations. A new voice was as important as a new appearance. Now he realized that Nikolai Nikolaevich kept reverting to French whenever he spoke about Tiucheva. And there was something else. A softening of the voice. For the moment, at least, he had no desire to speculate, or, to guess what this meant. Guessing was something special in Vasiliev's armory of detection. He had learned the art from Charles Peirce, the American philosopher whom he met in London. But he was not now being called upon to solve this little mystery of the Grand Duke's speech pattern. Nor did he wish to have it solved for him. It was enough to tuck away the impression in his memory.

When Vasiliev returned to his tent, he gave Serov a brief account. "And so we leave in a few days armed with a personal letter of the Grand Duke to the Russian minister in Cetinje, Aleksander Semenovich Ionin. I've heard of him, even more about his brother. They are ardent Panslavs, but favor the Serbs. So we are plunged into high politics, Serov, which, as you know, I try to avoid for fear of drowning. Ah well, one thing I learned from the Grand Duke that gives me hope. The hunting in Montenegro is reputed to be excellent."

Serov nodded, whistled and grunted in his usual style of approbation, then smiled for the first time that day. Vasiliev knew the symptoms. Serov also had news to relate.

"Yes, that fits," Serov paused for effect. "I was talkin' to some rankers while you was hob knobbin' with the greats of this world. They'd been volunteers with the rebels in '75 and then joined up with our regulars in '78. So they'd spent time in Montenegro. They called it by its right Slavic name *Crna gora*, couldn't understand why it got its Italian name. Anyways they told me it was the most beautiful land they'd ever seen. So really like your, what did you say, 'Elysian fields?' But we'd better hurry to see it, they said, for the locals are cutting the big oaks, some centuries old, faster than they can be grown again."

"Well, we've no order to stop the timbering, Sergeant. We Russians are not innocent on that score. God knows it will be hard enough to find out who killed a man two weeks ago in a place we know very little about and where they are still fighting over borders that every major power in Europe is also involved in trying to draw."

Chapter Two

Adrianople

"You have heard many times, I am sure Vasili, Clausewitz's aphorism that 'War is the continuation of politics by other means.'" General Franz Eduard Count Totleben was standing over a large map of the Balkans spread out on a camp table in his tent on the outskirts of Adrianople. Vasiliev followed the general's pointer as it moved west from the city across the Balkan Mountains. "But you see, here, politics is a continuation of war."

"I'm not certain I catch your meaning, Eduard Ivanovich"

"What I mean is that here the fighting never stops. It goes on in tandem with the talks. The two get so damned mixed up with one another that you can't tell where one stops and the other begins." He set the pointer down, sighed and turned to his orderly standing at rigid attention by the entrance to the tent.

"My God, Suchin, don't you have anything else to do. Go check on the horses. We are leaving this place this evening. Major Vasiliev and I are old acquaintances and need to have a private talk."

Suchin flushed, saluted and hurried out of the tent.

"So how is your father? When did you last see him? Now there was a true soldier and we could have used him at Plevna." Without pausing, Totleben continued, toying idly with the pointer as if he wanted to straighten the dotted colored lines that criss-crossed and intersected border lines all over the map. "Well, perhaps even he would be confounded by the politics of the thing." Totleben sighed again. "This brings me to the reason I'm having this private talk with you. Not that I wouldn't have enjoyed a chat. When did we last meet?" Once again he did not wait for an answer.

But Vasiliev remembered. He did not need the snap of a canvas tent flap to remind him of Totleben's speech at the graduation of the Page Corps. The man who had organized the brilliant defense of Sevastopol, only to see the city fall to the British and French, spoke with great force of Russia's renewal but also humility about his own exploits. After the ceremony, Vasiliev had been introduced as one of the top three in the graduating class. The few words Totleben had spoken to him then almost persuaded him to give up his determination to enter the police rather than accept a commission in the Life Guards. "I hope I shall have the pleasure of having you under my command, some day," is what the general had said. Of course, Vasiliev knew that he would not have been singled out had his father not been Count Vorontsov, one of the few living generals Totleben admired. But still, it was an honor, and only now could he repay it.

"Listen Vasili, as I have told you before, it's a pity you did not opt to enter a guard's regiment. Then I could have made you my adjutant. No one could ever figure out why you preferred the ordinary police. But it's too late for regrets." Totleben chuckled as he released the pointer and stared hard at Vasiliev. "My work here is over. But, as I said the fighting goes on, not like Clausewitz would have it. No, this is half hidden, all of it irregular, some of it dishonorable. I understand you've been given the task of clearing up the murder of Grigoriev. Never liked the man myself. But that's not important. It's just a waste of your talent. Even if you succeed, which given the situation as I see it is improbable, you will get no public recognition, perhaps not even another medal. Oh! I don't doubt your abilities, as you surely know. But there are too many powerful interests at stake. I have no inside information that leads me to this conclusion. But all you have to do is look at the map and think of Grigoriev's recent travels as reported by Aksakov's journalistic babble." Totleben picked up the pointer again and waved it as if it were a magic wand.

"Look here. Follow his path. The Dalmatian coast, into Bosnia, across the mountains into Montenegro and beyond to the northern Albanian tribes. So what does this tell us? That he was on some kind of special mission. And who might be interested in the fate of these lands, now that they are being fought over —yes, you see how carefully I choose my words—fought over, I repeat, in Berlin." The pointer passed off the northern edge of the map.

"Austria, Italy, Greece, the Bulgarians, the Serbs and, even the Albanians, though Herr Bismarck does not choose to recognize their existence. And, of course, we Russians and the Turks. The English, too, are involved. They cannot seem to keep their nose out of any crisis. Perhaps the French, as well, because almost everyone else converses in their language. Now you may ask why?" He smiled. "You *must* ask why to see the whole picture."

"You paint a broad canvas, Eduard Ivanovich. Now let's see. I will have to brush up on my languages. French, English and Serbian pose no problem. A bit of work will restore my Italian. My Greek is of the classical variety and I fear Albanian is out of reach"

Totleben chuckled again. "You inherit your sense of humor from your papa. Good, but you can be sure that whatever language people speak to you, they will, shall we say, dissimulate at best. The worst I leave to your imagination."

Vasiliev shrugged. "I did not mean to be frivolous, Eduard Ivanovich. Please continue."

The tent flap snapped open and Suchin poked his face in. "A thousand pardons, Eduard Ivanovich, but a message has arrived from the Grand Duke." Vasiliev looked up, but this time the trigger did not release a memory. The flap of the tent was just another random noise.

Totleben ripped open the envelope. He read the message quickly. "Yes, yes, I'll be there."

He turned to Vasiliev. "You are spared a further lecture in the history and politics of the region. Perhaps you know most of this? Just a few more words. Ionin, our consul general in Cetinje, Montenegro, is a good man but too close to the Italians. Don't trust the Austrians, still less their Hungarian lackeys and beware of the ambitions of Prince Nikola of Montenegro. Aside from the head-hunting tribesmen and Greeks bearing gifts you have nothing serious to worry about." Totleben's smile became more of a grimace.

"Now, the real reason for our little intimate chat. Our leaders are much divided over the future course of our foreign policy. The problems are many. A small group in the Foreign Ministry, who are not in agreement with what is happening in Berlin but are also not wild eyed Panslavs, wants to check Austrian influence. As you know, Vienna has betrayed us more than once. The Austrians are always ready to fight to the last Russian, and then pick up a piece of land here or there. Now they are poised to take over Bosnia and Hercegovina. There may be nothing we can do to prevent this. But our people have to know what resistance they may encounter when Vienna moves in, and how we might keep in touch with it. A delicate mission for you, Vasili. Also probably again no rewards except helping to prevent another war in the future. So I am asking you to investigate the situation on the ground. Get in touch with the local Muslim and Orthodox leaders and find out their intentions. You will report to me by telegraph, using a special code. Here it is. You can explain to Ionin that this is a means of communicating information about the Grigoriev murder.

"I regret the need to rush off. I did not expect this. Of course Vasili, you may choose not to accept this assignment. I cannot order you to do so."

"Your request, Eduard Ivanovich, is for me an order. You have never failed Russia, nor do I wish to do so. Thank you for your confidence." Totleben seized him by the shoulders, embraced him and without a further word left Vasiliev to pour over the map and make some notes. He did not relish the new burden. It smacked too much of spying. But he could not well refuse the hero of Sevastopol and Plevna.

Whenever Vasiliev returned to his quarters, he would involuntarily glance at the saber suspended from the tent pole, Petya's saber, and he would feel a rush of anguish. A vivid flash of memory would carry him back to the moment when Petya fell, mortally wounded in the trenches of Plevna, the saber an extension of his blood-stained arm, pointing toward the Turkish lines. Vasiliev recalled too how he had flung himself down beside his childhood friend in a vain attempt to staunch the wound as a hail of bullets passed over his head, as if Petya's last act had been to save his life by giving his own. Had he cried out and wept over the body? The next few moments were blotted out by a nearby explosion that knocked him unconscious and covered both of them with a thick layer of mud. They dug him out quickly enough to save him from being suffocated. Then he helped to exhume Petya's body and carry him back to the rear during a lull in the fighting. They buried him in the Russian military cemetery that already was crowded with the thousands of men sacrificed in the storming of the fortress.

But the most painful of his duties faced him when he returned to Russia. Tradition dictated that he should present Petya's saber to his father, the Colonel. But Vasiliev was never a slave to tradition, and instead he would place it first in the hands of Irina, Petya's younger sister, in memory of their childhood friendship and innocent games. Petya had always played the role of his faithful comrade-in-arms and Irina their loyal and resourceful nurse while Serov, just freed from serfdom, would serve as his orderly. They were all together for only a few years, but they were the most precious of his youth, and he was convinced of Serov's as well. When he entered the tent, Serov silently observed him, sensing that they both shared the same disappointment at not being sent back to Moscow.

Every night Serov would prepare the samovar. They would set out the chess set that Vasiliev's father Prince Vorontsov had given him on his tenth birthday. "It is more than a game, Vasya," he had said. "It trains the mind to anticipate the actions of others." Vasiliev had taught Serov and then been astonished at the agility of the younger boy's mind, and the son of a serf to boot. But Serov knew who was the master in their relationship and managed to lose the requisite number of games without making it obvious. He often reflected that his skill in losing was even greater than in winning.

Chapter Three

St. Petersburg, Russia. Two months earlier.

Ekaterina Countess Dolgorukova proudly bore the name of an ancient lineage of Russian aristocrats, although it was known that she descended from a minor branch of a noble family without ties to the aristocracy. Her claim to glory and, she hoped, to greatness was her long love affair with the Emperor of Russia, Alexander II, the father of her three illegitimate children. When the news reached her of the armistice ending the Russo-Turkish war, she was alone, seated at her dressing table in the comfortable apartment the Tsar had purchased and furnished for her and her three children. Peace was a momentous event, she thought, for Russia but more important for herself. It would end the mad Panslav fever that consumed much of the court. It would weaken the last emotional tie between the Empress, Maria Fedorovna, and the Tsar. Her own star, in the ascendant for fifteen years as the Tsar's mistress, would now attain its zenith.

Overwhelmed by the immensity of the future now opening up before her, she put down her hairbrush and stared fixedly into the mirror. She leaned closer and traced the slight furrow in her otherwise smooth brow. Still only just thirty, and despite giving birth to three children she knew her erotic power over Alexander remained unimpaired. She had been an innocent schoolgirl when he fell in love with her and now she was on the verge of becoming …what…? She hesitated to pronounce the word but watched with fascination as her lips formed the word "empress." Maria Fedorovna was dying. Ekaterina had persuaded Alexander to legitimize her children as nobles, albeit secretly under the name Iurevskii. He promised soon to grant her the title of Princess Iurevskaia. The imperial family detested her. She realized that years ago. But it made no difference to Alexander. He continued to be enamored, even besotted by her. She smiled. Princess to Empress! Not such a big step once the way was clear.

There was a commotion outside her door. She recognized the shouts of her dear "Gogo" and the door burst open. A five-year-old boy rushed into the room, having torn himself away for the gentle restraining hand of his English nanny. "Mama! Mama! Papa is coming."

She had been daydreaming too long and had not completed her toilette for the day. No matter, he wouldn't care. It was one of the most attractive things about him, his love of the intimate family life she provided. It was his escape from the stiff protocol which barely concealed the intrigue, rumor and even debauchery of court life.

Tsar Alexander Nikolaevich strode into the room, picked up his son, held him aloft and cried out, "This is a real Russian! In him at least only Russian blood flows in his veins." She felt a thrill surge through her entire body.

Later in the evening when the celebrations were over, she outlined for him her plan to secure the financial future of his second family. She had already been successfully dabbling in railroad concessions. She even involved him in some dubious deals, as a way of making him her accomplice. But this had caused some difficulties. Count Shuvalov, the head of the Secret Police had exposed her. But the Tsar, as she had foreseen, angrily brushed aside his evidence and sent him packing as ambassador to London. Too bad, she thought at the time. He could have been useful. Even now he seemed to be taking a sensible view of things in the Balkans. Yes, he could be useful as a counterweight to the Empress's friends among the Panslavs.

But the experience had shaken her. Perhaps Russia was not the best field for future speculations. She had been speaking recently to the Italian ambassador, who had no trouble with her "unofficial standing." He mentioned, casually it would appear, the opportunities to be had in silver mines in the Balkans. "Well, I am sure you know my dear *signora contessa*, being a person who is well-informed," the ambassador lowered his voice, smiling in an all too obvious conspiratorial way, "that negotiations are currently going on in Berlin over the distribution of lands in these remote regions. Yes?"

Dolgorukova nodded raising her fan to cover the lower part of her face. Two can play at this game, she thought.

"Ah, yes," the Italian ambassador continued. "The Turks in their slovenly way have neglected opportunities to exploit their natural resources. Old silver mines, for example, have been left idle for centuries. Now I am well informed myself. There are rich deposits located in an area that is being disputed as a result of the war. On the one side we have the Montenegrins, who despite the Italian name of their principality are Slavic. Indeed they claim to be better Serbs than the Serbs of Serbia. Not too confusing? No. On the other side, we have the Albanians, or I should say certain Albanian-speaking tribes, because there is no Albanian state. In the north they are Catholics, but they are Muslims elsewhere with a scattering of Orthodox villages. But the Albanians have long lived in the Ottoman Empire. They like to say they acknowledge the Sultan as their sovereign as long as he stays out of their affairs. Charming, no?"

"I am aware of these complexities, *signor*. But pray, continue, lest I lose track of your final destination."

"*Touché, contessa*. So to continue on my track, which takes me along a few sharp curves, you understand? The land has been awarded to the Montenegrins or the Serbians by your Russian diplomats who signed the armistice. A certain Count Ignatiev. A Pan Slav isn't he?"

"So I understand"

"Of course you do."

But, the Albanian tribesmen are in occupation of the area, it is called Kosovo, where the old mines are located. And they refuse to give them up. The mines have not been in operation for over a hundred years. An old story. Another sign of the Ottoman decline. No need to bore you with the history. So the war goes on there, although nobody likes to put it that way. And at Berlin they are trying to sort this out. Now, we have a tug of war as well. I am not boring you, *contessa*?"

"No indeed, I find this fascinating, if only because I now see the last curve in the track."

"*Brava, contessa!* So the powers, in a quandary turn to our eminent ambassador in Constantinople, Count Corti, to propose a compromise. There is no good way to settle this for the two sides. But I have good information that Count Corti is drawing up a border might well give the mines, originally assigned to the Serbians, to the Albanians as representatives of the Sultan. The Austrians are supporting him. They may end up occupying the area. Corti has travelled to Montenegro to investigate the opportunities on the spot. All to the good, because there are Italian businessmen who for some time have been exploring the possibility of investing in reopening the mines. And Count Corti has been encouraging the Porte to examine their bids. But he also reports that Russian agents, acting perhaps unofficially, are supporting the Serbian claims. Now, why am I telling you all this?"

"Because you have observed that I am what the English call a good businessman, although a woman. And because the Russians at Berlin would have to take a position that is opposed to the Montenegrins, that is fellow Slavs. But I should stop explaining you to yourself. We should talk again, *cher ami.* Yes, it is a conversation that needs to be extended and amplified. Besides, the Tsar is approaching, wondering no doubt what keeps us deep in conversation for so long a time."

The Italian ambassador bowed, kissed the extended hand of Dolgorukova and greeted the Tsar effusively.

"The Contessa has just been explaining to me that the floral arrangements were designed by our well-known florist, Paoggeli on the Nevsky. Exquisite, are they not?"

Later that week, Dolgorukova received a handwritten message from an official in Asiatic Department of the Foreign Ministry brought to her by her trusted maid. It read simply: "Your instructions have been carried out to the letter." It was signed 'R'. She placed it carefully in a reticule by her bed. An unsettling dream woke her in the early morning hours. She took out the message, read it again and then burned it.

Chapter Four

Adrianople

"The first part of your journey is risky, even dangerous," said Suchin. Stabbing the map with his forefinger, he restlessly shifted his weight to relieve the pressure on his left leg which had taken a Turkish bullet at Shipka Pass. Vasiliev and Serov, standing on either side of him leaned over to follow as he traced a path between a point on the coast and the great port of Thessaloniki across the Gulf of Thrace. "You see the Austrians haven't completed this railroad between Constantinople and Vienna. They call it the Great Orient Line. So the line operates only from Adrianople to this fishing village. The Greeks call it Alexandropolis and the Bulgarian call it Dedeagach. You have to understand there are at least two names for everything around here. Then it resumes again here at Thessalonika and goes all the way to your destination, that is Prishtina in Macedonia and then beyond to Mitrovitsa. Now you have a choice to close the gap in the rail line. Either you go overland and risk being shot by bandits or *bashi bazooks*, those crazy irregulars the Turks have imported from the Caucasus. Or else you go by ship and risk drowning in a one of those coastal storms that blow up sudden-like in the Gulf." Suchin straightened up, a triumphant smile on his face.

"Which do you recommend?"

"Glad you asked and happy to accommodate your wishes, Major. I would go for the ship. If you agree I can put you in touch with a reliable sailor." Suchin coughed apologetically before going on. "I am married to a Greek girl and her father is a ship's captain. He owns a small craft but reliable. It's a sloop, in Greek *trehantiria*. It's seaworthy enough, 'like a donkey' the Greeks say."

"How long is the voyage?"

"Much depends on the winds. Let's say, two days."

"And the cost?"

"To be negotiated with the captain. If I remember his craft is scheduled to sail in a few days. A cargo of olive oil."

"And two Russians."

Suchin was beaming now. "If you take the train tomorrow, you will be in Alexandropolis in a few hours. I will send a message to my father-in-law. He will meet you to arrange the rest of your trip."

"And the train tickets?"

"There is a young clerk in General Totleben's staff, a girl who handles this sort of thing. I can let her know. Her name is Elena Pavlovna." Suchin knew a great deal about her, but he did not bother to pass on his information to Vasiliev.

Elena Pavlovna had come to Serbia in 1875 from her hometown in Tula Province with her lover, an ardent Pan Slav who had joined up with Chernaiev's volunteers. After he had been killed in action, she made her way east and drifted into the Russian camp. Because she was literate and had a fine handwriting she was taken on as a clerk with the regular army. She had acquired a good knowledge of Turkish. She was not pretty, but possessed a lively sense of humor and a pleasing manner. Her best feature was her glossy black hair that hung down to her waist in two long braids, which when loosened, seemed to envelop her completely. Perhaps it was this that attracted a young Albanian with the face of an angel, as she described him to her friends, who served as a runner for the staff.

Instructed by Suchin, she bought the tickets that evening and had him deliver them to Serov in a sealed envelope, which also contained instructions on where to meet the Greek captain in Alexsandropolis. Then she celebrated with her young Albanian what he claimed was his birthday, making him five years younger than she was. He had chosen a small café in the neighborhood of the Rüstem Pasha Caravanserai. He ordered a pitcher of *hardaliye*, explaining to her that it was a non-alcoholic drink, as befitted a Muslim, made of grape juice, mustard seed and sour cherry leaves.

As they sat in the large courtyard dimly lit by torches, he regaled her with stories about the Caravanserai. It had been built three hundred years ago by order of Grand Vizier, Rüstem Pasha, a legendary figure because of his vast wealth. He commissioned a young architect, Mimar Sinan, who later became celebrated throughout the Ottoman Empire. Sinan's design placed the building in a grand rectangular courtyard with a marble basin the center. The façade had a great arcade with a row of shops. There were rooms for over a hundred visitors. Later a second courtyard was added. Of irregular shape, it originally served as stables for camels and a soup kitchen.

"Well, he concluded proudly, "you see how magnificent our public buildings were at the height of our glory. Sadly, much has changed."

Then he pointed to the ruins of a small mosque. "Destroyed by you Russians," he said, in a tone that startled her. Then he laughed, took her hand and squeezed it.

"But war brings good and evil and it brought me you." He then chatted about his family in the mountains south of Montenegro. She hardly noticed the passage of time. It was late when they left and some of the torches had burned down. As they turned into a narrow street, she felt suddenly uneasy. She took his arm and pressed against him.

After a few more steps, she was seized from behind and wrenched out of his reassuring arms. Before she could cry out, a rough hand covered her mouth. She was dragged into a doorway opening into a dark passageway and a room without a window. For an hour she was tortured until she had revealed what they wanted to know. Then the same rough hand pulled back her braids, exposing her throat to a very sharp curved knife. She died instantly. Her body was loaded onto a cart and carried to the river where a small rowboat was waiting. A bag of stones was tied tightly around her waist and in midstream she was released quietly into the water. She was reported missing only after Vasiliev and Serov had left by train. The Albanian had disappeared and was never found. After interviewing her friends, the investigating officials, a Russian officer and the Turkish police chief, concluded that the two lovers had either run away together or else he had disposed of her out of a fit of jealousy for which there was no evidence. The incident was officially closed.

When he was questioned, Suchin denied he had any information that might have helped the investigation. He had simply selected the girl as a reliable messenger. He had been too busily occupied with more important matters to inform General Totleben who, after all, was burdened with weighty matters of state and could not be bothered with these kinds of incidents. The General did not find out until much later how important Suchin's testimony had been.

Several days before the girl had been murdered, Suchin received a letter from his mother in the far north province of Vologda. It had been written by the priest. A fire in the village, dreaded by the peasants as the "Red Rooster," had consumed their hut, all her possessions, killed the cow and her chickens, leaving her destitute. She had made the pilgrimage to the Ferapont Monastery and prayed to the Mother of God icon in vain. She had no other means of living and pleaded for his help.

Suchin was bound to military service for another five years. In that time his mother would no longer be alive. He could not ask for money from his father-in-law and his wife was pregnant with their first child. He sought solace with the regimental priest and then with his immediate superior. The officer told him that he had heard of a man, a former Russian officer, who was looking for a soldier to help him with small daily tasks and paid well.

"This is a bit irregular," the officer winked, "but your situation is desperate, though not unusual." Suchin could meet him at a small tavern outside the army encampment. He would be easy to find: a very tall, muscular, heavily bearded man, with a prominent scar on his right cheek, probably wearing a military cloak stripped of its insignia.

The tavern was crowded with men in uniform, fortunately for Suchin no one from his regiment or the general staff. He looked about but did not see the man he was seeking until very late in the evening. He was an intimidating presence and for a moment Suchin hesitated to approach him. But then the picture of his mother kneeling before the Mother of God icon brought tears to his face.

The man, calling himself Andrei Gregorevich, called for a carafe of raki and led Suchin to a corner table. He was a taller man than any in the café and otherwise just as he had been described. His unusually broad shoulders and thin waist gave his upper body the appearance of a trapezoid. He imperiously waved aside the two men who hastily departed the table. So, concluded Suchin, a man of authority. The man asked a few questions about Suchin's duties. His eyes lit up when Suchin, intending to impress him with his worth, mentioned his assignment to General Totleben's staff.

"So, then perhaps you have knowledge of a person I seek, a certain Major Vasiliev? He has been assigned a task which is, I understand, very important for the future of our Motherland."

Suchin could not resist boasting about his responsibility for making Vasiliev's travel arrangements.

"Ah, too bad he is leaving so soon. I would like to have spoken with him, but I must leave tomorrow for a few days. An urgent matter. Perhaps you could tell me his travel plans, and then I could arrange to meet him later."

Suchin was only too happy to oblige. "Excellent," the burly man smiled. "You can be of even greater help to me, my friend. I would like to engage your services in the future. For the time being, here are a few rubles to help your mother. God alone knows why the good lord visits us with fire and brimstone. To cleanse our souls? But your mother is as you say a pious woman and does not need such an ordeal to test her faith." The man drew out a heavy purse and placed it on the table. Suchin could hardly contain himself, blubbering his thanks.

"So, when I return in a few days, I may have a few little tasks for you. We can meet here next Tuesday."

Suchin returned to camp with a glorious feeling that the Mother of God did in truth hear his mother's prayers.

When he heard that the girl had vanished, he felt a pang of regret. But he dismissed the idea that her disappearance was connected in any way with his conversation with Andrei Gregorevich. He said nothing about it to anyone. Shortly thereafter, General Totleben's staff was ordered to return to Odessa, and Suchin never again met his benefactor.

Chapter Five

Alexandropolis

'It looks like one of our garrison towns!" exclaimed Serov as they detrained at Alexandropolis. The streets were filled with Russian troops, many of them laboring to widen the narrow lanes and break through the cul de sacs. "They've been at it since they occupied the town, Totleben told me. They are trying to make it more serviceable for the movement of men and animals in wartime. But I'm not so certain who is going to benefit. The Bulgarians are supposed to have taken over by the Treaty of San Stefano. But from what we heard in Adrianople we may have to give it back to the Turks."

"Now why would that be, Vasili Vasilievich?"

"Sometimes high politics is beyond me…too high."

They made their way to a small café on the sea front where dozens of fishing vessels were tied up and flocks of albatross and dozens of other sea birds crowded the sky above them, swirling and plunging like ballerinas, their pure white bodies making arabesques that no dancer could have replicated. On the horizon a bright orange sun was sinking into the sea. They paused fascinated by at the swirl of colors, changing from moment to moment as if some master choreographer were determined to render them speechless with wonder.

It seemed to Vasiliev that the café hardly belonged to this splendid scene. It was a small building, almost a hut, with peeling whitewashed walls, a worn thatched roof, sagging in places, and few darkened windows.

"The perfect place for a rendezvous," muttered Vasiliev.

There were no Russian soldiers to be seen inside, only a group of Greek fishermen who stared sat them as if they had just emerged from the sea bottom. But a strong and cheerful voice rang out in heavily accented Russian, and Captain Popodopolis pushed aside a bead curtain leading to a separate room.

"Welcome, heroes of Shipka," he cried out.

Well, thought Vasiliev, no concern here for concealment. Popodopolis was a stocky man with powerful forearms; a short badly cut white beard and an unruly matching thatch of hair, standing up like spikes in all directions. He embraced them both and led them into the back room where a wooden table had been set with a bottle of wine at the center.

"*Xinomavra*," he exclaimed, "meaning sour black and holds up well over time. One of the few things to come out of Macedonia that is not in dispute." He laughed. "None of your common *retsino* for you, my friends. You'll have to drink too much of it here in Greece."

He poured the dark liquid into three tumblers and raised his arm to toast them. "You may wonder where I learned my Russian," he said as he leaned toward them. When he folded his bare arms on the table, Vasiliev worried it might not be able to stand the strain.

"Well, my father served at Navarino. He was a midshipman on the Russian flagship, you know, the Azov. A great battle. We destroyed the Turkish fleet. But my father told me that the English admiral in command of our joint fleets, Codrington was his name, was criticized for his, what do you call it, rashness? Still he is a hero to us. Helped us win our freedom. Well, you are not here for a history lesson. So you want to sail to Thessaloniki, Nothing simpler. I plan to leave tomorrow morning. The sea should be quiet, if we can judge by the sunset."

"Captain, we greatly appreciate you taking us on as passengers. We understand that is not usually possible, so we would like to compensate you."

The captain's face darkened. "No question of that, Major. This trip is in honor of Navarino!" he exclaimed and re-filled their glasses. "Yes, let us drink to victories over the Turks!"

The ship was, as Suchin promised, seaworthy and made good time under a favorable wind. But as they approached Cape Akrathos, a fog began to creep in from land.

Cape Akrathos and Mount Athos

Popodopolis cursed under his breath. "Well, I should have expected it. Fog's like some restless ghost. Comes up when you least expect it. Still there's enough light to see the Holy Monastery of Athos, and there it is to the west on that hill top. The ruins of the Tower of Kolitsou. Imagine! Built by the Byzantine Greeks in the twelfth century. Ah! Those were the glory days. Will we ever get back our Greater Greece?"

But Vasiliev's attention had been drawn to a dark shape emerging from the mist on their starboard side. He seized the captain's arm, "Visitors?"

"Oh my God!" Popodopolis exclaimed. He pulled out his telescope. "Hard to port!' he ordered. But the dark shape kept moving closer.

"What is it?"

"A Turkish craft, a caique, faster than we are, but otherwise worthless."

"And what might its purpose be?" Vasiliev was now looking through the telescope himself, impatient for an answer.

"Pirates," exclaimed Popodopolis. "Turkish pig swill." A series of curses in Greek followed.

"I thought they had disappeared since the Americans put an end to piracy long ago."

"Those pirates were Greeks. The war spawned some freebooters. Maybe Turkish deserters. May God wreck them!"

As the caique drew closer Vasiliev could see a dozen men arranged in a line on the deck, closely spaced apart. They were brandishing scimitars. A stocky figure in the prow raised a flintlock to his shoulder and fired. A bullet struck the mast close to Vasiliev's head. Vasiliev drew his revolver. Serov immediately followed suit and waited for the order to fire. Vasiliev took careful aim and shot the man with the flintlock in the shoulder. A cry of pain rang out. The wounded man dropped his weapon which fell over the side. Vasiliev hesitated. He realized it would be a massacre if he and Serov shot down the rest of the scimitar-wielding pirates. The Greek captain took the decision out of his hands. He roared an order. His crew scrambled into action. They pulled open a wooden door to a compartment amidships. Vasiliev watched in astonishment as three sailors manhandled a cannon of ancient vintage onto the deck. It looked like it had been salvaged from one of Codrington's frigates at Navarino. The Turkish caique had drawn abreast and was less than fifty meters away. Vasiliev could make out the features of the pirates, howling in rage over their fallen leader.

"Fire away lads!" the captain shouted. Two of the sailors primed the canon and inserted a solid round shot. A third one standing behind the canon aimed it and lit the fuse. The four-pounder exploded. The recoil struck the cannoneer who had forgotten in his excitement to jump aside. Screaming, he twisted in agony on the deck. His legs were shattered. But his aim had been true. A gaping hole opened up just above the water line of the caique, and the sea poured in. The Turkish craft shuddered and slowly fell back, listing to port. A cheer went up from the Greek sailors. Vasiliev bent over the recumbent form of the wounded man, but there was no chance of saving him. Vasiliev muttered a few words in his archaic Greek. "You are a real hero." The sailor's eyes widened. Then he expired.

The mist obscured the death throes of the stricken caique and deadened the cries of the pirates.

Vasiliev turned to the captain. "Don't you want to rescue the survivors?

"The Hell with them! I know their tricks. They'd knife our lads as they were being picked up," the captain gnashed his teeth. "So we'll never know," Vasiliev muttered to Serov, "whether this was anything more than a chance encounter."

****

The monks of Iviron Monastery on Mt. Athos had good reason to welcome the stranger from far distant Russia. He came bearing gifts from a benefactor and a message from Theophan the Recluse together with the first volume of his Russian translation of the great spiritual work, *Unseen Warfare* by Nicodemus of the Holy Mountain. This was no surprise. The Iviron Monastery had enjoyed the patronage of the Russian court since the time of Peter the Great. The stranger appeared to know whole passages of the work by heart. His only request was to stay alone in the tower of the monastery overlooking the Aegean. This was granted. In the morning, a monk related the news that a Turkish caique had been sunk by a Greek craft. The monks who saw the stranger leave remarked on his disgruntled appearance.

He crossed to the port of Dafni on the west side of the peninsula and hired a small *trihantiri* to take him across the Sigitic Gulf to land on a beach in sight of the town of Ierissos. He made his way to a small villa which had been built after the town had been burned by the Turks during the Greek war for independence. Three Albanians were squatting on the grass outside the villa, with four horses tethered nearby.

"He's a big brute," said one. "Good we managed to lift a big bay for him." The man threw his cloak over his shoulder, and as the men rose from their sitting positions, he shot them one by one in the forehead with the carbine that had been slung over his back.

He checked saddle bags and was pleased to find canteens filled with fresh water and some dried meat and biscuits. He untethered the horses and tied them together in a line before mounting the bay and setting off at a brisk trot. He would change mounts every twenty miles until he arrived at the outskirts of Thessalonika, one hundred and sixty miles away.

The countryside was deserted and he had time to reflect on his mission. He laughed to himself at the idea. Everyone he encountered seemed to have a mission in this God-forsaken region, men, women of power, whole governments, hired guns like himself. Then there was Vasiliev. He wondered, as he often had, why he resented this eccentric man. He had been two years behind him in the Page Corps and doubted that Vasiliev ever noticeed him. It puzzled him why this illegitimate son of a count and a peasant woman was the favorite of all the instructors and universally admired by the students. He was the one exception. Why was this? He could not be sure.

Or perhaps his feeling of resentment was not so strong then, in the corridors of the Corps, but later in the Caucasus where their two paths almost crossed. Again Vasiliev "the Blessed" was on everyone's tongue. But weren't his exploits just as remarkable? Of course, later there was his disgrace, the result of a betrayal by a fellow guardsman of a clandestine meeting with a Circassian woman who turned out to be a spy for Shamil. He would never forget the pain he had suffered at the moment the epaulettes had been torn from his uniform. Vasiliev was not involved. But his success at the same time rankled deeply.

Even so he was willing to serve as a common soldier and work his way up through the ranks. But luck was against him. In an attack on a mountain *aul* he had been badly wounded. A saber cut disfigured his face. A bullet injured his leg which refused to heal for weeks. Then, the added humiliation of being denied a decoration for valor, which he had earned, and his discharge as no longer fit for active service was enough to destroy any man. What had this to do with Vasiliev? He could not say.

Chapter Six

Thessalonika

Captain Popodopolis told the story many times, embellishing it as was his custom to heap praise on his men. But he always remembered to add at the end that this Russian officer had given him money when they docked at Thessalonika for the mother of the unfortunate cannoneer. He felt obliged to give Vasiliev in return the names of a few trustworthy Greeks. They would be able to serves as guides through the maze of streets and provide reliable informants about the teeming life of the city with its many creeds and languages.

Vasiliev thanked him but thought it best to start with the authorities, lest he be tagged as the spy he feared he had become. After he and Serov had installed themselves in the Hotel Olympus, he sent a message to Selim Bey, the chief of police. He was surprised by the return invitation to visit the chief at his home rather than at headquarters. When Vasiliev entered the spacious courtyard, he understood why. The old Turkish architecture had been suitable restored, and though the home was modest it blended Turkish and European, mainly French, features, a style that was, Vasiliev learned, becoming the fashion for the Ottoman authorities. Selim Bey welcomed him in his small but elegantly furnished reception room, with Turkish carpets strewn on the floor, a large sofa and an ornate Italian chest in the corner. He was smoking a *chibouk*, but put it aside. Just as Vasiliev entered the room, a servant was leaving, having placed a coffee urn and two cups of Bulgarian porcelain on a circular metal table inscribed with a verse from the Koran.

Selim Bey

Selim Bey had an aristocratic look, finely chiseled features, a broad forehead and high arched eyebrows that jutted out over widely spaced eyes of equally dark color. He graciously accepted Vasiliev's documents with a bow. His long tapered fingers with carefully manicured nails turned the pages carefully with the reverence normally reserved for a rare manuscript.

"Ah! An important man, this Grigoriev, it would seem." His French, only slightly accented, was otherwise perfect. "In these times of violence to send a high ranking and respected official to solve the death of one man…well, almost extraordinary, and all the way from Moscow."

"Not directly, your excellency. I was already in Adrianople."

"A lovely city. I hope you will return it to us. Ah, I apologize for my brusque manner. I am only a policeman and not a diplomat. So how can I be of assistance?"

"This is a courtesy call, your excellency, simply to inform you that a Russian officer and his orderly have descended upon your fair city for too short a time to appreciate its many attractions."

"So, an officer, but also a diplomat. Lovely! I fear our attractions are mostly of the remote past. You will see many ruined churches and other decaying monuments of even greater antiquity. To refer only to recent events, did you know Major that two thousand three hundred years ago the Persian king, Xerxes, stood on the mountain where the old citadel now crumbles away, planning his invasion of Greece? Mohammed the Conqueror used to say that we Turks succeeded where the Persian had failed. How can bitter memories last so long?" Selim Bey seemed lost in thought as he poured Vasiliev a second cup of coffee.

"You surely know that St. Paul...Ah, you must forgive me for launching upon a lecture. I did want to become a teacher, you see, and ended up pursuing rascals instead of the lives of great men. Now, I feel that I must spare you the history and become a practical man. There is surely some assistance I could render."

"There is one question I would like to ask you. You are probably the best-informed man in the city. Have you heard of the incident at sea which almost terminated my assignment before it began?"

"As a matter of delicacy I did not chose to raise the issue. But yes."

"And what did you conclude?"

"You know, Major, there have not been any Turkish pirates in these waters for decades. Greeks perhaps. But not Turks. We seem to have lost our navigational skills. Or else, we have come to rely too heavily on the talents of our Greek subjects. Did you know, Major, that at the famous battle of Navarino there were as many Greek sailors in our ships as on yours? No? So the question arises. If these were Greek pirates, why would they sail a Turkish caique, which is an inferior craft to their *tretantiria*."

"So as not to appear to be Greek."

"Exactly. Now what significance does that have? To answer this question we need sustenance."

Selim Bey clapped his hands and a servant immediately appeared. Selim Bey gestured vaguely. The servant bowed and within minutes a plate of almond cookies appeared.

Selim Bey leaned back in the depths of the cushions.

"Let me answer in an indirect manner, with another story. More than five years ago, a young Christian woman voluntarily sought to convert to Islam in order to enter a Muslim landowner's household. Not unusual even today. As you may know my government had forbidden forced conversion and sought to prevent and expose any act of coercion in these matters. On her way to the mosque, she was seized, her veil torn off, by an unknown man. With accomplices, this man commandeered the empty carriage of the American vice-consul, carried off the girl and, as it turned out, returned her to her mother, who opposed the conversion. The next morning a group of Muslims gathered at my headquarters and demanded her release. As in all such matters, I warned the agitators that they that they had no right to assemble. I also tried to calm them. I promised the girl would be found shortly and the culprits punished.

Unfortunately, the crowd rapidly increased in number and I hadn't enough men to disperse them. The self-appointed leaders threatened to storm the American consulate. But it turned out that the girl was not there, and the consul was out of town. News spread to the bazaar. Armed Albanians got involved. You must understand Albanians are always armed. Tempers flared. At that moment the French and German consuls *just happened* to pass by. Well, so it seemed at the time. The crowd incited by the hotheads turned upon them and beat them to death. The foreign community was horrified, as was I. All Europe was outraged by another example of "Turkish fanaticism." Foreign warships were summoned and anchored offshore with their guns trained on the Upper Town. We discovered the girl's whereabouts, locked in her mother's house, and organized a rescue mission. We recovered the girl, just in time. The frenzied mob was heading for the foreign quarter, intent on burning it to the ground, when the news arrived of the girl's release. The crowd dispersed. We arrested a number of the rioters and executed six of them. The justice of the Sultan, may god preserve him, had triumphed. Or had it?"

Selim Bey delicately bit off a piece of an almond cookie.

"Two small incidents five years apart. An attack on the consuls and now, one against you, a few years between a war and a crisis over the distribution of imperial Ottoman territory, with the great powers negotiating in Berlin. At the same time, fighting continues in the land where you intend to pursue your investigation of another murder, this time of a prominent agent of the Pan Slavs."

"The dots, as we say, are still far apart."

"Indeed. Now let me try to connect them."

Selim Bey placed his hands together as if in prayer, but he was not praying, thought Vasiliev, just summing up like a good prosecutor.

"The furor over the massacre of the consuls died down, but the battleships remained. There were too many unanswered questions. I decided to pursue another line of inquiry."

"Like a good policeman should."

"Thank you. Your country and mine may be bitter enemies, but professional men from both can and must agree to work together."

Vasiliev nodded

"So, first who were the abductors? Of course, they must have been Greeks, Orthodox Christians, sworn enemies of Islam. But wait, who had identified the culprits? The leaders of the mob? Dispassionate witnesses? The girl? I obtained permission of her employer, a respected Muslim landlord, to interview her. She told me two pieces of information that could not be reconciled with the accepted version of things. First, the men spoke what she called a 'strange language.' Remember the girl is Greek but comes from a village where Turkish is also spoken. Her mother worked briefly in the household of a German store owner, where French was spoken. She did not speak or even understand much in those languages, but she could recognize them. So what remains? Unfortunately, in our great city of Thessaloniki, a large choice. These men speaking a strong language were also strangely dressed in the '*Frankish*' style. Frock coats, floppy hats and short beards. They turned her over to her Greek family, and then disappeared. So who were they?"

"What is your best guess, Selim Bey? I myself am a great believer in inspired guessing. Have you ever read the theories of Charles Peirce on guessing? No? An American philosopher. You would find him a kindred spirit I think. His view in brief is that the mere accumulation of facts about a crime does not guarantee an understanding of its causes, why and how it happened. Facts have a habit of accumulating very rapidly. This is the curse of a determined investigator. What is needed is a connection that can be supplied by what Peirce called inspired guessing. He meant a process of linking the unusual or surprising facts in a causal chain, a hypothesis, then testing it. While there may be several possible explanations, the trained mind can seek the most plausible one by referring to what he called the nature of things. As an experienced investigator, you will seek the explanation or guess the outcome by exercising that faculty that lies just below the surface of one's consciousness. A conclusion is reached. This is the way it has to be. If there is no strong evidence to the contrary, then the chances are one has guessed right. I find that the method works more often than not. But of course no method is infallible."

"Well, I must look him up. So, let me continue to spin my story or, as you would put it, marshal the unusual and surprising facts then propose a hypothesis and finally test it. My next step was to find out why the European consuls just happened to stroll past a riot well under way. The explanation I heard at their consulates was that they had been summoned by the governor. But my visit to the governor drew a blank. No such summons or invitation had been issued. So who sent the message to the two consuls and why? A final point, if you will allow me?

"The murder of the consuls occurred three days after the outbreak of the Bulgarian insurrection which led to the terrible killings of Muslims by Christians and Christians by Muslims. By the way, it is most unfortunate that Europe learned only of the massacre of Christians. 'The Bulgarian horrors,' the English statesman Gladstone called them. The Bulgarians were also committing atrocities. But I then sought to explain this apparent coincidence in timing to fit a 'hypothesis' as you would put it."

"I am beginning to glimpse a line forming to connect the dots,"

"Excellent! Please let me have your best guess," Selim Bey chuckled.

"May I first add another dot?"

"By all means, I welcome your expertise."

"In Moscow we read in the papers in the spring of 1875, a year before the murder of the consuls, how Emperor Franz Joseph of Austria made a tour along the Dalmatian coast of his Empire. He received numerous petitions from the Christian population across the frontier in Bosnia, then under your, that is Ottoman rule. The petitions complained about the injustice and oppression of the

Christians at the hands of the Muslim officials. Within a year an uprising broke out in this province and then a year later another uprising in Bulgaria which brought us Russians into the war. Now all these events have one thing in common. Isn't that so?""

"Well, I agree but I would rather that you, a Russian officer who must have served in the army fighting against us would tell me what that is."

"Yes, first let me separate what I guess to be the case before the Russian declaration of war against your government and now. There may be a connection of course."

"All the better."

"The events we have sketched out suggest that before the war there was a concerted effort by some in Europe to discredit the Ottoman government as incapable of ruling over a Christian population. And now after the war, the incidents, still small compared to those preceding the conflict, suggest that this same charge, bolstered by new outrages against European representatives, will be used by interested parties to carve up your territory."

"Bravo Major! But should you let your government know what you have just 'guessed'? Oh, yes, before we finish this wonderful exercise, let me add one more dot. As the crisis was building, our enlightened Minister, Midhat Pasha, had succeeded in persuading the Sultan, may God protect him, to issue a constitution giving equal rights to all his subjects, Christians and Muslims. Only the Christian uprisings intervened. The constitution was suspended in the face of war. I fear it was the last chance to prove to Europeans that we intend to create a society similar to theirs."

"I have only one reservation, or rather emendation." Vasiliev said. "I believe that conspiracies of the dimension we are suggesting can only exist if there already exists in the minds of men a reservoir of fear or suspicion or hatred that can be exploited and released in a flood that carries away ordinarily rational people in a wave of emotion."

"So, officer, diplomat *and* poet. It has been a great pleasure to meet you, Major. Now, the important thing is to draw the right conclusion for yourself. Be aware. Emotions are riding high. Trust no one. Even after this all too brief acquaintance, I assure you I would rather have you fail in your mission than succeed if you then become another of its victims."

Chapter Seven

Thessalonika

The Russian consul in Thessaloniki, Alexander von Moritz, was in a lamentable state. At least this is the way his devoted body servant described him to the cook on that sultry morning when a small news item in the weekly gazette, *Salonik*, announced the arrival of Captain Popodopolis' Greek ship, *Kolitsou*, with a Russian officer aboard after an encounter with Turkish pirates. The paper lay scattered on the floor in von Moritz's study, giving the impression of a man with disorderly habits. This too was unusual, not to say downright disturbing, the servant continued his story.

"*Ja! Das war besser in Smyrna,*" von Moritz sighed. The scion of a Baltic noble family, he preferred to think in German and then translate his thoughts into Russian, not always gramatically. How he wished he had not left that safe mooring on the shores of Anatolia! The Greeks there were so civilized, free of the taint of Slavic blood. When he was given the choice of this post he had jumped at the opportunity, calculating the advantages he could reap from a community in the midst of a war economy. Now he would even settle for a prolonged leave in his hometown of Riga. It was dull there on the Baltic coast, but one could get through a week there without meeting a Russian.

"*Und das verdammt Grigoriev,*" he spat out the name. Von Moritz glanced at the lattice separating the study from the corridor, knowing full well that Efraim was concealed there. So time to reveal another eccentricity worthy of gossip. For several years, he had cultivated the impression of a man with strange if not bizarre habits. He understood that by providing Efraim with delicious tidbits to embellish and recount at the local taverns and bordellos, he enabled his servant to obtain, in exchange, morsels of valuable information. This was how he learned of the pirate attack, alas too late to warn anyone. From his network of informers, he had pick up other ominous signs of a conspiracy to prevent the investigating Russian officer from getting to the scene of the crime until all the material evidence and witnesses could be removed or destroyed.

In a flash of inspiration, he decided to invite the Russian officer to dinner. What was his name? Vasiliev or Vasilievskii? And he would invite the other consuls of the powers! A brilliant idea. What an uproarious dinner that would be. As if he was convening a Congress of Berlin in miniature. No better way than for this Vasiliev to be introduced into the labyrinth of Balkan politics. For surely the assassination of Grigoriev was a political crime. Yes, a labyrinth, But who was the Minotaur? Well, that would be for the officer to find out. If he succeeded. he would prove to be a modern Theseus. If not, he would be devoured.

We'll see then what this officer is made of. Von Moritz called for his cook.

"And where is our distinguished American colleague?" asked the French consul sipping his glass of Veuve Cliquot, after having been introduced to Vasiliev. Throughout the evening, he had the habit of waving one hand in the air as if to dismiss any objection to what he was saying.

"He excuses himself as usual from dining with me. He pleads an aversion to my cats. They cause him to sneeze." Von Moritz paused. "But you know, *cher ami,* his French causes me some discomfort as well." The consuls laughed appreciatively. The common language at the table was French and Vasiliev's Parisian accent was highly praised. But that ended the harmony of opinion.

Vasiliev found that he had no need to ask questions. He felt as though he were at a debate at Oxford where he had spent some time after his graduation from the Page Corps. Appropriately, the equivalent of a referee was the British consul, but a referee with an agenda. Von Moritz was content to let him start the discussion.

"I hardly need repeat…," he began.

"But you will, *mon ami*," chirped the Italian consul to general laughter.

"Well, I speak for the benefit of our recently arrived Russian representative, the hero of Plevna, isn't that right?"

"It pains me to disagree with your first point, *dear sir*. But no. The hero of Plevna was General Totleben, whose acquaintance the English first made at Sevastopol in the Crimean War."

"Oh bravo!" exclaimed the French consul, who seemed to have forgotten that the French took part in the siege of Sevastopol too, storming the Grand Redan for the glory of Napoleon III. The British consul quickly recovered his poise. "All right, then, let's hear what our Austrian colleague has to say."

The man on his left set down his cutlery and inclined his head to the Englishman, "Actually to be more precise, your Austrian colleague is Hungarian by birth and native language, representing his Imperial Highness, the King of Hungary and Emperor of Austria, Baron, Heinrich Karl Haymerle, at your service."

"Ah ha!" exclaimed the Italian consul, "a second riposte. And isn't another Hungarian, Count Andrassy, the representative of the Monarchy in Berlin?"

The English consul flushed slightly and also inclined his head as a form of apology. Vasiliev thought he looked like a spoiled portrait of the Duke of Wellington.

"The situation is clear enough…" he too was immediately interrupted by the German, or better Prussian consul.

"Not clear at all! He grumbled. "Or else Prince Bismarck would not have to act as the honest broker in Berlin." His thin lips were set in a straight line as if they had been drawn by on the command of his superior officer.

Von Moritz now saw fit to intervene. "Gentlemen, I invited you all to inform our distinguished guest who is on a noble and dangerous mission…"

But he too was destined to fail in completing a sentence.

"And what is this mission, if I am permitted to ask?" The Italian consul dabbed his moustache as if to conceal his expression.

Vasiliev displayed his habitual crooked smile.

"This evening my mission is to learn from all of you what the current situation might be in the highlands of Albania."

"To what end, may I ask?" It was the Italian again.

"To assist the cause of peace," von Moritz broke in. So, Vasiliev thought, this is to be the official line. He nodded.

"A secret mission then?" the Italian persisted.

"How could it be secret if I am meeting here tonight with the representatives of all the great powers?" Vasiliev held his smile in place.

"But your minister in Cetinje, Ionin, isn't it? He's already very well informed. An excellent man, I understand. Also a lover of cats, like our distinguished host."

"Of course. But as consul general he may not be able to travel to certain disturbed or disputed areas."

"Whereas you can?"

"But this is exactly why our distinguished host has invited me to meet with all of you, the most knowledgeable men in the region. In order to prepare me for this mission."

"So if you are satisfied, gentlemen, then let us proceed or better, start again from the beginning."

"All right, Alexandre," said the British consul. "The beginning is not easy to locate. But let me start by saying that in my many years here I have always thought my wife and I were living on the edge of a volcano, a volcano that is normally dormant. On occasion it becomes active, indeed explosive. So, my beginning is salutary warning. This does not refer to the current crisis. No, I refer to something more in the natural order of things, if I may continue the metaphor. At the risk of lulling my colleagues to sleep, an unfortunate habit of mine, let me remind you of how this volcanic activity is rather general in our world. Of course, this one is unique in ways I will come to shortly.'

"Shortly is the word, my dear fellow," said the French consul. "A most exquisite desert awaits us."

"Quite right. Generally speaking, three great empires, mine, yours Major and the Ottoman, have witnessed three great rebellions in the past twenty years: the Great Indian Mutiny, the Polish Rebellion and now the Serbian-Bulgarian uprising. And at the heart of all three are religious and racial conflicts. The violence has receded but all three volcanoes still bubble. This is what you face, Major, no matter what your mission of peace may entrain."

"And the unique element?" Vasiliev wanted to know.

"A brief story, I promise brief," he said, ignoring the shrug of his French colleague across the table.

"Several years ago, as you surely remember, two of our colleagues were murdered by a mob here in Salonika. I was almost the third victim. But more important for the point I am trying to make are the causes. You must also surely agree that one of the great disputes between our two empires arises from the treatment of the Christians under Turkish rule. We in England try to persuade the Sultan to grant reforms. We believe that the duty of the ruler or an empire is to bring peace and order and, I would add, civilization to our subjects. You Russians insist that the Sultan cannot be trusted to fulfill the promise of reform he makes to Europe. So, you favor supporting those who rebel against him. You suspect us of prolonging the life of a 'sick man', or was it a 'sick bear' that the late Tsar Nicholas I called the Ottomans? We suspect you of hastening his demise. Others represented around this table have their own perspectives. The trouble or uniqueness of this dilemma is that every time there is a crisis, here in this part of the world, Europe is drawn in. This is not true in India or Poland, you see. Here the plot thickens, as the great detectives say. Here is the uniqueness. Now, back to the murder of the consuls. You may wish to consult our chief of police, Selim Bey, on the details. A good man. Well, he saved my life so he must be good."

A slight ripple of laughter around the table. Von Moritz, sensing the need to bring an end to the consul's lecture signaled Efraim to bring in the *tarte au chocolat framboise façon charlotte*.

"Yes, yes. An abbreviated ending then." The English consul drew a deep breath. "A crowd of indignant Muslims gathered to demand the girl be released. By ill chance the French and German consuls happen to pass by on their way to the governor, isn't that right?" He turned to the French consul who had lost some color in his cheeks, Vasiliev noted, despite the appearance of the *tarte au chocolat*.

"The crowd seized them as hostages. The attempt to release them backfired. They were beaten to death in a small room off the street out of sight. I heard shots and feared that a general massacre was under way. We were only a hundred meters from the rioting.

Selim Bey pulled me from the window and allowed me to escape through his *haremlik*. I immediately telegraphed to Athens for a British frigate from Piraeus. Other ships soon arrived, but the girl had been released and Selim Bey had managed to arrest some of the rioters. Six men were hanged." The British consul paused to survey the effect of his recital. There were somber faces around the table.

"I see several lessons for me to learn, gentlemen, if I may speak while you devote yourself to this exquisite *tarte*." Vasiliev leaned forward speaking quietly. "A violent incident, crime if you will, may erupt spontaneously. It may be directed against an individual and the forces of order. It then easily spreads to ground already prepared by mutual distrust. Finally that no matter how responsible and fair minded the local authorities, public order may breakdown, giving a reason, perhaps even an excuse for outside intervention."

"Well put, Major," said Baron Haymerle, "but a bit abstract. And there is another dimension which we are all aware of. The Orthodox are also at one another's throats. Ever since you championed the Slavs, your unpredictable Pan Slav, Count Ignatiev, lent his support to the creation of a Bulgarian exarch, the hierarchy has been split. The Patriarch at Constantinople has his ideas and the Exarch his. They do not correspond. And then, the Catholic hierarchy... you see I am Calvinist, so I have no interests here...especially the Franciscans are at odds with the Jesuits, and the Sultan distrusts the Jesuits as instrument of Vienna, that is the Monarchy. Well, one of the reasons that Count Andrassy is seeking to have Bosnia and Hercegovina placed under the benevolent protection of Emperor and King, Franz Joseph, is to prevent more terrible attacks from happening

"And this is your Austrian mission? To bring civilization to the benighted Slavs?"

The Italian consul seemed to have hurried through his dessert in order to make this intervention.

"So too is your hope to revive the Venetian tradition, isn't that so?"

"Ah. Messieurs, I must intervene here." The French consul had recovered his poise. "The irony in the tragic death of my colleague is that he was responsible for helping to set up, the year before his untimely death, a branch of the Paris-based *Alliance Israelite Universalle*. Yes, we French too have a mission, but it is to educate, nothing more. And the prominent Jewish families have rallied to support the *Alliance*. Our enlightened initiative has caused the Chief Rabbi great discomfiture."

"Gentlemen, we have strayed from our sworn 'mission' which is to instruct and enlighten Major Vasiliev. I can only hope that we have enlightened rather than confused him. You see how we differ among ourselves, Major. So you have a fair picture of the tangled thicket into which you are venturing."

Vasiliev glanced around the table. "What I hear, gentlemen, is how clearly each of you presents the mission of his government. Fortunately for me, I do not have to reconcile these differences. As I understand it, this is the task of your representatives in Berlin. I am instructed to report on local conditions so that my government can make more informed decisions. You have helped me understand better the larger political interests of your governments. Now, all I ask is that your representatives on the ground will also share their views with me just as frankly."

There was a chorus of general approbation. Von Moritz then proposed that the company recommend some lively local music venues for the Major's entertainment during his brief stay."

"I was skating on thin ice," Vasiliev summarized the evening's events to Serov. "I had no way of knowing how much they knew about my assignment to investigate Grigoriev's murder. Obviously Von Moritz did not want to make it an issue. So, we will treat it as a part of my investigation of local conditions. It is a strange thing. But somehow I felt more at ease in discussing these matters with Selim Bey than with our European colleagues. Just the opposite of what you might expect."

Chapter Eight

Thessalonika

The following evening Vasiliev had returned late to the hotel after attending a concert recommended by Von Moritz. Serov was still out on his own special mission to make the rounds of the "watering holes" as he put it to pick up what he could from the lower depths of Thessalonika's night life. Vasiliev was waiting for him in the nearly empty dining room. The musicians were putting away their Turkish guitars when a commotion broke out in the kitchen. A waiter wrenched open the door and looked around wildly. Spotting Vasiliev, he rushed up to him. In a torrent of voluble Greek, he declared, insofar as Vasiliev could understand him, that there was a ruffian in the kitchen who demanded to see him. Vasiliev followed the man and found himself facing an irate kitchen crew surrounding a familiar figure, dressed in an odd manner. Vasiliev held up his hand to quiet the babble of voices.

"My dear Serov, what is happening?" Then he addressed the person in obvious authority, the French chef, explaining that this was one of his agents and should be allowed to accompany him into the dining room.

Vasiliev shook his head as Serov dropped into a chair. "You look as if you have been travelling in rough company." Vasiliev ordered two glasses of raki and a bowl of ice. "Fitted out in a Greek sailor's garb, a bit torn here and there, a cut above the eye, bruised cheek, but swollen knuckles. I would guess you were not the only one damaged. So take your time."

"Well, beggin' your pardon Vasili Vasilich, it wasn't my fight.

Just got caught up, as it were. But there's little importance in all that."

"What is important, then?"

"Well, I'm not sure. But you might make somethin' out of it. There's this tavern, called the Golden Fleece. When I passed in the morning, I was told by the doorman here, who has some Russian, that it was a hangout for Russian sailors. Well, you know, how you taught me to change the way I look, if need be. So here I am in a strange town, I don't speak any of these languages, and there are plenty of 'em. And I'm supposed to find what the talk of the streets is like. So, I pick up some duds at the bazaar to fit in, you know. And down I go to the Golden Fleece. Lucky to fall in with some boys from Odessa, Russians, they were but from Greek families. So they spoke the local tongue. Well, Vasili Vasilich, I've got enough stories to fill a week of tellin'."

"But you have one that is important, right?"

"Ah, you're always good at guessin', like you say, what I'm thinkin'."

Serov cast a longing glance at his empty glass. He had wrapped some ice in a napkin and laid it on his knuckles. Vasiliev signaled for another round.

"Well, it's about a girl who got caught in some religious fight."

"She was kidnapped on her way to converting to the Muslim faith. There was a riot. Two European consuls were killed."

"Ah! Vasili Vasilich. It's always the same. You're two steps ahead of me. So why do I get knocked on the head, if you know all about it." But Vasiliev knew Serov too well, not to hear the slightly ironic emphasis he placed on the word "all."

"Perhaps, not all, then."

"Well, I don't know all that you know"

"Sergeant, no more playing with words. What could I not have known?"

"Ah! there's that." Serov made a show of unwrapping his hand and adding some more ice to his bandage. Vasiliev knew the game. Serov, having been a serf, had no formal education. Much of what he knew of the wider world he owed to Vasiliev. But he reserved the right to reveal in his own time and fashion what he had found out on his own in their investigations. Even if the delay was only a few minutes, Vasiliev had learned to wait until Serov was ready to spin his tale.

"Well, my Odessa friends were tellin' about what they'd heard. Seems the local Greeks here are pretty angry about being accused of snatchin' the girl. They admit she ended up bein' hidden by a Greek family. But the boys who grabbed her was of a different sort."

"I heard the same thing from the chief of police. What else?"

"Some say the mother arranged it all. Hated to see her daughter wearin' a veil. But the local Greeks don't believe a word of it. 'Why stir up the Muslims?' 'Who needs another riot?' So goes the argument. Then someone asks, 'so who gains?' Everyone quiets down. Next thing I know, a big son of a bitch, beggin' your pardon, at the next table starts throwin' punches. And all Hell breaks loose. Maybe, I'm thinkin' as they try to bash my head in, he doesn't like the question. One thing though. He sure didn't look like a Greek or a Turk. Dressed different too. But I didn't hang around to find out who he was."

"Good question, Serov. Who gains? Too good a question, maybe, for the people who do gain."

Vasiliev woke up the next morning remembering what Selim Bey had said: "Trust no one." He checked that Serov felt restored and sent him back to the waterfront. In no time, Serov found the Russian ship anchored offshore, where his friends had told him it would be while the docks were being modernized. They had told him that a certain Sabri Pasha had been responsible for the biggest building project in the history of the city. One of them had even witnessed the famous ceremony ten years before when the Turkish governor had tapped the sea wall with his silver hammer, inaugurating its demolition. But progress had been slow, as always in the Ottoman Empire, due to the difficulties of financing. So the big ships still had to stand off shore while lighters transferred their goods to the docks. One of these craft was just landing when Serov arrived. Two of the men had been at the Golden Fleece greeted him as 'the man with the quick fists.' They went off together to another tavern to drink coffee and Serov asked his favor, passing over a small purse. Later that day a Russian-speaking Greek sailor bought two unreserved second-class tickets on the Austrian railroad from Thessaloniki to Skopje for the next Thursday, and two first-class tickets from Skopje to Prishtina on the following Friday.

****

The same day, Vasiliev paid another visit to Selim Bey and requested assistance in buying two firstclass reserved seats for the same trip on the preceding Wednesday. Having received the tickets by messenger at the Olympia Hotel, he notified the Russian consul of his departure. Vasiliev then checked out, making a fuss over the bill for the benefit of anyone who was observing him. Serov had managed to find two suitcases at the local market along with enough clothing to fill them, and these were sent off to the train station to be loaded on the Wednesday departure. Another set of luggage was checked in the railroad storage room.

That evening two men, one dressed as a Russian merchant of the second guild, the second as his assistant, entered a rooming house located in the tangled lanes leading to the old flour market, the *Oun Kapan*, at edge of the Jewish quarter. Their passports identified them with a trading house in Odessa. They had no trouble obtaining a room. Before turning in, they sat outside on the square under the plane trees and watched the villagers packing up the produce from their stalls, a few Vlach shepherds gathering their surviving lambs, and the last of the Muslim butchers folding up their chopping boards, blood-stained from the dismembered limbs and heads of lambs. Serov's attention was caught by a few wandering Albanian *yogurtdjis*. "See, those fellas over there," he nodded his head in their direction. "They're sort of dressed like that big fella in the Golden Fleece."

Vasiliev glanced over. The men were very tall, over two meters. All of them were belted with Mauser cartridges. They were wearing tight trousers, worn very low and extremely short waistcoats. The interval in between was tightly swathed in sashes and belts. Their faces resembled those of geese with weak chins and a beaky nose.

"Not armed, it would seem," said Vasiliev remembering Selim Bey's remark.

"Not so you'd see it," retorted Serov. "Who knows what's under those sashes?"

"And the man in the Golden Fleece?"

"Not sure. I think I saw the hilt of a dagger under his sash. But he didn't take it out. Maybe he was thinkin' it wasn't that kind of fight."

Vasiliev shook his head. "Unplumbed depths, Serov, you still surprise me. Yes, unplumbed depths."

****

The benefactor of the Iviron Monastery had long before set up an informal networks of armed irregulars throughout the region, and it was easy enough to find some of them in the bazaars. Some were Albanian tribesmen, former soldiers in the service of the Sultan who had been discharged after the war. Others were renegades from the Hungarian regiments who had not accepted the compromise of 1867 that created the Austro-Hungarian Empire. Like the Albanians he had left at the villa and like the men in floppy hats speaking a "strange' language, they were eager to pick up a few coins for whatever service was required of them. He knew their loyalty was a matter of a fiscal transaction. They would take his money, carry out his instructions and then drift off to the north, joining armed gangs known to the population as mountain bandits. He had no fear of running out of funds. The mysterious source in St. Petersburg had employed a string of Russians in subordinate positions at the consulates, keeping him well supplied without asking questions. What he did not understand was that his contempt for the mercenary motivations of the Albanians was badly misplaced. He would pay dearly for his ignorance. When it came to matters of honor, money lost its value. And honor was a family matter. The men who discovered the bodies of the horse stealers were cousins of the dead men. They vowed blood revenge.

Albanians on the March

Chapter Nine

Cetinje

Late on Wednesday, Selim Bey received information that the train to Pristina had been attacked by bandits. The terse message stated only that one railroad guard had been wounded. He immediately telegraphed to Pristina seeking more details. The next day the reply informed him that the bandits appeared to have targeted the first-class car where the guard was wounded and several passengers were robbed. There was no news of any Russian officer having arrived at Pristina. Selim Bey was distraught. Had Vaseliev been abducted? He confronted the gendarme who had ordered the tickets, but the poor man, shaking with fear insisted that he had told no one about his purchase. Selim Bey coldly relieved him of his duties and placed him under arrest.

Von Moritz was horrified to receive the news. He raged against his servants without having the slightest idea who else beside himself at the consulate knew of Vasiliev's plans. He too sent cables to Pristina and to Ionin in Cetinje, notifying him of the disappearance of the Russian major. On Friday evening two equally worded telegrams from Pristina arrived at police headquarters and at the Russian consulate.

"Happy to announce safe arrival at Pristina. Very grateful for all your assistance. Vasiliev."

Selim Bey was at dinner and erupted with a shout of triumph. "Now how by the power of Allah, who alone is great, did he manage that?"

Von Moritz was quick to reassure Ionin that Vasiliev was on his way, ending his telegram, "Understand now why V. was selected for mission."

When the telegram arrived from Von Moritz, Ionin was sprawled on a large Turkish divan covered with Persian rugs, stroking his Persian cat, Venus, with trembling fingers and murmuring endearments. What he said could not be heard let alone understood by anyone in his household. Even Venus sensed some something unusual in her master's rather frenetic stroking of her neck and back. But this was preferable to being lifted unceremoniously off the divan and banished. Across the room Vulcan crouched on the threshold. He was black, of uncertain lineage, and appeared discontented. Ionin called out to him. "Why so sulky. You can join us if you wish." Vulcan's tail twitched ominously.

Reading the message again and again brought Ionin a great sense of relief. He had been in a quandary for some days, anxiously awaiting the arrival of the detective but uncertain about the best means to gather information beforehand. Should he pursue his own inquiries? He consulted with his friend Count Corti who was about to return to Constantinople. Corti advised him to do nothing or as little as possible,

"There is always the danger of compromising the evidence," he pronounced grandly.

Ionin was not convinced. He had ordered the burial of Grigoriev's head in a temporary grave on the grounds of the consulate, in hopes that the rest of him would not be discovered. Beyond that, he thought it wise to show some further initiative. He decided to have the girl interrogated by his orderly, but not immediately. He believed she should have some time to recover from her shock. He had ordered her confined to a room in the consulate where she would be served by Anna Ivanovna, an older Russian woman belonging to his household for many years. Then in Anna's presence the girl would be questioned. It appeared that she knew some Russian, but she insisted on speaking directly to the consul general. He refused to give his consent. There was something intimidating about her beauty. Even Count Corti had been impressed when he watched her being brought into the consulate.

"She doesn't look like any other women in these parts." Ionin's voice had trembled at the spectacle which promised a scandal.

"Not Russian either?" Corti had asked. "Her skin is positively translucent, and pale to the point that it seems to lack color except for the rosy blush on her cheeks. The eyes... *dio mio*, pure blue. And her hair, long dark blonde. A goddess," was Corti's experienced verdict.

Ionin promised the count to reveal all he would learn. But he could not trust himself to question her. And he worried that word of her beauty would get to his wife, who preferred to live in Ragusa, known for her irrational jealousy, Venus excepted. No, his orderly would have to assume the burden, if that is what it was. Having reached this decision, he dumped Venus on the rug where she hissed to show her displeasure and then scurried off before something worse happened to her. Vulcan watched her pass and thumped his tail in approval.

Ionin ignored them as he wrote out the protocol to be followed.

The orderly would report to Ionin in the presence of his secretary who would write down a verbatim account of her answers. When the detective arrived, he would be handed the account. Ionin reassured himself that this procedure would be a persuasive demonstration of his dedication to solving the crime which seemed of such importance to high-ranking members of the government, the court and even the imperial family.

The orderly reported that at first the girl seemed reluctant to speak at all to him.

"She stared at me with those cold blue eyes like I was a serpent. It was disconcerting."

"Yes yes, but get to the point, my boy."

Venus, restored to favor on the divan, was startled, sensing danger. But he she relaxed again when he continued to stroke her

"After a while, the girl muttered a few words to Anna Ivanovna, who then passed on to me what she had said. It's all here," said the orderly, trembling slightly as he handed over a sheaf of notes.

"Well, a summary then. I am just off to shoot." Ionin had apparently forgotten his own instructions on the procedure to be followed.

The orderly was not prepared for this.

"Well...er," he stuttered, "she seems to have been...that is she had certain relations with the victim..."

"You mean she was his mistress. Well and then, what about finding the head?"

"Er, she didn't want to talk about that. When I mentioned...the crime so to speak... she shut down." The orderly lowered his eyes.

"What did she want to talk about?" Ionin demanded, flinging his shooting jacket over his shoulders and tapping the floor impatiently.

"Well, your excellency, she told me the story of her life."

"My God, my boy, we are not in the business of compiling biographies for an encyclopedia!" Ionin was beginning to have doubts about his plan. He thought about Count Corti's advice, the wily Italian. He slammed his fist down on the Venetian table.

Venus was sufficiently alarmed to seek out the company of Vulcan. They scurried out of sight. The rest of the day, no one could locate Vulcan. He had fled at the first cry of anguish by his master and only turned up at night to be fed.

The orderly was crestfallen when he returned to his quarters. Perhaps, he thought to himself, "I should have worded it differently, like 'she told me about her life with Grigoriev.' Oh well, let the detective work it all out. I hope he has better luck." After that there were no more interrogations. The girl was left alone to brood.

The secretary retained his record of the girl's testimony. But something bothered him about the instruction to bury the head. Shouldn't the head too be considered evidence that the detective would wish to examine? The cook was puzzled when he asked for a large quantity of salt without telling her the reason. In the dark garden that evening, he salted the head to preserve it, recalling the stories had had heard from his Montenegrin friend, the local gendarme. The man had related in grisly detail the taking of Turkish heads as trophies during the war. "Clean cut they were," he had boasted. The secretary had examined with some distaste Grigoriev's head he salted it. Not a clean cut he observed. Then he placed it in an airtight box and covered it with a thin layer of soil.

The staff treated the girl well enough. But she could not stand to be confined. Two days after the last visit of the orderly, she persuaded Anna Ivanovna to let her breathe some fresh air. They would walk together in the walled gardens of the consulate. After making a complete tour, she begged to make a second round. She had spotted at the far end a thick tree branch extending outside the wall. When they drew near, she dropped a step behind Anna Ivanovna and struck her with full force on the back of the neck. She stepped over the recumbent body and seized hold of the branch, lifted herself up with the agility of an athlete and clambered over the wall, dropping softly on the other side. Within minutes she was out of sight.

The building had been under surveillance ever since the word has spread throughout Cetinje that a girl had arrived at the Russian consulate carrying a dismembered head. No sooner had she fled down one of the narrow passages of the town then two men seized her, threw a cloth over her head and bundled her into a carriage. She struggled fiercely and the men were hard put to hold her down. A wild ride over a rutted track ended in front of a shanty in the outskirts. She was half dragged half-carried inside and thrust into a sparsely furnished room with bars on the only window. As soon as they left her, she tore the cloth off her head and fell to her knees, sobbing. She had escaped from one prison only to find herself in a worse one. She lifted her tearful eyes and stared in bewilderment at a bronze colored, metallic Latin cross that hung over the heavy wooden door that closed behind her.

Chapter Ten

Skopje

Skopje on the rail line from Thessalonika to Prishtina and Mirovitsa had been spared the fighting during the war. A small detachment of Cossacks had arrived after the Treaty of San Stefano was signed, ceding the town to the newly created large Bulgarian state. The *starshina* had received a telegram from the military attaché in Thessalonika informing him of the arrival of a Russian officer and his orderly traveling incognito. He was instructed to render all courtesies to the two men. When Vasiliev and Serov stepped off the train, the officer was waiting. For a moment he stood transfixed then burst out, "Vasya, for God's sake what are you doing here? And rigged out in that extraordinary outfit."

"Vitya! How amazing!" The two men embraced to Serov's astonishment. "And speak of outfits, you a Cossack *starshina*?"

"Plenty to talk about, just as in the old days"

Vasiliev turned to Serov who was standing rigidly at attention. "Sergeant, this is my old comrade from the Page Corps. Colonel now isn't?" he said, glancing at the shoulder tabs, "Vitali Semeonovich Kashinin and, if I'm not mistaken, judging from his uniform, of the Yaik Cossacks. We haven't seen one another in what, ten years?"

Serov saluted smartly. He would find out later what this was all about.

"A sergeant! Well you too have a different look," Kashinin laughed and he waved to several Cossack troopers to come up, ordering them to conduct the Sergeant, "despite appearances," to the barracks with the luggage. Then he called up two horses and he and Vasiliev trotted into town.

"So what is this, a new uniform?" the troopers snickered as they led Serov to an ox cart, where they piled the luggage.

"Now comrades, don't be too hard on me. You see it was a choice. Either wearing these duds or getting shot."

"Sounds a good story. So let's take a detour and see if we can quench your thirst."

Serov was pleased that, even without trying, he had already opened what Vasiliev would call, "a new line of communication."

After Vasiliev and Kashinin had brought one another up to date over several glasses of raki and a plate of dolma, Kashinin became somber.

"Not good, Vasya, not good at all. Overland to Montenegro? The land is teeming with bands, Albanian and Turkish irregulars, Hungarians too, if you can believe it. Many of them demobilized soldiers. Nowhere to ride safely now. We've only been here a several weeks, but I can tell you, I would prefer service in the Caucasus. At least there you knew the enemy.

Kashinin drank off his raki. "And then there are the Austrians. It seems that they have orders to occupy the district to the north separating the Montenegrins and the Serbs. They call it the Sanjak of Novi Pazar. But it's not clear how far south they are going to get. There's been fighting around Mitrovitsa at the end of the rail line. Last word is the Austrians have not been able to occupy the town."

"But surely the Bulgarians and Serbs were our allies."

"Yes, but they distrust one another. Both of them lay claim to what the Serbs call Old Serbia. But that's the trouble, or one of them. It used to be part of the Serbian Kingdom several hundred years ago. I mean how historic can you be? And the Bulgarians, few though they are in this area, say we Russians have given the place over to them. You know at San Stefano. And God help us, the Albanians, the worst of them all. Sometimes they fight the Turks. Sometimes they serve with them. They claim that the *vilayet*, you know the district of Kosovo, has been their home for centuries after the Serbs fled the Turkish conquest to the north."

Kashinin shook his head and ordered another round.

"But all I have seen in the streets so far and here in this tavern are Muslims, by the looks of them. We passed plenty of minarets, but no churches."

"Exactly. And in the fighting, the Turks and the Albanians defended the place against the Serbs who didn't get closer than Niš just to the north. So who's to have it?"

"And you are here on what kind of a mission?" asked Vasiliev.

"To keep them from slaughtering one another."

"How many men"

"The usual, a *sotnia*, squadron of a hundred."

Vasiliev whistled. "Hardly enough."

"I've already lost five men wounded on patrol and sent back. Ten men sick, in the dispensary, so-called, a filthy place. The rest sullen and ready to bolt."

"But they are Cossacks?"

"From another one of the newly formed hosts, no tradition, no spirit."

"I have no choice, Vitya, but to press ahead. So I need your advice."

"They should have sent you by ship to Scutari. The local Albanians call it Shkodër, just a day's ride from Cetinje."

"Listen, old friend, there's been something wrong with this assignment from the beginning."

Vasiliev told him about the pirate attack at sea and the ambush of the train. "That's the reason for the elaborate disguise."

"So you can expect more trouble. I'm really sorry, Vasya, I can't spare any men to escort you. Maybe at Prishtina you'll have better luck."

"Seeing you was almost worth the trip!"

"Yes, 'almost' is the word."

The next morning, Vasiliev and Serov changed into their uniforms before taking the train on to Prishtina. On the way, Serov related what he had learned from the Cossack rankers.

"They was surely unhappy. Kept repeatin' the same thing. Didn't like the Turks. But if the town was to go over to the Bulgarians, then only a Russian army could keep it in their hands. And they didn't want any part of that."

Vasiliev fell silent, and Serov knew better than to break in on his thoughts. Vasiliev was 'puzzlin' things out. What he did not know was that Vasiliev was more puzzled than puzzling. He kept asking himself what if anything did all this mean for tracking down the murderer of Grigoriev? He was beginning to get the queasy feeling that the suspects in this murder might not be individuals, but nations or even empires.

Chapter Eleven

Prishtina

For reasons known only to God who alone is great, as Selim Bey had said, the railroad from Thessalonika to Mitrovitsa bypassed the town of Prishtina, six kilometers away. A carriage ordered by Selim Bey met them at the station, driven by an Albanian coachman. Two Albanian guards, seated opposite Vasiliev and Serov, were armed to the teeth. There was no way of communicating with them, but they handed Vasiliev a telegram from Selim Bey assuring him of their loyalty and the necessity of protecting him against robbers during the hour's drive. Their first view of Prishtina, nestled in a valley between two low hills, made a pleasant impression with its bright red roofs. The cottages interspersed with clumps of green trees and white minarets. But the impression quickly evaporated as they entered the town. The streets were dirty and the facades of many of the tumbled down houses were no cleaner. They passed the partially roofed bazaar in a bad state of repair. The stalls were crammed with shoddy foreign merchandise, the benefits of easy transport by rail. A whiff of rotting meat drifted over from the butchers' section.

They stopped at an inn, run by a Vlach. The two Albanians mounted guard in the corridor outside their rooms. They did not seem to require food or sleep. A policeman showed up, introducing himself as Admir, presenting his credentials and another message from Selim Bey who gave his assurance that the man was trustworthy. He invited them to his home for dinner, with the Albanians trailing behind and resuming their guard in the street outside. The women of the household were only partially veiled and dressed in the Turkish manner.

The policeman who also turned out to be Albanian spoke creditable French and was eager to present the claims of his people over the Kosovo *vilayet*.

"As you will see, *monsieur l'officier*, we are able to keep order if left to ourselves. Why just recently an Englishman came here all the way from Shkodër, Evans was his name. By foot, monsieur! Through the mountains and without a scratch."

"Have you had any other foreign visitors lately?"

"What do you mean by foreign?" a note of caution had crept into his voice.

"Well, like us, Russians."

"Not here, but..." he hesitated, recalling the message of Selim Bey.

"There were stories, of course, always stories about mysterious strangers. But these come from the mountains where they love to tell tales."

"I would be grateful to hear such tales. You see, my government wishes to be fair to all parties in drawing frontiers. The more information we have from those who have travelled in the region, the better informed we will be and the fairer our decisions can be."

"Ah yes, of course. Well, let me tell you about fairness. You have spent only a few hours in our town. Even a few days or weeks will not be enough to learn everything about us. As a sworn official, let me assure you that we live in peace here, the majority who are Muslims and a large number of Orthodox, even some Spanish Jews. I say Spanish because they came from Spain long ago. The Orthodox are called Vlachs not Serbs, as you might be told elsewhere. The Serbs all left with Archbishop Arsenius, many years ago. It was after the Great Morean War. Imagine, in the 1690s! So why do the Serbs want to come back?"

"I know this history, *mon ami*, but I would like to hear the tales."

"Yes, the tales...." The host clapped his hands for the remnants of the veal stew to be removed and sweets to be served.

"One such tale speaks of a man, perhaps a Russian like yourself, but not an officer, who was seen at the Devich Monastery, some years ago, before the war. It is said that he spoke our language. This is hard to believe, but so it is said."

"And that is all?"

"It is said, he travelled alone"

"Anyone else?"

"There are always the Franciscans."

"And what is their purpose?

"Why, to minister to the Albanian Roman Catholics, but they are losing ground."

"Why is that, then?"

"The Franciscans are agents of the Austrians, or the Italians. So they are not welcome."

"Do your tale tellers say anything about the mysterious Russian and the Franciscans?"

The Albanian's eyes shifted again.

"Not that I heard, but, of course, the tellers of tales do not reveal everything they have heard or seen, lest..."

"Yes?"

"...lest they may not be believed."

The next morning a sharp wind was blowing out of the hills as Vasiliev and Serov mounted their horses, waiting for their guide. The two guards had vanished in the night. A young Albanian rode up and bowed to them.

"I am your guide. I am called Skoro, which in your language means 'the swift one.' I try to live up to my name."

He was unusually tall for a local Albanian, with piercing grey eyes betraying a Slavic admixture. He wore a gold embroidered waistcoat and several colorful sashes with two pistols and a dagger thrust in the bands. He spoke a Slavic dialect that Vasiliev understood but could not imitate so he answered in Russian. "We go to the Devich Monastery."

Chapter Twelve

Devich Monastery

They rode for several hours over a great plain where all the unploughed land was covered with blood red flowers. In the lead, Skoro swept his hand over the vast expanse, exclaiming, "Kosovo Pole, the blood of heroes."

Serov rode up beside Vasiliev. "What does he mean?"

"A battle fought here centuries ago between the invading Ottoman Turks and the Serbs. It has become a legend."

"Is everythin' around here centuries old?" Serov shook his head.

Skoro burst into song, an ancient ballad.

> "Thy Milosh, O Lady, fell by the cold waters of the Sinitza, where many Turks perished. He left a name to the Serbian people that will be sung as long as there are men and Kosovo field…"

"So who won this famous battle?"

"Depends on what you mean by 'won.'"

"Vasili Vasilich, please, no more riddles."

"Just listen for a moment."

Skoro had regained his breath.

> "Over this dreary plain spread the Turkish army; steed by steed. Warrior by warrior; the spears were like unto a black forest; the banners like the

clouds, their tents like snow; had rain fallen from
the heavens it would have dropped not upon earth,
but upon goodly steeds and warriors."

Skoro raised his head to stare at the cloudless sky and fell silent.
He turned in the saddle.

"Perhaps after Devich you will go south and you will see the
tomb of Sultan Murad I who perished on the field."

"So what is the legend?" asked Serov

"What I know is little enough. Perhaps Skoro will tell you more.
But sometime in the late fourteenth century two armies met here,
one commanded by Sultan Murad I and the other by the Serbian
Prince Lazar."

"So, Muslims against Christians."

"The legend or the ballads are not clear about this. It seems
there were Christian bowman in the pay of the Ottoman army. That
was not unusual for the time. Whatever the case, the fighting was
fierce and both Murad and Lazar were killed.

"So, one thing is for sure."

"The Serbs commemorate this as the great tragedy of their
nation, the end of their independence, the triumph of crescent over
cross."

"Vasili Vasilich, beggin' your pardon, you sound like a ballad
yourself."

Vasiliev laughed. "They're catchy, these ballads."

They turned north and rode up onto a plateau where they
passed a group of several houses surrounded by a huge palisade
of thick stakes sharpened into spikes at the top. Vasiliev marveled
at the way they were tied together with twisted branches, creating
a stout and solid barrier. At intervals on the outer perimeter, thick
oak trunks buttressed the wall. A dense mass of blackthorn ran all
along the top.

"Place looks like a fort," muttered Serov

"Serbian *zadruga*," Skoro called back to them.

Vasiliev explained. "The Serbian families left in the area still
practice a form of communal agriculture like our commune at
home. But theirs is restricted to an enlarged family. I learned at
camp that sometimes a man would have ten or more children who

then married and with their children and other relatives continued to live and work together."

"And maybe fight together."

"Good thinking, Sergeant. Maybe that's why they've survived."

They passed a ruined church and then the road improved and individual houses of Muslim landowners began to appear. Below them a group of people, including women and children, were scattered along the banks of a stream.

Skoro shouted a word and then spat.

"I think he said gypsies, sounds the same in all Slavic languages."

"And just as unpopular in all of 'em, too, eh?"

On the steep descent to the monastery they began to meet pilgrims, who swarmed around the two men in uniform.

"You've come to free your Orthodox brothers!" the men shouted. The women raised their hands to make the sign of the cross. Vasiliev waved and they pressed on to the monastery.

A monk pushed his way through the crowd and greeted them. Then he ran to summon the Archimandrite or *Hagi*, as the locals called him.

Vasiliev and Serov made their way into two connecting yards, the first jammed with pilgrims, jostling one another and pointing to the visitors with astonishment and enthusiasm, The second yard was crammed full of horses, carts, oxen and buffaloes with their owners, shouting and gesticulating wildly. They dismounted and were taken up the narrow stairs of a large white-washed *hospitium* into a rabbit warren of rooms. Skoro whispered to Vasiliev.

"They know me here. We'll meet in the morning," and he disappeared.

The *Hagi* came to their rooms as soon as he finished conducting services. He was an impressive figure, with a strong jaw, aquiline nose and a thatch of dirty blonde hair. He was delighted that Vasiliev spoke some Serbian. It turned out that he had been born into an Albanian Muslim family but converted to Orthodoxy and had forgotten much of the tongue he had spoken as a child.

"So here, it is the faith that determines what you are."

Vasiliev wondered what faith Skoro professed. He seemed to be welcome everywhere.

"Only one other Russian has visited us in my lifetime," the *Hagi* continued, "Before that, who knows."

"Yes, it is about him I have come to visit you."

The *Hagi* nodded thoughtfully.

"Good, we shall speak after our meal together."

A fast day, but the food was abundant. Fresh trout from the nearby Drin River, tomatoes from the monastery garden, balls of rice and herbs rolled in vine leaves, which was called here *japrak* and not dolma. The spices were different too, and green peppers stuffed with rice, also spicy. Bowls of clotted cream (*kaimak*) were placed in the center of the table. The meal was topped off with sheep cheese and fruit.

Vasiliev and Serov were seated at one end of the table raised on a low dais. Below them on long benches were seated a vast number of pilgrims, piling food freely into their copper bowls. The *Hagi* told them there was enough room for a thousand or more pilgrims. Vasiliev notice Skoro feasting with a group of male pilgrims. He had left his weapons somewhere else. After dinner Skoro joined Serov and some of the men in dancing the *kolo*. They were much cheered for their elegant style.

The *Hagi* took Vasiliev by the hand and led him to a small office off the nave of the church.

"So, the Russian," he began without being asked any further. "His name was Boris Grigoriev, and he was very devout. He spoke excellent Serbian, having learned it, he told me, at the Ipatiev Monastery outside Moscow and then, I would say, perfected it here among us. He spoke to me frankly, but there is no reason to hide what he said. He was a member of the Slavic Benevolent Committee in Moscow. He wanted to help us, Orthodox people, sustain and defend our faith. He asked me many questions about the religious life here in Kosovo *vilayet*. What can I tell you that you may not know?"

"You may assume I know next to nothing about the local situation. But first I have something to tell you that will shock and disgust you. I too will be frank in all matters concerning Grigoriev. We have information that he was brutally murdered in Montenegro."

"Sweet Mother of God," the *Hagi* crossed himself and clung to the cross around his neck.

"My assignment is to find the murderer."

"May God speed you on your way," exclaimed the *Hagi*.

"But also, I have been asked by the military authorities to find out what I can about the situation, or plight, if this is the case, of the Orthodox in the lands that are being disputed by the great powers in Berlin."

"So we may not come under the authority of the Bulgarian exarch?"

"Is this important to you?'

"You see, Major, the 'situation' as you call it is very complicated. My own allegiance is to the Patriarch of Constantinople, and not to the Exarch of Bulgaria. This is a minor difference, perhaps, compared to our relations with the Muslims. But up until the recent war our relations have been rather peaceful. Sometimes I think that there are greater problems in dealing with our Latin brothers. The Franciscans have been very active ministering to their flock. But the number of Catholics has been declining recently. Many have converted to Islam. Or, they appear to have done. There is much talk of 'Crypto-Catholics.' You see, dear Major, the far away diplomats have no understanding of what is happening here. So there will be more violence, God preserve us."

Skoro was still cavorting with the pilgrims when Vasiliev and Serov returned to their room. There were no beds. But they had no trouble sleeping on the two straw mattresses laid down on the floor.

They left the monastery early in the morning with the blessings of the *Hagi*. They were riding three abreast, approaching a dense clump of woods when the first shot rang out. Vasiliev's horse stumbled and fell, pitching him over her head. He fell heavily on his side narrowly missing a large boulder. For a moment he lost consciousness. Serov was out of the saddle in an instant and covered Vasiliev with his body. He drew his pistol and fired into the woods as he dragged the semi-conscious Vasiliev behind the rock. A second shot struck Serov's horse, killing it immediately. Behind him he heard Skoro gallop off into the trees. Vasiliev's horse lay on its side thrashing and screaming. Serov turned to shoot it in the head. A third rifle shot kicked up dust by the side of the rock.

"Vasili Vasilich, can you hear me? We are pinned down and Skoro has run off. Both our horses are dead."

Vasiliev opened his eyes, grimacing with pain.

"It's the shoulder, dislocated. You know what to do."

Serov seized the arm holding the shoulder tightly and gently massaged the bones back into place, but the pain was excruciating. Vasiliev fainted. In a few minutes he opened his eyes again.

"If you cover me, I can make a dash for the trees," said Serov.

"Not a chance. The man's a sharpshooter. I would be firing wildly and he would have a clear shot. Our flanks are out in the open, so he'll have to stay concealed. Our only recourse is to wait for darkness, and then try to make our way back. On foot."

"Do you think Skoro was in on it?"

"No, or else he would have made certain to finish us off. I'm hoping he rode for help. We can only wait and see. For now, try firing over the rock at intervals, see if our man is still out there."

They let an hour pass. Staying well concealed, Serov reached over the top of the boulder and fired. His shot was immediately returned, sending a stone chip flying over their heads.

"He may be a good shot, but he's not very smart. He should have held fire until we thought he had given up and then shot us down as we broke cover."

Serov fired again with the same result.

They waited again. Suddenly two muffled shots rang out from the trees, followed by what sounded like an exchange of gunfire. Then silence. A few minutes later they heard Skoro shouting.

"It's safe now. We killed him."

Serov stood up to see Skoro and the two Albanian guards who had led them to the monastery riding out of the trees, waving and leading a horse.

"Well, where did they come from?"

Skoro explained while wrapping Vasiliev's bruised shoulder with one of the own sashes. Vasiliev did not understand all his words, but enough to translate for Serov.

"The two Albanian guards had been sent ahead to reconnoiter.

They missed the lone rifleman in ambush but spotted a band of ten horsemen on the other side of the woods. They rode back and met Skoro who had circled behind the sharpshooter. They shot him. When the band rode in to see what was happening, they drove them off with a volley. As I understood Skoro, they did not want to kill any of the band for fear of starting a blood feud."

"But what about the sharpshooter? asked Serov. "Didn't killing him count as bloodshed?"

Skoro shrugged "He did not belong to a local tribe. They could tell by his dress."

"Must be hell to be a policeman here," Serov grunted.

Chapter Thirteen

On the Road to Mitrovitsa

Skoro insisted that they return to the monastery at Devich. The way ahead to Ipek was too dangerous. He pointed out that the town was almost all Muslim but surrounded by Serbian villages. Vasiliev translated word by word: "the Serbs are like an island surrounded by Albanians. Now it is not clear whether they will belong to Serbia or to us."

"You remember, Serov, that many of the pilgrims at Devich monastery were Serbs from Ipek. They were the ones calling for our help."

"I don't understand," said Vasiliev turning to Skoro who was holding the bridle of the horse the Albanians had retrieved from the dead sharpshooter. "Why suddenly is it too dangerous when we set off for Ipek from the monastery only a few hours ago?"

The guards had ridden ahead. Skoro seemed confused and mumbled. "They found out that there are disorders there. And then there is the band we met. More trouble ahead. Also we have only one extra horse. This is not good."

There was nothing Vasiliev could do. He depended upon these men. They would have to turn back.

The two guards rode the dead man's horse turning their mounts over to Vasiliev and Serov. The procession slowly made its way back to the monastery. There another surprise was waiting for them.

The *Hagi* came out to meet them a worried look on his face.

After Skoro had told him what happened, he exclaimed that there was even greater trouble on the horizon to the south.

"The Albanian chiefs have gathered at Prizren. You must come inside and rest, Major and I will tell you more about this."

"For some time," he explained, "there have been rumors among the Albanians about what may happen to their lands when the great powers settled the new boundaries. It seems there were no Albanians at the Congress of Berlin where their fate was decided. Now word has reached us that the some of the land to the north, beyond Ipek, where you were planning to travel, has been given to Montenegro. The Muslim chiefs are angered. This is their land inhabited by their people. They have met to form a League. It is intended to defend the Albanian lands against foreign occupation. They have sworn allegiance to the Sultan. They promise to respect the life and property of all his subjects, including non-Muslims.

"That was in June this year while you were on your way. Then terrible news just today from Gusinje. This is to the west of Ipek, a district of the Kosovo *vilayet* near the old Montenegrin border. Terrible news," he repeated. The *Hagi* had lost his noble bearing and seemed somehow physically diminished in Vasiliev's eyes.

"What do we know? Two men have told the tale. An Ottoman official by the name of Mehmed Ali Pasha, a man known to me… he came from a Huguenot family, born in Germany. But he jumped ship in Istanbul and joined the Ottoman army. Became a field marshal no less. You see how many different people serve the Sultan? Yes, Mehmed Ali Pasha had been at Berlin. I heard he worked hard to prevent a loss of Ottoman land. But then he was sent to the north, to Kosovo *vilayet* to persuade the Albanian chiefs to accept the decisions of the Congress, to approve their becoming part of Montenegro. A brave but foolhardy effort. He arrived at Djakova…you see I am telling you this because that is the only other overland route you can follow to complete your mission. And at Djakova he was attacked and a massacre followed. The men say they saw his head on a pike paraded through the town bazaars."

A slight sob escaped the Hagi's lips. He quickly recovered and grasped Vasiliev's hand.

"You understand what I am telling you? Another murder, but not a mystery. On all sides violence. May God preserve us.

"Major, all paths are blocked for you. You must not try to reach Ipek or you too will fall victim to this violence. The railroad is still open. You should return to Thessaloniki."

Vasiliev haggled with a dealer in the crowded yard of the monastery to purchase fresh horses. After another uneasy night's tossing and turning on the mattresses, they set out again early in the morning, having changed back into civilian clothes. His shoulder still ached. He wondered why the Albanians should help him. As they moved out, Skoro was in the lead and the two Albanian guards brought up the rear. There was no singing. Skoro took a small detour on the plain of Kosovo to the tomb of Murad I, the Turkish hero of the great battle.

"On the hill there, is the burial place of his standard bearer." They drew up beside a small mosque surrounded by a walled-in plot containing several graves. A guardian emerged from a small shelter. He seemed as old as the tomb. He held a staff in his hand as if that would protect the holy site, or perhaps it was merely to hold him upright. He coughed and mumbled a few words.

Skoro told him these *giaours* had come to pay respects to the fallen hero. The man hesitated, screwing up his eyes and staring at Vasiliev. Vasiliev passed a few coins to Skoro.

"Tell him this is to help maintain the garden."

The guardian stepped aside and with an expansive gesture waved them in. Serov had no interest in visiting a Muslim's tomb and turned back to wait for Vasiliev in the garden. As a mark of respect, Vasiliev did not cross the threshold. A large coffin stood on a rich Turkish carpet in the center of the mosque. It was covered with a black cloth overlain with several colored draperies of crimson and silver. The whitewashed walls were beginning to peel. And now it seemed, Vasiliev thought, as if the Albanian Muslims were rebelling against their Sultan. Or was the Sultan using them to resist the decisions he had agreed to at Berlin? Murad had been the terror of Europe and now the Europeans were dictating the boundaries of his shrunken empire. Vasiliev recalled a line from Shelley's poem, *Ozymandias*. How did it go? "Look on my work, ye Mighty, and despair."

The journey back to Prishtina was uneventful and the men rode silently. Vasiliev wondered how he would draft his report to Totleben. Ancient quarrels, never resolved. Could any outside forces impose their will? As if to confirm his fears, Admir, their policeman friend, warned them conditions were bad at both ends of the rail line.

"If I had to chose, where there is no good choice" he said spreading his hands in a gesture of helplessness, "I would go back north to Mitrovitsa. The chances are that the Austrians will have arrived. But it is hard to predict. To the south the Albanians are too excitable and no one knows what they want. You will have to go to the station and wait for the train coming from Mitrovitsa. It will probably not proceed any further south but will return to the north."

The train arriving from Mitrovitsa was jammed with people fleeing the Novi Bazar where the Austrian troops were moving in. They had been authorized at Berlin to occupy the corridor between Serbia and Montenegro created to keep the two Slavic states apart. Vasiliev wondered whether the Serbs and Montenegrins had gotten anything in return. He would soon find out. How would all this affect his assignment? It seemed to him more and more futile. He silently cursed the high born at court in St. Petersburg who had sent him on this impossible mission.

As the engine came to a stop short of the town, the crowd milling about on the station platform surged toward the cars that were disgorging its passengers. In this tangled mass of humanity, all shouting and screaming, a man in the uniform of a railroad guard was trying to enforce some kind of order. In desperation, he drew his revolver and fired into the air.

"People, listen to me! You will be taken south but not on this train. We have to return to Mitrovitsa now to pick up more passengers who fear for their lives."

"And how will we all fit in, then," a woman's voice rang out.

A few men were trying to force their way back on the train.

"Don't be foolish," cried the conductor. It you stay on board you will be carried back to Mitrovitsa."

Vasiliev feared the man might be beaten to death. But he was rescued by several other railroad guards who jumped down from the first car and also fired into the air.

Vasiliev and Serov managed to clamber aboard waving their tickets.

Very few passengers stayed in their seats, gaping out the window at the crowd milling around the station platform.

When they arrived at Mitrovitsa, the station platform was also crammed with passengers, mainly Serbian families, fleeing in fear of their lives.

"My God, they're just jumping from one fire into another," groaned the conductor.

Mitrovitsa, the terminal point in the line from Thessaloniki was a railroad town still under construction. But it had a clean new look in comparison to the rundown condition of Prishtina. There were vegetable gardens around a few of the houses and, the conductor had assured them, there was a good supply of fresh water.

The streets were patrolled by troops of the Austrian-Hungarian army, although Vasiliev immediately noticed that their uniforms identified them as Hungarian hussars. As they descended the train, an officer and two men stopped them and asked politely for their documents. The officer spoke German. He told them that the town had just been secured but there were Serbian bands in the neighborhood.

"So I advise," he switched on a sardonic smile, "that you do not promenade outside the town limits."

He accompanied them to what looked like an administrative building, its two wings still under construction. Major Peter Barga of the Fifth Hussars was in command. He too spoke to them in German.

"I am happy to say that our two countries have agreed at Berlin on all contested points. Let me explain." He rolled out an old ordinance map on his desk.

"I apologize for the inaccuracies on the map but you know our Turkish friends have not the habit of being exact. So here we are on the extreme limit of what the Ottoman officials have called the Sanjak of Novi Pazar. I understand from the latest dispatches from Vienna that it was one of the most hotly discussed topics at Berlin. It remains under Ottoman sovereignty but we are permitted to occupy it in order to maintain order and keep the railroad open. Otherwise...well I believe Captain Polyani probably told you that the local Serbs are very unhappy about the arrangement. You can see from the map that this Sanjak actually forms a corridor separating Montenegro and Serbia. Our representative at Berlin, Count Andrassy, insisted that this was necessary to keep the two Slavic states apart in order secure our communications. Fortunately, your Tsar Alexander accepted this plan."

Major Barga stepped away from the map.

"Let me speak frankly, Major." Vasiliev was tired of hearing the phrase. It was as if most of the time he could only expect to be deceived.

"In the recent past, our mutual, official relations in these wild regions have been troubled by unofficial and irresponsible elements."

"You mean Panslavs?"

"Your word, Major. Frankly I do not know exactly what the term means. Sympathy for the Orthodox population? Fine, we are all Christians. Agitation to unite all the South Slavic people into a great state? That is something different and, I think you would agree, threatens us all. I fear the illusion that this was not only possible but desirable was first advanced by Napoleon Bonaparte. You will recall that after he destroyed the Republic of Venice, he seized the entire Dalmatian Coast. His generals cultivated the idea of an Illyrian state, unifying Croats, Serbs and others. A revolutionary idea, don't you agree? Well, for us it was inflammatory and dangerous."

"Yes, I have read my history. Count Metternich, at Paris in 1815, insisted that Austria annex the Dalmatian Coast."

"Exactly, and your tsar at the time, Alexander the first of that name agreed. And now we have his nephew, Alexander the second of that name, again agreeing with us that the new version of this revolutionary idea must be suppressed. And it is up to us ..."

"Now Austrians and Hungarians."

"Exactly. Which means that our Emperor in Vienna has the benefit of us Magyars, if I may use the name we prefer, who have had more experience in dealing with the Slavs. Especially the Croats."

"The Austrian mission."

"If you wish."

"This is what your consul in Thessaloniki called it."

"So it must be then that I am not a diplomat."

For a moment the two men stood facing one another over the map. Many years later Vasiliev would remember this conversation. He was then in America, a retired sheriff in the town of Duluth, Minnesota. A very hot August day in 1914. His son had just rushed into his office waving the local newspaper.

"It's war, Dad! The Austrians have bombarded Belgrade. They are determined to destroy Serbia."

Chapter Fourteen

Vienna

It was already late when Benjamin von Kállay rose from his desk in the Foreign Ministry at No. 2 Ballhausplatz in Vienna. Rubbing his tired eyes, he stood for a moment gazing out the window at the streetlights of the Square. It was late and Vilma and the girls would be waiting. He closed a folder with the label 'Current situation in Hercegovina' submitted by General Filipović and he shook his head disapprovingly. As the chief of the first department in the Ministry, Kállay did not have any official responsibility for the Condominium of Bosnia and Hercegovina, as the occupied province was now called in Vienna. But he was preparing himself for the position of chief administrator. He had already served as consul general in Belgrade and had visited Bosnia before the rebellion. It was said by those who knew that his Serbian was as proficient as a native due to the devoted attention of his mother, who was of Serbian descent. Von Kállay, or Kállay de Nagy-Kálló in the original Hungarian, saw himself as fulfilling a mission he would prefer to call Habsburg rather than Austrian.

He glanced at the portrait of Emperor Franz Joseph. What would he do without us Magyars, he thought to himself. The Austrians had been involved with the German and Italian states for centuries. He would call it an obsession. Now, they had been kicked out of both for their trouble. The legacy of Metternich had turned to dust. It was the turn of the Magyars to restore the prestige of the empire, now baptized the Austro-Hungarian Monarchy. And Count Andrassy was the chief architect. Kállay had admired his work at Berlin. To maneuver among Bismarck, Disraeli, Shuvalov and all the rest required the touch of a genius. To get Bosnia and Hercegovina without a war and force the Russians to abandon their absurd dream of a great Bulgaria! Yes, pure genius. He himself had witnessed the effects. As a member of the European Commission to draw the boundaries of two Bulgarian states, he had lined up with the English. Time and again they had achieved good results. Just like Andrassy at Berlin.

He rang the small silver bell on his desk and the door opened immediately.

"Gabor, have this dispatch sent at once to General Filipović in Sarajevo."

Now it was necessary to put his plan into operation. He had no doubts that his methods would meet with the approval of the local population, if only Vienna supported him. He knew his wife, Countess Vilma Bethlen, would back him to the hilt, even though she would have to give up living in Vienna for provincial Sarajevo. But the military! Of course they had to repress the resistance, but then they hadn't a clue what to do afterwards. As for the Duke of Württemberg who was tapped to succeed Filipović, he knew nothing about the region. But he, Kállay, knew his turn would come.

He rehearsed his speech to Andrassy. First, it would be necessary to correct the abuses, the lack of discipline on the part of renegades who obeyed only their paymaster. Those idiots in Thessaloniki who had staged those incidents. And God only knew whether they were involved in other plots and conspiracies to embarrass the Turks and the Russians both. Next, he would tell the Count we can fulfill our mission by constructive measures, not provocations and assassinations. Yes, he would become a builder and weld the people together into a Bosnian nation under the benevolent rule of the Monarchy. Perhaps another arrangement like that between Hungary and Croatia; control from Budapest but a degree of autonomy in Sarajevo. That would confound the Panslavs and the Serbs in Belgrade whom he knew only too well. So, third, encourage the Serbs to set their sights on the south and turn their backs on Bosnia. Get the Montenegrins to go along. Keep them both away from the coast. Finally, dear Count, he continued his inner monologue, with our railroad through the Sanjak to Thessaloniki and our command of the sea lanes in the Adriatic we will dominate the economic life of the entire West Balkans. So let the Russians try to do the same in the East. They will fail, of course, as they have in their misnamed Kingdom of Poland, whereas we have succeeded in our Polish province of Galicia. Yes we shall demonstrate to all of Europe, that it is we who are the civilizers and Russia only a false claimant to the title. Would the Count not appreciate his thinking which adhered so closely to his own?

Chapter Fifteen

Livadia, Crimea

Outside her small cottage near Livadia, Ekaterina Dolgorukova strolled in the gardens. She loved this retreat from the stiff protocol of the Winter Palace. She felt the soft air against her cheeks, stirred faintly by the breeze off the Black Sea. She only wished that Alexander would spend more time here with her and Gogo. But now she was waiting impatiently for the arrival of her Italian hat maker. The girl was always full of gossip from the Russian court where she had many customers for her services. But this time, it was not about hats or gossip that excited Ekaterina. The girl had managed to convey a carefully worded message through an intermediary who served as Ekaterina's major domo. It promised exciting news from the Italian ambassador. This could only mean one thing, a financial opportunity.

The girl was a perfect *intriguante*. She arrived with a dozen hat boxes. The two women strolled in the garden where the Countess' borzoi bitch was rooting about. Ekaterina use to say that even if the dog could talk, she was too stupid to understand anything. But one does not scorn a gift from his Imperial Majesty, the Tsar of All Russia.

"*Eh bien, ma chère, j'ai des impatiences dans mes jambes; dites moi vite quelque chose d'extraordinaire.*"

The girl explained that the Italian ambassador had hoped to present the glad tidings in person. It had been a long time since he had been invited to Livadia. But he sent his warmest regards. Ekaterina fidgeted while the girl spoke.

"Très bien, très bien, mais des nouvelles! "

The ambassador had recommended several years before that the Countess buy some Ottoman bonds. She had hesitated. The proposal seemed risky in political as well as financial terms. In the end, she had agreed. Now, the girl reported that at the Congress of Berlin Count Corti had inserted into a protocol prepared by the French and English for the creation of an expert financial commission at Constantinople a proposal to examine the claims of the Ottoman bondholders and to recommend satisfactory steps to be taken to assure that they be met.

"The profits will be enormous and guaranteed forever!" the girl exclaimed.

Ekaterina clapped her hand so loudly that the borzoi bitch lifted her head and howled in distress.

"Maintenant, montrez moi des chapeau, qui ont du vrai chic."

She felt she was at her best when Alexander came to visit a few days later. But she sensed immediately, despite his effort conceal his feelings that he was depressed by news from Berlin, the very place from which she had such glad tidings.

After he had fondled Gogo and the other children, he sank back into his chair and covered his eyes for a moment with a shaking hand.

"What is the trouble, my darling Sasha?"

"Shuvalov has given away everything at Berlin."

More good news; she caught herself in time.

"But surely the Prince could have intervened."

"Ah, Katia my darling, Gorchakov is no longer the man he was ten years ago. First, he let that insane Panslav, Ignatiev, bully him into violating the agreement I had with Franz Joseph and now he succumbs to Shuvalov's intrigues."

"Oh my dear, you have been ill served." She would not remind him that she had spoken against out against the Panslavs and had also worked to remove Shuvalov from his dominant position at court. She was more astute than any of his advisers. But she could not say this. Her dear Sasha must be allowed to learn for himself the truth of what she told him.

She held him in her arms and stroked his forehead.

"At least there is peace, and that is due to you, my darling.

Others would have dragged you into war with all Europe. That hateful Disraeli was just ready to pounce, and the wily Magyar, Count Andrassy, belongs in a gypsy bazaar not in the Habsburg Foreign Ministry. Even the great Bismarck was a disappointment, wasn't he?" She had never ventured to express her political ideas so boldly.

"So you see it all," he murmured. She led him off to bed and cradled him in her arms until he fell asleep. She counted this as one of her most successful days.

Her sense of triumph was short-lived. An attempt was soon made on the tsar's life. A bomb had derailed a train in which he had been scheduled to travel. She was absent, of course, but now all her plans seemed threatened. Alexander had become in the words of one minister, "a semi-ruin." He complained that he sat in the Winter Palace almost all the time and whenever he dared to go out, his carriage was accompanied by a convoy of Cossacks. When the Empress, Maria Alexandrovna died, Dolgorukova saw this as her last chance. She persuaded the tsar to marry her in secret, violating the Orthodox Church's prohibition of a new marriage for one year after the death of a spouse. Shortly after, she made her first appearance at a public ceremonial by his side. The diminutive Gogo stood beside them in his Cossack uniform.

The Italian ambassador had already informed her that Count Corti had proposed a new boundary that left the silver mines in Ottoman territory. "Of course, the situation is still very fluid, as we say. The Austrians are to occupy the area. But I can assure you, Most Serene Highness, that if the settlement is reached along these lines your bonds will have greatly increased in value."

Dolgorukova was thrilled more by his use of the title the tsar intended to bestow upon her publicly than the idea of increasing her wealth as a hedge the against any eventuality. What did it matter now that her marriage was morganatic, violating the taboo in force since Peter the Great that forbade rulers from taking Russian wives. Her children could not inherit the throne, but they would be safe. There was nothing she could do to stop the rumors. Her maid had reported a particularly ominous one. Two hundred years earlier, a peasant prophet had predicted a violent death for any tsar who married a Dolgorukova. She shivered when she heard it.

Chapter Sixteen

Berlin

Count Peter Andreevich Shuvalov sat at his desk staring out the enormous window of his study at the flickering lights of Berlin. He found the city provincial compared to St. Petersburg. The only point in common was the abundance of mosquitoes. And now after days of wrangling with the great men of Europe over the Balkans, he was exhausted and dispirited. He picked up his quill and addressed an envelope: "Lady Mary Derby, the Knowsley." He paused, his thoughts going back to the happier days when he first arrived in England as Russia's ambassador and found in Lord and Lady Derby great friends, each in a in a different way. He conducted his official business in a relaxed atmosphere with Lord Derby as Foreign Minister, but wrote informally and more intimately to Lady Derby, sharing his hopes for reconciliation between their two countries. In return, she supplied him with bits and pieces of information that could only have come from someone privy to discussions in the British cabinet. They did not hide their cordial relations with one another. The gossips whispered that there was more to it than met the eye. Reportedly Queen Victoria had expressed herself. "We are not pleased."

"Chère Lady Derby," he wrote, continuing his letter in his perfect French, "Lord Salisbury and I have grown to respect one another, although it took some time to overcome his reserve. I badly miss the former ease of manner and frankness of my discussions with Lord Derby. His resignation was a terrible blow to Russia and to me personally. Here at Berlin, Lord Beaconsfield holds sway over the British delegation. He speaks only in English which not all his interlocutors understand and then, being half-deaf, he fails to understand what they reply. But Prince Bismarck holds him in high regard: *"Der alte Jude, das ist der Mann"* he says, repeatedly. But Lord B. is no friend of Russia, as you know. As for the rest, I could write volumes. Our most fervent opponent is Count Andrassy. Lord Salisbury has described him as "thinner and gypsyer than ever." He is very friendly, playing the knight in his tête-à têtes with me. But in the presence of the English he hangs on every word of Lord B. and Salisbury like a slavish admirer. They often work in tandem. They have connived to deny Montenegro and Serbia a common border. With the support of Count Corti they had have insisted that corridor separating the two countries, which the Turks call the Sanjak of Novi Pazar, remain under the rule of the Sultan while the Austrians retain the right to occupy it. I have strongly opposed their maneuver. But I just received a message for St. Petersburg to concede the point. Where does that come from? We have already agreed to the Austrian occupation of Bosnia and Hercegovina in return for some small concessions. The trouble there is that our Panslav enthusiasts have been stirring up armed resistance to the Austrian troops in occupation of Bosnia. You know my enemies are at work here, in St. Petersburg and the Balkans. Prince Gorchakov is of no use. He lost his grip on foreign policy long ago. There is no firm hand in control. My dear friend, I press your hand and thank you for the seven good days at Knowsley. Please pass my warmest greetings to Lord Derby." He scrawled his signature, "Schouvaloff."

He read it over and put it aside. Perhaps too frank? Of course, there was still more to be said. I do not name my enemies, he mused. So many of them. But why the demand to occupy Novi Pazar? Andrassy whines that it is to secure communications. What he means is the railroad. When the Austrians complete it from Mitrovitsa to Budapest they will have the only overland commercial link all the way down to Thessalonika. They already control the sea borne traffic on the Adriatic. And they wished to deny Montenegro a seaport. The gallant, foolish Serbs and their Montenegrin brothers feel betrayed by us. So then the whole of the Western Balkans falls into the hands of Vienna, or is it Budapest? But what do the Italians get out of this all? A secret promise for Albania in the future? Or is there something I am missing. It is to be regretted that I know so little about the region. Perhaps Colonel Bogoliubov can enlighten me. He knows the Montenegrin frontiers. And Bobrikov, Grand Duke Nikolai Nikolaevich's representative in Serbia, didn't he warn us that a big Bulgaria stretching to the Aegean was less important than a link up between Serbia and Montenegro?

Shuvalov sighed and turned over the letter in his hand. Yes my dear Lord and Lady Derby, there is no strong hand to coordinate things. And we will be blamed for the resistance to the Austrians in Bosnia. God spare us from another war. He glanced once again outside the window to the growing darkness as the lights of the city were extinguished. He read through the letter again. How true, how futile. He held the letter to the flame of the candle and watched it burn.

Chapter Seventeen

Gusinje

In the valley of the Tsem River a few miles from the Montenegrin border, three men sat around a fire, roasting chunks of lamb on an iron spit. They were dressed in the traditional garb of Circassian tribesmen. Their caftans were criss-crossed with cartridge belts sown into the fabric. They wore sheepskin caps and soft-soled, knee-high boots of quality leather. They spoke in hushed tones the language of the North Caucasus Mountains. There was no reason to whisper. No one else could understand their complex tongue. The older man, Hadji Murad, had served under the banner of the legendary Shamil who had fought the Russians in the thirty-year holy war called the *ghazavat*. Soon after the defeat of Shamil in 1860, tens of thousands of Circassians had been expelled into the Ottoman Empire. The Sultan gladly accepted these fierce warriors and resettled them in colonies from the Black Sea coast to Kosovo. In the exodus, Hadji Murad had lost his wife to disease but brought out his three children and raised them in the egalitarian spirit of the mountains. The second great tragedy of his life had been the loss of his daughter not to disease but to the seductive wiles of a Russian. He cursed her and tried to drive her out of his mind. She was the perfect recreation of his wife, a woman so beautiful that even in the land known for the beauty of its women she turned heads and inflamed the minds of young men. And though her twin brothers, Kustan and Hayder Hassen, also cursed her, they suffered her loss so greatly that they quietly forgave her. And now they had learned that the Russian had been murdered and their beloved Tamara had disappeared. Twice they had crossed the border in search of her.

When they returned to their father, they related what they had learned. He listened quietly, but they saw the tension distort his battle scared features and watched his hands fiercely grip the dagger sheathed in his waist band. He had sworn to kill her and her Russian lover. Now they pleaded with him to allow them to win her back.

Hadji Murad sat in silence. The brothers hardly dared to breathe. The lamb slowly turned black on the spit. He stood up and walked slowly to the dried riverbed. There he knelt in prayer. When he came back, they had portioned out the burnt lamb and placed pieces on cooked rice from a copper pot.

"We will bring her back, God willing. We will do this together in the memory of your blessed mother."

"We'll have an armed escort, Serov. They will convey us across this strip of rugged terrain, called the Sanjak of Novi Pazar, and deposit us on the Montenegrin frontier, or what passes for a frontier these days."

"Who would have thought it? And no ticket necessary."

"No disguise either."

"Someday, Vasili Vasilich, perhaps in old age, you will explain it all to me. But right now I am on my last legs and want only to sleep on this real bed."

The convoy escorting Vasiliev and Serov had skirted the Devich Monastery and the town of Ipek to descend on Lake Plava from the north.

Captain Polyani was riding beside them, when he called a halt, pulled out his telescope and surveyed the rugged country ahead. "We'll camp here and send a courier ahead. They should be prepared to receive you."

"Who is 'they' Captain, if I am be so bold as to inquire?"

"Ah, of course. My orders are to establish contact with Ali Pasha, the commander of the Albanian League's forces defending Gusinje which is a few kilometers to the south of us. It is impossible to cross over into Montenegro to our immediate west."

He handed Vasiliev the telescope.

"Over there are the 'Accursed Mountains', the Prokletija. You see the problem."

"So, Gusinje Where Mehmed Ali Pasha was massacred! Does not sound like a welcoming place."

"Yes, the confusion in names is unfortunate," Polyani seemed to have missed the point, thought Vasiliev.

"Our latest information is that the town is safe right now. The Turks no longer have any authority there. Ali Pasha is a Muslim but most of the tribes around here are Roman Catholic. Thus far the feelings of being Albanian have erased the differences in faith. God knows how long that will last. But long enough to let you slip across the border, unless, of course, the Montenegrins and the Albanians start shooting at one another."

"Excuse my naiveté, Captain, but why would that be?"

"Shooting, my dear Major, is the universal sport in these mountains. There do not seem to be any other forms of entertainment."

Vasiliev held his tongue but the thought on the tip of it was 'so the need for the Austrian mission.' Then he thought again. This is the area of the silver mines. The next morning the courier returned leading two white mules.

"I think this constitutes an invitation to place yourselves under the protection of the League."

Vasiliev related the conversation to Serov, imitating the officer's voice dripping with sarcasm. "Well, the Albanians have been decent to us so far. We have no choice but to mount our mules and enter Gusinje."

An irreverent thought passed through Serov's mind as he reflected upon Jesus astride a mule heading into Jerusalem.

Theirs was a short ride along a ridge before they saw an armed escort waiting for them in the valley.

A young Albanian officer dismounted, saluted Vasiliev and addressed him in French. Reading surprise on Vasiliev's face, he quickly explained.

"Until a week ago I was an officer in the Ottoman Army and trained in Thessaloniki where I learned French. We have all gone over to the League here. We shall have our own prince, too." He spoke breathlessly as if he could hardly contain his enthusiasm.

"And perhaps you have come as an emissary of the Tsar to help us?"

"My congratulations, lieutenant. I have been authorized to draft a frank report on the new situation here."

"If you speak the truth, then you can only help us."

Gusinje was filled with Albanians who a few weeks earlier had been wearing Turkish uniforms. When the League was formed at Prizen, they had all defected from the Ottoman Army.

"Berlin seems farther and farther away every time we move," Vasiliev muttered to himself as he was conducted into the presence of Ali Pasha. Serov had been taken off to prepare their quarters.

"Welcome hero of Plevna!"

Vasiliev thought it would be ill-mannered to deny this again. He certainly could not have wished for a more robust welcome.

The headquarters of the aspiring prince was a converted stone cattle shed. A pile of blazing logs illuminated most of the cavernous hall. The walls and wooden posts supporting the roof were hung with cartridge belts, swords and pistols. Two dozen men crouched down around large platters of fat lamb. They wore heavy silver chains around their necks and silver mounted pistols at the belt.

Vasiliev was seated next to Ali Pasha who murmured, "better is talk when the belly is fed."

Vasiliev could hardly object. The deafening noise of men laughing and singing to the accompaniment of the tambour made conversation impossible in any case. The men plunged their hands wrist deep in the lamb stew. Vasiliev rolled up his sleeves and follow suit.

When the warriors were sated, they lay down in a row while the women who had been crouching in a dark, far corner, fell upon the remains of the meal, Ali Pasha led Vasiliev past the recumbent forms and outside to an orchard of plum trees. He picked a few of the overripe fruit and launched into a long monologue.

Later Vasiliev gave Serov a summary.

"The reason the Albanians welcome us is that we defeated the Turks. That gives them the chance to demand self rule," he said handing Serov a plum.

"But they was fightin' us during the war," Serov objected.

"Right. But now the Turks are weak and the Albanians think they can defend themselves better on their own. The regular Turkish forces have retreated to the south, freeing most of the country where the Albanians live. This includes the Kosovo where we have ended up. There are other areas to the south they claim around Scutari, or Shkodër as they call it. But there are problems. The Albanians hope the powers will grant them their independence or something like it. The boundaries with Montenegro are still contested. Some sniping goes on."

"And are we goin' to be the targets of that snipin' again?"

"Ali Pasha tried to reassure me on that score. He has a plan to get us across the frontier."

"Why should he do this?"

"Remember, Sergeant, so far every one we've met hopes we'll support their side of the story when we make out our official report. Everyone, that is, except the Austrians..."

"...the one's we've met call themselves Hungarians or Magyar."

"You are right, Serov. I stand corrected. I wonder whether it makes a difference anymore. You must understand, a decade ago they came to an agreement after many years. So now their empire is called Austria-Hungary but they both served the same emperor, Franz-Joseph."

"It's not for me to understand, Vasili Vasilich. I accept. But it seems to me that there is a lot of switch' sides goin' on in these parts."

"Well put again. I think that 'switchin' too will have to go into the report to Totleben."

"So what is this plan, beggin' your pardon?"

"Ali Pasha says that there is a short stretch on the frontier along the Tsem River that is not well guarded on either side. There's a sort of unspoken agreement to keep open an old trail used by smugglers between two villages inhabited by Roman Catholic Albanians. They keep the peace for a Franciscan priest who ministers to both sides."

"But Ali Pasha is a Muslim, no?"

"Today, being Albanian counts for more than religion."

Serov shook his head. "I can't keep track of who believes what."

"It changes fast. Right now the situation is to our advantage. We head out tomorrow night."

Ali Pasha gave his last order of the night to his most trusted men.

"Let the Franciscan, Father Gian Petro, be their guide."

Chapter Eighteen

Crossing into Montenegro

A sliver of moonlight was all the light they had as they wound down the rocky trail to the riverbed. Father Gian Petro had sent word earlier. There would be no trouble. Once across the border, several villagers would be waiting to take them further into Montenegro. Still, the priest warned them, "It would be best to avoid speech, make no sound."

They began to cross the river when muffled shots rang out on the other side.

Serov's first thought was 'not again!' but he quickly realized that they were not being fired upon.

Father Gian Petro seized Vasiliev by the arm. "I don't understand. There was to be no violence."

"Perhaps others were trying to cross without permission. What do you advise?"

The Franciscan hesitated. Then they heard a cry.

"Someone is calling for help. We must go to their assistance."

He plunged into the shallow stream. Vasiliev muttered to Serov, "We have no choice. We have to follow him." He drew his revolver as they waded to the other side. The cry had fallen to a whimper. Father Gian Petro led them up the riverbank. Vaguely they saw the figure of a man struggling to rise, then another sprawled in the brush.

"What has happened, my son?" The Franciscan was on his knees cradled the head of a man who was gasping for breath.

"Father! Hear my dying confession." The priest bent over and began to administer the last rites. Vasiliev could not hear the man's mumbled words.

Serov had gone ahead a few steps. He too had drawn his Colt, peering into the brush before crouching over the second man.

"He's a goner. A shot to the head."

Father Gian Petro stood up.

"Three men attacked them," he spoke softly. "I'm not certain I heard clearly what the dying man said after that. He wanted to confess first. Something about 'strangers' but what could that mean? Unless…"

"Yes?"

"I don't think he would use that word to describe a Slav or Albanian, or even a Turk. But there are other men, 'strangers' who came years ago from beyond the Black Sea, near your land, Major. They settled in small colonies and call themselves Adyge. The Turks call them Cherkess. The Europeans call them Circassians. Perhaps it was they. But why did they shoot to kill?"

Serov approached. "I saw no weapons, Vasili Vasilich. Is it possible the men were unarmed?"

The priest raised his hands to his face. "Defenseless! My doing. I told them, no firearms." A catch in his throat, and then, his voice hoarse, "I must go to their families. I can take you to the village and then you are on your own."

Vasiliev thought for a moment. "Perhaps their weapons were taken by their assassins. I cannot image an Albanian going unarmed into a disputed border. Even at your request, father. Besides, we heard more than two shots."

The Franciscan seized Vasiliev by the shoulders. "You are right, of course. Thank you for easing my conscience."

"Father, we cannot pursue these killers at night. But I believe Ali Pasha should be warned. This may be just an incident, but it could mean more trouble along the border. Also, we can ask him for mules to carry the bodies of the men back with you to their village."

"You are a good soul, Major."

Vasiliev hardly felt like one. Every step of the way seemed marked by violence and blood.

****

The three Circassians rode silently on the mules they had captured from the dead men. They had also acquired several revolvers and a Martini-Henri rifle which Hadji Murad strapped over his back.

"How did they know we were coming?" asked Kustan.

"We know not. We know only that the power of God, who alone is great, has preserved us. Our enterprise has received his blessing." The two young men bowed their heads.

"We will avoid the villages and find our kinsmen to the north. God will guide our way."

During the ambush, Hayder Hassan had brushed his arm against a tree branch, opening the wound. Hadji Murad had heard of the skill of Montenegrins in treating gunshot wounds. But there was a risk in trying to find a native surgeon. Kustan slipped into an Albanian village at night. Yes, there was such a man, he reported. "He might come if he were told a good story and shown a heavy purse."

A diminutive old man showed up with a bag and a dog. The dog waited outside the hut. The surgeon had very fine fingers, but there was no need to cut. No bones were broken. The bag contained his curative salves. He washed out the wound with extra strong raki, muttering that they had waited too long.

"You should have applied right away the white of an egg and salt, never water. Well, it can't be helped."

He moved his tongue over the only two teeth left in his head as he mixed together an extract of pine resin, the green bark of elder twigs, white beeswax and a few drops of olive oil. Then he used the mixture to clean the wound. He covered the wound with a swatch of pure white sheep wool soaked with the salve. He gave them a small container of salve and a bottle of raki.

"You have to change the dressing at night and in the morning. If the wound begins to stink, then wash it out with raki again"

He refused to give them the exact proportion of the ingredients of the salve, claiming it was an old family secret. He grinned at his patient

"Now if you're foolish enough to get a broken head, I can fix that too."

He weighed the purse in his hand but did not count the coins. His dog was waiting as he left the hut, and they vanished into the night.

As the sun rose over the mountains, the three men stopped to pray and break bread at a small steam where they filled the gourds they hung from the necks of the mules. They washed the wound with raki and applied the salve. The climb became steeper but then leveled out on a plateau and then they descended to the lush Morača river valley. They avoided the strong points held by Montenegrin troops. They travelled at night skirting the villages, stealing a sheep when necessary and eating the flesh raw. But the river was abundant in fish and they did not want for food. It was only by chance, or as Hadji Murad said, the will of God that they came across a small settlement which they recognized by the shape of the huts as belonging to their kinsmen. Here they were able to rest, listen to the gossip and heard stories of the wanderings of the Adyge, called Circassians by the Europeans.

One night Hadji Murad burst into song, his voice strong and expressive but the tonality sounded strange to the ears of his audience. They had been away from the mountains too long. And who could remember the epic battle of Kurkizhin when the Kabardians had fought the terrible Avar invaders hundreds of years before. The men bent their heads to listen and marvel.

On a cold fall day when torrents of rain fell in the valley, a traveler from the south sought shelter in their hut. As he warmed himself at the fire, he spoke of a strange occurrence in Cetinje. A girl, it was said, resembling one of their tribe, had been taken into the Russian consulate, but then had escaped. Nothing more for certain was known. But a rumor had reached him that a beautiful girl, perhaps not the same one, was being held at the foot of the Lovćen Mountain that towers above Cetinje.

Hadji Murad knew at once that God had sent this man. But now another problem. They had run out of raki and the wound was beginning to stink. They decided to leave Hayder Hassan with one of the Circassian families who promised to obtain more raki and dress the wound twice daily.

"When you are well again, follow us. We will leave signs which only you can read of the trail we take." He and Kustan left the next morning to retrace their steps to the south.

Chapter Nineteen

Cetinje

Vasiliev was surprised, not to say astonished, as he and Serov rode down what was the only wide street in the Montenegrin capital of Cetinje. There were about forty stone houses on either side. They stopped at the only hotel, a converted seminary where rooms had been reserved for them. The desk clerk proudly pointed out that the largest stone building opposite the hotel was the palace of Prince Nikola the ruler. He also told them that the prince administered justice beneath the elm tree outside his palace.

"You know of course that we have never been conquered!" the clerk exclaimed, a statement Vasiliev was to hear often.

"Well Sergeant," Vasiliev frowned, "it would be hard to circulate in this town without being noticed, no matter what your disguise might be."

"That sounds like I'll have nothin' to do, beggin' your pardon."

"We'll find something to occupy you. Never doubt it."

A black cat scurried past Vasiliev as he entered the consul's study. He was surprised again at the elegance of the furnishings. He wondered whether the rooms of the palace were so lavishly appointed.

Vasiliev noticed immediately that Ionin was nervous. His hand was moist to the touch and he kept caressing the neck of the Persian cat that crouched next to him, glaring at Vasiliev.

An older woman brought a tray with cups of strong Turkish coffee and slices of Greek sour milk cake with almonds called *Yaourtopitta*. She kept her eyes averted from Vasiliev.

"Thank you, Anna Ivanovna." Ionin glanced at her with what Vasiliev took to be a conspiratorial look. Perhaps he was over interpreting, a bad habit of his.

"What can you tell me, Alexander Semeonovich, about the murder of Grigoriev?"

"Very little, I fear." Ionin leaned forward in his Venetian chair and relaxed his grip on Venus. She uttered a sound which Vasiliev interpreted as more a growl than a purr and leapt to the floor. She ran to the threshold where Vulcan, ever faithful, was waiting. They scurried off together. Vasiliev felt unprepared to interpret that little drama.

"I have had some notes taken of her preliminary interrogation." He handed a sheaf of papers to Vasiliev. "We had too little time to follow up. You see, she escaped soon after. I deeply regret the lax security. I assume full responsibility." Ionin seemed to be reading from a script.

"Was there no attempt to find her? Surely in a town as small as this…"

"Small, yes, but the people can be secretive and suspicious of outsiders, which unfortunately, includes us."

"And the Prince?"

"He was at the front with his troops. I did not think it appropriate to trouble him. This is our affair."

"So, no search was undertaken."

"We made a few discreet inquiries." Ionin seemed evasive.

Vasiliev was leafing through the pages.

"Thank you, Alexander Semeonovich, I will take these minutes and study them. Perhaps we could speak again."

"With the greatest pleasure, Major Vasiliev. I understand the concerns in St. Petersburg."

Vasiliev was not impressed with Ionin's show of concern over opinion in the capital.

"By the way, who took these notes?"

"My secretary. A most honest man."

"And what was done with the head?"

"I ordered him to bury it, to avoid …complications"

"I would like to interview him, to get his impressions."

"Of course, but you have the account in writing.

"Ah! Alexander Semeonovich, in my business it is as important to know the writer as his writings."

The secretary took an immediate liking to Vasiliev who treated him with respect, a pleasant change from his usual experiences with officials. He was delighted when Vasiliev asked to see the head. He had been right to preserve it.

"You would make an excellent detective," Vasiliev said as he opened the box. "Taking care with the evidence. Good. The wound is ragged as if the head were sawed off. Not a clean cut."

"This I saw too," said the secretary flushed with pleasure at Vasiliev's praise.

"I must tell you a friend of mine, a Montenegrin gendarme who fought in '77, saw many Turkish heads roll. He said most were cut off cleanly with a *hanzhar*. This is a short heavy weapon used for the purpose."

"So it is not likely then that a Montenegrin did the deed."

The secretary shrugged.

"We will replace the head as you preserved it. We may need to use it as evidence."

After Vasiliev left, Ionin called for Venus but she failed to appear. He sighed. He had second thoughts about inviting Vasiliev to go shooting with him. He had decided to follow Count Corti's advice and say as little as possible about the incident. What could this detective do weeks after the crime? As for the girl, God knows what happened to her. There were more serious matters to absorb his attention. Corti was right. The Petersburg court would quickly forget all this. Compared to matters of peace and war...well, there was no possible comparison.

Serov had already wormed himself in the good graces of the Russian cook who plied him with Greek cakes as he told her stories of crossing the Balkan Mountains.

"So, plenty of excitement here," he said, munching loudly.

"Always is in this crazy country."

"Crazy is it?"

"This girl, a real beauty, shows up with a severed head in a bag. Now, I tell you."

"And that was the late Grigoriev."

"Late is right. God knows where the rest of him lies."

"But I don't see her around."

"She escaped."

"Oh, ho! Sounds like a play or somethin'. And where did she go?"

The cook waited a moment until a servant left the kitchen. Then she lowered her voice. "Well, Anna Ivanovna might know. She let the girl get away. And they didn't look very hard for her neither."

"So what do you think?"

"I heard, but you mustn't say I told you, that someone saw her being taken."

"Taken? You mean someone grabbed her?"

"I would say that is a good way of putting it."

"Your cake was delicious, Maria Alexandrovna. I envy the consul-general."

"Well, he does love his food."

Serov took great pleasure from relating the cook's story to Vasiliev.

"So, what we have to do next is to find this 'someone' who saw her taken. Serov, Do your best. I'll question Anna Ivanovna."

Serov had already made up his own mind on how to do exactly what Vasiliev wanted. For a few coins he had one of the servants loan him his worn clothes. He practiced limping and holding one arm rigid by his side. Then he made the rounds of the smaller wooden houses off the main street, pretending to be a former volunteer in the fighting against the Turks in the great Serbian rebellion of 1875, now reduced to poverty and begging in Christ's name.

After a few hours he found out what he wanted and came back to the hotel, making sure to enter by the back entrance.

"Well, Serov, you look as though you've been combing the streets."

"I had to find somethin' to do, as you said. Funny, how it was, Vasili Vasilich. Some turned me away like as if I had the plague. Others thrust a crust into my hand, but weren't too happy about my comin' round. Seems that the volunteers weren't so popular as we thought. But one old timer was different. He'd fought on our side back in '54 in the Crimea. One of the few who made it all the way out there and back. Here's what he told me. He was out in the fields by the road leadin' north, lookin' for a stray buffalo.

Along comes a coach drawn by a pair, hell bent for somewhere. The coachman looked peculiar, like he wasn't from these parts. When he got back to the town, he heard the story of the girl. So, he thought...but nobody asked him, and why should he say anything. He'd learned to avoid trouble.

"Good work, Sergeant. In the morning, we head north. I've requested another set of passports from Ionin. Travelling here may mean showing up as someone else." Vasiliev pushed the sheaf of papers over the table.

"In the meantime, you might want to read this, but perhaps a summary would do."

"I'm much in favor of your summaries, Vasili Vasilich."

"The girl was born into a family of Adyge, in Kabardia in the mountains of the North Caucasus. Her father was a tribal leader who had fought for Shamil. When Prince Bariatinskii captured Shamil, he decided to parade him in Russia to honor the chief so as to keep the peace and to celebrate his victory. The girl's father, Hadji Murad, was chosen as an attendant. In that way he learned some Russian. But later he grew disillusioned with Russian rule and in '64 left with thousands of his countrymen. The girl was still a child then. Her mother was already sick and died on the ship crossing the Black Sea. The Sultan welcomed them in the Ottoman Empire, calling them Cherkess, and settled them all over the Balkans.

The girl had twin older brothers. She said they treated her more like a prince than a princess. That is, they taught her to ride and shoot with the best of them. But they discouraged all her suitors, dismissing them as unworthy. She felt constrained. One day while out riding with a few friends, they met a Russian who was injured in a fall when his horse had stepped into a hole and broke its leg. He was not armed so she shot the horse. She helped him on her mount and brought him to native surgeon who treated his injuries. This was Grigoriev. They fell in love. She realized their love was doomed. He was Orthodox, she was Sunni Muslim. Her family would not accept him. He had no family but was devoted to the cause of the Slavs. They ran away. They lived together but prayed separately, travelling all the time. In Hercegovina they came to understand that they shared a common desire to see their people, the Muslims and the Orthodox reconciled and united in one country. When the rebellion began against Ottoman authority, they helped rally the rebels. When after several years the war broke out, they supported independence for Bosnia and Hercegovina. But the Austrians opposed them and sent in troops. Her lover had ties to the Russian volunteers and begged for Russian intervention. But, she said, the Russians betrayed their hopes in exchange for Austrian recognition of Bulgarian independence. Grigoriev lost faith in St. Petersburg and together they began to organize bands to resist the Austrians. One day when she returned from visiting a Muslim village, she found his head impaled on a pole in front of their tent. His companions had fled. She could not find his body. She felt she was going mad. She could only think of shaming the Russians into supporting their fight. This is what brought her to Cetinje and the consul-general. Ionin had a reputation for sympathizing with the Slavic cause in the West. But she soon found he did not want to meet with her. She felt despondent. The interrogation ends here."

Serov listened intently, as was his custom, emitting his characteristic range of sounds, sighing, softly whistling, gasping, all eloquent expressions to those who knew how to interpret them.

"What a sorrowful tale," he finally said. "So, you think she escaped to return to the fight?"

"This is what Anna Ivanovna concluded. The girl spoke to her about the need to seek revenge. But Anna Ivanovna could not find out the answer to the crucial question, revenge on whom?"

"And we are supposed to find the answer?"

"That and to report on the extent of the resistance to the Austrians in Bosnia."

"So first we search for the girl."

"Ah Sergeant, always the romantic."

Chapter Twenty

Morača River Valley

When the Franciscan, Father Gian Petro, had left them, the Albanian elders gathered in a *medjlis*. They had just come back from the graveyard where they had buried their two tribal members under large wooden crosses, beautifully carved with arms ending in rays of the sun. An old man stood at the head of the two graves with a rosary in his hand and shouted scraps of Latin. The women wailed while the wife of one of the men sang the death lament.

Drawn up in a circle, the men fell silent for a few moments before the oldest man spoke: "Blood for blood," he intoned to nods of assent. They had listened dutifully to the Padre who had admonished them not to follow the tradition of the blood feud. They liked him but not his name. Like other mountain tribes, they gave him a new one. Also they did not always follow his advice. As he left them he said, "Why imperil your souls with pagan rites when you can save them by behaving like Christians. Our brothers must be avenged," another man declared. Then they selected four young men to carry out the sentence. One had already shot two men in a feud with a neighboring tribe. But no stigma attached to him. The four men rode out at dawn to seek justice.

They were good trackers and they knew the killers were 'strangers.' The *Rus'* officer had told the Padre that there was an exchange of gunfire. They expected nothing less from their fellow tribesmen. More important, it meant that one of the assailants might be wounded. That would slow them down. Perhaps they would even seek aid. The hunters would question all the native surgeons on the way north.

They too had to avoid the Montenegrin camps. It took them several days to reach the Morača River Valley. They knew they were on the right trail after they found the surgeon who had treated the wound of one of the killers. He confirmed that they were Circassians. So they had to be approached with caution.

A Vlach shepherd told them a wounded man had been taken in by a Circassian family on a ridge overlooking the river. Two other men had left him and gone back south.

They waited in the wooded area on the edge of the river and then climbed the ridge in the dead of night. They had discussed how to distract the watch dogs. They had bought a lamb from the Vlach and butchered it, cutting out the choice fatty parts and drenching them with a mixture they had the surgeon prepare. One of them crawled up the wooden fence around the hut and threw the meat over. The dogs barked as they ran up to the fence, but then fell to devouring such savory flesh as they had never tasted before. In a few minutes all was silent again. The men waited another few hours, until they were confident that the household had forgotten about the barking and sleep had overcome them.

As they passed the bodies of the dogs, they applied their curved knives just to be certain that they would not be disturbed. They judged that the door would be too stout to force, and they could not break in through the narrow windows. So they waited, stretched out on the ground as close to the hut as they dared. The hours passed slowly for them, and their bodies began to ache from lying on the rough ground. When the first light of dawn broke over the horizon, two of them moved up to each side of the door. They expected that someone would come out to get water from the river. Probably a woman. It would be an easy matter to knock her aside and cut down the men still asleep in their beds.

A soon as they heard the wooden bar removed, they drew their revolvers. A young woman appeared holding a large bucket strapped across her back. They struck her down and charged into the house. The bucket crashed to the dirt floor and the first man to enter stumbled over it, accidentally discharging his weapon. The others jumped over his body. Unexpectedly, they faced two closed doors on opposite sides of the narrow corridor. One man pushed open the door to the left and was met by a volley of gunfire that riddled his body. The other two men burst into the room on the right, firing at the forms huddled under the blankets. An old man and his wife died immediately, while a child crawled out of the bloody bed and expired on the floor.

The two men whirled to face the shooter in the other room. There turned out to be two of them, one getting off five quick shots from his colt six shooter and another blazing away with a rifle. The Albanians fell to the ground with fatal wounds. The fourth man, momentarily stunned when his head struck the edge of the bucket, lay in wait for one of the shooters to emerge from the room. Behind him the young woman recovered consciousness and screamed:

"There's another one out here!"

He shot her through the heart.

He realized that alone he had no chance to winning this fight. It would be suicide to charge the room now. And the shooting would have aroused neighbors, also armed to the teeth, possibly even a Montenegrin patrol. He backed out of the house, turned and raced toward the top of the ridge. Before he reached protective cover, a single shot from a Martini Henry rifle blew off the back of his head.

Chapter
Twenty-One

Kotor and vicinity

Rain had fallen a few days before, and the dirt road was still soft enough to bear traces of the coach and pair. When the terrain became rocky, the wheel tracks vanished. Only occasional wooden crosses marked the trail to Kotor. The land around the foot of Lovćen Mountain was sparsely inhabited. At a distance from the nearest stone house, Vasiliev reigned in and pulled out the telescope he had borrowed from Ionin. There was no sign of a coach or any movement. They made a wide circle around the four dispersed houses and saw only one woman driving her pigs into a fenced in area.

They dismounted under the leafy cover of a copse of beech trees. Vasiliev handed the telescope to Serov.

"Do you see anything unusual?"

Serov took his time. "Pigs isn't out of the ordinary, but there's one house I can see that has slits in the walls. Gun ports?"

"Exactly what I think."

"Looks like there's also a trench surroundin' the house half hidden by bull rushes."

"So a small fortress, it would seem. That's our place. Now how to get inside without getting the girl killed."

"Night attack?"

"Too risky. We don't know the inside layout. Our only chance is deception. Best thing, Serov, is to have you resurrect your 'begging veteran' act. You still have the rags in your saddle bags?"

At dusk Serov made his way, limping painfully it would appear to any observer, across the open fields to the house where the pigs were crowded in a wooden pen, snorting and munching on their feed. In his practiced way, he managed to ingratiate himself with the peasant woman who by chance had lost her husband in the war. Life was hard she said as she bathed her two children and fed him a tasty stew. She allowed him to pass the night in the barn in return for helping her butcher a pig and prepare the parts for sale at the local market. He found out what he wanted to know and left early in the morning to meet Vasiliev who had spent his uncomfortable night in the open fields.

"So, Vasili Vasilich, here's what I can tell you. The old couple that lived there before the war was gone sudden-like one day, no one knew where. 'Strangers' came and hired her husband to help them dig a trench and cut slits in the wall. They hardly spoke to him but paid well. 'What kind of 'stranger?' I asked. 'Ones that spoke oddly,' she says. 'And they were dressed 'strangely.' How 'strangely'? I asked. 'With vests and floppy hats and low boots not fit for hard work.' And then they left. Only they came back awhile ago. This time three of them. In a coach. She saw them carry a large bundle into the house. Then one of them drove off with the coach. And no one's been in or out in these past few days except once a week when the coach comes back and the driver brings in what looks like provisions. She was curious. So she asked at the local market. They told her he bought a lot of food. And that the driver spoke a 'strange' tongue."

"Did you find out when the coach comes next?"

"Of course, Vasili Vasilich. I knew what you'd be thinkin'."

Vasili had been thinking a great deal during the hours when Serov was tending pigs. Ever since Mount Lovćen had come into view his mind had been wandering over its contours. He remembered his first glimpse of mountains, riding across the territory of the Terek Cossacks and marveling as the outline of the splendid North Caucasus Range emerged from the blanket of the morning mist. Then as now he recalled his favorite story by Pushkin, *Prisoner of the Caucasus*. And he also thought of the first Circassians he had ever encountered and how beautiful the women were. Now one of them was captive in the fortress-like house. The problem for him was not so much in freeing her, though that would not be easy. But what to do with her captors, then where to take her, and how to find a place of refuge in this wild country.

He was not a killer, yet how could he leave her captives alive to pursue them? Serov's information had given him more time to plan. The coach would not be coming back for another two days. He mulled over different escape routes. He would ride to the Bay of Kotor beyond the mountain and hire a boat. Overland they would be vulnerable, but at sea? No one could track them or know their destination. All he would need to do, then, was incapacitate her captors. This would give them a head start.

On the appointed day, Vasiliev and Serov were waiting in the market. They had put on clothes bought in the bazaar and packed their uniforms in two large bundles. They watched the coach arrive and followed the driver as he made his purchases. Where the stalls pressed closely together and the aisles were crowded, Vasiliev took hold of a young boy dressed in rags and pressed a coin into his hand, whispering instructions. At a signal the boy pushed over a table with copper kettles, pinched a stout merchant's wife who screamed, and darted down an alleyway. A fight broke out. Suddenly the place disintegrated into a mass of seething humanity, Serov contributed his share of the pushing and shouting, striking out at the hands that tried to restrain him. Vasiliev stifled the coachman's cry by fiercely gripping his throat and dragging him down a dark passageway. He quickly stripped him of his vest, boots and floppy hat. Then he took out of his pocket a small flask and poured its contents down the man's gullet and over his recumbent form. With a deft move he twisted the man's ankle, not so hard as to break a bone but disabling him nonetheless.

Serov had shaken free of the crowd and picked up his own purchases. He met Vasiliev by the coach and pair tied to a post at the edge of the market. Serov, whose build was more like that of the driver, quickly donned his clothes while Vasiliev piled the packages of food and their uniforms into the coach. It had taken them only a few minutes before they were flying down the road toward Mount Lovćen.

Then, an unexpected piece of luck. A menacing black cloud appeared over the mountain as if by command and carried by a blustery wind descended with full force, dumping buckets of rain on the market and the houses outside the town. Visibility had fallen to zero, when Serov jumped down from the coach seat and pounded on the door of the fortress house. Vasiliev left the cab on the far side and flattened himself against the wall between a slit and the threshold. When the door began to open, Serov hurled himself against it, striking the man behind it with full force, and then flattening him with a savage blow to the head. Vasiliev was right behind and leaping over the man's slumping body he rushed down the corridor where he encountered a second man emerging from a room, a look of astonishment on his face. Vasiliev hit him twice and the man fell to the floor.

For a moment all that could be heard was the rain lashing the roof and windows. Then Vasiliev cried out in Russian:

"We are friends of Grigoriev! We have come to free you. Don't be afraid." He kicked open a locked door and peered into the room as Serov busily bound the hands and feet of the two recumbent men. Vasiliev shouted again: "We are friends come to rescue you."

He saw her crouched in the corner, a rough blanket wrapped around her. A soft moan escaped her lips.

Her hair had fallen over her face and when she brushed the long blond tresses aside, he was struck by her beauty even as he saw the fear in her eyes.

"You are Tamara, Boris Andreevich's great love. And I am Vasiliev, a fellow Russian come to avenge you."

She stood up, the blanket falling to her feet. He extended a hand, but she brushed it aside and threw her arms around him, an embrace he would always remember. She held him tightly as he muttered some words of comfort, whatever came into his head, even as he felt a surge of desire for her.

He was startled by Serov's voice behind him.

"We are secure," he said.

Vasili released her. "We must hurry now. Can you walk?"

She nodded.

As they turned toward the door, a flash of lightening lit up the gloomy room and for an instant the Latin cross of polished bronze shone over their heads.

Chapter Twenty-Two

Kotor and Ragusa

The storm lasted two days. When it had abated, three horsemen emerged from the dense woods to the east of the mountain and rode into the valley. A moon shone brightly on the few stone houses but there were no lights anywhere. They sat in their saddles for a long time. Then the older man signaled an advance. From far off the smell of the pigs filled them with disgust. Hadji Murad decided few people except for *giaour* peasants would expose themselves to that abomination. He sent Kustan ahead to investigate. Hayer Hassen had joined them only two days before, He was still weak but had ridden fast to catch them up. Now he sagged in the saddle. They would rest tonight, but not with the smell of pigs in their nostrils.

Kustan knocked softly on the pig woman's door, holding his scarf against his nostrils.

A faint voice answered, sounding like a gasp.

He spoke in his best Serbian. He was looking for a friend who came in a coach. Which house was his?

There was a long pause. Then she whispered so softly he could hardly hear.

"The stone house with the trench and slit windows."

"We wait until dawn," said Hadji Murad

As the edge of the sun came over Lovćen Mountain, they were already mounted. Hadji Murad scanned the valley and was surprised to see in the distance the coach approaching from the market town.

"This is the key to the fortress, "he said.

As the coach passed below they fell in behind, maintaining a distance of a hundred meters or so. When they were close enough to the stone house, Hadji Murad signaled again and the two brothers spurred their horses, cantering to draw even with the pair of coach horses. With drawn revolvers they motioned the coachman to move forward without stopping, across the narrow wooden planks that bridged the trench, then coming to a halt. Hadji Murad came up from behind. With a surprised look on his face, he ordered the coachman to climb down. The man was hatless, dressed in ragged clothing. He was barefoot and his right ankle was bound up in a dirty rag. He looked terrified. Climbing down from the coach box his ankle gave way and he fell in the mud. They picked him up and frog marched him to the door. Another surprise, the door was ajar.

Half dragging and pushing the coachman ahead of them, the two brothers advanced slowly down the corridor. Hadji Murad muttered a command and they paused on the thresholds of the two rooms. Another gesture and they burst into the room on the left, holding coachman in front of them. Hadji Murad kicked open the door on the right. The room was empty except for a pallet and blanket on the floor. His keen sense of smell detected the odor of his daughter. He trembled, rooted to the spot, until his sons cried out.

"Papa, come."

They had thrust the coachman aside and he collapsed again on the floor. Against the wall two men were stretched out, both bound hand and foot. Pans of water, half empty had been placed next to them so they could bend over and drink. The place stank of human urine and excrement. Hadji Murad and his sons set to work.

No sounds, even those of men screaming in pain, could pass Beyond the thick stone walls of the fortress house. The woman pig farmer could only say later what she had seen, not heard. She watched the coach arrive with the three Cherkess riders —oh yes, she knew their dress well enough—just as the sun had risen enough to free itself from the shadow of the mountain. She was among her pigs when the three men came out again. By this time the sun was at the zenith. One of them climbed on the coach seat and the others mounted their horses, tying the third horse behind the coach. They rode off toward the market town and she saw them no more.

It was none of her business. But it all seemed strange. The coach coming on the odd day, strangers visiting other, different strangers. She loaded her cart with two piglets and harnessed her mule. The sun was low in the horizon when she arrived at the market town. The first thing she saw was the coach and pair tied to a hitching post. She told her story to her aunt who always put her up for the night on market day. The older woman sensed trouble, having known plenty of it in her life. She passed the word to a neighbor who knew the local police officer.

When the officer and his deputy rode out the next day, the sun was masked again by lowering clouds.

"It was as if it was hiding its face from a sight none might see," he later told the police chief in Kotor. There were three severed heads fixed on sharpened sticks thrust into the ground at the muddy entrance to the house. Their noses had been cut off. Inside they found the bodies, cut and sliced like badly butchered animals. The odor was indescribable. So, the officer did not attempt to describe it to his chief.

Inquiries were made. But no one knew or did not acknowledge that they knew the identity of the men or how they had come into possession of the house. The pig woman farmer would only say that the old couple who had lived there for years vanished one day and the three men move in with their bundle. But she was afraid to tell them about the other men who had been interested in the stone fortress. Her aunt warned her, "Say as little as possible."

With his keen military eye, Vasiliev was impressed by the medieval fortifications built by the Venetians to defend Kotor, which they had called Cattaro, against attack by sea. But Serov was fascinated by the number of cats that swarmed through the streets of the old town. They were everywhere, perching like birds of prey on the walls. From what he could judge they were pampered, even idolized, or at least tolerated by the inhabitants.asiliev had more important things than cats on his mind. Vasiliev sent Serov to find a boat, preferably Greek-owned and operated. Meanwhile, he did what he could to relieve Tamara of her fears and anxiety. Questions could come later. Perhaps she would venture answers before he had to pose them. He took her straight to what passed for the most fashionable shop just outside the entrance to the Old Town. The Italian proprietress exaggerated her show of discretion.

"Listen to this, *caro mio*," she gushed to her husband later that evening. "A Russian officer comes to the shop with his mistress, a stunning girl who looked as though he had just snatched her from a brothel. My dear! Her dress was half torn and her hair, beautiful but tangled, her shoes, muddy! Can you imagine? Oh! What an adventure that must have had. Well, I took her in hand. When I finished with her, she looked like royalty, don't you think?"

Her husband, the manager of the Rialto, the only decent hotel in Kotor, laughed as he rolled his portly body on top of his wife, whispering in her ear. "I have an even juicier bit for you. This same officer shows up with his adjutant and this 'princess' in tow, decked out in one of your most charming creations. He demands two rooms, one for her and a double for the two men. Well, I didn't blink an eye. But, oh, these Russians! They seem to have learned everything from the French, from Voltaire to the Marquis de Sade."

Serov reported back from his visit to the port with an amused expression on his face.

"I tell you, Vasili Vasilich, these Greeks seem to have happy memories of us. We seem to have done everythin' right by them. Down at the dock, I asked around. Everyone seemed to understand me, but I couldn't always get what they were sayin'. So, one young fella takes me by the hand and leads me to the old codger sittin' in a chair that looks like a pilot's seat from an old ship. Just torn out, you see and him sittin' in it, like he was still steerin' a ship. He takes one look at my uniform and greets me in Russian. A bit rusty you know, but the real thing."

"It turns out he was a lad when our fleet came 'round in 1813. He signed on. There was high hopes the local Slavs would get the port then. But it turned out not. 'A damned shame,' he called it. 'The Austrians took over. And who's happy about that?' he says and spits on the dock."

Vasiliev had taken out a cigar and was lighting up, thinking to himself how Serov always made ordinary life a little more interesting. He blew out the match.

"And the boat, Sergeant?"

"I'm gettin' to that. Just settin' the scene as you would say. Well, this old sea dog has a nephew who runs up to Ragusa once a week on his own craft, just like the one we sailed on with Popodopolis. So tomorrow it leaves at noon. Gets to Ragusa in five hours. I tell him we need a couple of berths. He says, 'It's done.' He draws me a map of where it leaves from."

"Perfect, my friend. Ragusa is perfect."

The following morning Vasiliev accompanied Tamara back to the dress shop and purchased a travelling outfit for her. Then the three of them took a cab down to a side bay where the Greek *trehantiria* was tied up. The captain greeted them in Italian with a hearty voice, casting a searching look at Tamara. Well, thought Vasiliev, there would be no way to disguise her short of a *chador*. Serov had arranged for her to stay below in a small cabin out of sight of the crew. Vasiliev paced the deck restlessly, as he had not slept well thinking of the girl in the next room.

On a sudden impulse he went below. There was no one in the companionway. He stood at her cabin door for several minutes. He even raised his arm to knock but then lowered it. What made him turn around and go back to the upper deck? A vague memory of another time in distant Russia? The fleeting vision of a young Sonia running across field to greet him and her brother after a hunt. It was the first time he had seen her as a more than a childhood friend. Was it that or of something more prosaic that made him hesitate? The muffled sound of seawater lapping against the hull? Or the creaking of the ship's timbers as if giving forth deep sighs? For a long time afterwards, he would relive those moments, alternatively cursing and congratulating himself. Was it a lost opportunity or admirable restraint?

As the ship approached the harbor of Gravusa, which served as the port for Ragusa, Vasiliev sent below for Tamara. When she joined them, they were passing the gorge that the captain called the Valle d'Ombla. She gasped with pleasure. Vasiliev too was moved by the magnificence of the scene. A smaller boat picked them up and they sailed through a winding channel between rocky heights, below which the slopes were covered with cypress and olive trees. A few white cottages were scattered along the shoreline.

They landed at a mill fed by the energetic pulse of the Ombla River. A limestone mountain towered over them, forming the boundary of Hercegovina. The helmsman spoke a strange Slavic dialect, but Vasiliev understood enough to translate. "He says that during the revolt, there was a fierce engagement just beyond the mountain between the Turks and the mountaineers." The helmsman called out to two young men lounging on the shore who were happy to pick up a few coins carrying their few bags.

They ascended a narrow strip of high ground that brought the harbor of Ragusa into view. They stood for a moment, stunned by the beauty of the tropical vegetation, a palm tree, thickets of rosy oleander and a public garden filled with masses of flowers. Their porters gestured at a small hotel just outside the Porta Pille, the land gate of the city, called the Albergo al Boscetto. Vasiliev thanked them in Italian and they responded volubly, wishing them a good stay and offering their services in the future as guides.

When they were settled in their rooms, Serov leaned out the window overlooking the shimmering water and breathing in the air perfumed by hundreds of flowers.

"Vasili Vasilich, I think we should make this our base of operations."

"You'd soon become lazy and lose your sharp edge. Look what happened to the Venetians."

"Ah but they hung on here for three hundred years."

"My goodness, Sergeant, now where did you learn that?"

"You'd be surprised, begin' your pardon, how much a fella can pick up on the streets."

Vasiliev was satisfied to stay outside the town in the belief that the less Tamara was seen in public the better the chances of keeping her out of danger. He explained to her that she was not being confined as she had been in Cetinje. She appeared to understand. She would lock herself in her room and not be locked in. The three of them would take their meals together. Slowly, slowly, he thought. It would take time to gain her trust. The first dinner was a promising start.

"Did you notice how striking the women are who serve us?" she said. "They don't look like the Slavs I met to the north." Tamara was staring out to the bright water. Her features seemed to Vasiliev to have softened in the few days they were together. She turned to him and her smile sent a dart straight to his heart.

"These women," she went on, "they look more like the faces I remember when we landed in Anatolia. I was only a little girl but I remember my brothers saying how some of the women in the marketplace were 'oriental' in appearance. How many different races there are here too? And why cannot they all live in peace?"

Vasiliev knew she was thinking of Grigoriev again, and he buried his own feelings. For his peace of mind, he decided to assume the role of a teller of tales.

"It is said these women are descendents of an antique people called Phoenicians. They are reputed to have worshipped serpents."

Tamara shivered.

"Well, no longer, no need to worry. But there are legends about a Greek hero, Cadmus, who was metamorphosed into a dragon in one of those caverns we passed below the rocky cliffs."

"A place to hide, maybe," said Serov.

Vasiliev was startled to see the look of fear that suddenly distorted Tamara's features. Now what had he said that could possibly produced that effect?

"Indeed! The Cadmus legend was just meant symbolically," he said, hoping to dispel what fears his story might have stirred up. Later Serov would recall this part of the conversation and give himself some credit for what happened shortly afterwards.

Vasiliev felt confident in leaving Tamara alone while he and Serov arranged for the next stage of their travel into Hercegovina. Entering Ragusa through the Porta Pille, the gate that cut through the massive city walls, they found themselves in the *Stradone* or *Corso*. On both sides of the street, there were fine stone buildings, limited in height to four stories after the great earthquake of 1667. The slabs of the paved street were made of polished marble, causing them to slip several times.

"Now I understand why Peter the Great wanted St. Petersburg to look like a Venetian city," said Vasiliev.

Serov glanced up at the pure blue sky. "Too bad he couldn't get the sun to go along with him, begin' your pardon."

"It's good you only share these sentiments with me, Sergeant."

The abundance of churches made it clear that this was a Catholic town. In the streets, they heard mainly a dialect of Serbian being spoken. But the better dressed people spoke Italian. They even saw a few Vlachs in their shepherd's dress. This was Ionin's main base, although, as he had confided to Vasiliev, he preferred Cetinje. There he could deal directly with Prince Niko, support his views and commiserate with him when his plans to occupy a port on the Adriatic were frustrated. Vasiliev thought that in his place, he would never trade Ragusa for Cetinje, but then admitted to himself once again that he was not a political creature.

Tamara was still not certain how far she could trust the Russian major, Vasili Vasilevich Vasiliev. He had rescued her from her wretched abductors and treated her with respect. But she had learned that trust was not something you distributed casually. And never wholly, except perhaps to her beloved Borya. Even with him, she held back something. What did this Russian officer want from her? He promised revenge, but why? The others in Cetinje, that fat consul with his cats and sly Anna Ivanovna trying to pry secrets from her. She made a mistake in escaping, but only because she fell into the hands of those horrible men. And what did they want? They hardly spoke to her, as if waiting for some order. Every night she feared for her life. Or worse. She knew how they sold girls like her into some pasha's harem. Is that what they were waiting for, a bid on the possession of her body?

She gazed at herself in the gilt-edged mirror in her room and fingered the fringes of her elegant dress. She thought of her father and brothers and, lowering her head, silently wept. She had betrayed them for love and then lost her love too. The Russian officer was her only hope. But she had to be careful. It was good the others knew so little about what she and Borya were up to. But what did he mean by mentioning Cadmus? How much could she tell this Russian officer?

Chapter Twenty-Three

Ragusa

Vasiliev sent off two telegrams at the Russian consulate and then went off to register with the Austrian police. They seemed polite enough. Apparently, the danger of war had receded now that the Treaty of Berlin had been signed.

A handwritten message was also waiting for him at the consulate, addressed to Major V.V. Vasiliev. The envelope bore the official stamp of the *Manchester Guardian* with the initials AJE scribbled below. Written in English it invited Vasiliev to meet a certain Arthur J. Evans, who identified himself as a correspondent for the newspaper, on the terrace of a small hotel behind the Palazzo Rettorale any day in the late afternoon. As soon as Vasiliev arrived, he spotted Evans. In his eyes, the Englishman fit the stereotype. He was well built and carried himself like an athlete. He had a bemused look about him, but his eyes darted from object to object and person to person as if taking a series of snapshots with a hidden camera. He carried a book which he handed to Vasiliev.

"I have heard about your exploits," he smiled. "Here are mine, at least up to now. And I would like to hear more about yours."

Vasiliev glanced at the cover, *Through Bosnia and Hercegovina on Foot*, London 1877. His first thought was, 'a messenger from the gods.'

"In that case we may need more than one session. May I invite you to share some refreshment?"

"With pleasure."

"Shall we toss a coin to see who goes first?"

"But, I've already begun," Evans objected, tapping his book which Vasiliev now held. "Your turn unless you have a manuscript hidden about you. Oh, and I will take a gin and tonic with a slice of lime. A very English drink, I fear, but they do have the ingredients in stock, just for me. An old customer."

"A cognac, please," Vasiliev ordered. Then, not to be outdone, he added, "Armenian ten-year-old *per piacere*! If not? Ah, I see not, then a Courvoisier."

The exchange made Evans wonder whether this Russian preferred foils or sabers. But he just laughed. After all, they were just verbally fencing.

Vasiliev related his adventures, properly edited, leaving out nothing of what he had observed of the politics but everything else. He thought about how to introduce Tamara into the conversation. The Englishman was too well informed not to know she had arrived with him.

"As for my personal life, not to be spread across the pages of the *Manchester Guardian,* I will only say that I have been entrusted by my consul, Ionin, whom you know I am sure, to conduct a beautiful Circassian girl back to her people. More exactly to her father, a tribal chief whose support we would like to cultivate."

Evans peered into his glass, to mask his expression.

"I can think of worse missions."

"Another round?"

Evans nodded and then began his recital.

"No need to repeat what I wrote more than two years ago. But since then, much has changed. What exactly do you want to know?"

"I will have to follow your footsteps, or some of them, and preferably not on foot. The Circassians I am looking for may no longer be in their villages. So, what can you tell me about the situation over the border in Hercegovina and beyond into Bosnia. All I hear are rumors of resistance to the Austrian occupation. How unstable are conditions?"

"Hard to say, at least from my perspective. I've been travelling recently along the Montenegrin Ottoman borders to the east, where you have already been and the south where things are still 'unstable' to take your word.

"Let me explain. In the recent war, the Montenegrins drove the Turks out of Antivari and Dulcigno on the Adriatic coast. They want to keep them. Unless they do, they'll have to continue to trade through Kotor, which makes them dependent on the Austrians. I can personally testify that the local Muslim population in the area was willing to accept the rule of Prince Nikola in preference to Austrian control. But the Austrians were adamant, no sea coast for Montenegro! Instead, they proposed that Montenegro would acquire the area around Gusinje, where you have also been. You know that this area is overwhelmingly populated by the North Albanian tribes. And since their new unity in the League of Prizen, they are determined to hold on to their hereditary lands for dear life, and I mean that quite literally. But you have already observed that.

"Enter Count Corti on center stage right. His supposed compromise solves nothing. It cuts back the area in the north but still leaves substantial Albanian tribal areas under Montenegrin rule. It adds still more Albanians of the Hoti tribe to Montenegro in the Tuzi district bordering on Lake Scutari. It gives Montenegro the port of Antivari or rather its ruins. The town was completely demolished in the war. What a tragedy that was. I've described it to my readers as 'the most perfect representative Venetian city of the Adriatic or the Levant' before the Montenegrin bombardment. The Montenegrins will have to build an entirely new one. They are to be denied the port of Dulcigna which survived its siege virtually intact. Why do I tell you all this when you will be going north into the turmoil in Hercegovina, rather than south into the turmoil of Albania?

"Because it is all of a piece."

Evans was leaning forward now, his eyes no longer darting around the crowded bar room but fixed with fierce intensity on Vasiliev.

"My dear Vasili, if I may call you that. I feel a kindred spirit. You see before you an English Slavophil, not to say Panslav. Oh! Not your Ignatiev type, no. But a believer in the right of the Serbs and Montenegrins as Christian people to have their own country and not to be subject to the Turk or the Austrian. I feel certain sympathy for the Albanians, especially the Christians but even the Muslims among them. The Turk plays them against one another. But let me return to your northern expedition."

He glanced as his watch.

"Damn! I've lectured you too long. You warned me about our needing more than one session. Now I have to finish writing a dispatch for the *Guardian* and sending it off by wire so that it can appear in tomorrow's paper. Short if not sweet, often bitter. But it has to go or my editor will ream me out. You see, I'm the only English reporter on the spot. the others sit in Istanbul and Vienna. They can't help but be influenced by 'official circles.' Perhaps tomorrow, same place? Good."

Evans vigorously shook Vasiliev's hand.

Vasiliev sat on the terrace, pondering what Evans had told him. Still much to learn, he concluded, perhaps more than he could understand in this land of fierce loyalties which we mistakenly call primitive.

He had arranged to meet Serov back at the consulate.

As they walked along the Stradone, Serov reported on his inquiries among the boat owners recommended by the Greek master of the *trehantiria*. Since the war, the Austrians and the French had discontinued their weekly service up the coast. It was possible though to hire a small sailing boat, called a *trabaccolo*, which would take them to Stagno, a small town at the entrance to the Narenta River in Hercegovina. Upriver lay the city of Mostar.

"That's where you wanted to go, Vasili Vasilich. I was lucky. In the Austrian Lloyd office, a young woman spoke a few words of Russian. Though, begin' your pardon, she hadn't ever served on one of our battleships," he said with a straight face.

"Sergeant, you're getting out of hand."

"She told me that I should be careful because the area was still not pacified by the Austrian troops."

"I think you'll be happy to return to Moscow."

"True enough. The population there all speak Russian. At least that's my understandin'."

Vasiliev later reflected that it was the last moment he would have occasion to smile for a long time.

The next day a telegram arrived from Ivan in St. Petersburg with a note attached that a copy had been sent to him at Cetinje.

Serov knew it was bad news as soon as Vasiliev had torn open the envelope. Sent *en plein air*, not in code, it informed him in official language of the death of the Empress, Maria Alexsandrovna. It ended with the words, "More forthcoming."

A dark train of thought raced through his head. This could only mean one thing. A realignment of forces at court. What would become of the urgency behind his mission? Or even any further interest in it, or worse, opposition to it continuing. He put this together with what he was hearing about the change in attitudes in high places toward the Serbs and Montenegrins. Is that what Evans had been about to reveal as well? And what about the lovely Tamara? What was he to do with her? Had he just lost the official reason for pursuing her murderer?

Serov stood next to him, mute. But his expression confirmed Vasiliev's own doubts and fears. Vasiliev was often surprised by Serov's uncanny ability to read his thoughts. Or was he doing his boyhood friend an injustice? Hadn't Serov, a young household serf in the service of Count Vorontsov, Vasili's father, learned a great deal by silently observing the high-born as they pursued their petty intrigues and calculated flirtations, weaving their deeper conspiracies in the drawing rooms of the Count.

But all he asked was "What do we do now?"

"We'll not wait for what's 'forthcoming' from Ivan. We need to ask Tamara some hard questions, together, Sergeant." Vasiliev did not trust himself to be alone with the girl, not now, more than ever.

Chapter Twenty-Four

Outside Ragusa

She sat in the high-backed chair in the garden, poised and expectant, her hands folded demurely in her lap. Regal, thought Vasiliev. How many courts in Europe would be enriched by her presence!

He had given some thought about how to begin, how to avoid flattery, condescension or, God forbid, veiled threats.

"Tamara, we need your help in bringing justice to Grigoriev. If you wonder why a Russian officer has been given this assignment, then I can tell you there are important people, high ranking people who valued his work. They want to honor his service."

"Perhaps they should have given us more help, then, when it could have mattered."

"Is the cause lost, then?"

"Without him, it has lost much."

"Do you think with our help you might recover part of this loss?"

"If you had his spirit and you could be trusted, perhaps."

"Ah, his spirit. I can't claim to match that. But surely he prepared the ground for others to follow?"

"I seek only revenge."

"Surely, he would honor you for that. But perhaps he would hope for more?"

"All right, first revenge, then …." She hesitated, searching for the right words. "Yes, to build, to go forward."

"To what end?"

"Liberation."

Vasiliev decided he would risk it. He would like to have caught Serov's eye. But he only felt the presence of the Sergeant who was standing behind him, absolutely motionless. The *stolb*, the pillar as he was known in his youth. Someone who could appear to be an inanimate object, without any discernible sign of breathing, without the flicker of an eyelid, staring into the void. And this he could do for hours. Vasiliev had heard of Indian fakirs who could perform this discipline. But Serov had no knowledge of yoga. The result was that people forgot he was there. The perfect witness, the ultimate impersonation — a non-person.

"Tamara, excuse me for saying this. But why should you devote your life to the liberation of people who are not yours? I have read the account you gave of your life. Are you telling me you have undergone some conversion?"

"Not in your meaning of the word."

"So, in what meaning?"

"Borya showed me how people can keep their own faith but find another way of joining together."

"Please explain."

"We went together into Bosnia. There we found Muslims and Christians who spoke the same language, joined by the same blood. On the holy days, they go into different places to worship. But they all worship a single god. Only his name is different. Borya told me, 'we are all peoples of the Book.'"

"And there are those who do not agree?"

"Yes. In the old days, so it is said, the Sultans tolerated all the faiths. Borya said the Great Catherine in Russia also accepted all who swore loyalty to the throne. Now, it is different."

"And Grigoriev wanted to create such a community?"

"He said there were among your people those who supported the idea with money and arms. That was the time of the great rebellion."

"You mean four years ago, in Hercegovina, then Bosnia. And Grigoriev volunteered to help."

"Yes, and to stay after the idea was betrayed."

"Tamara, can you tell me who might have killed Grigoriev?"

A tremor passed through her.

"There are many enemies of his ideas. Borya warned me that they are powerful and clever and act from far away."

She brought her hands up to cover her eyes and held them there for a moment.

"Those who…the murderers, tried to make it look as though they were tribesmen, perhaps Albanians. You understand?"

Vasiliev knew she could not pronounce the word *beheading*.

"But you do not think so."

"No. Borya had no quarrel with the tribes. Let them have their own homeland, he would say. The Albanians too are of several faiths and will be united by language and blood."

"So who were his enemies?"

"This is hard to say. There are those from the north. When I was held by your consul in Cetinje, a woman who watched over me said that they were Austrians come to occupy the Bosnian lands. But Borya told me too that the Russians who had helped in the great rebellion were losing interest. His comrades who came with him to fight were leaving. I came to your consul's house…"

"You mean Ionin in Cetinje."

"Yes. To shame him into revenge! In the beginning, Borya said, he was with us. But then he turned away. No one knows why."

Vasiliev knew, but he was reluctant to tell her. The powers at Berlin had arranged things in their own interests. The Russians had made concessions. Austria was to occupy Bosnia and Hercegovina and the Sanjak. Perhaps the Montenegrins would get a port, perhaps not. But they would be saddled with hostile Albanians on their frontiers. The railroad would be built and all the Western Balkans would fall under Austrian influence. Russian influence in Bulgarian would be recognized, and they would get former Ottoman territories in the Caucasus. How could he explain all this? It would be like casting his government among the enemies of Grigoriev who was intent on carrying on the struggle. Or were there still Russian agents who were on the side of the rebels, as Totleben had hinted? Now that the Empress was dead, who at the center would support the Slavic cause? He was determined to find these things out. And to uncover the murderer or murderers for reasons that were becoming more and more personal.

Chapter
Twenty-Five

Ragusa

The Iron Colonel's "forthcoming" telegram arrived late in the evening. This time it was in code.

After he had decoded the message, Vasiliev read it out loud to Serov in a resigned tone of voice.

"'Katia's star in the ascendant', Ivan means Dolgorukova, of course. 'Still not clear how much her advice on negotiations with Austrians has influenced the final delimitation of Serbian borders. What is clear is that she has set herself against the Panslav sentiments of the late empress. No longer any interest at court for discovering fate of Grigoriev. Our support for rebels in Hercegovina at risk. Your report on situation urgently required. Ivan.'"

Vasiliev held the telegram to a candle and watched it burn.

"At this point, Serov, I usually ask you to prepare the samovar, or as this news requires something stronger, a *riumochka* or two of vodka. But since these vital aids to dispel depression are not available, let us adjourn to the bar for a cognac. Perhaps Evans will show up again and further darken our mood."

The next morning, Serov was out early to buy provisions for the trip into Hercegovina. The manager of the hotel told him that he would find a colony of Hercegovian refugees from the time of the rebellion outside the Porta Placce, where there were a few markets. By this time Serov had picked up enough Serbian to buy what was needed. In his uniform he was an object of interest but no one spoke to him until he was standing in front of a stall selling dried figs, dates and nuts. He was startled when a middle-aged woman addressed him in halting but correct Russian. She was wearing the characteristic dress of a Hercegovinian, a bright crimson fez covered by a light white kerchief falling to her shoulders, a reddish blue colored jacket and an apron of red and orange hues tied about her waist. She held in her hand a girdle studded with semi-precious stones, agates and carnelians.

"Would you care to buy this? Very cheap."

Serov thanked her politely but said he did not have a woman who deserved such a beautiful item. After he bought his figs, she was waiting for him.

"Russian officers are so polite to us, not like the Austrians." She had strapped the girdle back around her waist.

"May I speak to you for a minute, in private, away from this crowd?"

Serov followed her past the Turkish market to an abandoned building that looked like a former stable.

She turned to him in the shadows.

"Have you come to save us?"

Serov glanced around but there was no one near them.

"I don't understand."

"Why are you here then, if not to save us?"

"I have been ordered here." Serov wondered where this was leading but decided to play for time.

"Yes, of course, you are a soldier. But as a soldier you must want to defend your Slav brothers."

"We want to help. But this is Austrian territory. We are not free to act. But to learn."

"Learn? What is there to learn? First, the Turks drove us out and now the Austrians have occupied our land. There were some brave lads from Russia who fought with us but that was years ago. We sought refuge here three years ago. We want to go back home."

"Yes, we know this. What else do we need to learn? I will tell you, friend. A soldier must know the terrain, you understand what I mean? The lay of the land, before he engages in battle. But also the strength of the enemy."

Serov feared that he was already saying too much.

"I see. Well, we have been here too long to give good information about all these matters. Things are bad. But we do not know how bad. There are rumors. But there is someone who can help you."

"This is good news. But we must be careful."

"I know you have no reason to trust me. But I am also taking a risk in speaking to you so frankly."

"All right. Let me tell you what I have to do. I am only a Sergeant. My superior officer is in the city. I will ask him if he agrees to meet this person. And then I will return with him to talk again with you. You can also speak with this person. We will then arrange to meet him in a place agreed on by both sides."

"My, my, such careful preparations! But you are right. We must proceed cautiously. You must be vigilant. Take care no one follows you. The Austrian police are suspicious of everyone now. Perhaps it would be best if you did not wear uniforms. Is that possible?"

"It is possible. But I have to ask."

"Thank you, Sergeant. We have no one now but the Russians to trust, and we can no longer be sure about even you."

Vasiliev was waiting for Evans who arrived breathless at the hotel.

"A real crisis is blowing up on the Montenegrin border," he exclaimed as he sank into his chair and waved to the servant.

After gulping down half his gin and tonic, Evans leaned over conspiratorially, as Vasiliev fully expected, and with great intensity related his news.

"An Italian newspaper, *Gazette Piedmontese*, has published a scandalous story. According to Count Corti's, compromise, you will remember, the Tuzi region on the southern border of Montenegro and inhabited by the Albanians was assigned to Montenegro in return for Prince Nikola giving up lands to the northwest where the old silver mines are. Alright. Now the Albanians, or rather the chiefs of the Hoti tribe, who are Catholic, declare that the Austrian consul at Scutari had urged them to resist and promised Austrian support. The *Gazette* then published several dispatches from the Austrian consul in which he reported to Vienna that he had discouraged the chiefs from resisting. Now the drama heats up. The Hoti persist in maintaining their position. The Austrian consul demands they answer eight questions in order to prove he did not encourage them. The chief snapped back, refusing to answer the questions and reiterate their original position. Now listen to this, I quote exactly. They 'set their seals to this declaration and swear to its truth with stones on their shoulders.' This is, of course, their most sacred oath. So take your choice, a minor Austrian diplomat or seventeen of the great Hoti chiefs!"

"I believe I already know where you come down."

"Perceptive of you."

Vasiliev glanced around the terrace. Nobody seemed to be taking an interest in them.

"What do you think the Austrians are up to?"

"As much of a mystery to me as to what the Russians are up to." Evans smiled.

"My guess," Vasiliev took a sip of his cognac, "and I am a great guesser when I don't have all the evidence, is that either this is a game of thrusts and feints on both sides, or else people on either side are working at cross purposes with one another."

"So deception or confusion."

"Nicely put. Of course one does not necessarily exclude the other."

"You like puzzles, don't you?"

"Only to solve them."

"And you think the solution may lie in Hercegovina and Bosnia."

"And what is your best guess?"

"As to guessing, I am an amateur archeologist, fallen on hard times as a journalist. As a journalist I always have to be certain of what I write. As an archeologist I face a different set of problems. There are gaps in the records of ruins, and languages no one has yet deciphered. So I form hypotheses, like the one you have just proposed as the basis for your guess. And then I test it.

"My very method."

"In your case, the testing is going to be rather dangerous."

"Your book has helped enormously. But you say much has changed since you left two years ago. Where do I find more recent information?"

"There are the refugees, mainly Serbs from Hercegovina, that is Bosnians of the Orthodox faith. They started coming in '77, fleeing the killings. Since the end of the war, the flow continues. Most of them are crowded around the Porta Placce, you know, the sea gate. You might inquire there. But I would not show up in a

Russian uniform. The Austrian police would not take kindly to your interest."

Evans lifted his eyes for a moment as if he were trying to read the future.

"And you? What is your plan?"

"Right now, the Albanians fascinate me. The Prizen League has a good chance of uniting all of them. In the same way, I think that the Serbs have the best chance to uniting the South Slavs. But they both face formidable enemies. The Austrians and the Turks who, as we have been discussing, seem to play both against one another. Then back to England for a brief visit. But I'll return to Ragusa. This part of the world is a treasure house of classical antiquity. Roman ruins quite literally underfoot. And then there are all the Venetian works of art. Nowhere else is quite like it, even in Italy. But between earthquakes and wars, much has been destroyed. I fear that every year more will disappear. I must try to make a record of what has survived before it is gone. This is the archeologist in me. If I were only rich…"

Nodding his head, Vasiliev gazed across the square at a beautiful building in Moorish Gothic style.

"Yes, the Dogana and Zecca, the Mint of the old republic," said Evans as if reading Vasiliev's thoughts. "One of the few buildings that survived the great earthquake in 1667. Now, alas, a granary. Still, the façade is magnificent even if the interior has been stripped."

The two men stood up as if in unison and shook hands.

"You know, Vasili, if you get to Sarajevo and need assistance, my friend from Eton and Oxford, the *chargé d'affaires* there, is the man to see. I'll let him know you might be in the vicinity. I have come to believe, like Lord Derby, that if the English and Russians keep in touch, we might avoid another war in the Balkans."

"You have been a great help to me, Arthur. I hope your travels bring you to Moscow some day. Another city with great Italian architecture. The Kremlin you know was built about the same time as the Mint here, by an Italian architect in the style of the Palazzo Sforzesco in Milano."

"I'm sure that it will never be turned into a granary."

"Not in our lifetime, surely."

Three years later when Vasiliev had returned to Moscow, he

learned from Ivan that Evans had been arrested in Ragusa as a spy and after a short stay in an Austrian prison released. The nothing again for many years until Vasiliev had left Russia for the United States. One morning in 1897 he came across a pamphlet in the Duluth Public Library by Evans entitled "Letters from Crete." It was a plea for an international peace-keeping force to regulate an autonomous status for Crete after the Greco-Turkish War of that year.

Still the fighting journalist, thought Vasiliev. I wonder whatever happened to the archeologist in him.

Vasiliev had his answer a few years later, when the American papers were full of how Evan had been knighted for his great discovery of an ancient civilization at Knossos in Crete.

"Good for him," he muttered.

"For whom?" asked one of his sons.

"A splendid chap I knew long ago."

"Chap? How English, Dad!"

"Yes, he was every bit an Englishman."

Chapter
Twenty-Six

Outside Ragusa

Vasiliev had scarcely returned to the hotel when Serov arrived with that look of anticipation he knew so well. They sat in the garden with Tamara and exchanged their stories. She swiveled her head from one to the other, saying nothing until they had finished. Then they had their first quarrel. No shouting, screaming or weeping, but a serious disagreement, nonetheless. Tamara insisted on being the one to make the next contact. Vasili firmly contradicted her. Being left out of it, Serov watched the exchange and slowly realized to his astonishment that he was witnessing something resembling a lovers' quarrel. And to his even greater surprise, he thought Tamara was getting the best of it.

"All right, Vasili, here is my compromise," she was saying. "The Sergeant and I go back together. If the two of you go, then I will be left here alone for some time. You say you want to protect me. But I have to tell you, and the manager can back me up, that when you were both gone, a strange person showed up, asking for you. He did not give his name. The manager seemed to be intimidated by him. I was in the garden and then went up to my room and locked myself in, as you ordered. Someone tried the door. I don't even have my knife with me. I fear he will come back. Perhaps with others. Police? But perhaps not."

Vasiliev jumped to his feet. "I'll…"

"Please Vasili, hear me out."

"You think getting in touch with Serov's contact will be dangerous? I think not. It was an accidental meeting, don't you think so Sergeant?"

Serov nodded despite Vasiliev's villainous look.

"If we show up together, they will know that you are back here ready to intervene if we disappear. If you go with Serov, then both of you could be taken, and that would be the end of me as well. My last point, if there is a Russian refugee in hiding, then he is more likely to agree to meet with me, as a woman, than two Russian army officers. You forget. The Bosnians feel let down by your government. You are a representative of that government. They will be less suspicious of me.

"If you stay behind you can explain to the manager that I am going with the Sergeant in order to buy the fabulous girdle this woman offered to sell. It's the perfect disguise."

She turned again the Serov, who was dreading what she was about to ask him.

"What do you think, Sergeant? Isn't my plan the best one?"

How many times in his life had he been asked to oppose Vasiliev openly on this kind of question? How could he answer that she was right without angering the one man to whom he owed everything in life. 'Begin' your pardon,' was not going to get him through this.

"No need to put Serov on the spot, Tamara. I can tell from his expression that he agrees with you."

Vasiliev stood up again. "I'm going to ask the manager a few questions."

Tamara watched him walk away.

"Thank you, Sergeant," she said quietly.

While Serov was putting on civilian clothes and adding a false moustache to his modest disguise, Vasiliev looked on dubiously.

"No risks. Don't let her do anything rash. And when you have arranged a meeting with the source, come right back, and with her."

"I've never had any difficulty getting' up like a servant. That's what I was brought up to be, isn't that so?" He knew it was a feeble attempt to mollify Vasiliev. What else could he say? 'I'll guard her with my life?' That would be a stupid thing to say, even if it were true. "At least I know where to find the woman wearing the girdle with the jewels. I always struck a good bargain too," he said, flourishing the purse with Austrian kroner Vasiliev had handed him.

Tamara was wearing her travel outfit. She had put up her hair in coils and placed a transparent white veil on her head. If she thought that constituted an effective disguise, thought Vasiliev, she was mistaken. But was there anything she could do to produce that effect? She would have had to cut off all her hair and blacken her face. Even then…, he mused and brought himself up short.

"It's a good day for a shopping expedition." He ground out the words in the hope of covering up his anxiety. He had never felt quite so useless.

Serov kept looking behind them to make certain they were not being followed. Tamara asked him about his life, and he told her a few stories about his boyhood friendship with Vasiliev, the serf boy and the son of Count Vorontsov (he did not tell her the bastard son). She had a lovely laugh, especially when he told her how they used to wrestle one another in the fields of his father's estate, to the horror of the village peasants.

The woman was where he had last seen her.

"Very good, Sergeant. You look just like a native. And who is this beauty?"

Tamara had agreed with the deception.

"This is the fiancée of my commanding officer. She was interested in the girdle. Is it still for sale?"

"Is that all you have for me?"

"Of course not. But you warned me we should be careful. So, we're bein' careful. Let's move over there by the old stables and make as if we're hagglin'."

Serov took out his purse and opened it.

Tamara took the girdle in her hand. "Fine work," she said "Who was the craftsman?"

"How would you know his name even if I could tell you?"

"Oh, you'd be surprised. It looks like the work of a master in Travnik."

The woman was startled. She snatched back the girdle and looked as though she were about to run.

"Don't be frightened," Tamara said in a low voice that Serov had never heard her use. "We are friends, looking for followers of Cadmus and you are one." She took the woman's left hand and touched a ring in the shape of a dragon on her fourth finger.Then she drew a thin silver necklace out of her blouse, at the end of which was an identical ring.

The woman's eyes went wide with astonishment.

"Then the man you told the Sergeant about, isn't he one of us?"

Serov was startled. He recalled Vasiliev telling them about the myth of Cadmus but what did it mean here? He decided quickly to intervene. "Stay calm, friend, and pretend we have agreed on a price. How much do you want? My commanding officer authorized us to arrange another meeting."

The woman handed over the girdle and took the purse without counting the money.

"But who are you? How did you find us?" She seemed to have recovered her balance.

"It's not important for now. Later, when I can meet your comrade, I will tell you everything." Tamara spoke with a voice of authority.

Serov was as much baffled by Tamara's commanding tone as he was about the matching rings. But he could not think of a way to prevent what he saw happening. Vasiliev would be furious.

"We need to meet now," said Tamara. "We cannot fool the police forever."

The woman raised her hand to her face and looked around wildly

"No one is following us. We were very careful. Lead us to him. We can bring food too. What do I call you?"

"Maria." The woman nodded. Tamara took her by the arm and they went from stall to stall buying two bottles of the local wine, dried fruits and nuts. Serov felt he was in the hands of a female Vasiliev.

"In the caves," the woman whispered, "we have to take a boat. Wait here."

She returned in a few minutes with an older man. Serov glanced at his left hand, the dragon ring. He nodded to them but did not speak.

The boat was carried by the swift current against which they had battled when sailing upstream a few days earlier. The boat man kept close to the shore and beached the boat in front of a large cavern in the rocky cliffs.

Maria spoke a few words to him in a Bosnian dialect.

"She says to wait for us. We will not be longer than an hour."

Maria stared at her. "So you speak our language, too. Tamara smiled. "I like the way it sounds."

"Be careful, the ground is rocky and there are sharp stones on the side of the cavern. I must warn you he is not well."

They smelled him before they saw him. He was lying on a bed of straw. He had been a large man, Serov estimated, but his body was emaciated. His long hair and heavy beard almost obliterated his features.

Maria knelt beside him and handed him one of the wine bottles which she had already uncorked. He took a long draught, coughed violently, all the while nodding his thanks.

Only then did he peer at Serov and Tamara. With a sudden, jerky motion he swept to one side the curtain of hair hanging over his face. At the same time he raised his hand in what looked to Serov like a salute.

"Tamara!" his voice cracked with emotion.

"Is it you, Stanislav? By the prophet, what has happened to you?"

Serov felt an odd sensation as if the ground were shifting under him. He could only think of how he was going to tell Vasiliev was had happened.

"Ah, my dear Tamara, how beautiful you look, a vision appearing before a dying man. And who is this?"

"A friend who has come to help me seek revenge."

"For Borya. What can I tell you? I ..." He was seized with another spasm of coughing.

"Gently, gently. Sip the wine. There is bread and fruit here. You need strength to talk, to tell me about his last days."

Maria held his head as he took another swallow. She tore off a piece of bread and fed him, pushing away his filthy hands. He ate a few figs and lay back on his pallet.

"Yes. I will speak gently. So little time left. Maria has kept me alive this long. It must be just to await you." He pushed aside his curtain of hair again. Serov took notice of the dragon ring on his left hand. It shone in contrast to the darkened fingers that looked as if they had been burned

Mostar Bridge

"It must have happened outside Mostar. I left him outside the town."

"Yes. The last I saw of him he was crossing the Mostar Bridge. He said he had a meeting with some of our group in one of the towers of the old fortifications." Stanislav closed his eyes, and Serov feared he might not open them again.

"Yes, the Mostar Bridge…" Tamara bent closer. Serov could not imagine how she could stand the odor of putrefaction. The man must be rotting from the inside.

Suddenly, the dying man opened his eyes wide and gnashed his teeth.

"It was Omar who betrayed him. I am certain. I saw him slink out of the tower and disappear in the stalls of the town. I shall never forgive myself for not pursuing him."

"But you were the lookout, Stanislav. You were watching for enemies coming from without, not from within. You cannot blame yourself."

Stanislav had raised himself on his elbows and stared at Tamara as if he no longer recognized her.

"I waited too long. When I sought him out, I think the terrible deed had been done. He was…missing. There was blood and the others had fled."

"Did you see…?"

His body began to shake. Serov wanted to close his eyes as she grasped the shoulders of the dying man. Stanislav moved his head, but was it a sign of yes or no? Then he fell back and lost consciousness.

Maria was weeping. There were tears in Tamara's eyes but she brushed them away.

"Let me see," said Serov, holding his neck cloth over his face. He forced himself to take hold of the man's wrist and found no pulse.

"He is gone," he muttered.

Chapter
Twenty-Seven

St. Petersburg, Russia

Katia Dolgorukova's plans were moving ahead steadily. There were those at court who would have said stealthily if they had known the details. She had convinced the Tsar that she and her children deserved to become an official part of the imperial family. He was helpless to resist her entreaties, especially when she whispered in his ear as he was penetrating her. Her only fear was that he would cease to desire her. But to the amazement of the court, this did not happen. It was rumored that she had cast a spell over him. They called her "the blonde witch." She reveled in the epithet.

With practiced skill she urged the Tsar to persuade the heir, Alexander Alexandrovich, or order him if necessary, to introduce her son Gogo as his younger brother. Torn between his filial duty and his contempt for Princess Iurovskaia, as he was obliged now to call her, he agreed to carry out his father's will to act as protector of "the young family." To the dismay of other members of the family, especially Grand Duchess Maria Fedorovna, the former Princess Dagmar of Denmark and wife of the heir, Dolgorukova began to appear at family dinners with her children. But no one dared to say anything. The next step, she calculated, would be to appear with the Tsar at an imperial ball after the period of mourning the late Empress had ended. In the meantime, she was determined to pursue her business interests.

The Italian ambassador had informed her that the Austrians were now in firm control of the site of the old silver mines in the Sanjak of Novyi Pazar. An Italian consortium was in Vienna negotiating for a lease on the property. And a preliminary survey had turned up traces of gold in the vicinity as well. She doubled her investment in the project, always acting through the intermediary of a Swiss banking firm.

Still, disturbing rumors reached here from other sources that the Italian group was concerned about the stability of the region. The alleged "firm control" of the Austrians could be jeopardized by small bands of former participants in the resistance to the Austrian occupation in neighboring Bosnia and Hercegovina. They were now scattered but active. It was said that among them were survivors of the Russian volunteers of earlier years who now served as leaders of some of these bands. She was annoyed that her previous efforts seemed to have failed to eliminate the criminal activities of these adventurers. The Russian consuls in the region would have to be brought to heel. Their sympathies with the old rebels and Panslav volunteers of Chernaiev were well known. Hadn't they read the publication of the Treaty of Berlin?

Count Shuvalov returned from his first audience with Tsar Alexander since his return from Berlin in a deeply depressed state. His August Master had dismissed all his efforts to reach an equable settlement with the European powers over the postwar ordering of the Balkans. In the cold and distant manner that Alexander had lately cultivated to express his disapproval, he had declared his disappointment in the Treaty which Shuvalov had painstakingly help to negotiate. That he had probably saved Russia from a renewed war, facing a coalition of powers as in the Crimea a generation earlier went unacknowledged, unappreciated and even misunderstood. Yet, he had won the respect of the English, Derby, of course, but even Lord Salisbury, though not Disraeli, that madman who had poisoned Queen Victoria against him. He had drawn closer to Prince Bismarck who offered Russia the best guarantee of her security and greatness in Europe and Asia. Didn't they see that?

He glumly peered out the window of his carriage, hardly taking notice of the snow-bound streets of the capital, a frigid world that seemed an extension of the atmosphere that surrounded him at the imperial court. He buried his face more deeply in his fur pelisse and silently cursed his enemies. First and foremost was the Dolgorukova bitch. What did they call her now? Princess Iurevskaia, a ridiculous title having no connection with anything in Russian history. And she the offspring of a minor gentry family. Was there no end to the woman's scheming?

Well, he would see who ended having best served Russia. He still had his men in place from the days when he was Head of the Third Section, first class secret agents whose identify was unknown even to the Tsar, not to speak of the sycophant courtiers and ministers whom his men had long had under surveillance. They had picked up some juicy bits from the garrulous Italian ambassador, too inflated with his self-importance to guard his tongue. Yes, a greater scandal was in the making than his discovery that she had been dabbling railroad securities. A pity, in a way, for she shared with him his disdain for the Pan Slavs who had pushed Russia into the war that even his enemies among the so-called liberal ministers, like Miliutin at War and Reitern at Finance, had opposed. If only the Tsar had been consistent. But he was afraid of becoming dependent on one or another of his advisers. If he had only listened to him, he could have been Russia's Bismarck. But what was the sense dwelling on that dream, although he thought at one point he had come so close. But the serpent Dolgorukova had reared up to force him into honorable exile at the Court of St. James. Could he manage a comeback?

No, there was no chance of an alliance with her even against the Pan Slavs. She was thoroughly corrupt. Now he would prove it Beyond the shadow of a doubt. He could count at least on Menzentsov, his former subordinate in the Third u. c. Yes, Nikolai Vladimirovich would organize his best men to expose the Dolgorukova's intrigues with the Italian capitalists. He was convinced that she had been instrumental in persuading the Tsar to concede on the issue of Novi Pazar. Leaving a territorial corridor between Serbia and Montenegro in Ottoman hands with the right of Austria to occupy it made political sense. But the real reason in his view, confirmed by the Italian ambassador's indiscretions, was to grant the Italians access to the old silver mines that the Ottomans had abandoned for want of capital. He had evidence that she, the greedy wench, had invested in the future exploitation of the mines.

Of course, he would have to move carefully. He constantly reminded himself how confronting the Tsar with proof of her dabbling in railroads had cost him his position in 'seventy-four. There were other ways to expose her. He would have to work around the Tsar, perhaps leaking information to the press. Katkov's *Moskovskie vedemosti* would love to snap up the bait. Or else, an approach, indirect, to the heir Alexander Alexandrovich who despised her. In for the long run, then...

His spirits were beginning to rise as his coach drew up to his palace on the Embankment. By the time he had settled in his study, a brandy in hand, he had almost recovered from the shock of his audience with the Tsar, almost for the painful impression would never leave him. There were sealed reports from Menzentsov on his desk. It had taken his men less time than he expected to conclude their work. The Italian ambassador had foolishly assumed that the diplomatic pouch was immune to searches. The details came as something of a surprise on one aspect of the intrigue. The letters revealed a clandestine relationship between Dolgorukova's personal maid and the deputy foreign minister. She was the go-between carrying messages from Dolgorukova, which expressed in veiled terms the need to neutralize a certain Pan Slav agent, named Grigoriev, whose activities threatened to disrupt the plans to re-open the mines.

"Astounding," gasped Shuvalov.

He needed more information about this agent. A few days later, a chance encounter at court with Anna Tiucheva, the former lady-in-waiting to the Empress provided him with a totally unexpected source. It still rankled that her father, the poet Tiuchev, had caricatured him in the 1860s as "Peter IV," implying that he wielded unprecedented power as the Head of the Third Section and confidant of the Tsar. Shuvalov, as always when necessary the perfect courtier, expressed his regrets at the death of Maria Fedorovna, the late Empress. She had always been a personal friend to him, despite her mystical Pan Slav dreams. And he spoke warmly of her other qualities. Tiucheva responded, not without a touch of asperity.

"Yes, Maria Fedorovna had a great heart and a special affection for the plight of our Slavic brothers living under Turkish rule. You may know, as you know most things, that she greatly mourned the death of one of my own friends and her champion in the Balkans, Boris Andreevich Grigoriev. His brutal murder in Montenegro has never been solved. Have you ever wondered, Count, whose interest this atrocity served?"

Shuvalov suppressed an exclamation. Quickly regaining his composure, he excused himself with a few banal phrases. He hurried back to his palace where he scribbled several messages. He instructed his body servant to deliver one at once and in person to Menzentsov. The following morning he had his answer. A certain Major Vasiliev of the Moscow police attached to the Grand Duke's Danube Army had been ordered to investigate the murder at the instigation of the late Empress through the good offices of none other than Anna Tiutcheva. But shortly after the Empress's death the instructions had been cancelled and Vasiliev had been called off the case.

Shuvalov felt a surge of excitement just as he experienced on a hunt when a wild boar emerged from the brush into the sights of his rifle. He needed to get in touch with this Vasiliev. The one man in St. Petersburg who might help him was a somewhat mysterious figure nicknamed "the Iron Colonel" who had never been under his authority but was known to have his own network of informal agents. Was Vasiliev one of them? But an approach had to be carefully arranged. He sent out more messages and within twenty-four hours learned that General Totleben had also been in contact with Vasiliev. He made certain to attend a reception in honor of the hero of the storming of Plevna. In a brief exchange with Totleben, he confirmed that Vasiliev was on a double mission, personal for the Empress and political for Russia's future course in the Balkans.

"And how was it possible to get in touch with Vasiliev?" asked Shuvalov, implying he had information that could help the major fulfill his larger mission.

"I could supply you with a special code that will enable you to bypass the normal lines of communication. But his whereabouts at any one time are not known to me. The man who could help you in locating him is his trusted friend, the 'Iron Colonel.'"

Shuvalov was now convinced that he was closer to tightening the web of conspiracy around Dolgorukova. Again, caution was the watchword. If Vasiliev could be persuaded that continuing to pursue the murder of Grigoriev could be constrained to fit the larger mission sanctified by Totleben.... Shuvalov had no love for the Pan Slavs, quite the opposite. Whether the murder of Grigoriev would discourage them, a result he could only celebrate, was of secondary importance. He was convinced that Pan Slavism was dead or at least slumbering deeply. No, the critical issue here was his obsession with Dolgorukova's involvement in the crime. The identity of the assassin was the last link in the chain that would fetter her, overcoming the Tsar's passion. There were things even the supreme autocrat could not ignore, especially now that he was being hunted by revolutionaries who seem to have gained sympathy in Russia's fickle educated public.

Chapter
Twenty-Eight

Cetinje

Consul Ionin was devoting most of his time trying quietly to persuade a stubborn and, in his eyes, unreasonable Prince Nikola to accept a new proposal by the great powers over the boundaries of Montenegro left unresolved by the Treaty of Berlin. It would be a great advantage for the country, he argued, to exchange the barren and wild northern territory around Gusinje inhabited by fierce Albanian tribes for the district and port of Dulcigno on the Adriatic on the southern border of Montenegro. He was deeply disappointed by Count Corti's plan to carry out just the reverse. And he could not understand why his own government supported this idea. Oddly enough, he found himself arguing on the side of the Austrians. But on second thought, and Ionin was always having second thoughts on this matter, the Austrians wanted to prevent the expansion of either Serbia or Montenegro toward the north where their troops were in the process of occupying Bosnia and Hercegovina and the Sanjak, intending to dominate an area weakly controlled by the Ottoman Sultan and to encourage the Slavs to expand to the south where the Austrians had no interests.

Now, like snow falling on his head, instructions came from St. Petersburg to hasten to the European Boundary Commission meeting in Ragusa. There he was to announce a reversal in the previous official Russian policy and endorse the solution he had been advocating all along. Well, splendid, even if it would ruin his relations with Prince Nikola. What was going on in St. Petersburg? But it was the second telegram that struck him not like a snow fall but rather a blizzard. He swore loudly.

He had been sitting at his desk with Venus in his lap. She reacted, as always, from his sudden outburst by jumping down and scurrying for cover. He looked up knowing full well that Vulcan would be sitting on the threshold of his study, thumping his tail in glee.

"It's not possible," he growled. He reread the cable. Could the message have been garbled to express the opposite of what it said? He would ask for confirmation. He fretted for several hours, unable to sit still. The confirming cable arrived. No mistake had been made. He was ordered to intercept Vasiliev who was in Ragusa, abort his mission and recall him. What was worse was the instruction to provide a former Russian officer, who had lost his papers, with a passport and exit visa to leave Montenegro. No name or description was provided. It was signed by the deputy minister of foreign affairs.

His order threw the consulate into an uproar. First, the demand for a carafe of two hundred grams of vodka, then an order to pack a bag and another for a fast coach to Cattaro, a boat to Ragusa. But these things could not be arranged overnight. More swearing and counter orders. Should he send a cable to the ministry of military affairs? What of Totleben's instructions? Were they to be disregarded? And who was this mysterious Russian officer without a name that had to be spirited out of the country? A nightmare!

Both Venus and Vulcan had disappeared. But they were not forgotten. Ionin's final orders as he hurried out of the consulate the next morning were precise instructions on feeding them. This time he could not carry them along, an ominous sign in his view.

Ragusa

Tamara brooded all the way back to Ragusa. Serov rode silently beside her, respecting her painful memories. He decided it was up to Vasiliev to question her further.

While Vasiliev had been waiting impatiently for their return, a courier arrived from the Russian consulate with a telegram from Ionin that stirred a feeling of uneasiness. "Arriving shortly. Urgent business. Do not take any further action."

Then he felt a flood of relief as two riders came into sight. He was always reassured when Serov returned from a mission, but this was different, seeing Tamara, a quickening of the heartbeat. His uneasiness returned when he saw the look on their faces.

Serov let Tamara tell the story. He took note of what she left out and stored it away for future reference. It was more a matter of recording her moods and emotional reaction. He already felt that Vasiliev was becoming involved to the point where his normal cool-headed judgment was in danger of failing him. Mulling this over, he was surprised that he could detach himself from Vasiliev's way of looking at things. Then again, it was Vasiliev who had taught him how to develop a critical view of people and events. Whether he would now approve of being an object of this method was a different question.

What Tamara told Vasiliev persuaded him to ignore Ionin's message and press ahead into Hercegovina. She explained that the organized resistance to the Austrians may have crumbled but Grigoriev, Stanislav and others had been working to establish an underground network. The dragon rings were the sign of recognition. Cadmus was the code name of the organization. Someday it would break out again. The Austrians had already alienated many Bosnians both Christians and Muslim. The resistance had cost them the lives of several hundred men if not more. Those who had welcomed them would soon regret their views. Vasiliev was determined to find out as much as he could about Cadmus, carrying out the instructions of General Totleben. He had a feeling that the lines drawn at Berlin were not going to last forever, perhaps not even for very long.

They hired post horses, rode up the coast to Metković and then along the left bank of the Neretva to Mostar. While Vasiliev extolled the beauty of the mountain scenery, Tamara recounted how well the terrain had suited the tactics of the insurrectionists. A true daughter of the Caucasus, as if he needed to be reminded of it! They had to pass through an Austrian custom post where they were treated with much greater suspicion than had been the case when they left Montenegro. The customs officials seemed jittery. They made a thorough search of their few bags, and asked innumerable questions. Vasiliev had the impression that things were not as stable as they were reputed to be, by Vienna of course.

As they approached the great stone bridge over the Neretva River. Vasiliev recalled Evans's ecstatic description of the scene in his travel book: "the steep banks tiered with rocks, contorted, cavernous, festooned with creepers and wild vines above the arcades of Turkish stores, filled with brilliant oriental wares; the peaks, towers and gables of the quaint old fortifications…," the likes of which he had never seen. But the scene left Tamara gloomy and depressed. Her mood, shifting dramatically as it often did, settled over all of them in spite of the vibrant colors and medieval silhouette of the city, evocative of a fairy tale out of the thousand and one nights.

At Evans's recommendation they stopped at the only decent hotel, run by an Italian. He was delighted to see them, complaining that the old days had gone when European tourists would fill his rooms. Still, the dining room was crowded with Austrian officers, a few telegraph operators and Turkish officials. They were served a fiery red wine, the chef's special lasagna and bowls of fresh fruit. Toward the end of the meal a young man came over to their table and introduced himself in bad German as Robert Hamilton Lang. Vasiliev invited him in his impeccable Oxford English to join them.

Lang was clearly taken with Tamara, and happily related stories of his travels in Bosnia, dutifully translated into Russian by Vasiliev.

"The Austrians would like to bring civilization," he began, "but right now they are having trouble convincing the local population that their administration is efficient and fair. The Muslims begs are finding it difficult seeing their authority replaced. Even Christians in the towns are complaining of high taxes. The Catholics are particularly disappointed. They're not happy with General Josip Filipović, the commander of the Austrian forces in Bosnia and Hercegovina. He is after all a Croat! He appointed mainly Croats to the local administrative posts, so earning the distrust of the Serbs. Still, I believe in the long run the Austrians and their Croatian and Hungarian administrators will bring order and prosperity to the region."

"How long will that take, do you think?" asked Vasiliev.

"Hard to say, of course. Much depends on whether they'll be allowed to get about their business without the intervention of outside powers."

"By which you mean…"

A Croat Official

"The Serbs, primarily but, sorry to say, old chap, you Russians as well."

"My impression was that 'we Russians' have agreed to turn the country over to Vienna."

"In principle," said Lang coloring slightly. "But there are still these bands, with a few Russians in charge. At least that's what the Austrians maintain."

"You mean renegades," Vasiliev continued without translating.

"That's one way of putting it. Another way, I hate to say it, is that they are getting unofficial encouragement from the outside."

"For what purpose?"

"To keep alive the spirit of rebellion in case it is needed again later."

"Interesting. Well, I can assure you Mr. Lang, we are not here to give any encouragement to bands officially or unofficially."

"Of course not, of course not, I didn't intend…"

What precisely Lang did intend was never stated because an Austrian officer came over to the table at this point and saluted Vasiliev.

"My compliments, major, isn't it," he asked glancing at Vasiliev's shoulder tabs, "I have the honor to request that you present your credentials and documents of your companions to the commissioner of police, when convenient. Let us say tomorrow morning?"

"You see," said Lang sotto voce, "efficient but officious. It will take some time to import some Viennese *gumütlichkeit*."

Chapter
Twenty-Nine

Mostar

"My dear Major! All your documents are in order. I assure you of our good will and willingness to accede to your just requests in accord with the solemn agreements signed at the Treaty of Berlin. Now how may I be of assistance?"

"*Monsieur le commissaire de la police*, I appreciate your expressions of good will. I am here at the request of my government in order to discover the whereabouts of a subject of his Majesty the Emperor of All Russia. He may have been engaged in illegal activity. Since these acts would have taken place under the sovereign rule of the Sultan, and in light of agreements signed between his government and mine, I would ask that he be turned over to my authority for judicial proceedings under Russian law."

"And the name of this subject?"

"Boris Andreevich Grigoriev."

The commissioner gestured to his deputy who left the office and returned within a few minutes, handing a slim file to the commissioner.

"This is a report from our agents. I am pleased to share with you. But as you will see, the last information we have of him is his brief appearance in Mostar, on June 14, 1879. The report covers three years of his previous activities, or rather, I fear, rumors of his activities which were quite extensive."

"My own information confirms much of what is written here," said Vasiliev, after scanning the few pages. "What particularly interests me now is what happened to him on or after June 14. I see there is nothing more here after that date. So he disappeared?"

"From our sight," said the commissioner tersely.

"Was there any incident reported at the tower by the Mostar Bridge, on that date?"

"If there was it would be recorded in a different file. Why would that interest you, if I may ask? Does this have any bearing on the disappearance of Grigoriev?"

"According to an eyewitness, he was last seen entering the tower."

"And the incident?"

Vasiliev felt he was nearing the end of what he could admit of Stanislav's dying testimony without revealing the existence of Cadmus. This would compromise Tamara.

"I confess to making an assumption here, although a reasonable one, you may agree. If this Grigoriev was last seen entering the tower, the question remains whether anything occurred to prevent him from leaving of his own free will. Hence my question about a possible incident."

"Reasonable, possibly, but your assumption is based on the premise that an eyewitness can be found who had the tower under observation for an extended period of time. I can assure you that there was no police report on an incident taking place in the tower on that date."

"Thank you for your cooperation, commissioner." Vasiliev bowed slightly and left with the copy of the report.

"You see our problem, Tamara. We cannot produce any written evidence by a living person. Not even a secondhand account. We have only this one slim lead about a certain Omar who betrayed Grigoriev. But this is a common name. How can we find out who he is?"

"We would have to find another member of Cadmus in the city."

"And how would we do this? Was there a clandestine meeting place, perhaps a public one where members could identify one another by the ring?"

"I do not know. Borya kept me out of the city. He said it was too dangerous. We agreed to meet on the outskirts. If he did not turn up then, I was to return to our camp in Montenegro. That is where… I found his…remains."

"But you never recovered his body?"

"No."

"So we do not really know whether he was killed in Mostar or abducted here and then killed across the border in order to avoid committing a crime in an area under Austrian administration. I have to ask you a question which I should have done earlier. But I wanted to spare you. I can't do that any longer because we have run out of leads."

"Go ahead," she said lowering her eyes.

"I'll put this as delicately as I can. What was the condition of the head when you found it? I must ask for exact detail. Had the blood congealed? You have been trained to use the scimitar and knife. Can tell me by the nature of the wound what kind of a weapon might have been used?"

Vasiliev hesitated and then took her wrist in his hand.

She did not flinch or pull away.

"I was so horrified. I only remember that later I found a small amount of blood on my clothes. As for the cut…it was not a clean one."

"So the murder might not have taken place there in the tower but somewhere else. Possibly later. The blood that Stanislav saw… we do not know how much there might have been, perhaps he had only been wounded. Perhaps it was not even his. He might have fought his attackers.

"In any case, how did they get him out of Mostar?" he mused. "And who else knew of your camp in Montenegro?"

Hearing loud voices, Vasiliev went to the open window. The Italian manager was arguing with a tradesman who had drawn up his cart in front of the hotel.

"You're new, all right," the manager shouted, "but you should have the good sense to make a delivery in the rear!"

"Of course, that's it. Surely a cart and not a carriage!" Vasiliev exclaimed. He called in Serov from the adjoining room.

"We are going to hire a cart. We'd best do this as civilians."

Vasiliev carefully questioned the manager who explained that there were six shops in the vicinity of the Tower where carts might be hired. Vasiliev rehearsed Serov in Serbian and then changed his own clothes. They would each take three renters. It was a long shot. They would ask the price, then whether a cart had been hired for a long-distance trip earlier this year, perhaps to cross the border, and whether the man in charge of hiring had been named Omar.

At the second address, Vasiliev stood for a while studying a dilapidated wooden sign 'Carts for Hire.' It was hanging over a gaping hole in an ancient stone building that must at some time have been a gate. But only traces of the iron work could be seen affixed to the walls of the entryway. Two men lounged on a bench made of a rough-hewn wooden board resting on two granite blocks.

"Is the owner around?" Vasiliev asked, adjusting the fez on his head and scratching himself.

The man, sucking on a blade of straw, jerked his head over his shoulder.

"Inside," he rasped.

The place was cool and dark and pervaded with the odor of manure. Vasiliev let his eyes adjust, gradually making out the outlines of two carts filled with hay and a pen. Several mules stirred uneasily at the appearance of a stranger.

"Hello!" he shouted.

"Yeah, yeah, coming your worship." A voice followed by a small man wearing a cotton blouse and coarse pantaloons emerged from the recesses of the shop.

"You hiring or just selling those mules?" Vasiliev drawled.

The man leaned up against the stall, holding one hand behind his back.

"Well, now, depends on what your wants might be."

"My wants depend on whether you can meet the order."

"And what is that?"

"I've heard you're what they call a discreet man, as well as a shrewd man of business."

"You may have heard right."

"I have some goods I'd like to send along."

"And where might that be?"

Vasiliev jingled the purse in his pocket.

"I pay well."

"Sounds as if you're looking for a discrete way to move them.

That's what you said, didn't you, 'discrete'? Not many around here use that fancy word."

"But you understood it right away."

The man nodded.

"Let's just say I'd need to have a guarantee that you can cross over without difficulty, if you get my meaning."

"Let's say you're asking to get your stuff across the border while the customs official is looking the other way."

"How much per day?"

The man leaned forward, peered into Vasiliev's face, and stretched out both hands. Before he could speak, Vasiliev saw that the right finger of his left hand was missing.

"Omar, isn't it?"

The man staggered back, reaching for a pitchfork on the wall, but Vasiliev was too quick. He pinned the man against the pen, twisting his arm behind him and covering his mouth.

"Not a sound, or your throat is open to the world."

The mules became more agitated.

"You denounced Grigoriev and then supplied the cart to remove him from the Tower. Was he still alive?"

Vasiliev relaxed his hold over the Omar's mouth but pressed the dull edge of his knife against his throat.

"Not me, it wasn't me, I didn't touch him," Omar bleated.

"Stanislav saw you running away."

"They forced me…threatened to kill my wife."

"Who is they? What did they do to Grigoriev?"

"They looked like Albanians, but covered their faces."

"Albanians? Really, that is too much. Where do you see Albanians in Mostar? What language did they speak?"

"Serbian but with an accent."

"So you set him up. What did they do to him?"

"I don't know. They seized him and I ran— that was the deal— they let me go."

"And the cart?"

"They told me to drop it off at the south entrance of the Tower. They promised to leave it in Cetinje."

"Did they tell you exactly where, an address?

"Yes, but I don't remember. I was too afraid. I never saw it again."

"And your hand! When did you cut off the finger with the dragon ring?"

"After...." His voice broke.

"Where is the ring?"

"I threw it in the river."

"No you didn't. You still have it, in case your comrades come for you inquiring what happened. And then you will give them some cock and bull story to cover yourself. I want the ring. It's the price of your life."

Vasiliev was guessing again and taking a big risk. If he was wrong...but he knew he could not kill the man in cold blood. He turned the blade and made Omar feel the cutting edge. A trickle of blood trickled down the man's neck.

"Please, please! Without it I am a dead man."

"No! You will be if you don't give it up now. You can tell whoever comes calling that they, these so-called Albanians, cut off your finger to steal the ring. It's a better story than the one you told me."

Omar sagged, whispering: "In the back, in a box under the ledge below the window."

Vasiliev frog-marched him to the rear of the shop. The box was locked. Vasiliev used his knife to pry it open, all the while holding Omar's arm in a tight grip. The ring was there but not the finger, for which Vasiliev gave thanks. Then he hit Omar on the back of his neck with a blow he had learned from Serov in the old days. The man would be unconscious for an hour or so. But he would not suffer any permanent damage.

Vasiliev pocketed the ring and strolled nonchalantly out of the shop.

"Your boss is a hard bargainer. I may be back and I may not." He left them staring at his back.

When he returned to the hotel, Serov was still out hunting for carts. The manager was dealing with a recent arrival who looked like an Austrian businessman, He gestured to Vasiliev to wait for him. He wore an apologetic look.

"While you were out a messenger arrived, asking to see the young lady."

"And you discouraged him as I told you."

"Well, he was only a boy, you know, quite clean and tidy he was."

"For God's sake man…"

Vasiliev rushed up to her room. She was not there. A wave of panic surged over him. Then he heard a noise in his adjoining room. He tore open the door to find her packing his things.

"Did you find the cart…? Oh! You look terrible. What happened?"

The questions tumbled out of his mouth in no good order

"Exactly my question to you! The boy…and the packing?" He sank into the nearest chair.

"Vasili, nothing happened. The boy had a message for us. He said that 'the men you are looking for have gone to Sarajevo.' He showed me a dragon ring. And so I am packing for you and Serov."

Vasiliev ran his hands through his hair.

"It's just that I…"

She came to him and placed her hands on his shoulders. He looked up, his crooked smile had never seemed more attractive to her. Footsteps resounded in the corridor and Serov burst into the room. He stopped dead in his tracks. Tamara slowly dropped her arms. The three of them stood as if rooted to the spot.

"And what luck did you have with the cart, Sergeant?" Her voice was steady, if a bit husky.

"Sergeant," Vasiliev said with a sheepish look on his face, "this time I think I've had better luck." The possible double meaning of his words suddenly came over him. Serov had rarely seen him blush since boyhood.

"This is generally the case," Serov was enjoying himself.

Vasiliev recovered at once and spun his tale. Tamara told hers. Serov reported his running around had been a waste of time, "exceptin'," he added, "for one small thing." Vasiliev recognized Serov's dissembling style, just like his classic opening gambit in a chess game, followed by an unexpected move.

Serov was satisfied that he had their full attention.

"This cartin' fella at the last place looks me up and down and then says: 'well, sir, if you was wonderin' about rentin' one of my carts for a long haul, then I'd give you piece of advice for free, as it were. Say you was intendin' to cross the border, that's one thing. I'd not favor that. And if you was intendin' to go to Sarajevo, say, then I'd warn you about that. The road's so bad they shake you to pieces along the way. Why an Englishman tried it several years ago and he arrived a wreck. Took him four weeks to get so he could walk straight. If there's business to be had goin' that way, better not to rent one of my carts. Better to find some good saddle horses.'"

"So, Vasili Vasilievich, how does this fit in, d'yuh think?"

Tamara had retreated to the window and scanned the street as if she were looking for watchers.

"I'd say that we have a little puzzle. Someone could be trying to put us on the wrong trail by sending us off to Sarajevo when the cart we're looking for went in the opposite direction into Montenegro. Or we're dealing with two separate trips, the first by cart across the border to Cetinje where it still might be and the second, later by the same people on horseback to Sarajevo where they might still be."

"And you're guessin'?"

"Not yet. Too little evidence. But one thing is clear, our disguises have not worked."

Tamara turned away from the window.

"Whatever may have happened in Montenegro or on the way there," she said, "the murderers would not have stayed in Cetinje. The town is too small. And they would have been foolish to come back here."

"The scene of the crime, at least of the abduction," said Vasiliev.

"Is that the term you use? All right, the scene of the crime then or one of them. But there is more to go on. I know that the major center of the Cadmus group was in Sarajevo. It was there that the greatest resistance to the Austrians took place. Borya was involved. It seems possible that they picked up his trail there and followed him to Mostar. And now the beasts have gone back to their lair. What do you think?"

Serov was on the point of saying 'that's as good a guess as I've heard recently.' But then he thought better of it.

Chapter Thirty

Cetinje

"Vulcan is missing!" Anna Ivanovna cried out frantically, as she burst into the secretary's office.

He cursed as his pen slipped, ruining a perfectly good copy of a petition to the Montenegrin foreign office.

"My God woman, that creature is always missing or in trouble. He'll turn up."

"This time is different. He disappeared two days ago. He hasn't returned for his food. I have never seen Venus in such a state. She has been prowling all over the consulate. If we don't find him, Alexander Semenich will have our heads."

"Please do not use that expression here. Now what do you propose? That we organize a search in the capital? Or perhaps put up a wall poster giving a full description of the escapee. We would become the laughing stock of Cetinje."

"Please, Igor Vladimirovich, I only ask you to send someone to look for him. Perhaps we can hire the cook's son and the gardener. They know the streets and can ask around if Vulcan has been seen without compromising us."

"I'm putting you in charge. This is the second time, let me say, that a creature has escaped your surveillance."

"A treacherous thing to say. But I will accept the responsibility."

Within in few hours, several local employers of the consulate were dispatched under secret instructions to find Vulcan at any cost. Inquiries were made. Small financial incentives were offered, and by the end of the day a few sightings had been reported. But when relating his findings to Anna Ivanovna, the gardener was embarrassed and hesitated to speak frankly.

"Putting together what we have learned, Anna Ivanovna, I can only conclude that Vulcan wandered into the wooded ravine to the south of the town. The locals say the place is enchanted, others say haunted. Years ago a young couple, a Muslim boy and a Christian girl, ran away together. They were pursued by parents on both sides, captured and murdered in the ravine. Since then, the few bold enough to enter in search of firewood have seen their ghosts, lamenting their fate. So no one goes there now."

"Oh, my God! That monstrous cat!"

"If he has disappeared there, we will have to go looking for him ourselves. No amount of money will persuade people to help us."

"And you? Do you believe in this nonsense?"

"Well, Anna Ivanovna, the stories are pretty scary."

Anna Ivanovna reported to the secretary who scoffed at the tales.

"You'll have to go yourself. Well, what do you want an armed guard? Take Mishka with you."

"But he is just a boy and not all there in the head."

"So much the better. Anyway, he knows how to fire a shotgun. That should be enough to disperse the ghosts," the secretary laughed evilly.

Anna Ivanovna waited until noon of a cloudless day when there would be fewer shadows. But once in the wood, with Mishka trailing behind her, the gloom enveloped them. For decades no trees had been cut or pruned. Anna Ivanovna carried a big stick with which she brushed aside the dense undergrowth. It seemed to her preternaturally quiet. There were no bird cries or other forest sounds. Mishka was the one who first saw the tracks and the broken branches on the other side of a screen of high bushes to their right.

Anna Ivanovna's heart was beating rapidly as she followed the trail. The ground sloped sharply so that she had to cling to the low hanging branches, many of which had been broken off. They came to the edge of a steep drop. As she peered ahead, a slight breeze stirred the leaves of a giant oak towering over the ravine and letting in a shaft of light. At the sight below, she uttered a scream and almost fainted. Mishka raised his shotgun and fired both barrels.

"No! no!" She screamed again this time at him. But it was too late. The double charge had caught Vulcan fully in the chest and blew him away. He had been perched on a wrecked cart, its wheels smashed to pieces. The decayed body of a headless man hanging out of the straw bedding shuddered slightly as some of the shot gun pellets struck his torso.

Mishka uttered an unearthly cry, dropped the shot gun and fled into the dense undergrowth.

Anna Ivanovna fell to her knees and cried out again, as the sharp stones cut into her flesh. She could not remember later how long she must have stretched out on the ground, sobbing.

The secretary gave way to a violent rage and then fell into a depression. A host of questions assailed him. How was he going to inform the consul general? Where was that great detective now? He muttered to himself. He sat immobile for some time and then shook himself, drew a telegram form from a desk drawer and wrote several words, tore the blank up and started again. He would not mention Vulcan. Just the discovery of the body, no other details. He would explain later, in person. Or perhaps not. If he could swear Anna Ivanovna and Mishka to silence, he would simply order the boy to bury the remains of the cat in an unmarked grave and leave his disappearance a mystery. As for the torso, he assumed it was Grigoriev. It too would have to be interred, but in a marked grave. If they wanted to dig it up, that was their business, but he could not leave it rotting somewhere. The cart he would leave. Suddenly, he realized that the decent thing to do would be a mistake. If he covered up the body, he could be accused of tampering with the evidence of a murder. God forgive him for failing to do his Christian duty. He rose from his chair as Venus entered the room. She cast an accusatory look at him, or so it seemed. Then she quietly padded to the sofa, jumped up and settled down on her favorite cushion as if resigned to her loss. Was he going crazy?

Ionin received the telegram as he was returning from his consultation with the Austrian consul in Ragusa. He was told that Vasiliev and "his party" had arrived in Mostar, but then left, presumably for Sarajevo. He swore under his breath. He could not be sure Vasiliev had received his order and now he was going to have to chase him all over Bosnia and Hercegovina.

The Austrians proved helpful in providing him with a carriage and escort along the Dalmatian coast to Klek. There he could make arrangements to cross the country to Mostar and, if necessary, continue to Sarajevo. But they warned him that the farther he penetrated into Hercegovina and Bosnia more dangerous his trip would become, even under their protection.

Unknown to Ionin, the dangers facing him were multiplying. Hadji Murad and his sons had ridden back across the Montenegrin border with Hercegovina in search of Tamara. They had learned from her captors that she and Grigoriev had last been seen in Mostar. They rode for three days over rough terrain, arriving in the outskirts of the town two days after she had been seen there with two Russian officers. Hadji Murad sent Kustan to the main mosque to learn more. Then, seeking information at the bazaar, he found out that a Russian official had just arrived, having made inquiries through the Austrians about the whereabouts of the officers and a Circassian girl. It was said that he was the consul from Cetinje, the very man who had kept Tamara prisoner.

"If we follow him, he should lead us to her," said Hadji Murad.

They spent the night in the open by the main road leading out of Mostar. Early in the morning, they spotted a coach with an escort of six Austrian cavalrymen. It would be a simple matter to follow, if they kept to the hills overlooking the track.

Chapter
Thirty-One

Sarajevo

Vasiliev had taken seriously Lang's advice to keep well off the beaten path from Mostar to Sarajevo as bandit attacks made it unsafe. This meant riding through heavily wooded hill country before crossing the border between Hercegovina and Bosnia. Lang also mentioned the existence of Christian *zadrugas* thoughout the region, well hidden on the high ground in order to avoid raids by Turkish irregulars. Toward dusk Vasiliev and Serov came upon one of these and halted about fifty meters away. Vasiliev shouted greetings in Serbian. An older man emerged from the large central dwelling flanked by two younger men holding rifles. Vasiliev dismounted and slowly walked towards them.

"We seek shelter for the night, good Christians." Vasiliev held out his hands in supplication.

"Have you come to liberate us?" asked the old man. It seemed it was the same everywhere.

"We seek information about your life in the name of our August Master, Tsar Alexander Nikolaevich." Vasiliev hated himself for this kind of pronouncement, but it was not altogether untrue.

"Enter and be welcome, brothers." The old man's voice trembled with emotion.

The central building was surrounded by sheds and barns. They could hear the bleating of sheep and goats. One of the young men handed over his rifle to his brother and led their horses into a stable.

"They will be fed and watered," the old man said.

He gestured grandly and led them into a chamber where huge

loaves of bread were baking in a large hearth surmounted by a stone chimney that reached the high-pitched roof of wooden timbers, blackened from the smoke of years. Seated on stools along the walls were a dozen women spinning wool. They wore embroidered jackets over sleeveless waistcoats and long tight shifts. Tamar later remarked on their colorful socks which she had never seen before. An equal number of men were engaged in working leather.

When they were seated at the communal table with about thirty members of the *zadruga*, the old man explained that they had been a self-sufficient community for hundreds of years. The times of war and revolution were over, he hoped. In the old days, the women slept in the windowless inner room and the men lay out in the entrance hall with their wepons. This was no longer necessary. Vigilance, yes, but they no longer lived in a state of constant alert.

Tamara was taken in hand by the younger women, who bathed and fussed over her, taking great delight in brushing her long blonde hair. After a sumptuous meal of rice soup with milk, a well-broiled trout and a roasted chicken and the famous *kaimak*, or clotted cream for desert, Vasiliev and Serov joined the younger men in the courtyard to smoke. Vasiliev handed out his last cigars to the men who joked about the contributions of Turkish tobacco and coffee to the progress of civilization. When the laughter and bantering subsided and the men left them, Vasiliev held Serov back for a few minutes.

"How am I going to make sense of all this in my report to General Totleben, even leaving aside the politics? I still know too little about the lives of these people. They are all so different, entwined with one another in a state of armed peace or open conflict. Is it possible that an external power, like Austria-Hungary, can accomplish what the Ottoman Empire obviously failed to do? Can they pacify the warring factions and convince them to give up their weapons and their ideas of blood feuds?"

Serov knew better than to interrupt, let alone offer his own opinion. He could only think of the stories of the old men in his village in the Moscow province about the time of enserfment; the great rebellions of the remote past, of the exploits of Stepan Razin and his Cossacks enshrined in song and the lesser outbreaks against the worst of the landowners; the barn burning and illegal timbering;

The Road over the Bosnian Hills

the occasional murder and savage reprisals by government troops. Would that all also come to an end under the benevolent rule of the tsar-liberator, Alexander Nikolaevich? Now there were other stories, of the attempts to assassinate him by revolutionaries, no longer composed just of peasants but also young, educated people. He had seen some of them in the mad summer of '73 when they went to the people and were met, he heard, with indifference, hostility or sympathy, all depending on the district. He recalled how he had saved Vasiliev's young noble friends, Irina and her brother, who was later to die at Plevna, from a crowd of enraged peasants. But there was good reason not to speak of all this, and Serov remained silent.

In the morning, they resumed their trek over the hills. Occasionally, they passed a caravan. At other times they were forced to dismount and lead their horses down precipitous slopes into deep valleys surrounded by high mountain peaks. Having read Evans's account of his trip in the opposite direction from Sarajevo to Mostar, Vasiliev had ensured that they had an ample supply of fresh water in gourds that they suspended around their necks. They would not suffer from thirst the way he did in crossing the picturesque but waterless terrain. Their first view of Sarajevo contrasted sharply with Evans's rapturous description. A great fire had devastated the 'Damascus of the North.' The best part of the town was a charred ruin. The once great emporium of a hundred thousand inhabitants, with its great bazaars roofed with colorful tiles, where fine jewelry beautiful leather goods and the superb workmanship of the knives, sabers and cutlery had been displayed in hundreds of shops, had been reduced to a shadow of itself. They entered the town across the one of the several stone bridges that spanned the many rivulets that flowed through the valley. Passing through the gates in the massive walls, Vasiliev remembered they had been built by a Hungarian general in 1270 when Bosnia was under the protection of the King of Hungary. The great quadrilateral fortress surmounted by twelve stone towers stood unscathed. Looming above the half-destroyed city were dozens of minarets. But what struck them immediately were the dilapidated houses and dirty condition of the crowded streets infested by packs of dogs. Most surprising of all was the appearance of the women who carelessly let slip their veils and insinuated by the movement of their bodies a provocative invitation. None of them had ever before seen the like of this wanton display in a Muslim community.

Their entry into the city went unremarked by the guardians of the peace. Vasiliev and Serov were dressed in civilian clothes and Tamara was modestly garbed in a long dress, her hair swept up and concealed by a fez and semi-transparent veil that also covered the lower part of her face. They made for the British consulate where the consul, Edward B. Freeman, alerted by his friend Evans, was expecting them. Vasiliev knew he was taking a great risk in avoiding the Russian consulate and relying on the English. But he was determined not to allow Ionin and whatever powers lay behind him in St. Petersburg to abort his mission.

The British consulate, located on the rivulet, Melaka, resembled what Vasiliev remembered as a typical English country home with its expansive gardens filled with English flowers, roses and petunias. The previous consul, Holmes, had imported fruit trees from Malta. At dinner they were served the most delicious peaches they had ever tasted, while Freeman entertained them with stories about the history of fires in the city.

"I have high hopes for a revival of the grandeur of the town now that the Austrians appear to have taken hold," said Freeman. "They were intelligent enough to appoint a Muslim mayor. But it will take time. My own feeling is that they could display a bit more energy in patrolling the roads. The countryside is still infested with robber bands, you know, they call them *haiduks*. The trouble is that the peasants still regard them as heroes and patriots. Just last week they shot up an Austrian military post in a nearby town. If I had been in Evans' place, I would have strongly discouraged you from coming. He is quite a daredevil, but he wasn't traveling with a lady." He smiled at Tamara who, fortunately, did not understand English, and Vasiliev did not translate his reference to bandits.

"You are right in wondering what possessed us to venture into such dangerous waters. We have undertaken what may be a quixotic enterprise." Vasiliev cringed inside as he spun his fabrication." We have promised a close friend to help Miss Murad find a dear relative who has been missing since the outbreak of the rebellion, but who was last reported in Sarajevo. So we will do our best. But we do not wish to impose upon you and can find rooms in a local hotel."

"No imposition. I live alone. Holmes had a large family to fill up the place. Besides the local *khans*, which pass for hotels, are filthy places. No! There is ample room here. But I must warn you that I have an obligation as consul to report your presence to the chief of police. You will have to present your passports. But that should be no problem."

Chapter
Thirty-Two

Sarajevo

The weekly Post to Sarajevo had been delayed by the crack in the rear axle of the coach. The driver explained to his sole passenger, the Russian consul Ionin, that the problem had arisen from the unusually heavy load he was obliged to transport, a chest of *kreutzers* in coin which was intended for the local garrison. This too, he added, explained the unusual escort of six dragoons. What he did not reveal could not have reassured the consul. Ionin had no reason to take notice of the glove worn on the driver's left hand. Even if he had seen the dragon ring it concealed, he would not have understood its significance.

For some time, the carriage and its escort had under close observation by other men wearing similar rings. About ten kilometers from the city, a band of thirty *haiduks* under the command of Stojan Kovačević, a former leader of the insurgents in Hercegovina, ambushed the Post. They rode out of concealment behind a small hillock and rapidly shot down the escort, losing only one of their own. They saluted the driver and began to unload the chest of coin when Ionin, having crouched inside the coach as bullets whipped the roof over his head, cautiously peered out, catching the eye of Kovačević.

"Great God! Alexander Semenich!" the bandit leader exclaimed. "A bit late for you to show up. And not another *Rus'* in sight. Only dead Austrians. What kind of assistance is this?"

Ionin pushed open the door riddled with bullet holes and stepped out. His face was ashen. He stood shaking in the bright sunlight, squinting at the grotesque face of the man in the saddle. There was something familiar about him. But one eye was dead white, and a terrible scar twisted his mouth into a grimace. Long, dirty hair fell to his shoulders.

"Ho! He doesn't remember!" Laughing hoarsely, Kovačević turned to one of his confederates.

"Let me remind you then of a day six years ago when you came into Hercegovina and called our chiefs together, promising rifles and ammunition for the 'great Slavic cause,' as you called it. Quite the revolutionary then, you were. And what has happened since? We Serbs went to war twice against the Turk, remember? The second time, though, you disdained our services. And then you cut some deal with the Austrian dogs. So now we have to fight again. This time without your rifles and ammunition."

Ionin realized there was no way he could explain the twists and turns of European politics that required Russia to reach a compromise with Austria-Hungary in order to salvage something from their great military victory.

"We won Serbian independence for you at the Congress of Berlin," he managed to gasp.

"Oh ho! Berlin! My, my. What a long way from Sarajevo is Berlin. So our Serb brothers are tossed a bone and the choice cuts of meat in Bosnia and Hercegovina go to the Austrians who have never fought with or for us. Clever chaps, aren't they?" Kovačević was now addressing his men, gathered around him.

"All right. This is no place to resolve these weighty questions. Tell us instead what you are doing here."

Ionin had had time to prepare his explanations.

"You think we have betrayed you. But no. I am here in pursuit of your enemies. I am responsible for hunting down the murderer of Grigoriev."

"What! Borya dead, murdered?"

"You did not know?"

"We heard only that he was in hiding, that he had gone to Montenegro to rally Prince Nikola to the cause." Behind him a chorus of murmurs rose to a frenzied pitch. The cry of 'revenge' was shouted by more than a few voices. Kovačević raised his hand and a sullen silence fell over the band.

"Yes, revenge. Who are those responsible?"

"This is what I am here to discover." Ionin found it all too easy to lie surrounded by more than a score of cutthroats, whatever patriots there may have been among them.

"Ah, Alexander Semenich, if we could only believe you. So many lies, so much deception. But we seem to have no choice. It would do no good to kill you now. We will send you on your way. But you are mistaken if you think the Austrians will help you in the name of some European idea of justice. It is more likely that they will do everything to conceal their part in the crime. Who else benefits?" Kovačević shook his head. He turned his horse away from Ionin and shouted back.

"You can tell your Austrian friends that we are not bandits, but fighters for the freedom of Bosnia." He spat on the body of one of the dead dragoons: "Of course, they will not believe this. Even if they do, they will not allow you to spread this word. Someday, perhaps, we will extract an even more terrible revenge than that we seek for the death of Grigoriev, our comrade and a true patriot."

The band had lifted their dead companion onto his horse, stripped the dead dragoons of their arms, and tied their horses to their own. At a signal from Kovačević, they rode off silently into the hills.

Ionin's nerves gave way, and he began to tremble uncontrollably. Then he retched at the side of the road while the driver watched without expression before helping Ionin back into the coach.

"I think it best, Consul Ionin," said the driver, "to leave to me an account of the attack and say nothing of what then transpired. Let me remind you that we have many sympathizers in Sarajevo and whatever you say to the Austrians will be soon known to us. It would be wise then, to remain silent. We will have to leave the bodies of the dragoons here. They will bear witness to what I say happened." It took him only a few minutes to repair the 'cracked axle.'

Ionin nodded and fell back exhausted against the cushions as the coach drove off.

From the top of another hill overlooking the road to the south, three men had been sitting on their horses watching the spectacle below them.

"Should we intervene?" asked one of the young men.

"Too many," growled Hadji Murad." Let's hope they are only after the money. We can only wait."

When the coach started up again, Hadji Murad spoke again.

"Now we have to be even more careful. The army will send out a party to scour the area. They will find nothing, of course, except six dead dragoons. But we will have to make a wide circle in order to avoid them. This means losing sight of the Russian. Perhaps we can ride fast enough to reach the gates to the town before he does. If we lose his trail now, it will be very hard to find him again. We have very few of our own in Sarajevo. It is doubtful that any of them even know where the Russian consulate is. But, with the help of God who alone is great, we will prevail."

Chapter
Thirty-Three

Sarajevo

"Where are we most likely to find survivors of Cadmus?" Vasiliev asked Tamara. "We have to act quickly before Freeman learns that we are here under false pretenses."

"The town has changed so much since the war and the fire. But perhaps our friends still gather on Thursday evenings in a Turkish bath just beyond the northern wall of the fortress where in former times the Pasha provided wanderers with food and lodging at the Sultan's expense. Also there was a small restaurant on one of the narrow streets leading to the synagogue. I might be able to find it again. But I cannot go alone. You or Serov must accompany me."

Vasiliev pondered for a few moments, agonizing over the choice he knew he had to make. It would be too conspicuous for all three of them together to search the town for members of the Cadmus. But he hesitated to send Serov out by himself. Without knowing the language he would arouse suspicion if he displayed a dragon ring. He could not expose Tamara to grave danger again if he were to send her out by herself. The only practical solution was once again for them to separate. Serov would accompany and protect Tamara, who had her ring and spoke Bosnian. He would keep the second ring he had taken from Omar and make do with his good Serbian. He did not like his plan, but there was no good alternative.

"Tomorrow is Thursday. I will go to the north wall of the fortress. Sergeant, you will go with Tamara to survey the area around the synagogue. Tamara, you can introduce Serov as a Russian friend of Borya's. Sergeant, you know my methods. Apply them."

The next morning Vasiliev showed up at the office of the director of police, a certain Herr Oliva, carrying with him a note from Freeman and his own and Serov's passports. As Freeman explained, one of the first acts of the Austrians was to appoint members of their diplomatic service to administrative posts in Bosnia. Oliva was, as Freeman had described him, a tall, dark-haired, youthful looking Croat with an unpleasant manner.

He glanced at Freeman's note and then asked in clipped, strongly accented French: "What is your purpose in coming to Sarajevo?"

"A personal matter of honor. We were asked by an old friend to help a resident of your town, a Miss Tamara Murad, locate a relative missing since the war."

"And why was this request not made to my office as the superintendent of all police matters in the Condominium?"

"It is not clear that this is a police matter. No crime has been reported. I felt it would be an imposition to bother the authorities here. Your consul in Thessalonika, Baron Haymerle, confided in me that your administration was deeply and creatively engaged in restoring order to Bosnia. I was presumptuous enough to conclude that your time was too valuable to be spent on such an insignificant matter."

Oliva's eyebrows shot up but he did not comment.

"And how long do you propose to stay?"

"With Mr. Freeman's kindness, only a few days. I think we will find out what we want in that time. Miss Murad is an Orthodox Christian convert. As far as I understand, the Orthodox population in Sarajevo is quite small, no more than five or six thousand. I suspect that the Orthodox priest of the *Nova crkva* should be able to point us in the right direction."

"You are well informed, Major Vasiliev."

Oliva rang the silver bell and an orderly immediately appeared.

"To be stamped with a seven-day pass." Then turning to Vasiliev, "That should be ample time, *n'est-ce pas?*"

Thank you, *monsieur le directeur,*" Vasiliev bowed himself out.

"Now, he thought to himself, just so long as the busy Herr Oliva does not bother to communicate this 'insignificant' request to the Russian consul, we have time to ferret out the truth or what passes for that illusory ideal in the narrow streets of Sarajevo.

****

As they approached the synagogue, Tamara drew out her silver necklace and detached the ring, giving it to Serov.

"It would be better if you wore it. Otherwise it would arouse suspicion."

As they walked, Tamara took his arm and said, "We should give the appearance of being preoccupied with one another, so tell me more details of your youth with Vasiliev." Serov enjoyed relating stories of these years which seemed to belong to a different age. His recited them in the folksy manner he had perfected, savoring the ring of her laughter. He found himself struggling with feelings that he knew he could never express. He had observed how even the worldly Vasiliev was having similar difficulties with his self-control.

They circled the synagogue twice without eliciting any response.

"The inn must have been destroyed in the insurrection. We had better go to the *Nova Crkva*."

"I hope it is now a quiet quarter," Tamara explained. "Men of my faith, especially the Sufi sect, bitterly opposed the construction of the church. It was greater and richer than the mosques it overlooked. There it is! You see the pictures of the saints that cover the outer wall. They were a present from your Tsar. They say that when it was consecrated, a great protest was planned. But the Governor of Bosnia, Dervish Pasha, surrounded the church with soldiers and promised terrible punishments if the riots broke out. So you see, not all Muslims are bad."

As they stood admiring the gilt frames of the portraits, a beggar approached them extending his hand with a dragon ring turned to the inside of the fourth finger.

Serov dropped a few coins in his palm. The beggar did not lift his eyes from the ground but muttered a few words and then limped off.

"He says to follow him," said Tamara.

They made two quick right turns into a lane with a wooden terrace painted blue and green.

"We don't want to give the impression of being in a hurry so as to avoid the slightest suspicion that a message has been passed." Her smile dazzled him, even as her manner redoubled his respect for her self-possession. Again he felt completely under her sway.

Keeping the beggar in sight, Serov looked back to make sure they were not being followed. He took the same precaution after a second turn. The beggar vanished under the eaves of the wooden terrace. Just as suddenly, they were accosted by a diminutive old woman wearing a shawl over the lower half of her face and who held up a piece of embroidered lace so that the dragon ring on her left hand came into their view at eye level. Tamara smiled, fingering her own ring and asked for the price. Serov kept his gaze fixed on the turn in the corner. The woman muttered something. Tamara asked whether she had other samples.

The woman answered, "Inside."

The interior was very dark and smelled pleasantly of wood resin. The woman took Tamara by the hand and guided her down a corridor. Tamara reached back seized Serov by the wrist, pulling him along. Her touch sent a tremor though him.

They came into what appeared to be a large room, but the flickering flames in the hearth did little to illuminate its dimensions.

Two figures sat cross legged in the shadows on either side of the small fire. The woman let go of Tamara's hand and vanished.

"Where did you get the dragon and what do you want?" A hoarse voice speaking Serbian came out of the gloom.

"I travelled your land for years with Boris Grigoriev. I shared his hardship and his hope. He was brutally murdered and I seek revenge. Can you help me?"

"And the other one with you?"

"He is a friend, a former officer in the Russian army. I trust him as I would my brother. He speaks our language badly, but he understands it well enough. He knows better than I do how to gain information that will help me."

The man with the hoarse voice shifted to Bosnian in addressing his compatriot, but she interrupted him in the same language. "I will understand everything you say."

Serov was astounded, but she was right, he quickly realized. Now they would have to trust her.

"All right. Tell us about Grigoriev, his travels and his hopes and then if you speak the truth, we will tell you... we will answer your questions."

Chapter
Thirty-Four

Sarajevo

Tamara spun her tale, throwing her head back as if imagining once more the exploits of her beloved Borya and weaving them into a heroic epic. Serov understood little of what she said but was mesmerized by the rhythm of her voice as it rose and fell, ending in a heart-rending diminuendo. The flames in the hearth seem to imitate her recital, blazing up and dying down, almost flickering out at the end.

For a moment or two there was silence. The man with the hoarse voice coughed quietly, or was it a sigh, and leaned over to toss a few twigs onto the embers. The fire revived and Serov felt as though he had been pulled back from immersion in a magical realm.

"So what are your questions?" the voice steady now.

She nodded to Serov. He knew what Vasiliev wanted to know and asked where Grigoriev had last been seen, with whom and whether he mentioned any specific threats to his life.

"We last saw him in Travnik. He was to meet with a group of *bunjevici*. You know who they were?"

"Please tell us," Serov said, with Tamara translating throughout the exchange.

"They were Catholic Serbs. The Hungarians claim they were unified and loyal in their struggle for independence in 1848. But Grigoriev knew that some of them had fought against Kossuth and the patriots. Many who resisted learning Magyar after the Ausgleich in 1867 drifted down into Bosnia. Grigoriev believed they could be won over to the cause. He warned though that another group of

Hungarians were disaffected by the compromise with Vienna that created the Dual Monarchy, He called them renegades.Tthey owed allegiance to no one but were available for hire."

"Do you understand, my friend?" Tamara asked Serov.

"Is it possible that the Hungarian renegades could have infiltrated these *bunjevici*?" asked Serov. Tamara did not translate immediately.

"Wait a minute," her voice changed abruptly, becoming harsh.

"What is wrong?" asked Serov.

"*Valahal!*" she exclaimed.

"Who is she cursing?" growled the man who had been silent up to this time.

"It is nothing," she quickly regained her poise. "An old memory." Repressing the image of the Latin Cross in her place of detention, she recalled the 'strange' language of her capters. When she regained control of her voice, she translated Serov's question.

"Anything is possible in these times," the hoarse voice answered. "The answer lies in Travnik."

"Did Grigoriev mention any other enemies?" Serov continued to probe.

"Rumors abounded. Borya once told us that he had been warned in the bazaar by one of us wearing the ring, though, cautious as always he did not mention his name, that a man speaking Serbian with Russian accent had been inquiring about him."

"Did nothing come of this?"

"Who knows? You asked for possible enemies. An unknown man, probably Russian, is asking questions. For what reason? To join us? Or to harm us?"

The silent man uttered a few words.

"What did he say?" asked Serov.

"He mentioned the Austrians."

"Well, of course," the hoarse voice spoke with a trace of impatience.

"There is no need to remind you that the Austrian army of occupation took Borya to be an insurgent and put a price on his head."

"Did anyone collect the bounty?" asked Serov.

"If so, we would have told you," the hoarse voice spat out.

Serov realized his error too late. He had sounded like a fool. This conversation was over.

Tamara thanked the men profusely. The old woman materialized out of the gloom and guided them back to the street.

"Please Sergeant, give her some *kreutzer* for the lace. It is the least we can do."

Chapter
Thirty-Five

Sarajevo

As they passed the *Nova Cjirka* again, a commotion broke out near the entrance to the cathedral. A voice behind them cried out. "What is happening?" They turned to see an elderly blind man who was holding on to a stout-looking oaken cudgel with two shaking hands.

Tamara spoke softly to reassure him. "Nothing, just a few young hot heads." She touched him lightly on the shoulder. They moved away from him.

"Let's get out of here," whispered Serov. But it was too late. Three of the men detached themselves from the group who had been shouting insults at an Orthodox procession leaving the church. They rushed toward them, knocking aside the blind man who dropped his cudgel as he fell to the ground. Serov stepped forward and met the first man head on. He ducked, blocked the wild blow aimed at his head, kicked the man in the groin and hit him so hard in the face that he was thrown back against the other two. Tamara seized the cudgel and with practiced skill brought it down on the second man's skull so that he too collapsed in a heap. Serov was so astonished he almost forgot to keep an eye on the third man who had drawn a knife. Tamara brought the cudgel down on his forearm. The man screamed in pain and dropped the knife as Serov struck him a savage blow that spun him around before he fell to the ground. Tamara seized hold of the blind man's arms and raised him up.

"You're safe now," she said as they took hold of him and half dragged, half carried him down a side street. No one followed

A Coffee House in Sarajevo

them. A door opened and a woman, completely veiled so that only her eyes shone, gestured to them from the dark interior. "Bring him in here and go!" she cried out.

Serov reached out to take Tamara's hand but she was already racing ahead, and he had to make an effort to catch up.

They made several sharp turns in the empty narrow streets and finally slumped against a wall, gasping for breath.

"I'm lost now," Tamara said catching her breath.

Serov stepped out into the street and searched the sky.

"The minarets can guide us from now on. I took a bearin' on them before we got in this mess." He shook his head "That was quite a performance, I mean with the stick and all."

Tamara laughed, holding on to her side.

"I told you, Sergeant, that my brothers brought me up like a boy. They violated every rule of the Sharia, you know, our law. They taught me to use a scimitar, so how different is a big stick? And the running, well that too. You see they need me for their games. They were disappointed that I was not a boy. So they tried to make me into one. I think too that they wanted to discourage suitors. What good Muslim would want to marry a wild girl like me?"

Serov had several answers to that question, but delivered none of them.

Toward dusk on Thursday, Vasiliev made his way to the fortress and entered one of the many Turkish coffee houses in sight of the walls. He sat down on one of the wooden benches surrounding the room which was furnished with Turkish rugs and cushions. He took out of his pocket a small volume of poetry that he had borrowed from Freeman, ordered a coffee and a *cibouk* and devoted himself to reading Pushkin. The thick coffee was served boiling hot, with a small bowl of sugar on the side. Milk, he had learned, was never provided. It was dubbed by a medieval Arab physician as "an unheard of sacrilege." He raised his eyes from time to time as if savoring both the beverage and the verse. He noticed that in one corner there was a finer and higher cushion. No one was seated there until an obviously wealthy *aga*, who was greeted as a regular, eased his bulk down onto it as if it were a throne. There was a low babble of voices in several languages, only fragments of which reached Vasiliev. What surprised him most was to see a billiard table in the corner, one of the artifacts of "European civilization," he assumed, that had been introduced by the Austrian occupation. He ordered a second and third cup, but realized that without food he could not continue drinking at such a rate. No dragon ring had popped into sight. He paid and left, determined to find an inn where he could get something to eat. He had taken no more than a few steps, when a small boy ran up to him, waving something in his hand.

"Sir, sir," he exclaimed in broken English, "you forget." He pressed a rolled-up newspaper into Vasiliev's hand, and then he vanished in the crowd.

Vasiliev kept on walking, understanding that contact had been made. He continued walking close to the shadows of the fortress walls until a man with an extravagant moustache and red turban accosted him.

"You are looking for someone?" he asked in Serbian.

"Yes, a comrade," said Vasiliev and held up his hand.

"You come alone?"

"Yes."

"Then go to the coffee house on the corner of the next lane and wait."

The place was smaller darker and without a billiard table. Vasiliev sat down on the bench. Only a few men were sitting cross legged and smoking *chibouks*. Slowly one by one they got up and left until the place was empty. A short fat man sat down next to him. He was dressed in a strange costume which Vasiliev could not identify.

"Now friend, what is your business?"

Vasiliev decided it would be best to be frank and open. He took out his passport and placed it on the bench beside him.

"My business, as you put it, is to discover the murderer of your comrade in the Cadmus organization, Boris Andreevich Grigoriev. I'm an Inspector in the Moscow City Police on leave as a reserve major in the Russian Army. I am also authorized by the highest military authorities to report on the extent of resistance to the Austrian army of occupation in Bosnia and Hercegovina. I obtained this ring from a traitor to your cause, a certain Omar Ali in Mostar."

"We have heard about Omar. He has been liquidated."

"Frankly, I wear the ring to make contact with you, not to join your organization. I apologize for the apparent deception. But I need your help and perhaps you would benefit from mine."

The fat man had picked up the passport and scrutinized it.

"This seems genuine enough. And your story is plausible. But you must understand that we have paid heavily in the past for trusting our enemies in disguise."

"What I ask from you is not trust but information that will not compromise your organization. If my questions offend you and the answers exposes some aspect of your work you wish to conceal, then I do not expect a reply."

A waiter appeared out of the back carrying a tray with a pot of coffee and two cups. There was no sugar.

Vasiliev steeled himself for another dose.

"Fair enough," said the fat man. "Ask your questions."

"Did Grigoriev suspect anyone in particular of being an enemy? I know many opposed his work. But I am looking for one man, the killer, or perhaps several killers."

"Let me say one thing before I answer. If we knew who had committed this terrible crime, we would have punished him in our own way. Even if we had a strong suspect, we would have extracted the truth from him by our own means. But there was no one who Borya mentioned. One clue he left us was a rumor. Information had reached him that he had become a threat to powerful interests in his own country. So he became wary of any stranger from Russia. After his death we searched but found no such man. But our reach is limited. Beyond the border into Montenegro our actions are limited. Another curious hint of deception. The Austrians had put a price on Borya's head. No one ever showed up to claim the bounty. But we discovered quite by chance that the money may have been paid out secretly. Our source was not reliable. He said that the bounty hunter may have been a Hungarian renegade. But this is unlikely. They are not known for courage or intelligence."

"What about personal enemies, rivals for leadership?"

"For us there are no leaders. Exceptional men like Borya, yes. But no one gives orders."

"As a detective, I must ask another question that you may find irrelevant at best, offensive at worst."

"Go ahead, I have strong nerves," said the fat man, swallowing his cup of coffee in a single gulp.

"A rival for sexual favors?"

"Ah, Tamara! Not a chance. She gave no one else the slightest encouragement. No one I saw even came near her. Strictly forbidden fruit.

"I fear we have not helped you at all. I can only suggest that you go to Travnik where Borya was to meet some of the *bujnevici* before he went to Mostar."

Vasiliev told him about the death of Stanislav.

"You must have questioned Omar then, before you took the ring."

"Yes. He said only that two men, looking like Albanians and speaking Serbian with an accent, hired his cart."

"That kind of a description is worthless."

"Possibly. But I share it with you in the name of our pledge."

"Yes, thank you. But the men who hired the cart might not have been the killers."

"Also possible."

The fat man poured himself another cup but Vasiliev declined.

"Yours is a noble but difficult task. We might be able to trace the movements of the cart up to the Montenegrin border. Perhaps Borya was still alive when it was driven across. It would have been smart to avoid killing him in an area under Austrian jurisdiction."

"My idea as well. But I have no proof."

The fat man stood up and adjusted the sash over his sagging belly.

"We will go our separate ways, now, Major Vasiliev. If we find anything of value for your investigation, we will be in touch. It will not be hard to find you in Bosnia and Hercegovina. Please give me the ring now. And, forgive me, but I will leave first and ask you to wait for a few minutes before you follow. Perhaps you will have another coffee?"

The fat man inclined his head and waddled out the door.

The next morning Vasiliev awoke to find a folded slip of paper under the door to his room. Crude bloc Latin letters spelled out: "You seek Selim 'the Lame' at the Gate of Delight."

"Sounds like the Arabian Nights," he said to Serov.

Chapter
Thirty-Six

On the road to Travnik

Ionin was badly shaken when the carriage drew up at Austrian Police Headquarters in Sarajevo. He let the drive tell the story of the attack, carefully avoiding any mention of his previous knowledge of Kovačević and his band. The Austrian Police chief gave orders to organize a force to hunt down the *haiduks*. Ionin was relieved to be escorted to the Russian consulate. But his relief was short-lived. It stunned him to learn that Vasiliev and the girl had been reported by an informant to have spent a day or two staying with the English consul. His first reaction was to curse the English for interfering, once again, in purely Russian affairs. His second reaction was to submit an official protest. But then he thought better of it. He did not wish to appear to have lost control of the situation. When he was then handed the telegram informing him of the discovery of the body in the forest, in his back yard as it were, he almost collapsed. How was he to explain this? He would have to rush back to Cetinje and leave Vasiliev and his girl to the mercy of the Austrians. He spent a painful night worrying about his future career.

The Austrian punitive force had split up into three detachments in an attempt to encircle the area where the ambush of the Post had taken place. But Kovačević had followed the unmarked trails in the hills, and evaded his pursuers. Instead, the Austrians picked up the trail of Hadji Murad and his sons. In the mistaken belief that they had been part of the raiding party, two of the detachments closed in on them. The Circassians' horses were in a lamentable state; they had not been properly fed and watered for several days and moved slowly over the sharp rises and steep declines. At the top of a hill where they stopped to rest, they could see their pursuers still at a distance but closing fast.

"We have to break through on one of their flanks before they join forces," said Hadji Murad. "Quick! Gather some of those large stones and scatter them on the trail. That will slow them down. We'll take cover in that grove of oaks. We'll strike at dusk, widely spaced. I'll take the center position. Remember, rapid fire, keep moving off to your right and left. We shall meet on the hill over there where you can see a ruined castle.

"We are closing in now. They're right ahead. We'll catch them before darkness," the Austrian officer bellowed just before his horse stumbled on one of the stones, almost pitching him out of the saddle. The others drew up sharply and then the firing began. The dragoons began to dismount but only after two of them toppled from their horses, shot through the head. The officer rallied the rest and ordered concentrated fire into the trees. But another bullet caught him in the chest. He cried out before falling face down into the dirt. Panic set in among the rest of his men.

The Sergeant called out: "Fall back. There may be many hidden in that grove." Another dragoon fell.

The two brothers had run out of ammunition, but they were able to catch two of the horses of the dead dragoons with carbines still in the saddle holsters. They called out to Hadji Murad. Receiving no answer, they galloped up to the castle as the sun sank below the horizon. They waited for what seemed like hours. Then they heard a shuffling noise outside the ruined walls. Kostan motioned to his brother to cover him as he went into the darkness. He saw the recumbent shape of a man, his extended arm gripping a scimitar.

"Papa," he cried out. "Quick Kustan, papa's been badly hurt."

They carried the old man into the castle and laid him on the saddle blanket stripped from the dead horse of a fallen dragoon. They moistened his lips will water from the dragoon's canteen.

"Listen, my sons. Listen and do not interrupt or oppose my wishes. I am going to die of this wound. You must carry on alone. Your only duty now is to find Tamara. Leave me a weapon. I will last until morning and will draw their fire until my own inner fire is extinguished. Start now, by the light of the moon. Go with the speed of God who alone is great."

Hayden Hassen started to speak but Kustan seized his wrist.

"Listen and obey," he said to his brother.

"Staunch the wound. Then lift me to a sitting position by an embrasure overlooking the trail." He reached out and touched the forehead of each brother.

They left him reluctantly, barely holding back their tears. They believed that they would suffer the pangs of deep remorse for the rest of their lives for having left him to die alone. Early in the morning, when they had already ridden several miles on their new mounts, they heard the distance sound of gunfire. Then silence.

On their way to Travnik, Vasiliev, Serov and Tamara broke the arduous ride over the mountainous terrain by resting overnight at Catholic monasteries that had survived the war. The monks greeted them cordially but with some astonishment. Before midday the next morning, they caught sight of telegraph wires signaling they had reached the road that led to Travnik. As they descended into the Valley of the Lasra River, the great Muslim cemetery that Evans had mentioned as a landmark came into view. Just as he had described it, a field of tombs covered a wide expanse stretching over terraces built into the hills so that bones of the Muslim dead would not be washed down from the hillside by heavy rains. Even so, a few large sarcophagi had been overturned by the mountain torrents. Some of the tombstones were crowned with turbans, dating from the days of the Janissaries. A few more imposing tombs contained the bones of notable Muslims, former governors of the Ottoman province when Travnik was their residence. Vasiliev saw Tamara avert her gaze from the cemetery a shiver running through her body.

At a bend in the road, they passed one of the familiar ancient stone cisterns and then suddenly Travnik came into view. Towering over the town on two sides were the Vlasic Mountain to the north and the Velenica Mountain to the south, providing a magnificent setting for the assemblage of mosques, minarets and chalet-like houses that sprawled in the valley. In the midst of the town, a craggy acropolis reared up, crowned by another ancient castle.

"It quite takes the breath away," exclaimed Tamara.

"Not surprising that it was the political capital of Bosnia for several centuries," said Vasiliev. "Picturesque it is. But just let's hope the hotel where Evans stayed has improved under the Austrians."

"You are soundin' like a spokesman for the Austrian mission, beggin' your pardon, Vasili Vasilich," Serov muttered.

"You see how he treats a superior officer?"

The Sergeant has a noble soul," Tamara said gaily.

"And he does not blush easily," said Vasiliev.

They exchanged glances and in that moment they savored a rare, fleeing moment of intimacy.

Chapter
Thirty-Seven

Travnik

Vasiliev began to wonder whether they had been following the wrong trail. The scene of the crime was Mostar, or was it? Grigoriev had been attacked there in the Tower, but did he survive? Had he been carried back to Montenegro? Who were these men who spoke Serbian with an accent? What kind of an accent? There were so many possibilities. It seemed to him dubious that they were Albanians. If they had been, then they would surely have killed Grigoriev on the spot or turned him over to the Austrian authorities, claiming the reward. The Austrians themselves would hardly have gone to such lengths to conceal the circumstances surrounding Grigoriev's death. Vasiliev was puzzled that no one had claimed the reward. And what was the explanation for the transportation of Grigoriev, dead or alive, across the frontier into Montenegro. All these peculiarities suggested to him that the motivation for the crime had been political, but that still did not answer the question of whose politics was being served. Vasiliev kept these thoughts to himself.

He kept coming back to the idea that he may have made a bad guess in having been drawn deeper into Bosnia. Or were they being led there? They were moving away from the scene of the murder, where it was finally committed, in Mostar or across the border in Montenegro. Something else was nagging him as well, something Serov had mentioned when he reported the conversation with the Cadmus man in Sarajevo. He glanced over to Serov who was concentrating on the road. Then it came to him.

Serov always gave a full account of his investigations, omitting no detail however insignificant it may have appeared to him. He knew that Vasiliev would see deeper, find clues where they were invisible to others like himself. So he took pains to memorize what people told him. It would be as if Vasiliev himself had been present at the conversation. Tamara had, at one point, uttered a violent curse. What had triggered this outburst, so uncharacteristic of her? He was determined to find out once they were settled in Travnik. Perhaps he was exercising too much caution in questioning her, waiting until the right moment in order to avoid any appearance of conducting an interrogation. He really knew so little about the way her mind worked.

Now, they were riding into Travnik in search of some of the people who had last seen Grigoriev alive. Catholic Serbs no less. Travnik seemed to be an odd place to find them. All his informants had agreed that it was a still a Muslim town. The vast cemetery, famous for its imposing tombs of notable Muslims, confirmed this. But what about the living? As Vasiliev so often had an occasion to observe, the past survived only in its monuments, like the tomb of Murad. Who now inhabited the grand palaces that formerly housed the Turkish governors? These thoughts brought him back to the nature of Grigoriev's mission and the idea that Turkish agents might well have been his assassins in hopes of averting another rebellion that would bring Russia back once again in the name of protecting their Orthodox Slavic brothers. This would explain, too, the attacks of the pirates at sea and the bandits on the train. Yet Selim Bey had been genuinely helpful. There seemed to be no consistency in the operations of the representatives of all the governments involved, and he remembered Selim Bey's warning:" trust no one."

He shook himself out of his reverie. For the moment more practical problems required his attention. He was concerned how the locals would regard Tamara who was only lightly veiled. The first women he caught sight of were virtually encased in a shroud like covering revealing only the eyes. But then a few younger women, who were only lightly veiled, appeared on their way to the market; perhaps because this was a Friday and traditionally, they had been told, unmarried women in some towns were allowed greater freedom of movement and dress on Fridays and Saturdays. Travnik

Travnik

The buildings they passed still displayed the signs of importance that Travnik had occupied under Ottoman rule. The palaces of bygone Viziers loomed over narrow streets next to imposing barracks formerly housing Turkish troops. The wooden houses were decorated with a colorful variety of effects. Next to them, from time to time, solid edifices of stone appeared with rosettes carved in the pandrils of the arches.

At the end of the main thoroughfare, a long straggling street, they found "the best hotel in Travnik," as Evans had described it with tongue in cheek. But since he had come through several years earlier, the place had undergone a modest renovation. To their delight, there was a complete absence of vermin. The walls were newly whitewashed and the meals proved to be an improvement over the pilaf Evans had been served. The manager, a jolly fellow with a twinkling eye, greeted them with almost boisterous cordiality. It was soon apparent to them that Europeans, including Russians, were treated with courtesy everywhere in the town. War and rebellion had by passed Travnik and hopes had revived for an increased influx of tourists.

Tamara expressed her surprise at the tattoos that some women displayed on their arms. The manager was happy to explain that the custom had a long history. It seemed that at the time of the Turkish conquest, Catholic priests introduced the practice as a way of protecting their flock from being converted to Islam. By displaying images on their skin they would be regarded by the imams as violating the precepts of the Koran and permanently excluded from being acceptable as converts to the true faith.

"And the practice continues?" Tamara inquired.

"Yes. Old women have been designated as the official tatooers," the manager gurgled. "If you are thinking about having it done yourself, I can recommend an excellent person, a relative of mine, who is highly regarded for her skill and the beauty of her designs."

To Vasiliev's surprise, Tamara smiled sweetly and asked where the woman could be found. The manager promised to provide her with instructions, as the woman lived just outside of the town.

"Don't look so surprised, Vasili. Old women are a great source of information, as you know, and it is better to have some legitimate reason to visit one of them in order to find out what we need to know. This woman will surely know how we can get in touch with the *bunjevici*. And to ask the manager might create problems. But we mustn't seem too eager. Find out whether women are permitted in the coffee houses here. We might as well act naturally."

Serov had to smile to himself. He would never have dared take charge the way she did. And Vasiliev seemed perfectly willing to accept her lead, at least for the moment.

The coffee house the manager recommended was bright and clean with colorful rugs and comfortable divans. The clientele were mainly upper class Turks but there were a few Europeans accompanied by their wives.

Tamara played her role to the hilt, praising the thick coffee, though she found it too strong, and waxing genuinely enthusiastic over the quality of the cool fresh water, a glass of which was always served with the coffee. She was told by the waiter that Travnik could boast of an abundance of fresh spring water, unlike many towns, which explained the profusion of flower gardens. "You must know," whispered the waiter that "the name of our town, Travnik, means 'plot of grass.'"

"So another mystery solved," muttered Serov who also found the coffee too strong. Tamara gave him a reproving glance. He wished he had kept his mouth shut.

As they strolled through the market acting like curious tourists, they passed a strange looking figure carrying a large blue stick. He stopped from time to time, sampling the produce brought in from the countryside, apparently to check on its quality.

"Not a bad way to make a livin'," remarked Serov. "P'haps we should have such a one in the Moscow Central Market."

"Why, Sergeant! I thought you were a Russian patriot. How could you think of importing a foreign custom?"

Serov chuckled. He was back in her good graces and would long remember her bantering familiarly with him.

True to his words, the manager supplied them with a hand-drawn map of the approach to the old woman's place in a poorer section of the town near the ruins of the old castle. "At some point, you will have to ask for the hut of Nadia, the tatooer. Everyone up there knows her."

This time Vasili insisted on accompanying Tamara.

Chapter
Thirty-Eight

Budapest

Baron Kállay returned from the dinner party and grand ball at Count Andrassy's in a high state of excitement. The Count had confided in him the terms of the new two power treaty he had negotiated with Prince Bismarck. Now the Monarchy would take precedence over Russia in Berlin. The Russians would be brought back into a triple alliance of the three great eastern empires. But for the Germans the Austro-Hungarian Monarchy would now come first. This enormously simplified his forthcoming appointment in Sarajevo. He could proceed without fear of a Russian revival of the Pan Slav excitement that had plunged Bosnia into revolution and war.

He promised his wife he would not stay up beyond dawn. She inclined her head in a charming gesture of acquiescence, keenly aware of his duty to the throne. He sat down at his antique desk and stared for a moment, as he always did before commencing to work at the portrait of the Emperor, Franz Joseph. Then he turned to the pile of official documents awaiting his attention, neatly arranged by Gabor. There was much to do in preparation for taking up his duties in Sarajevo. Lately, he had been reading the recent accounts by the English travelers. If only we had such enterprising lads like Mr. Arthur Evans, he mused. Of course there was Vambery, but his interests had taken him to Central Asia.

Kállay considered his main task was to devise a plan to keep the Serbs and Croats divided and the Muslims satisfied by guaranteeing an economic revival on their landed estates. Above all, he was determined to restrain his hot-headed countrymen from commiting blunders that alienated everyone on the ground. He had to smile inwardly reflecting on the words of the great Count Szeczeny, what was it, fifty years before? He had sworn to transform Hungary from "an Asiatic colony in the center of Europe" by civilizing its nobility. Now it was the turn of Hungary to carry out the same great task on the newly acquired lands. He opened again the file on the *bunjevici*. They had to be won over again. They had complained to local authorities in Travnik about the activities of renegade Hungarian nationalists who were involved in stirring up trouble among the Orthodox Serbs for which they were being blamed. Kállay felt a flash of anger. This sort of thing had been going on far too long. He had to put a stop to it. Who could he send as his personal representative? He did not yet have official authority. It had to be someone like himself who had a good command of Serbian and a firsthand knowledge of the province. No one came to mind by the time the faint purple tint of dawn touched his window.

It was only two days later, a chance encounter in the corridors of the Ballhausplatz on a trip to Vienna reminded him of his old friend, Baron Haymerle, now consul at Thessaloniki, who knew the region well and shared his views on the Hungarian mission in the Balkans. Surely he would be able to recommend a capable agent to intersect with the *bunjevici*. When Haymerle responded to his inquiry, he was surprised and delighted that the man was a fount of knowledge about the Hungarian renegades and their harmful influence. By cultivating his acquaintance with Selim Bey and other Turkish officials, he had pieced together a disturbing picture of their activities based on careful intelligence and some speculation. It was clear that the Russians had sent a well-known Moscow detective, attached as a major to staff of Nikolai Nikolaevich of the Danubian Army to hunt down the assassin of Boris Andreevich Grigoriev, a Pan Slav who had helped to organize the Bosnian uprising in 1875 and who continued to operate in the area, putting together some kind of secret organization. From the beginning this major's mission had been plagued by a series of "incidents" as Haymerle phrased it, to interrupt or wreck his mission. First, there had been the alleged pirate attack on a Greek vessel carrying him to Adrianpolis; then a bandit attack on a train which, according to Selim Bey, he had anticipated and avoided by a skillful deception.

Then, according to information from a Major Peter Barga, Vasiliev and his orderly were ambushed outside the Devich monastery on their way to Montenegro by way of Ipek. The band that attacked them was never officially identified, but the body of one of them recovered by the Hussars of Major Barga was a former officer in the Hungarian Army who as a young man had fought against the Russians during their suppression of Kossuth's revolt in 1849. A tangled web!

Kállay shook his head in disbelief, stood up, streched and went to the window and looked and looked out on the square where the guard was being changed. "Such order, discipline and serenity," he said half-aloud, projecting the scene on the entire empire. And to the south a handful of irreconcilables could threaten it all. The urgency of his mission came back to him in a rush. He returned to the file, slowly reading Haymerle's elegant hand. Another twist in the plot, like a bad Parisian stage play; "*cherchez la femme!*" Grigoriev's mistress, a reputedly beautiful Circassian girl, shows up with his decapitated head at the Russian consulate in Cetinje, demanding revenge. This information obtained from the Italian consul who had it from Baron Corti who was present at the spectacle. She is then abducted by persons unknown who are later slaughtered, also by persons unknown. The girl was apparently freed by the Russian major, but his role in the killing of her abductors was not confirmed. In any event, an inquiry by local officials in Kotor established that the decapitated bodies of three men found in the house where they detained the girl were of Hungarian origin.

The trail of Vasiliev, who seemed to be a moving target of the renegades, picked up in Ragusa where the police registered Vasiliev, a young woman and his orderly. An agent of the Austrian Lloyd Line sold them tickets to Mostar. A report by the commissioner of police in Mostar provided information obtained from the Russian major, Vasiliev, that the Pan Slav agent Grigoriev was last seen entering the tower of the old fortifications by the Mostar River on June 17, 1879, before disappearing. Vasiliev must have had learned something there that drew him deeper into Bosnia, first to Sarajevo where a Croat in Austrian service, a certain Oliva, had given him a seven-day pass. After his departure from the city, his whereabouts were unknown.

Kállay was puzzled by several unanswered questions. He asked himself: 'Why this obsession of the Russians with the death of one man who represented a policy they now had abandoned of supporting the Serbs against us? Why were Hungarian irreconcilables so determined to prevent him from finding out the identity or identities of the assassin?

Perhaps some light might be shed on these questions, he mused, by finding out what the Russians were up to in the region. Were they playing a double game by pretending to give up on the Serbs and let Vienna dominate the western Balkans while they supported clandestine groups in expectation of future upheavals?

He drafted a message to be sent to all the imperial consuls asking for any information on the movements of Russian diplomats in the region, men who might be in touch with any clandestine groups that existed. At the same time, tracking Vasiliev might be the best way to uncover the network of the irreconcilables who at some point would have to show their hand in another attempt on Vasiliev and his lovely Circassian girl.

Yes, he would have Haymerle recommend a reliable agent to track down Vasiliev and crush the renegades.

Kállay's message reached Haymerle as the baron was about to set off for a dinner at the French consulate where he would meet Selim Bey. Over an after dinner cognac, which Selim Bey indulged in only among Europeans, Haymerle steered the conversation to recent events in Bosnia and inquired whether Selim Bey had any news of Vasiliev.

"Ah, the elusive detective, a true original, as you Europeans would say. The man seems to turn up in the most unlikely places. I believe he was last seen in Sarajevo. But that was several days ago."

"Several days! My dear Selim Bey you are kept well-informed."

"He interests me. He seems to be gathering intelligence while pursing his criminal investigation."

"Yes, my sources point in the same direction. Confidentially, Vienna is also interested in making contact with him for mutual advantage. If you hear of his whereabouts I should be grateful to have that information." Selim Bey bowed, declined to refresh his drink and soon made his excuses. Surely, he thought on his return to his villa, there would be no harm in letting the Hungarian know that Vasiliev, his orderly and the Circassian girl had already been located by his men in Travnik. Sooner or later Vienna would find out; their troops were in occupation of the region. He might as well gain a few points in giving them the information before they learned it from their own people.

The same courier who brought Haymerle's intelligence to Kállay, also delivered a message from the Austrian consul in Cetinje with the more surprising news that Ionin, the Russian consul, had departed from his home in such haste that he had left his cats behind, a true sign of an emergency. Then the following day a message apprised him of Ionin's arrival in Sarajevo, having survived a murderous ambush by bandits. The attack added a new complication. Who were these men? And why did they spare Ionin? Another complication. Beyond that, Kállay had to wonder why Ionin did not simply send a telegram to reach Vasiliev in Sarajevo but, instead, felt impelled to rush off in order to meet him in person.

Finally, Haymerle sent a name, courtesy of Selim Bey, of a man in Travnik whom he could vouch for, to locate Vasiliev, hopefully Kállay prayed, before Ionin or more desperate men could find him.

Chapter
Thirty-Nine

Travnik

Vasiliev was putting the final touches to his disguise as a civilian while explaining to Serov his plan of action.

"Tamara and I will slip out at dusk and make our way to the old castle district. We may or may not be under observation so it is best to take at least minimal precautions. A uniform would be too conspicuous. And what will you do, Sergeant?"

Serov was amused that Vailiev implied that he really had a choice. He knew the routine. He too would assume some sort of disguise and prowl the streets and coffee house of Travnik, seeking to pick up a lead as to the meeting place of the *bunjevici*. He tried to banish the thought that he would prefer to be the one to accompany Tamara or at least to join the two of them. But he also prided himself on rooting around in the shadowy worlds that suited his own style of 'uncoverin' things' as he called it. Vasiliev always appreciated his contribution, though it was a challenge to discover something that his chief had not anticipated. He knew his value but also his place. Their childhood friendship, unique in his experience, had changed over the years as Vasiliev went on the Page Corps and higher grades in the police. But he carried Serov with him and the old bond had not so much weakened as assumed a new and unique character.

Tamara had also made an effort to change her appearance so that when Vasiliev called upon her, he was struck by the effect. She had acquired a more severe and somber look. He reflected for a moment on the many disguises she must have assumed when traveling with Grigoriev. And then, in an effort to break the tension, he joked how the three of them could easily form a troupe of wandering players, if only they could find a suitable musical accompanist. She smiled wanly as if she too had been thinking of happier days with Grigoriev.

Serov made his own preparations carefully. He had already dropped by the armourer's shop nearby, assuming correctly that the proprietor must speak a Slavic tongue, given his profession and contact with soldiers from all parts. He made a ceremony of examining *yagatans* and quaint ornamental guns and struck up a conversation with the owner. After a pretending to haggle over the price, he purchased a small, ornamental, antique dagger which he tucked in his waistband. Casually, he inquired about the location of the Gate of Delight. The armourer chuckled and spread his arms wide as if to encompass the world.

"This is what they used to call our town!" Then he waggled a finger at Serov and grinned evilly.

"But perhaps you are referring to another Gate of Delight, a place of peculiar distractions, though not one I would advise you to enter alone, in uniform or speaking with a Russian accent."

Serov shrugged. "Perhaps not. Tell me about it."

The armourer glanced hurriedly out the door and lowered his voice in a conspiratorial manner. Serov thought he was overdoing it.

"It is not something to discuss here. All I can say is that the delights it offers are not approved by our guardians of the Sharia, the law. If you are tempted by the prospect of new experiences, then I might be able to help you find your way there."

"This all sounds very mysterious, my friend. But yes, I am interested in 'peculiar distractions.' Of course I am a stranger here and would need a guide. Can you recommend someone?"

"Wait a moment," said the armourer, and he disappeared behind a screen. Serov hear a door open and shut. A few minutes passed. When the armourer returned he had a small boy, dressed like a ragamuffin, in tow.

"This is Ali. He will guide you. You may give him a few coins. He will meet you here in front of my shop after it closes, at the time of the last evening call to prayer of the muezzin. The mosque is on the next street so the call will be clear. You must not be late."

Serov left a note for Vasiliev who had already left with Tamara for the place of the tattoo woman, and dressed in non-descript, vaguely European costume, for he could hardly disguise himself as a Muslim. At the last minute he tucked the ornamental dagger under a sash around his waist so that it would be concealed but easily accessible. He met the boy at the appointed time. Ali led him down a broad avenue flanked by stone buildings. Suddenly, he veered off abruptly. Breaking into a loping gait, he plunged into a rabbit warren of lanes, past wooden houses with curious latticed windows and pillars, painted in faintly discernibly blue, holding up the central bays of the upper stories beyond which stretched dark gardens. Behind a screen of trees, a massive building loomed out of the darkness, a small lantern illuminating a carved, wooden, double door. Slivers of light could be seen through cracks in the shutters. Ali mumbled something which Serov interpreted as the Gate of Delights. No sooner had he slipped a few coins in Ali's outstretch palm than the boy took off, vanishing in the gloom of night.

Serov hesitated. Wasn't this enough, to have discovered the place? He was sure he could find it again because just before they entered the garden he notice a dilapidated wooden mosque with its pinnacle awry and next to it a cupola supported by four columns and curved arches covered by a canopy like the tombs in the cemetery. Perhaps the burial place of a holy man. He could not just knock on the door without knowing how to respond to a question or challenged to give a password. No, it would be better to wait, and return with Vasiliev, although he was sorely tempted to explore farther on his own. Still, something held him there, standing in the shadow of a great oak. A few minutes passed. Then from the back of the garden a group of men, possibly ten or more, approached the building. Serov saw his opportunity. He hurried to join them as they pounded on the door, shouting some incomprehensible words. The door was flung open and they crowded in, gesticulating and continuing to shout, with Serov at their heels. The place was dimly lit and smoke filled. Serov slipped away from the group and found an empty place against the wall next to a low brass table. He slumped down on a heavy carpet and stared at the rich geometric design to accustom his eyes and to avoid appearing inquisitive.

Shortly, a servant approached and mumbled a few words that Serov did not understand. He began to cough violently and gestured to the man as if ordering coffee. The man nodded and returned with a tray bearing a steaming cup of coffee. Serov nodded in turn and grasping his throat as if he could not speak, swallowed hard and held out his cup for another dose of the thick liquid he had learned to dislike.

Suddenly, the loud talking in the room dropped off and a stringed instrument and flute began a mournful duet followed by the sound of lilting, female voices coming from behind a screen at the far end of the room. Serov was surprised, as he had heard from gossip at the Danubian camp that strict Muslims looked with disfavor on music in general and female singers in particular. More surprises were to come. A lightly veiled girl clad in pink muslin trousers emerged from behind the curtain and began to weave and sway to the music. Suddenly, she threw up her veil and allowed it to float down on her shoulders. There were shouts of approval. Then she whirled out of sight again.

What followed surprised Serov even more. When the voices stopped, a number of boys dressed in female costumes appeared, also singing in high pitched tones and dancing with mincing steps. There was a rumble of approbation from the clients. One of the boys approached Serov who waved him away brusquely. Ribald laughter followed.

"Not to your taste, friend?" A voice from the corner spoke words in a Slavic dialect that Serov barely understood. He peered into the semi-darkness, picking out the figure of a heavily bearded man with a shock of unruly white hair falling over an elongated, furrowed forehead. His legs were crossed under him but Serov noticed a shape like a crutch leaning on the wall behind him. He shifted his weight and drew closer. No mistake. Well, why not?

"Selim 'the Lame?'" he asked, having learned to pronounce the name in Serbian.

"Who asks?"

"A friend of Grigoriev."

"Ah, not many of you left here," the man had shifted to strongly accented Russian. It was too dim to see whether the man wore a ring.

"I have come a long way to find out what has happened to him."

"How should I know?"

"It is said that you may not but might know those who do."

"Has my fame reached so far?"

"The trail was not easy to follow but it has led me to you."

"So you are not here to share the delights of the gate?"

"No."

"They are of both kinds, you know."

"And you, Selim, what are your tastes?"

"The coffee here is reputed to be the best in Travnik."

"May I ask where you learned your Russian?"

"That my friend is a long story. But you did not seek me to hear it."

The singing and dancing stopped, and all that could be heard were the murmur of voices. Several men had risen from their cushions and disappeared behind the screen with the singers.

Serov thought he could not avoid asking a direct question.

"You are right. I have heard that you may know of where some of those called *bunjevici* may be found."

Selim uncrossed his legs and Serov noticed that one foot was missing. Well, he wasn't going to ask how that happened, because it would not doubt involve another long story.

"A curious quest."

"I have also heard they might help me discover what happened to Grigoriev."

"I might be able to help you. But first I must know more about you, for this world is full of evil men."

Serov spun out his tale, adopting a version of Vasiliev's assignment, while Selim consumed two more cups of Travnik's best coffee.

Selim grimaced as if he were unconvinced.

"A noble mission. But why entrust it to a man who speaks like a peasant."

"I can bring you one who is nobleman, if you insist."

"I do not insist or demand. I have learned to be careful, though."

Selim reached down to rub the length of his wounded leg.

"Will you be here tomorrow night again?"

"If fate does not decree otherwise."

Serov motioned to the servant and handed him some coins.

Selim smiled and raised his hand in a gesture of thanks. Then he slumped back against the wall.

Serov left the Gate of Delight, making his way past the dark gardens. He had taken no more than a few steps when he heard a rustling sound close behind him. With the instinct of a man who survived many sudden attacks, he whirled, fell to his knees while drawing his dagger and sweeping it in front of him. A heavy blow struck him on the shoulder just as his dagger cut into the leg of his assailant. A man cried out and fled, leaving Serov partially dazed, groping for his dagger which had been knocked out of his hand. Then he lost consciousness for a moment. He recovered expecting another and perhaps fatal blow. But he heard only a distant crash of foliage and then silence. A few minutes passed while he struggled to regain his balance. On his knees he scrabbled around in the dirt for his dagger, but could not find it. Then another sound reached his ears, someone was coming down the path from the Gate of Delight.

Chapter Forty

Travnik

When Vasiliev and Tamara left the *khan*, he looked more like a retired European official than a robust Russian officer. He had applied a light dye to his sideburns and wore a small goatee also dyed grey. He walked slowly with the help of a stick, arm in arm with Tamara. Along the street, they would stop and he would point to one or another of the buildings they passed by. The many mosques appeared to interest him in particular. Against the walls of some of them were the booths of tradesmen, now beginning to close for the evening. Vasiliev pointed out to Tamara how the stone cupolas and the porches of the larger mosques differed little from the architecture of the early Christian churches built in the Byzantine style. However, their walls were painted in brilliant colors depicting the Muslim view of paradise, palm trees laden with dates and vines sprouting from elegant vases or occasionally a ripe melon with a carving knife inserted. Tamara had to smile in appreciation of Vasiliev's knowledge of her religion. It was a credible performance, at least in deceiving any but the most discerning observer. As they began to climb the first of the hills separating the two parts of the town, the sun cast just enough light to catch the tops of the minarets. They counted thirteen mosques.

Vasiliev had memorized the map and although the streets were not named, the way was clearly marked and after one or two inquiries they found the shack of the tatooer.

"She doesn't look like she is terribly successful," said Vasiliev as they knocked on the sagging wooden door.

The old woman who answered gazed from one to the other as Tamara explained her interest. The woman took Tamara by the hand and led her into a a single room partitioned by a heavy, frayed cloth curtain. She signaled to Vasiliev to remain where he was.

Vasiliev took the opportunity to open the door quietly and peer into the darkness outside. There was no sign of movement, only a few lights scattered over the hill. He heard the distant cry of the muezzin. He wondered whether the old woman and Tamara were kneeling together in prayer. There was no sound. He counted the minutes and began to worry until the curtain parted and the two women emerged.

Tamara addressed him as a friend would.

"My dear, Selima is a wonder. She showed me many patterns and I selected one. Tomorrow morning she has time to apply the tattoo. We should, however, pay her in advance, don't you think?"

Vasiliev took out a purse and counted out a generous sum. The old woman bowed and opened the door. She called out a few words in a tongue that Vasiliev did not understand. Almost at once a young man appeared bearing a lighted torch.

"He will be your safeguard. The night is dark."

They had only taken a few steps from the old tatooer's door when Tamara whispered to Vasiliev that the boy had been instructed to lead them "to those who know," in the words of the old woman.

After taking many turns down darkened streets, the boy stopped before a stone building. In the dying light of the burning torch, they could barely make out the details of an enormous ornately carved wooden door.

"They are waiting," is all he said. Then he rapped out a pattern of loud knocks before plunging his torch into a barrel of water by the wall and vanishing into the darkness. A few minutes passed before the door creaked open, as if reluctantly thought Vasiliev. A hooded figure appeared, silhouetted by a flickering light at the end of a long passage. The figure gestured as if to usher them into a holy sanctum and led them into a large room where several men were seated on cushions placed along a bare, whitewashed wall. The only light here came from a small fire in an open hearth.

"Please be seated. We apologize for the lack of comfort, but this is only a temporary refuge for us." The man who addressed them was speaking in Serbian. The voice was mellifluous, each syllable clearly articulated. He was dressed in a costume that blended European and Bosnian styles with a long sword held by an ornate sash tied around his waist.

"We know something about your movements. You seek information but we do not know your purpose. You travel with a young woman, not of these parts, but we do not know why. So before we can help you, you must be open and frank with us."

"Gladly," answered Vasiliev. "But I too have questions. I have heard about you, but only rumors. So I would like to know how things stand with you, your politics most of all. Then I can tell whether and how much you can help us."

One of the men chuckled. "So no one wishes to make the first move. As a Russian you must play chess, of course. All right, I will advance my king's pawn two spaces. We are Serbian speaking Catholics, veterans of the Military Frontier, subjects of His Majesty the Emperor of Austria. But we are worried, even fearful about the ambitions of the Hungarians in the other half of our Empire. So, a certain respect for our Slavic bretheren in Bosnia and their fate under Hungarian rule. I believe I have inadvertently moved out not only my pawn but my knight as well."

Vasiliev had to smile. "I am a Russian officer assigned to find the murderer of Grigoriev. He was well-known to you I am sure, as a former leader of the Russian Pan Slavs during the uprising against the Turks in Bosnia. No friend of the Austrians, still less of the Hungarians. But devoted to the idea of liberation of the Bosnians from outside powers."

"Do I detect a Sicilian Defence?" the voice playful now.

"Your move," Vasiliev answered.

"It has been said that we were supporters of the Hungarian revolution of 1848 under Kossuth. But this was not true. We are disappointed that under Austrian military occupation the civil administration of Bosnia is being handed over to the Hungarians. We had hoped for a union with our brothers in Croatia-Slavonia and the creation of a third equal Slavic member of the Monarchy."

"So a Trial Monarchy to replace a Dual Monarchy, an Austro-Hungarian-South Slavic Monarchy."

"Exactly! So we had some sympathy for your Grigoriev, although we did not agree on all matters."

"You should know then that my mission was supported by Pan Slavic enthusiasts in St. Petersburg, but whose preference was for a large Orthodox Serbia, not a large Catholic Croatia. Still, I believe we have a common enemy and a common purpose."

"To find the murderer."

"Yes."

"And the young lady"

"A friend of Grigoriev who seeks justice."

Vasiliev fell silent. He was not about to reveal his instructions from Totleben.

The mellifluous voice had just begun to speak again when a muffled sound reached them from the entrance to the building. As if on a common signal they all stood up and faced the darkened corridor. Two *bunjevici* drew their weapons. Vasiliev drew Tamara behind him.

"Friends! It is your very own Selim 'the Lame.' And I have brought you an interesting specimen."

When two men emerged from the darkness, Vasiliev gasped. Tamara stifled a cry.

Selim had his arm around Serov's waist and gently helped him to sit down on an empty cushion.

"I fear that they know now and will soon attack us," said Selim before anyone else had a chance to speak.

"So, dear Selim, from the beginning," said the man who had imagined a game of chess with Vasili Vasilievich.

"First, let me attend to my friend," Serov looked up at the word 'friend.' Not often did he hear this from his superior officer, not since childhood.

But Tamara was already on her feet; she rushed to Serov's side, calling for hot water and clean rags.

A sharp order from the man in charge cut through the babble of voices. "First, we will hear out Selim. Then we shall talk quietly not like cackling hens."

Vasili stood over Serov as Tamara washed the blood off his head and cheek.

"Not serious," she whispered to Vasiliev, who took note of the expression on Serov's face as Tamara administered to him. Now he considers himself lucky, he thought. But he said nothing, only gently squeezed Serov's shoulder and slid down next to him on the bare floor. He would listen to Selim and then hear Serov's version of what had happened.

Selim spoke in Serbian, slowly, pronouncing every word as if he had deliberated beforehand on what he would say. Serov, propped up against the wall, understood almost every word and nodded in agreement with Selim's account of their meeting.

"And now the Sergeant, if you please, the details of your misadventure."

Serov told them in a few words.

"Anything else, Selim?"

"Yes, a moment after the Sergeant left me, I spotted one of our enemies. He was half hidden in a dark corner. I saw him rise and follow the Sergeant out. I was slow to follow. You know how I move like a three wheeled cart. I heard a scuffle but did not see the man's face clearly before he fled. The Sergeant was on his knees in the lane. I think the attack was a warning."

"Who are your enemies?" asked Vasiliev. "Or perhaps I should ask who among your enemies do you suspect?"

"Well put, Major. We have received several warnings, indirectly and not always from reliable persons. But their meaning is clear enough. The enemies are a group of Hungarian renegades. I call them renegades for good reason. They do not agree with Vienna or even Budapest about the future of Bosnia. They want to drive out those of the Orthodox and Muslim faith. They claim to be acting in the name of the Pope. This is not true. We too are Catholic but seek peace with all who live here. We have heard rumors that our beloved monarch, Franz Joseph, has appointed a decent man to administer the new province. But he faces a difficult task."

"We should attack first!" a young voice rang out. A murmur of agreement filled the room.

"Boldly stated, Pavel. But we are heavily outnumbered."

"The Muslims will support us!"

"Perhaps, if we are attacked first. But they do not want to turn their town into a battlefield. They want us to leave and fight it out elsewhere."

"Now we have a Russian officer to help us!" Another voice cried out.

Dmitry Alekseevich

"And so do they," the head man said. Vasiliev felt his muscles tighten, but he kept his voice calm.

"And who might that be?"

For a moment no one spoke.

Then the head man coughed lightly as if to clear his throat for a long disquisition.

"Well, Major, if you will join us in organizing a defense, we can tell you a great deal about this man and much else that will surprise you."

"I agree to your terms, but it would be useful to begin if I could address you by a name. It need not be your real one. A *nom de plume* will suffice."

This brought a chuckle. "Good, my name and patronymic, actually a real one, is Dmitry Alekseevich. Still, I will reserve my family name for a later stage in our acquaintance."

"So then Dmitry Alekseevich, what secrets have you to confide in return for our joint defense?"

Dmitry Alekseevich saw no point in revealing at this point that he had received a request from Baron Haymerle to make contact with Vasiliev. He did not wish to be taken as an agent of the government in Vienna.

"Let us start at the beginning. Or rather a few words about our sources." He had already prepared this little speech in anticipation of meeting Vasiliev. "When Vienna began to dismantle the Military Frontier, which will be abolished in the very near future, our people fanned out throughout the Balkans on their own initiative. We have a srong group in Sarajevo. Some even reached as far as Saloniki. We are concerned about the fate of our fellow Slavs, Catholic as well as Orthodox. You understand the prospect of war always hangs over us. The situation in the mid-seventies began to seem more and more threatening. Our people were without a central organization. But they kept in touch with one another. They took up different trades and entered service wherever they could find a place. Their purpose was to gather information, not to evaluate it, but to pass it on so that it reached us."

"So you might say your group served as a sort of central committee?"

"You might put it that way. But remember we did not issue orders or act as spies. And the group, as I prefer to call it, changes its membership as our lives change."

"Sounds like an ideal government, if rather utopian."

"But you see, we do not govern."

"I am sorry, but the concept is quite alien to me."

"It is unique, I think. Let me continue. Once Serbs revolted in '75, it was hard to keep in touch. Some of our people joined in. Others kept aloof. Then, two years later, the war between you Russians and the Turks further complicated our position. Again, let me emphasize that we did not all share the same political views. What united us was our devotion to the greater Slavic cause. We we did not give much thought to whatever final shape it might take. If we had, the movement would have fallen apart.

"Extraordinary! Men were fighting and dying to achieve this final shape as you put it, yet you did not know what that might be or even should be. I must confess, my dear Dmitry Alekseevich, this is a formula for civil war."

"Perhaps. We trusted in our love for our brothers. Our experience in the Military Frontier had welded us into a kind of brotherhood and we...well, no reason to go on with that."

The voice of Selim broke in. "You see, major, even a believer in the true faith, may Allah be praised, like myself was part of it! For my Slavic blood still runs strong." With those words he handed back Serov's dagger.

Serov spoke for the first time, nodding his head as a sign of thanks, "Thank God, in whatever name, for that strength!"

Vasiliev was to think about this conversation for a long time afterwards. What was more important to a man or perhaps a woman, language, religion or blood? He was unable to come up with a convincing answer for himself if only because in his case he had to add class into the mix. What cause would he be willing die for?

"Since the war ended," Dmitry Alekseevich went on, "we reknit our ties where they were broken or frayed. And many bits of information kept coming into us concerning our Russian brothers, ever since General Chernaiev's volunteers appeared in '75. Of course, we knew there were good and bad men among them. This is always true when men seek to fight. Now, to come to your case. After the war we lost our greatest friend from your country. This man was fearless and devoted to our cause. He too did not ask about the shape of things to come.This man called himself Grigoriev." He turned toward Tamara and nodded several times as sign of compassion. She raised a fist to her mouth. "Yes, my dear. We observed with sympathy your closeness to him though you knew nothing of us.

"Then you, Major, arrived on the scene, a fellow Slav from distant Russia, with instructions to find the killer. I regret that our customs prevented us from helping you. Perhaps now it is not too late. Whatever! All along your long trail, our people followed with their eyes. We marveled at your escapes from danger. We understood from the day you set out that those who attempted to stop you were also our enemies. They planned the attack on your ship going from Alexandropolis to Thessaloniki. They were behind the ambush of the train to Prishtina. They stauked you during your ride to the Devich Monastery."

"I find this hard to believe. I am tempted to ask where your agents or whatever you call them were posted, to know all this."

"Not agents, Major, please! Of course, they did not witness all these incidents but learned from others who may not even have known that their stories were being recorded and passed on to us. You must understand that information about your adventures was only a small part of what we were hearing about many other events. But they struck us as important and even odd. I mean we could understand the murder of Grigoriev. He was a real leader in the Slavic cause. It is a simple matter to assassinate a man in these parts. Men have had plenty of practice. But the determination to stop your investigation, the planning and organization? This seem out of all proportion to the desired result. Unless..."

"Unless some higher authority initiated the murder of Grigoriev for other reasons than appeared to be the case."

"A good guess, Major." This brought a smile to Vasiliev's face.

"Yes, I have been accused of being a good guesser."

"Accused? Surely not."

"A private joke, Dmitry Alekseevich, which I will share with you on another occasion."

"But can you guess what that other reason might have been?"

"Not yet, but you might help me."

"I fear that I cannot. Oh! I wish I knew. But you see, we only observe."

"But you started to say, 'unless' and I unfortunately interrupted."

"Nothing lost here. I merely meant that I personally found this whole operation odd. We have not discussed this as a group.

"One other point, if you will permit me," Dmitry Alekseevich continued.

"Everything you say is of the greatest interest."

"This concerns our dear Tamara."

Tamara had long turned toward Dmitry Alekseevich from having nursed Serov. She followed his every word with rapt attention. Now she gave a start and leaned forward so that her lovely face was brilliantly illuminated by the firelight.

"The people who abducted her are our common enemies. But let me prove this by asking a few questions. Do you mind, my dear?"

"Of course not."

"What did you learn about your abductors?"

"Very little, they were dressed in the European manner, they spoke a language not familiar to me and...oh yes, there was a Latin cross hung over the doorway."

"Hungarian renegades," said Dmitry Alekseevich.

"But for what purpose?" she asked.

"I am not sure. I would have to engage in what our Major calls 'guessing.' I think that you were not part of the larger plan to eliminate the Major and his faithful Sergeant. No, these men were utterly unscrupulous, even departing from their instructions. From what we know about them, at least these few men, they saw you as, if I may use a coarse word, booty. They intended to sell you to a caliph for his harem. You will forgive me for my boldness, but a rare beauty like yourself would have commanded a very high price. These men were not only renegades but bandits. They deserved their fate."

"What fate would that be?" asked Vasiliev. "We left them battered and tied up but otherwise well enough, considering."

"They were found or rather parts of them by a neighbor. Their severed heads were impaled on stakes outside their house."

Tamara cried out and buried her face in her hands.

Vasiliev felt a wave of disgust overcome him. Serov swore softly.

They both turned to Tamara.

"Do you know the meaning of this?" Vasiliev had lowered his voice to almost a whisper. She was shuddering. He wanted to reach out to her. But once again he held back. It was not his place, he thought, to take her in his arms and comfort her.

She threw back her head and, clenching her fists, blurted out,

"This is the vengeance of mountaineers."

Chapter
Forty-One

Travnik

Hadji Murad stood on the heights **of** Vlašić Mountain, staring down at the town of Travnik. As the setting sun touched the horizon, he sank to his knees to pray, giving thanks to God, who alone is great, for his guidance. When he rose again, the red disc had all but vanished and the gloom of night quickly settled over the rocky hillside. His thoughts went back as they often did at the end of prayers to the miracle of his survival, thanks to the power of God. His heart had been heavy sending off his sons but they were obedient to the last, leaving him to fight the rear action. He had not counted on surviving. He could only attribute it to divine intervention.

He remembered how the inspiration had come to him like a bolt from heaven. He had fired off the last of his cartridges, not without effect, he believed. What was left to be done? He rolled on his side and peered down the sharp decline behind him. Yes, he would appear to die there. He pulled out his dagger and cut a vein in his arm letting the blood flow over the ground. He tore off a strip of cloth from his robe to make a tourniquet. Then he inched his way to the edge of the precipice He placed his sword reverently on the ground bent to kiss it and smeared the handle with his blood. He removed his turban and wrapped his bare head tightly in one of his sashes, covering all of his face except a narrow slit for his eyes. He replaced the turban, jamming it down to provide added protection. He muttered a short prayer and then rolled over the edge, clasping his arms tightly to his body. The rocks seemed determined to tear him apart. Pain shot through his legs and ribcage. The fall seemed endless. For a moment he lost consciousness. When a large rock brought him to a violent stop, he could hardly breathe. The pain surged like a mighty wave, spreading throughout his entire body. Dazed but aware of the need to perform the final act of deception, he unwound his turban and wrapped it around a fragment of a rotting log that lay within his reach. Then he stripped off his outer robe and wrapped it around the rest of the log to give the impression of a body. He arranged the improvised head and torso so that they appeared to be attached. Summoning all his remaining strength, he crawled into a nearby clump of bushes where he could not be seen from the edge of the precipice. There he waited.

He may have lost consciousness again, but soon became vaguely aware of human voices coming from a far distance above him. It had grown darker since he had taken his fall. Peering out from his hiding place, he watched as several silhouettes appeared over the edge of the precipice. Then a volley of shots rang out and he saw the bullets tear into the dummy lying next to the big rock. He heard a muffled exchange of voices, then silence as the night closed in.

Hadji Murad would have been pleased if he could have heard the conversation among his attackers. But it was enough that they left him alone.

"He is dead," said one of the shooters.

"How can we be sure?"

"So, do you want to risk your life or limb to climb down there? Look at the blood trail. This means he was already seriously wounded. Then the sword. Just look at it? I know weapons. This is a family heirloom, sacred to the warrior who bears it. Better death than giving it up. And now we have riddled his corpse with more bullets. Perhaps you want an autopsy?"

"The colonel may be skeptical without the proof of a body."

"We give him the sword. He'll love it and all four of us testify to the death. No risk for us and the promise of a reward."

"Well, we all have to agree."

"So who is opposed? If you are then you can go it alone down there. And how the Hell are you going to get the body back up here?"

The voices faded away.

Hadji Murad loosened the tourniquet on his arm. He had

lost a lot of blood. He slept fitfully. Before dawn he retrieved his bullet ridden turban and robe, painfully inching his way along the ground. His eyes saw only dim shapes; was he passing through a dreamlike state or was this death? He had heard the faint murmur of water. After crawling a short distance, which seemed to take a hundred years, he came upon an underground steam that gurgled forth from a crevice in the rocks. Another miracle. He drank eagerly, washed the wound and then bound it tightly. Hunger gnawed at him. Would God, who alone is great, provide food as well? He staggered to his feet but a great dizziness overcame him, and he slumped down again. The pain in his ribs was almost unbearable. He knew he had broken something. He dragged himself over the rocky terrain which gave way to soft mounds of earth. As it grew lighter, he spotted what could only have been a rabbit hole. He sat by it, immobile, his dagger raised until a head appeared. A quick stroke. He spent the next half hour skinning the animal and making a fire by the age-old method of rubbing sticks together to generate a spark and then gradually adding leaves to catch the flame. He had to chuckle. Roasted rabbit wasn't so bad for a beginning. For the next few days he gathered berries, caught another rabbit and reached a river where there was an abundance of fish to catch. He began to feel as though he could begin to pick up traces of the boys' trail.

He did not retrace his steps but thought carefully of how he had trained them and what course they might follow. It took him two days to find the first signs of their passage. It was too easy; he would remonstrate with them. They should have taken even more precautions to avoid being followed. The pain only gradually subsided and he long longer spat blood, though it was hard to breathe deeply. He concluded that he had not in fact broken any ribs but only bruised them. He began to sleep for longer periods without awakening. Now he could walk with the help of a tree branch fashioned into a staff. At the first sight of a gravestone of his faith, he thanked God who alone is great, for having guided his steps to salvation as He had throughout his life. The cemetery of the faithful spread out before him.

Overlooking Travnik, he felt a rare wave of pleasure come over him. A town filled with devotees of the true faith. Surely this was the place where he would be reunited with his sons! Was it here that they would find their beloved sister? And what dangers would face them? It would best, he decided, to be patient, to conceal himself until he had a better idea of how matters stood. There were always enemies lurking where one least suspected to find them.

From his perch above the town, Hadji Murad had located the largest mosque with its twin minarets. Slowly he desended the sharp incline, and headed straight for it. He hoped to find an armourer along the way to obtain a new sword and perhaps a rifle as well. But he had no money. There was only the ruby ring of his grandfather, handed down to him and cherished as his last tie with the mountains. He would have to sell it. The pang in his heart was only relieved by the thought that now he would not have to decide which brother would inherit the family jewel. Scant consulation, he muttered to himself. Then another thought crossed his mind, the loss of a jewel to gain one of higher value. He had long ago forgiven his daughter for her connection to the Russian.

As he made his way toward the mosque, he kept looking for a jeweler's shop. Again his faith guided his steps. At a prayer house, he discreetly made inquiries. He was helped by a young man to find a store run by a Circassian who had emigrated from the Caucasus in 1866. The proprietor knew the true value of the stone and its silver setting.

"I am not a pawnbroker, as they call them in the West, but I shall put this treasure aside for one year. By then, God willing, you can redeem it for the same money I now pay you."

The armourer was a local man who knew his business. His shop was crammed with *handshars*, Bosnian cutlasses, elaborately embellished ornamental guns, pistols and a few foreign made rifles. They discussed the fine points of the blades with expert knowledge. He bought a Damascus sword with no frills, but the blade was exceptionally well honed, as sharp as a cat's tongue. He pocketed the remaining coins, enough to keep him alive until he had completed his mission.

Evening was falling when he approached the mosque. He was surprised to see a few Muslim women with a covering that concealed their entire face except for tiny slits for the eyes. When he passed them, they bowed their heads so low that the fringe of the upper veil which curtained their heads fell forward closing down the last glimpse of their corporeal being. What a contrast to the Christian women he had seen earlier prancing through the merchant quarter. They were dressed in European clothing that he hardly recognized any more, although their style resembled what he had seen years before during a visit to Belgrade. His thoughts turned again to Tamara for whom fine garments meant little. Without a mother to select the proper clothes, she followed the example of her brothers who encouraged her to dress with a freedom that scandalized the women of his generation. But he was reluctant to interfere as he marveled at the bond that united his three children. "So," he would snap at the old crones: "where is the sin in that?"

Hadji Murad walked slowly, memorizing the more distinctive details of the buildings along the way, making a mental map of the town. He passed several palaces which could only have belonged to high Ottoman officials, and also barracks, now empty which must have housed Turkish troops. So, once upon a time, this had been a great administrative center, he concluded. Even the wooden houses showed distinctive characteristics, latticed windows in the central bays of the upper stories, colorful designs painted on the outside walls. He would remember the house with the blue pillars. Most impressive of all was a solid stone building supported by arcades of masonry embellished with rosettes carved in the spandrels of the arches. A few streets beyond that building was a wooden mosque in bad repair, its pinnacle leaning dangerously to the side, as if anticipating a great gust of wind that would come some day to topple it into the street. Beside it was an elegant mosque of more recent design. A crowd had gathered and men were passing under an elegantly carved portal. It was a time for prayer. He joined them. Glancing up, he was thrilled by the brilliant deep blue color of the cupola overhead. When he lowered his eyes, he caught sight of them, two unmistakable figures kneeling in the back row, and his heart thudded so violently that he thought it would burst.

Chapter
Forty-Two

Travnik

"The plan is a good one, only a bit risky," said Vasiliev when they had returned to the hotel. Serov nodded. Tamara had gone to her room after their escapade and remained there for several hours. When she appeared again she seemed preoccupied, as if she were drifting away from them. Vasiliev went on as if he had not noticed.

"Let's go over it. Dmitry Alekseevich will make contact with the renegades and negotiate a meeting. He will explain that his men do not wish to be involved with the Austrian police who are determined to break the truce. He will insist that both sides produce their leaders. No seconds-in-command. The meeting will have to take place on neutral ground but under tight security. Each side will limit their numbers to no more than half a dozen men. Dmitry Alekseevich will propose the cemetery of Travnik as the meeting place at midnight on Monday. Each side will send two men an hour beforehand to reconnoiter the ground to make sure that the rules are in force. He will arrange a series of signals by torches to illuminate the scene. We have to count on the Russian showing up. Now we have a good description. We're lucky that he is a big man, bearded with a prominent scar on his right cheek, apparently a wound from a saber cut. Dmitry Alekseevich will engage in some inconsequential banter as if he were testing the waters and ask for another meeting. You and I, Sergeant, will be heavily disguised and waiting, concealed outside the cemetery.When the meeting breaks up we will trail the renegades back to their lair. Once we know where they are, we can notify the Austrian police. It will be up to them to organize a raid."

"And you intend to leave me here in the hotel?" asked Tamara, staring at the floor. Vasiliev was surprised at her tone. She sounded submissive and resigned to sitting things out. Not like her. He had prepared an eloquent speech to persuade her. Now it was not necessary. He should have been alerted that her change in behavior signified something serious. He subsequently cursed himself for failing to question her. Instead, at the time, he was relieved.

Before Vasiliev donned his disguise, he spoke to the manager who seemed less jolly than when he arrived.

"My friend, I have to ask for your assistance, once again."

"Excuse me, Major, but I have just done you another great favor and fear that this can be the last one for a long time. Actually, the same favor twice and it may cost me dearly. But as you are a friend of Monsieur Evans…"

A commotion broke out on the stairs at the end of the reception, interrupting them. The manager glanced anxiously in that direction and his face lost color. A German speaking guest was scolding the page who was manhandling a bulky portmanteau almost as large as he was.

The manager rushed over, apologizing profusely. Vasiliev glanced down at the hotel register, a matter of habit with him, testing how quickly he could read a name upside down. What he saw startled him. He waited for the manager to come back, determined to find out how much he could trust him.

"My dear Major, I apologize. Yes, well, just a few hours ago the Russian consul arrived from Cetinje, a certain Ionin, and took a room. He asked about your whereabouts. But I pleaded innocence, following your instructions to keep your presence here a secret. Then just before you came down another gentleman inquired after you. His documents identified him as a diplomat from the Austrian embassy. I also pleaded ignorance of your whereabouts. He left without reserving a room, but instructed me to inform his office if you were to show up. I must ask you then, please, either leave immediately or let both your consul and the Austrian official know you are here. You understand my position."

"Of course. I'm very grateful for your discretion. We'll leave as soon as we can pack. You need not continue to prevaricate on our behalf. Can you recommend another *khan*?"

"So a council of war," Vasiliev declared to Serov as they put the finishing touches to their disguises. "We have to rely on Tamara to arrange the move. I have the address. We'll rendez-vous after we track down our prey and inform the Austrian police. Then we can reveal ourselves to all those who are so eager to find us."

Vasiliev found Tamara standing by the window in her room, staring vacantly into the garden behind the hotel. He gave her careful instructions to move their belongings and to wear a heavy veil when she left the hotel.

"I can think of no better disguise," he chuckled, but Tamara did not share his gaity. Again, he misinterpreted her solemn look. He tried a joke

"You mustn't worry. I'll take good care of Sergeant Serov." Still no reaction. Then she extended her hand and silently shook his. For an instant, he felt an overwhelming desire to embrace her, but the handshake was firm, as if to keep him at a distance.

"The gods favor us, Serov," Vasiliev muttered as they took up their position in a ruined stone house across from the main entrance to the cemetery. A quarter moon shed a faint glow on the tombs and illuminated the path leading to Travnik. A slight breeze came from the east, but there was no threat of rain. They watched as the representatives of the two sides walked slowly toward the meeting spot and, brandishing torches, carefully surveyed the ground. One man of the two advance parties left to notify the rest of his group while the other stood guard at the opposite end of the burial grounds.

Half a dozen men emerged from the darkness, cautiously making their way toward the the tomb of Mehmet Ali Pasha. Vasiliev focused his binoculars. It was easy to spot the figure of Dmitry Alekseevich as he approached the entrance of the tomb. He shifted the glasses. A very tall figure, hatless, with dark hair falling to his shoulders and a Russian army officer's cloak flung over his shoulders, approached to meet him. They bowed to one another but did not shake hands. Apparently, neither man was armed, but those spread out in a semi-circle behind them had rifles slung over their shoulders. A conversation began. The torches held by three men on each side fluttered in the breeze, but they did not cast enough light to enable Vasiliev to distinguish the features of the men standing behind the two leaders. They appeared to be speaking calmly without threatening gestures, keeping a distance.

After fifteen minutes, they bowed and began to turn away from one another when the firing began. Where was it coming from? None of the men on either side had raised a weapon. A volley immediately cut down the tall figure. Dmitry Alekseevich shouted, "NO! No! No shooting." But men on both sides had unshouldered their rifles and were firing wildly. Torches fell to the ground. In the darkness Vasiliev could faintly see shadowy figures collapsing as the fusillade cut them down. Suddenly, it was over. A few dim shapes slipped away in the gloom.

Vasiliev and Serov watched helplessly. Then Vasiliev seized Serov by the arm.

"Quick Sergeant after them, the men who survived, the shadows running back toward the town. We'll meet back at the *khan*." Serov was off like a shot. Vasiliev made his way cautiously to the killing ground. There were no sounds. He stumbled over several bodies before finding an extinguished torch. He ignited the branches and search for the tall man in the Russian cloak. When he found him, he lowered the torch over the body. There were several wounds in the chest and throat, but the face was untouched, the eyes staring as if in wonder. There was no scar on his cheek. Vasiliev muttered a curse.

He could not guess what had happened. He would have to notify the Austrian authorities, but gripped by a surge of anxiety, he felt the urgent need to find Tamara at the *khan*. He feared now for her safety.

He walked briskly back to town, meeting no one. The shots had not been heard, or else people were too frightened to come into the streets. Memories of the war were too recent. He quickly found his way to the *khan* where he had sent Tamara. A dilapidated place, far different from the elegant hotel they had left. He roused the night manager, who grumbled as he handed Vasiliev an envelope along with a key.

He lit a candle and directed Vasiliev to a room on the first floor at the end of a corridor that smelled of various cooking odors none of which was able to prevail over the others.

"And the girl? Has she settled in?"

"In and out," he muttered. "In and out."

The air in the room was stale. Their bags had been set on the floor next to an ancient wooden wardrobe

The manager left grumbling. Vasiliev threw open the window and glanced at the envelope. The address, "Major V.V. Vasiliev" had been scribbled in Cyrillic but not by a Russian hand. He dismissed the idea that Ionin had tracked them down. Who then had written him?

Vasiliev tore open the envelope. A gust of wind from the strong eastern breeze that had sprung up extinguished the candle. Vasiliev fumbled for a match. He lit the candle again, shielding the flickering flame with one hand while he shook open the folded piece of paper.

Vasiliev read the few words in astonishment. Then a wave of anguish swept over him. The candle sputtered and went out again. His first impulse was to crumple the paper and throw it on the floor. He relit the candle and studied the words, trying to guess their meaning.

'My dear friends! Forgive me. I have betrayed you. But vengeance is mine. Farewell, Tamara'.

"In and out, in and out," isn't that what the manger said? He rushed back to the front desk

"Where are the horses stabled?"

"In and out, in and out," the manager repeated.

"Damn you!"

"Well, no need to take that tone. She must have taken one of the horses. The stables are out back."

"And she reserved only one room?"

"As I said."

Vasiliev struggled to get himself under control. He asked directions to the Austrian Police Headquarters.

At the stables, as he expected, he found only two horses, his own and Serov's.

She must have planned this as soon as she moved us here, he angrily reproached himself. I should have guessed from the way she behaved, distracted, restless; yes, in spirit she was already beginning to move away from us. I should have…but I attributed it all to her unpredictable moods.

Vasiliev saddled his horse himself, mounted and rode out into the night.

His thoughts kept racing ahead. She had heard us discuss all the details of the meeting tonight. She knew the killer would be there. But, at this point his habit of guessing failed him. He could not imagine her mounting the attack herself. But if not alone, then with whom? Were the shooters member of the Cadmus circle? But they would not fire on their own men. Hungarian renegades? It seemed to him they were everywhere. Why didn't she trust us to track down the killer and arrest him? Perhaps arrest was not enough for her. A mountaineer's blood vengeance. Was that the only kind she would accept?

There was one other possibility. Perhaps, knowing that Ionin had arrived, she feared that he had come to prevent us from carrying out our mission. After all, she had reason to doubt him in the first place. Isn't that is why she escaped his protection in Montenegro? He was desperate to excuse her, forgive her, while a moment before he wanted to curse her.

Could Ionin be involved? Orders from Petersburg to silence a man who may have had compromising information about someone in high places. Could she have found a renegade among the renegades? Or the Austrians…unlikely.

There was something else in the message that fed his despairing mood. She had used the word *'proshchei'* not *'dosvidanie.'* So, 'farewell,' *'adieu'* not 'goodby' or *'au revoir.'* Was he reading too much into this word? No, she was letting him know she would never see him again. Had he waited too long to tell her of his feelings?

Chapter
Forty-Three

Travnik

The night porter at Austrian Police Headquarters was reluctant at first to rouse Captain Schroeder, who was known for his quick temper.

"We're talking about a massacre, my dear fellow," Vasiliev finally said.

The man looked flustered, "Well in that case, of course," He scribbled a note, and handed it to a sleepy looking boy dressed in an ill-fitting Austrian uniform who ran off. Let him feel the wrath of His Excellency, thought the porter.

Schroeder showed up within the hour, shaved and dressed impeccably as if attending a reception at court. Bringing civilization to Bosnia, Vasiliev raged inwardly.

"A massacre, Major! Surely those sorts of thing belong in the past."

"I can asure you, Captain, I am not exaggerating. I went over the killing field myself."

"In the Moslem cemetery you say. Well. We'll have to send out a party to gather up the bodies. This could trigger disorders. What more can you tell me? It would be important for my report to state how you came across this 'massacre.'" Schroeder had fallen into the habit of prouncing the word disdainfully.

Vasiliev had rehearsed a careful response while waiting for the captain. He briefly described his arrangement with Dmitry Alekseevich, "a loyal servant of the Austrian crown," to flush out a Russian deserter who was known to be in the area. The meeting was designed to end peacefully. Once it was over, the idea was to follow the renegades and the Russian into town where Vasiliev would arrest the deserter and the Austrian police would have the chance to deal with the Hungarian renegades however they wished "You should have informed us of your plan," Schroeder said after listening patiently.

"Perhaps you are right. But I was concerned that any premature action by your men might prevent me from capturing the deserter."

Schroeder flicked an imaginary dust particle from his sleeve.

"You should give us more credit," he pronounced his words in a tone of mild reproach. "So now you have your dead deserter and we are saddled with the bodies of unidentified *bunjevici* and renegades. Is that the picture you want to draw of your 'massacre?'"

"In a word, yes."

"You leave me with many unanswered questions. Who began to shoot, and could you guess why?"

Vasiliev flinched imperceptibly at the casual use of the word 'guess.'

"I cannot say for certain. Someone was hidden in the gravestones behind the *bunjevici*. As for guessing. I have too little to go on."

"But you as a trained detective might give us a clue, however, slight."

"Armed men in the dark are always unpredictable."

"Excellent, Major, a memorable truism. I shall include it in my report. Now, I assume you will wish to examine the body of the deserter more closely. Perhaps he has left some identification papers? Or is that too much to expect? Perhaps a distinguishing mark"

Vasiliev again felt a sense of unease. Was this another casual remark, or something else?

"And we will ask you to identify the body of Dmitry Alekseevich. That was his name, no?"

"I will be happy to assist in any way," Vasiliev pronounced the usual formula in a normal tone of voice, which took an effort.

"Good. Let's say a rendez-vous in the morgue tomorrow morning. By that time I will have a better idea of who might be involved besides your principal characters."

A curious way of putting things, thought Vasiliev. Perhaps he cultivated the style to throw people off balance, or to impress them.

****

Early the next morning, Vasiliev paid a vist to Ionin who was just sitting down to his breakfast in the *khan*. He had sent Serov off to find out more about the victims of the shooting.

"I must say, Vasili Vasilievich, that you have led us a merry chase, yes a merry chase." Ionin's paunch moved up and down as his voice rumbled in the imitation of a laugh. But Vasiliev knew he was not amused.

"Would you care for coffee? I can tell you already that the knockwurst here is almost up to provincial Austrian standards. Another year and the Austrian mission may raise even that level." Ionin chuckled as he tucked into the wurst and six fried eggs.

Vasiliev shook his head, having had his fill of Turkish coffee. He was undecided how much to tell the consul. Ionin took a cigar from a silver case, trimmed the end and examined it carefully before lighting up. He did not offer one to Vasiliev. Vasiliev thought of the gesture as a small indication of the the consul's displeasure. But he hardly cared any more. He felt drained of all emotion. The words of Tamara's note kept coming back to him in a disembodied voice, as if she had spoken them to him in a dream

After a few troubled hours lying awake in bed, he had felt more confused than angry. What was Ionin rambling on about now?

"...so the problem, I should say the dilemma, I face is what to do with you. I cannot tell whether you deliberately ignored my instructions or whether they did not reach you. So let me be clear. Orders have come from the highest authorities in the ministry of foreign affairs, that your mission to find the murderer of Grigoriev must be terminated forthwith...." He paused for an instant then added pontifically, "..... . on grounds of state security. Any further action on your part would be considered a serious breach of the law and leave you open to prosecution."

It was at this point, Vasiliev later told Serov with a his crooked smile in full display, that the sight of a half finished sausage on Ionin's breakfast tray exasperated him to the point where he shook off his melancholy state and burst out in anger:

"Too late! Aleksander Semenovich, too late!"

Ionin started and half rose form his chair, his unattended cigar tumbling into the ashtray.

"What do you mean? For god's sake, Major!"

Vasiliev lowered his voice, conspiratorialy.

"Hear me out, Aleksander Semenovich. Let me reassure you that I never received your message ordering me to cease my inquiries. So I am not guilty of violating your instructions to say nothing of the law. Next, I have to tell you that last night there was a firefight between two groups of men in a local cemetery. I have good reason to believe one of the men who was killed was the murderer of Grigoriev. I am still waiting for details. I sent Sergeant Serov to police headquarters to find out what he could. If I may be permitted, Aleksander Semenovich, I would advise at this point that we should wait here until we have more information. It would probably be unwise for you to get involved until we have a clear understanding of what happened."

Vasiliev closely observed the changes taking place in Ionin's expression and guessed that he was fearful of how this news would rebound on his own reputation and career. Good, thought Vasiliev. Now perhaps we can cut a deal.

"Too early to speculate. But we can plan for several eventualities. It would be best for your situation if the identity of the man shot dead last night would be, shall we say, left undisclosed to the world. What I know about his situation here in Travnik suggests this is not impossible. The Austrian authorities in charge do not, I believe, know who he is. At least they do not know about his role in the Grigoriev affair. So we'll not enlighten them. What was this fight in the cemetery, then? Again I know enough to blame it on a struggle between two factions. One group, Hungarian renegades from the Austro-Hungarian army, bandits, if you will. The other Catholic Serbs loyal to the monarchy, calling themselves *bjunevici*. The leader of the bandit group was reputedly a discharged Russian officer.

Ionin gasped.

"No need to worry. Unless the authorities know a great deal more about him than I suspect, he can simply be identified as a former member of General Chernaev's volunteers who as you know only too well were active in the region during the uprising of '75 in Serbia and then, after the suppression of the revolt, deserted to form a criminal band. Much depends on whether he carried identity papers which would belie that story. So let us wait for Serov."

Ionin had sunk back in his chair. His hands were shaking as he tried to light a new cigar. At a knock on the door, he dropped it unlit onto the floor.

"Come in," he managed to say in a strangled voice.

A waiter entered, bowed and picked up the tray. Not noticing the cigar he stepped on it, crushing it. He muttered an apology and left, a perfectly ordinary act but it seemed to have the effect on Ionin of further diminishing his stature.

"Let's agree to meet later when Serov arrives with news," Vasiliev repeated, not expecting a response. He left Ionin slumped in his chair like a broken doll. He took no pleasure from Ionin's discomfort. The words of Tamara's letter kept intruding on his thoughts, pushing out with cruel insistence his attempt to make sense of the scene at the cemetery. He took out his notebook with his coded reflections on the situation in the region. But his eyes would not focus on the numerals.

Several hours later Serov quietly entered the room. Vasiliev could not tell from his expression whether he was the bearer of good or bad news.

"Vasili Vasilich," his voice gave nothing away. "The first thing I have to tell you will pain your ears."

"It could not be worse than the note from Tamara."

"That's not for me to say."

Serov was grateful that Vasiliev had not lit a candle, so his face was in shadow. He knew Vasiliev was impatient for his news, but he could not bring himself to blurt it out.

"Best I can say, is that at first the Austrians gave me no trouble. Maybe I was in luck. Or as you always say, 'by chance.' A lot of millin' around at the hospital. People runnin' this way and that. Someone, looked like nurse but was a man, p'haps an orderly, told me where the bodies were. His white smock was splattered with blood. No one stopped me. I went into this large room. The bodies were laid out in rows. I didn't count 'em. I asked the orderly to show me the biggest 'un, thinkin' it must be the Russian. He pointed to the end of a long table. An officer came up to me and asked what I was doin' there. I told him the Russian consul asked me to find out if any Russians were involved. The officer shrugged. He was called away and left me alone for a few minutes. The body wasn't covered yet. He was big, all right. There was wounds in the chest and throat. But none in the head. I have to tell you, Vasili Vasilich, there was no scar on his face. Not a trace, as you would say."

Vasiliev sighed, "I'm afraid Sergeant this is not news to me. I examined the dead bodies after I sent you to town. No scar. But he sure as hell tooked like Russian."

"Ah Vasili Vasilich, you're always ahead of me. Sometimes I wonder what use I am."

"Come now, Serov, I wanted confirmation. It was dark in the cemetery and I needed you to make sure. Did the police find any documents on the dead man?"

"Well, I can tell you for sure they didn't. A tag was hangin' round his neck. I couldn't read it. Written in German it was. But the nurse or orderly, whatever he was, translated it for me. It said, "unidentified and unknown person."

"Thank God! So the news is not all bad."

"No, Vasili Vasilich, not all."

Vasiliev caught the gleam in Serovs' eyes and knew that he was up to his old trick of withholding information until the last moment, just to dramatize the effect of his discoveries. Of course, Serov wouldn't put it that way. But it was his method of proving his worth.

"And now Sergeant you are going to feed me some precious bit of information that will change my life."

Serov suddenly grinned. "Well that's sayin' too much. But I am thinkin' it might do you some good."

Vasiliev folded his arms and waited.

"You might be wonderin' why I didn't come back to the hotel right away. The thing is, that I got talkin' to this orderly who wasn't Austrian after all, but a local man. He told me the men brought in were not all dead when they arrived. One of the renegades was badly shot up, but still breathin.' They was pilin' up the corpses so fast that no one noticed, 'cept my orderly friend. He bent over the dyin' man and heard his last words."

"And he told you what they were," said Vasiliev, knowing that Serov enjoyed prolonging these rituals of revelation.

"Well, it was more than that and less," said Serov. "They managed a few words between the two of them, just a few words."

"Good, a regular death bed confession, perhaps?"

"You might call it that, Vasili Vasilich." Serov cast his eye on the caraf of vodka standing on the table next to him.

"Ah, a little treat I ordered earlier to celebrate the success of our plan and now all we have are a few precious words. But you deserve a shot, Sergeant."

Serov filled a *riumochka*, tossed it back, smacked his lips and wiped his mouth.

"So, as I was sayin' the man was sputterin' a few words in a tongue the orderly couldn't make out. So he told him to speak in Serbian. The man was coughin' and chokin' and whisperin' so that the orderly had to bend his ear to hear and the man's mouth is tricklin' blood. And he said, 'tell Andrei....' Then he made a few sounds the orderly couldn't make heads or tails out of. So the orderly wet his lips with some water, he mumbled, 'a trap...flee.' The orderly, bein' no fool, asks: 'Where is Andrei, that I can tell him?' And the man tells him, 'a watch-maker's shop behind the old cloth hall.' Then he breathes his last."

"Serov, this is vital information. Why didn't you bring it to me right away?"

"Well, it's this way, Vasili Vasilich, it's as quick as I could. But on my way out of the room with all those bodies lyin' there, the officer comes back. He stops me and asks for my documents. I shows him and he says he has to 'detain me', as he put it, to check with his superior. I tries to talk him out of it, but his Serbian was as bad as mine, and you know I don't speak German. So I get cooped up for several hours waitin' to be questioned. I told them that the Russian consul was waitin' for my report, so they let me go. Then I rushed over."

"How damnably ironic!" exclaimed Vasiliev.

Serov put down his empty glass and waited for a translation.

"You see, Sergeant, this is what we planned for, not the massacre of course, but how the meeting would give us a chance to track the murderer back to his lair. And now we have the information but cannot act on it, can't arrest him. He can prove he wasn't there, at the cemetery."

Vasiliev was pacing up and down, his eyes searching the floor as if to find a way out of the dilemma.

"Ionin's coming with his order to end our mission and Tamara's flight has cut the ground under our feet. We lack both the official and personal reasons to arrest Andrei Gregorevich as we now know he is called. The Austrian police will not act without Ionin's approval, and he will not give it. If Tamara was acting on her own, improbably, or with others unkown to us, then she must believe she has exacted her revenge. She'll disappear forever. It's unlikely an Austrian investigation into the shooting will lead them to her. A proper mess, you understand?"

Serov nodded. "But maybe..." he muttered, then hesitated to suggest an opinion of his own. It was not his place to interfere with Vasiliev's ruminations.

Vasiliev scarcely heard him.

"I don't know. Somehow I have the feeling that this is not over. I mean, I'll write my report for Totleben, but I cannot let this killer go scot free."

He whirled and placed a hand on Serov's shoulder.

"I am after all a policeman," and then quickly added, "we do what policemen do, Sergeant. We do not close our eyes to crime."

Chapter Forty-Four

Travnik

It was not difficult to locate the watch maker's shop. The hotel manager gave them clear instructions to reach cloth hall. It had been the store house of a merchant prince from Ragusa in olden times. A stone building with arcades in the style of the old Venetian Republic, it stood some little distance from the old wooden mosque with its bent pinnacle, leaning next to an elegant cupola. The watch maker's store was housed in a wooden dwelling with latticed windows and an overhanging upper floor supported by a faded blue colored arch.

Vasiliev sent Serov around to the rear of the building to check for a rear exit into the garden while he entered the shop. He glanced around before asking about an antique silver watch that was displayed in the ground floor window.

The man appeared nervous at the sight of an officer in a Russian uniform. He was short, stooped and gray-headed, a pair of spectacles perched on his beak-like nose. As a mark of his profession, his fingers were stubby and gnarled, the nails dark but closely trimmed.

Vasiliev indolently bargained over the price, watching the man's reactions Then abruptly he leaned over the counter and whispered in a conspiratorial voice.

"Is Andrei at home right now? I have an urgent message for him. I fear his life may be in danger."

The man grew pale and snatched the watch out of Vasiliev's hand.

"I know of no Andrei," his voice betraying him. "Does the watch interest you or not?"

"Listen my friend, I come on an unofficial visit, but there is an Austrian patrol by the mosque, within shouting distance. They could be easily summoned and arrest you for housing a wanted man. I'm here to warn Andrei, but I need to see him in person so I can help him arrange an escape."

"I know of no Andrei," the man repeated. But he was shaking now and almost dropped the watch.

"Perhaps you know him under a different name, a tall Russian with the bearing of a soldier. He carries a full beard and there is a prominent scar on the right side of his face. We were soldiers together, you see, in the great war. He may have had visitors, men speaking with a strong accent, coming from beyond the frontier to the north."

"He's gone," the man croaked in a broken voice.

"Perhaps he left me a message. Take me to his room," Vasiliev spoke sternly and unbuttoned his holster.

"Please...." The man was barely able to utter another word.

"No one will hurt you if you do what I say. Just take me up to his room without a word or a signal. I have a man in the rear watching. So no tricks."

The stairs creaked as the man led him up to the mezzanine. He pointed to a door.

"There," he said.

Vasiliev knocked and spoke loudly in Russian,

"Andrei, listen. I come from the meeting at the cemetery. A terrible affair. You must flee. I am here to help you."

There was no sound.

Vasiliev drew his revolver and grasped the watch maker by his shirt. He turned the handle and threw open the door, pulling the watch maker in front of him.

The room was empty.

Dragging the watch maker across the floor, Vasiliev leaned out the window overlooking the garden. He saw Serov half-concealed behind a large oak.

"So, no one has left?" he called out.

"No one. But there was a girl in the garden. She ran away when

An Unveiled Bosnian Girl

she saw me. I think I recognized her. She was a dancer at the Gate of Heaven."

"Who was she?" Vasiliev demanded from the watch maker who had half-collapsed against the wall."

"I don't know."

"Strange. You don't know who takes rooms from you, or who lurks in your garden. Not very observant, not at all curious. You are a liar and a rascal. I have no more patience with you. By the time the police arrive, perhaps you will have recovered your memory."

In another moment the watchmaker might have confessed everything. But Vasiliev released him. With a whimper of relief, he completed his slide to the floor.

"Lead on, Serov, to the Gate of Delight."

It was still too early for the usual denizens to crowd the coffee house and the music had not yet started. But Selim 'the Lame' was at his habitual place and solemnly greeted Vasiliev and Serov.

"By the Prophet, peace be with him, you bear a heavy burden of guilt," he spoke without inflection. "Why did you not foresee what would happen?"

"For the same reason, my friend, that you did not. The meeting was proceeding well. The shooting came from behind, out of sight, an ambush. It could not have been planned by either side. We do not know who was responsible.But we have not given up the chase. The killer of Grigorev was not there. We will find and punish him."

"Yes, I know," Selim said in the same tone of voice, rapping the table with his knuckles

"What do you know?"

A waiter brought three cups of coffee.

Selim sipped his, though the liquid was boiling hot.

"I know the names of the men who died on our side, and some on the other side. But the Russian had no scar."

"You had a Cadmus man at the hospital?"

"He saw your Sergeant but said nothing."

The coffee house was beginning to fill up and the voices of the singers behind the curtain rose up in a mournful Turkish lament. Vasiliev guessed that this was in memory of the fallen. Would the girl appear at such a solemn moment?

"Do you know the dancer, Selim? She may be able to lead us to Andrei, the killer."

"She has been questioned. Unfortunately she did not survive. Our friends were angry and impatient. We will dispose of her body."

Vasiliev suppressed a curse. Serov blew hard at the steam rising from his coffee.

Selim continued, anticipating Vasliev's next question. "We only found out she was this Andrei's mistress after the shooting."

Vasiliev knew better than to ask how this information was obtained. There were more important things to find out.

The music stopped. The boys did not appear. Only muffled voices could be heard.

"What has been learned, then?"

"The Russian had promised to take her with him when the time came for him to leave. He had given her rich presents, gold earrings. After he heard about the shooting, he told her he had to go at once. He told her where to meet him. She was reluctant to reveal the place. Extreme measures were necessary to loosen her tongue. What was last heard from her lips sounded like *Crna gora*."

"So back to Montenegro."

Vasiliev swallowed his coffee.

"Nothing else? What about the renegades. Any left?"

"She had nothing to say about them. But we know there were a few who did not go to the meeting. Perhaps they left with the Russian." Selim paused for a moment and then exclaimed:

"This man must have powerful protectors."

"I fear you are right. But we will bring him to justice, I promise you."

"God willing that you should not fail."

Chapter
Forty-Five

On the Way to Sarajevo

By the light of the moon, a lone shepherd saw four horsemen ride out of the cemetery, heading south. When the shooting had begun an hour or two before, he had stopped searching for the stray lamb and was making his way back to his hut, fearful that one of the horsemen had snatched it up in the dark. As for the shooting, it was none of his business. He thought the war was over. But then again, the wars never seemed to have a beginning or end.

Riding with her family again, Tamara felt her head was bursting with warring feelings. She had her revenge, but she agonized over the cost. She had betrayed the trust of the Russians, Vasiliev and Serov. She had sacrificed the good Dmitry Vasilevich and his gallant followers. And although she saw the man fall who had murdered her beloved Borya, she was torn with doubts that he was truly dead. Her brothers had both sworn that they had taken careful aim at the tall figure and they were crack shots. They had not fired at any other men. But that had been enough to set off the massacre. Hadn't she forseen that would happen? She kept turning in the saddle, peering in the darkness to discern the features of her father. He had not fired a shot and not said a word to her. Just a quick, reassuring pressure on her shoulder as he would reassure one of his sons. It was clear to her from the way he sat in the saddle that he was hurting.

She had felt a momentary impulse to examine the body of the tall man in the Russian cloak, but when she saw the figure of Vasiliev emerge from the darkness, she fell back. She could not sacrifice him as well. As she hesitated, her brother Hassan whispered. "We must go now. The police will surely come to investigate. We must put a distance between them and us." Then his voice broke. "Our dear father was badly injured when he escaped from the Austrians. We fear for his life. He had concealed his wounds from you, but now he is losing strength. We must get him to a safe place."

Hadji Murad groaned heavily as he dismounted for the evening prayers. His saddle was covered with blood. Hassan proposed they rest for the evening. By the rays of the dying sun, his face had taken on a sorrowful look that Tamara had never seen before.

"My children," the wounded man forced himself to speak firmly although the pain was almost unendurable. "I will soon be in paradise, God who alone is great willing. But my last wish to you is also a command. I wish my eyes would fall before my death on the great mosque of Gazi Husrev-beg in the holy city of Sarajevo and that my remains shall repose in the cemetery of Alifakovac. It is known that the mosque, one of the greatest in Islam has rightly been called the Pilgrim mosque...." His voice failed him for a moment and he coughed up blood which he attempted to staunch with his neck cloth. Tamara pressed a fresh cloth into his hand, tears running down her cheeks. Hadji Murad gasped and continued to speak in a horse voice. "....the Pilgrim mosque for it is known that it is from here that the seekers begin their journey to worship at the tomb of the prophet, may all honor be his."

The brothers glanced at one another in despair. Sarajevo was a good three days' ride over heavily wooded high ground. How could their father survive that long? But they joined hands with Tamara and swore that they would bring him to the great mosque.

At the end of he next day, Hadji Murad could no longer sit in the saddle. His three children took turns tying him behind them, changing the tired horses as they moved slowly toward Sarajevo. When they dismounted for the evening rest and prayers, holding him in their arms, they too were covered in blood. He no longer spoke.

Tamara was passing through the greatest anguish of her life. Even the death of Grigoriev had not driven her to these depths of despair. What had she accomplished by her passion for revenge? Betrayal of her savior Vasiliev and the agonizing death of her father.

On the morning of the fourth day, they entered the valley of Sarajevo surrounded by the Dinaric Alps. As they descended a steep path the clouds broke and a ray of sunshine struck the minaret of the Gazi mosque. Hadji Murad who had lost consciousness on the third day suddenly opened his eyes, a beatific smile on his lips. He tried to raise his arm to point but could only gasp, "I have seen paradise" and expired.

Andrei Gregorevich felt for the first time in years that he was not in control of events that determined his life. True, he thought, he had been suspicious of the meeting with the *bunjevici* and sent Tvardov in his place. It was always necessary to take precautions in dealing with unknown men. But what he had learned from the one survivor among his Hungarians puzzled him.

"The shooting came from behind the *bunjevici*." Tears ran down the cheeks of the young Hungarian as blurted out his description of the massacre. "The shooting came from behind the *bunjevici*," he kept repeating. "Our men just fired back wildly. It was every man for himself. I think I was the only one of ours to make it out alive. But I can't be sure. All of ours were down but perhaps some were only wounded." He gasped. "It was horrible." He was trembling but had nothing else to say.

Andrei Gregorevich dismissed him with a warning and ordered him to leave immediately for the north. He was tempted for an instant to kill the man. But why leave another body for the Austrian police to trace? As for the watch maker, all he could divulge was that he had rented a room to a tall man who spoke Serbian with a Russian accent. Was that enough to satisfy the police? It was not the same with the girl, Anna. He had gone too long without a woman, and she was ripe for picking. She had matched the passion of his lovemaking as if she too had been denied its pleasure for too long. He was sure he had bought her loyalty, at least long enough until he could extricate himself from this cursed region. She had tried to persuade him to stay with her.It was tempting but too dangerous. He hesitated to kill her, to shut forever those dark green eyes.

Before he took any further decisions which he knew from experience should wait until he had a full understanding of the lay

Selim 'the Lame'

of the land. He would exploit his last contact in Travnik, a young clerk in the Russian consular office who had served in the past as a channel of information with the deputy minister of foreign affairs in St. Petersburg. They met in a small café called Lutva's at the end of the bazaar. In the old days it had been the favorite gathering place of Ottoman notables, but had fallen on hard times. No one would take notice of them. The clerk passed him a bag of coins and related extraordinary news. The Russian consul in Cetinje had arrived on a mission to order the detective from Moscow to end his mission, "whatever that was," said the clerk gulping down his coffee.

"Yes, I know," Andrei Gregovevich lied, keeping up the pretence of having multiple sources of information so that his informants would believe he was omniscient and hardly needed their bits of gossip.

"The only thing I am not certain about is the time of Consul Ionin's departure for Cetinje."

"Oh, that has been set for tomorrow."

Andrei Gregorevich nodded sagely. "Of course, that is what I have heard as well. My dear fellow, it is always good to have confirmation of what others, perhaps not as reliable as you, have told me." He smiled condescendingly. "And have you any other messages for me?'

"None, sir."

Andrei Gregorevich passed a few Austrian kroners across the table. "I have heard the exchange rate for rubles is not good. These may help you get through the week, at least."

The clerk blushed and quickly stuffed the bills in his pocket.

Late that day, Andrei Gregorevich paid a visit to consul Ionin in his hotel room. He identified himself to the porter as a former Russian officer with important news for the consul.

Ionin was startled when Andrei Gregorevich entered the room. His colossal figure was wrapped in an old uniform without insignia. He resembled the man he had been sent to rescue from Vasiliev's ill-considered adventure and was thought to be dead.

Andrei Gregorevich quickly read the expression and saluted Ionin.

"No, Aleksandr Semeonovich, I have not returned from the dead. The information you received is incorrect and you can assure your superiors that you succeeded in your mission."

Ionin stepped back and gasped. With one hand he grasped the edge of the table behind him for support. With the other he reached out as if to stroke the warm comforting form of his beloved Venus, for him an automatic gesture at times of distress. He was overcome by conflicted feelings, torn between his repulsion for the deserter and reputed killer of Grigoriev and the realization that his own reputation as a loyal servant of the crown had been salvaged by some miracle. He could not force himself to congratulate this man or to condemn him. He drew himself up in an effort to appear his most official. Would this contemptible creature ask for his assistance?

"What do you want?" he blurted out.

"My request is modest. You know that I have been acting on the instructions from the foreign ministry and in the interests of our August Master, Emperor Alexander Nikolaevich. But I have been hunted by some detective from Moscow acting on orders from another source. The latest attempt to kill me was carried out last night at the Muslim cemetery here on the outskirts of Travnik. I need your assistance to escape this cursed country."

Ionin suppressed his impulse to dispute with this killer. The Empress was dead and her wishes had become invalid. Vasiliev was now discredited.

"I am returning to Cetinje in two days. If you wish you may accompany me." Ionin felt he was forcing the words out of his mouth.

"Yours is a generous offer. I would prefer to meet you in Sarajevo and then accompany you to Montenegro. First, I have urgent business to take care of. I wish to put an end to my associations here and leave the country and the whole of the Balkans with a clean slate. I only need your assistance in notifying our representatives here and on the way to Sarajevo to provide me with horses and arrange for my arrival there.

"I cannot authorize more violence," Ionin rasped out the word.

"I do not ask for it. Mine is now a private affair. I have no wish to involve you, but I simply wish to be frank as to my intentions."

Ionin realized that this man had powerful patrons. He could disclaim all responsibility for what he might do, but could not refuse to help him out of the country. With a heavy heart he nodded and then agreed.

"Your understanding will be given proper recognition." Andrei Gregorevich's smile was twisted into a rictus by the deep scar on his cheek.

As Andrei Gregorevich rode out of Travnik, he kept reflecting on his mistakes. If only he had not been forced to meet his Hungarian mercenaries in Travnik to pay them off. They insisted they felt safe here. What a colossal error! Now he had to make his way back to Montenegro and then leave the country. At least, he had been assured of official protection most of the way. Well, he had earned it. He wondered whether it was necessary to take more precautions. That would require him to change his plan. He never liked to do this. He thought again about what the young Hungarian has said. The firing began from behind and Tvardov was the first to fall. Was he the real target? At a distance, he and Tvardov could be mistaken for one another. Who would have been the shooters? There must have been more than one. Certainly, not Vasiliev. This was not his style. Nor could it have been the Austrians. Just a group of bandits? Highly unlikely. They would only have attacked for money. Suddenly, it occurred to him that the shooters were friends of Grigoriev. And who would that be? Of course, how stupid! He cursed himself. The Circassian girl and who else? The same men who had beheaded his agents outside Ragusa. More Circassians, probably still alive. Once they learned that they had not succeded in killing him, wouldn't they resume the hunt? But perhaps they did not know that they had failed. He had an advantage then. Yes, he would have to track them down before they learned the truth. Now he regretted he had sent the young Hungarian away. He was alone and could not tell how many he would have to fight. But he consoled himself that he had the element of surprise on his side. He had little choice and decided he would have to eliminate them before he reached Montenegro. He knew that he was a small fish in a large ocean where many unpredictable currents swirled in different directions. He could not trust that his patrons in distant Petersburg would protect him under all circumstances, despite his bold words to Ionin.

The shepherd was startled when two new riders accosted him outside of his sheep pen. It was early morning so he had been up for some hours. With the sun behind him, he could make out that these men were in uniform, but of a kind he had not seen before. His first thought was, why the sudden interest in him? For years he had not encountered a soul. Now his land was turning into a highway.

First, there had been the four, but they were too far away to recognize. Still, one rode badly as if he had been injured. Then a day later the lone rider, a big fellow well mounted looked like a military type. Spoke Serbian well but with an accent. He asked which directions the riders had gone. He did not seem to know how many of them there were. The shepherd had not told him, but pointed southwest. The man seemed in a hurry and threw down a few coins.

Now two more, in full uniform, but not Austrians. One of them raised his hand in greeting and in bad Serbian asked whether any riders had passed. The shepherd chewed on his lip. Why should he give any more information? He did not wish to become involved in something that might become dangerous for him. He shrugged and called to his dog

"Well now," he spat to the side, "my seein'ain't what it was. So I can't rightly say."

"You've got a good flock," Vasiliev said. "But too large maybe for one man."

"I've got Mordva here," he pointed to a large sheep dog who took up a position the gate of the pen."

"How much does a dog like that cost?"

"Me sell her? Rather a death sentence."

"No. I was thinking of helping you to buy a second one to ease your labors."

The shepherd stroked the stubble on his chin. Was this a trade being offered. "Say a hundred drachmas."

"All right. How about your telling me about the riders and I give you a hundred drachmas."

Vasiliev motioned to Serov who dismounted and took out a purse, carefully counting out the coins and offering them to the man.

The shepherd felt a tingling in his hands. Another Mordva! But what if he told them what he had seen and then they shot him down and took back the money? He decided to take the risk.

"Well there was a lot of comin' and goin' mainly goin' to be sure. First four of 'em there were. They was too far off for me to see 'em clear like. Just the four," he said, "comin' from Travnik direction. Then next day, a lone feller comes riding up and asks about any riders. He didn't know how many. I didn't tell him. But I pointed him southwest. Big fellow he was. Spoke a bit like you. Not from around here, then." The shepherd gave whistle and his dog trotted over to stand next to him.

"Thank you, my friend. You have helped track a criminal."

Vasiliev turned his horse and he and Serov headed south.

The shepherd counted the coins again. "Well Mordva," he addressed his dog. "how would you like a brother?" Mordva barked loudly.

Chapter
Forty-Six

Outside Sarajevo

Vasiliev realized that it would not be a simple matter to track the riders moving southwest across the mountains. He could only guess that the first four were headed for Sarajevo and the lone pursuer, most probably Andrei Gregorevich, in close pursuit. But there was too much he did not know to have much confidence in his guessing. There were several trails none well marked and the ground was stony leaving few traces of horsemen to follow. Perhaps the best course would be to choose what looked like the most direct and widest path, assuming that none of the first group and their tracker knew that he and Serov were coming up behind them. But it would be wise to take precautions in order to avoid being ambushed. Andrei Gregorevich was obviously a clever fellow and probably an experienced veteran of many fire fights. He would always be on guard.

Serov had gathered several large canteens of water which they hung around their necks, dried beef jerky flattened out on their saddles and loaves of black bread stuffed in their saddle bags. They carried bags of grain slung over their backs as fodder for the horses. Vasiliev was confident that Serov's purchases would last them for several days in the desolate countryside until they reached the great forests on the approaches to Sarajevo.

Andrei Gregorevich was thinking along the same lines as moved cautiously along the main trail. He made no fire and was well supplied with water and food. Soon after the ground began to rise, he spotted dark stains on the rocky terrain. He dismounted to take a closer look. "Blood," he muttered under his breath. So, one of them was wounded. Good that will slow them down, he thought. When he reached the next sharp incline he noticed a pool of blood and a trail of stains leading to the edge of a ravine. He led his horse to the edge and peered over. Far below a saddle was wedged between two boulders, half hidden by the brush around them. What did that mean? The wounded man could no longer ride. Possible he was dying. It was careless of the others to dispose of the saddle in this manner. He stood staring into the ravine for several minutes. Then he dislodged some stones and began to throw them into the ravine covering the saddle until it was no longer visible. Just a precaution, he thought. Then he dug into a mound of dirt and scattered the earth over the pool of blood and the stains leading to the ravine. When he was satisfied that these signs were no longer visible, he mounted again and rode on, carefully examining the ground. Whenever he saw a stain, he stopped and covered it up. The traces became fainter and fainter. Soon nothing more was to be seen. He kept riding until nightfall.

Serov was the first to detect the faint traces of an attempt to cover up the blood stains on the trail. But neither he or Vasiliev noticed the buried saddle. Vasiliev debated with himself over whether they should try to overtake Andrei Gregorevich, if indeed it was he, before he reached Sarajevo where it might be more difficult to discover his whereabouts. There was a risk of pressing ahead. It might, on the other hand, expose them to an ambush if he suspected that he was being trailed. Vasiliev concluded there were too many unknowns about the riders to pursue them, but he was not happy with his own decision. He did not consult Serov. When the trail divided and divided again, Vasiliev was reassured he had been right.

They reached the outskirts of Sarajevo two days later. Emerging from the heavily forested northern environs of the town, they crossed the Latin bridge spanning the river Miljacka, heading for the bazaar in the Old Town. Vasiliev was wearing the Cadmus ring. He remembered that Dmitry Alekseevich had mentioned there was a strong group of *bunjevici* in Sarajevo. They would be his strongest allies in tracking down the killers of Dmitry Alekseevich. He hoped that the ring would identify him. But what were the chances he would run across one of them in this large town? He was relying, perhaps too heavily, he reflected, on his proverbial luck. The bazaar in the Old Town might be as the most likely place to make contact with one of them.

Andrei Gregorevich was an expert tracker. And he knew Sarajevo from the early days of the Serbian uprising. As soon as he saw the summit of Mount Trebevic to the south, he spurred his mount. He hoped to arrive at the Latin Bridge before the four horsemen showed up with one of them badly wounded or dead and slung over the back of his horse. He didn't have long to wait. When they appeared, he was astounded. The Circassians! He was right in his suspicions. The woman, beautiful as ever with two look-alike mountaineers and the body of an older man strapped to the back of one of the men in an obvious attempt to disguise the fact that he was dead or dying. If they had ridden this far, carrying a dead man, they could only be headed in one direction, the Muslim cemetery of Alifakovac. The only question for him now was what preparations would he need to make to attack them there, while they were mourning and presumably most vulnerable? He would have preferred to keep them under observation until he could round up some renegades living in the outskirts to assure success. If he acted alone, he would have to be certain of killing them all. This meant three rapid shots from his Martini-Henry rifle. If he missed one of them, he would be exposed to accurate counter fire. Mountaineers did not disarm even for a funeral. He also had to worry about attracting Vasiliev's attention. He had to decide quickly.

The following morning Tamara and he two brothers stood at the edge of the gravesite reciting verses from the Koran. They had persuaded the imam that their father was a martyr and did not need to be washed before his body was wrapped in a shroud and placed in a plain wooden coffin. They had been fortunate that there was an open grave freshly dug. It would be necessary to commission two white stone stella with Arabic inscriptions to place at the gravesite. But there was time for that. They had loosened the knots of the shroud and gently lowered the coffin, making certain that the body lay on its right side and murmuring, "With the Name of Allah and according to the Sunnah of the Messenger of Allah."

Higher on the slope of the cemetery a large procession was silently accompanying the coffin of a pilgrim. A tall, bearded man was shuffling at the end of the procession, his regular gait hampered by the Martini-Henry rifle held barrel down along his right flank and hidden under his ample pantaloons. Near the center of the cemetery, he left the procession and concealed himself behind the tomb of Commander Jusuf Pasha Ćuprilić. From his position, he had a good view of the three Circassians. He estimated the range at 200 meters. He crouched, peering down at the vast field of headstones, keeing his eyes fixed on them, glancing from time to time at the procession as it wound its way toward them. He could not wait much longer before the foremost mourners passed in front of his targets and blocked a shot. He calculated the timing of his fire. The Martini Henry was a single shot weapon that required rapid re-loading in order to get off the three shots necessary to bring down his enemies before they could react.

The traffic on the Latin Bridge had come to a standstill, held up by a convoy of camels carrying bales of cotton. Vasiliev looked up into the cloudless blue sky and listened to the mullah calling for midday prayers. "Another cause for delay," he muttered. Serov later recalled how he had been staring over the river, his eyes caught by the bright reflection of the midday sun on the distant field of white tombstones when he heard the three gunshots coming from the land of the dead.

The camels stirred uneasily and a ripple of fear passed through the crowd. Vasiliev started, exclaiming, "Good God." He knew instinctively, no guessing this time, what three shots meant. "Quick, Sergeant. The cemetery before it's too late." But instinct too told him that it was already too late. In the far distance a wail of lamentations carried across the river.

Andrei Gregorevich was certain that his first two shots to the head had gone home with deadly accuracy. The two Circassian men topple over. He levered in the third shot but the rifle jammed briefly from his violent forcing of the bullet into the firing chamber. A matter of a few seconds. When he fired again he saw the girl fall into the grave but he was not certain that he had killed her. She had been a moving target, bending over to toss a handful of dirt onto the coffin. He heard a scream behind him, even as pandemonium broke loose in the procession of mouners. He whirled to see an old woman, who had come up silently to pay homage to the tomb of the Commander. He struck her with the butt end of his rifle and then tossed it down the hill side away from the milling crowd below. He did not want to be seen with a weapon in his hands. He needed to get out of sight as quickly as possible. He plunged into the screaming and frantic mass of people, shouting as loudly as possible. They scrambled down the steep path past the Gazi Husrev-beg mosque, dozens falling as they slipped or were pushed over the irregular paving stones. No one tried to seize hold of him or block his passage out of the cemetery. In headlong flight, the crowd rushed the Latin Bridge, colliding with the heavy traffic and leading to more injuries. A few bodies fell into the river. For all his strength, Andrei Gregorevich barely managed to stay on his feet. He forced a passage through the crowd. He did not hesitate to tramble the bodies of the fallen mourners. No one gave him a second glance: he appeared to be just another terrified survivor of a mass killing.

Vasiliev and Serov struggled against the crowd pouring out of the cemetery. Vasiliev seized the collar of a young man, shouting into his ear:

"Where did it happen? Who was shot?"

The youth struggled to free himself, his eyes wild with fear. "Let go! I don't know…over there in that direction…now let me go."

Vasiliev caught sight of the imam kneeling by a grave site, raising his hands to heaven and crying out "God who alone is great, be merciful and spare your devoted servants."

With Serov close behind him, Vasiliev stumbled upon the bodies of the brothers. He saw immediately that both has been shot in the head. He gasped with horror when he peered over the edge of the grave sight. Tamara's body was sprawled on the coffin of her father.

"Cover me, Serov!" he shouted as he slid down into the grave. Serov drew his pistol, pivoted on his heel, rapidly searching the backs of the fleeing figures for a glimpse of an unusually tall figure, but saw no one matching that description.

He heard Vasiliev cry out, "she's still alive."

Blood was coming from a wound on the side of Tamara's head but her eyes fluttered as he called her name. Vasiliev tore off a strip from the edge of her cotton skirt and pressed her temple to staunch the flow of blood.

"Is the imam still there, Serov?"

"Yes. But no sign of the shooter."

"Bring him to the edge of the grave."

The imam was trembling but did not resist Serovs rough handling of him.

"Listen, oh holy one, you must call a physician. We can save her life. Be quick."

"Go with him, Sergeant and drag the doctor back if necessary."

Chapter Forty-Seven

Sarajevo

"Major Vasiliev?" The doctor approaching him in the Austrian Field Hospital was a stocky, energetic man with large blue eyes and a thin moutstache. He was peeling off his surgical gloves, and removing his white surgical cap. His white smock was stained with blood.

Vasiliev had seen many terrible sights of wounded and dying men, but the thought that this was Tamara's blood sent a shock through his entire body. Only the death of his good friend in the trenches of Plevna had affected him so strongly.

"Yes, doctor," his voice breaking.

The surgeon shot him a quizzical glance.

"She is still not out of danger. If the bullet had passed a millimeter or so closer to the brain and she would have died instantly. If she recovers I do not foresee any permanent damage. But her face was badly bruised from falling into the grave pit, and her nose was broken. She lost a few front teeth. I fear she will never be so beautiful again." The doctor spoke in German but with a strong accent. Another Hungarian?

"I am grateful for your quick response for an operation and your skill in saving her life."

"Yes, well, it was unusual. You will have to wait a day or two before you can speak to her. I have another operation now. Good luck," his last words spoken in clipped English.

Vasiliev turned to Serov.

"Listen, my friend, you know I dislike splitting up. But I need you to stay here and make certain that there is no further attempt on Tamara's life. You must intercept any stranger who attempts to enter the ward. I will notify the doctor that I have placed you on guard. If we are to find Andrei Gregorevich in this town, we will have to have help. I am going to try to make contact with the *bunjevici*. Our only chance is to display the ring in the most popular places in the bazaar. It's a long shot. I can't think of anything else to do.

"Ionin has ordered me off the case. The Vienna authorities will have good reason to track down Andrei Gregorevich and arrest him if he was responsible for the murder of the Circassians. But here too, things are not conclusive. As far as we know Tamara and her family were Ottoman citizens, though the crime was committed in Bosnia under Habsburg occupation. The Austrians will want to know what I can tell them about those responsible for the killing of Dmitry Alekseevich. I don't even know who fired the fatal shot that killed him. Did it come from the side of Tamara and her brothers or from the Hungarian renegades? There is no way of finding out."

Serov listened in silence. He knew that Vasiliev had yet to touch on the question that must be bothering him the most. But, he made it a rule to wait until Vasiliev was ready to speak out on a matter close to his heart. It would come without his probing or pressing for answers on sensitive matters.

He placed his hand on Serov's shoulder.

"Don't let anyone get to her," he said.

"On my honor, Vasili Vasilich."

As Vasiliev left the hospital, his mind was in turmoil. A dozen different images flashed through his head. There were many things he regretted now. It was one of the few times in his life that he felt unable to decide on a clear-cut course of action. And had it really been Andrei Gregorevich who was the assassin, or some one else, an enemy of the Circassians unkown to him? Most important, it now seemed, was Tamara's fate. She bore some responsibility for the massacre in Travnik. Could he ignore that? She herself had admitted she had betrayed him. But now her entire family had been wiped out. Surely that was sufficient punishment for her. Did he need to pursue Andrei Gregorevich in the name of some abstract principle of justice when he was no longer a man hunted by official Russia?

As he was about to step into the street, a voice interrupted his confused thoughts, addressing him in the same way as the doctor and with the same accent

"Major Vasiliev?"

At the same time stretcher bearers carrying two injured victims of the stampede at the cemetery called out to clear the way. Behind them a nurse was guiding an old woman whose head was bandaged and and who kept whimpering," I saw him, I saw him!"

Vasiliev caught sight of a uniformed man coming up behind her. He raised his hand in response, and shouted "Wait!" turning to catch up with the old woman.

"Who did you see?" he demanded in Serbian. The nurse started to protest, but Vasiliev took hold of the old woman's arm gently but firmly,

"Who did you see, mother?"

She looked at him wildly. "The devil," she cried.

"Yes, the devil and what did he look like?"

"Major Vasiliev!" he heard the nurse's voice now more urgently.

"A monster. A terrible one. Huge…a great beard and scar straight from Hell. He had a gun."

"Please officer, she has been injured, we must get her…"

Vasiliev had turned away and did not hear the rest. It was enough. The shooter had been Andrei Gregorevich.

"Major Vasiliev!" the accent was stronger as the officer came up to him.

"I must speak to you. I am Tóth, Peter Captain of His Imperial Majesty's Army of Occupation." He was clearly flustered and blurted out his name in Hungarian fashion.

Vasiliev apologized, explaining that the old woman was a witness to the killings in the cemetery.

"Then I must speak to her was well. Do you know her name?"

"No, but I can tell you what she said. Let's find a quieter place to talk and you can tell me how and why you found me."

They emerged from the hospital into a large overgrown garden where they finally found one wooden bench with all its slats intact. Who had time to maintain a garden during the war? Vasiliev ruminated.

"Yes, Captain, I am at your disposal."

"I am sorry to have accosted you in that fashion. But I have been assigned an urgent mission by Baron Kállay, His Majesty's delegated administrative head of the Civil Adminstration of Bosnia and Hercegovina. The appointment is pending but assured. Baron Kállay has given instruction to make contact with you unofficially but urgently as a person of importance to the future of the province."

Vasiliev was astounded by this decription of his status. But he merely nodded.

"I was selected to find you because of my knowledge of the province, its languages and the recommendation of Baron Haymerle and Selim Bey."

"Ah, my old friend, Selim Bey. I am intrigued by your government's association with him."

"Baron Kállay has a vision for Bosnia and Hercegovina."

"Surely you mean an Austrian mission?" Vasiliev made an effort to avoid sounding sarcastic.

"Well, certainly a mission, but perhaps better called a Habsburg mission, since most of the creative thinking belongs in this case to us Hungarians."

"I have heard this before," said Vasiliev, "and I do not doubt that this is the case. But to answer my question...."

"Of course. To continue my thought... a vision to create a genuine unity among the Bosnians, both Christians and Muslims. And the Baron envisages turning the province into a model of modern life. You see, he even has plans to build a tramway system in Sarajevo, the first in Europe."

"That should surely win over the waring elements," Vasiliev said, unable restrain himself. But Tóth seemed impervious to sarcasm.

"This should all be accomplished with the benevolent endorsement of your enlightened emperor, Alexander II. The Baron has been deeply disturbed by the activities of two irreconcilable groups, the Pan Slavs and the Hungarian renegades."

Vasiliev wondered where this was going. His mind kept returning to the image of Tamara as she was wheeled into the operating room. A battered and deathly pale face was barely visible under the heavy bandages where the blood stain seemed to spread with every moment. He shook himself out of this daytime nightmare and struggled to make sense of Tóth's ornate speech.

"....so it seems that they are, what? And then there is the case of the murdered Russian, also a Pan Slav. I have spoken to Consul Ionin and he tells me that you have been tracking this man. What is his name? Andrei Gregorevich? But now you have been ordered to cease and desist. And what about these Circassians who have been murdered? I must say I cannot make head or tail out of it. So, I am asking for your help as the man best informed, though also, it appears you are also personally involved. My instructions were to locate and eliminate those elements threatening the stability of our rule over the provinces, whoever they may be. As you know we already had to put down a rebellion with some loss of life. Is there another uprising brewing?"

Vasiliev sighed heavily. How could he explain to this man what was happening in Bosnia? He did not even know what he would end up reporting to General Totleben. Yes, he was personally involved. He had to admit that this was a large part of the problem now.

He started to say,'Captain, the situation is very complex,' but immediately realized this banal remark was just that, banal. Tóth was staring at him. How much time had passed before he he could find the right words to satisfy the man without compromising Tamara. Was this even possible? 'All right,' he resolved, 'sketch the outlines of the broader picture and omit the the details or bury them by weaving a web of circumlocutions.'

"As I see it," he began, "the situation is very complex." He bit his tongue. "Surely, your own intelligence people are better informed than I could ever be about the rapidly changing allegiances of different groups in the population, Croats, Serbs, Albanians, Bosniaks. As I understand it from my conversations with Consul Ionin even the foreign governments, yours and mine in particular, have been shifting their positions. But I can tell you this much. It might help you pursue your inquiries. A certain Pan Slav militant named Boris Andreevich Grigoriev was murdered by a former officer in the Russian army acting on orders from one or more highly placed individuals in St. Petersburg. I do not know precisely why, perhaps in order to reduce the possibility of his organizing another uprising against your occupation. He was a popular figure in the struggle for Serbian independence. I was instructed to find his killer, arrest him if possible, eliminate him if not."

He now had Tóth's full attention. For a moment, though, he was distracted by the sight of a large plum tree bent under the weight of overripe fruit, visible beyond the shoulder of the Hungarian officer. An irrelevant thought crossed his mind. Who had time to pick plums in the garden of a military hospital? He shook himself irritably.

"I discovered that the killer had recruited a group of mercenary accomplices from disaffected Hungarian soldiers."

"You are certain they were Hungarian." It was more of a statement than a question.

"Yes, but they disguised themselves as Albanians, just to make things more...complex"

"All right, I will take your word for it."

"I believe these renegades also threaten to disrupt the stability you seek in the province. More complications. Are you aware of the existence of another group from your country, opposing them? They call themselves called *bunjevici* and declare their loyalty to your monarch, Emperor Franz Joseph."

"But they are Serbs!"

"True, but also Catholic and they served your Emperor in1848, when I must remind you, many of your Hungarian compatriots of the earlier generation rose in rebellion under Louis Kossuth," Vasiliev took some pleasure in noting a slight twitch in Tóth's face.

"Selim Bey, who is also a friend of your country is also eager for stability if you can guarantee toleration for the Muslim population..."

"Of course, of course," Tóth broke in, "that is part of Baron Kállay's vision, tolerance for all faiths..."

"...along with tram cars," Vasiliev added with a straight face.

Tóth shifted his weight on the bench. "Yes," he muttered.

"The *bunjevici* helped me track down the killer, and I devised a plan to arrest him and turn him over to the Austrian police in Travnik. He was guilty of other killings in Bosnia after you had occupied it. Hence his crimes fell under your juristiction."

"But Consul Ionin insisted that you had been called off the case."

"Exactly why I sought to hand the man over to your authorities. He was a killer, after all."

"Yes of course."

"The plan went awry when the negotiations between the *bunjevici* and the renegades was broken up by a group of Circassions who had their own scores to settle. The killer escaped and tracked the Circasians to Sarajevo. You know the result. Now he has committed fresh crimes which will be interpreted by the Muslim community as directed against them as a group. There is a danger they will blame your people for failing to stop him. This will cast a shadow on Baron Kállay's vision, or mission." Vasiliev made sure that he uttered his words in the most solemn tones.

"But can we be certain the man who fired the shots in the cemetery here in Sarajevo is the same person who killed your Grigoriev?"

"Excuse me, Captain, he is not *my* Grigoriev, although he was Russian. Yes, just before you called my name at the hospital entrance, and I seemed to ignore it, an old woman accosted me. She claimed to be an eye witness of the shooting. She was convincing. She described the killer who had a numer of distinctive features, tall, burly, bearded, a livid scar on his cheek. You may wish to question her, if you doubt me."

Tóth shook his head vigorously. Then he asked the question Vasiliev had been dreading.

"What do you intend to do now?" Always the same question.

Chapter
Forty-Eight

Sarajevo

When Vasilev crossed back over the Latin Bridge, the camel caravan had long since passed. The crowd had thinned; the injured and the few dead had been carried away. But he detected a current of fear in the hushed voices swirling around him. In the bazaar, there was much milling about. Many shopkeepers, doubtless fearing the outbreak of looting, closed the shutters on their shops, or covered the produce on their stalls with heavy canvas and stood guard clutching wooden staves.

Vasiliev gradually made his way down the quieter side aisles. As he hoped, men turned to look at him because of his uniform. Perhaps their eyes would be drawn to the ring. He entered a number of cafes and looked about as if searching for a familiar face. After he left, he paused in the alley as if uncertain as to his next destination, hoping his ring had been seen and a contact made with one of the Cadmus organization. For an hour he wandered about finally choosing to sit down at one of the outside tables of *aščinica* on a corner where he could be seen by the steady stream of passers-by.

He did not feel hungry even though he had eaten nothing for twenty-four hours. But he began to feel light-headed. He ordered a vegetable *burek*. It might have been the only positive thing that came out of the conversation with Tóth. The captain had recommended it as the favorite food of the region, a pita stuffed with meat or vegetables. Perhaps this was the officer's way of demonstrating his local knowledge.

The young waiter suggested an *ayran* to go along with the *burek*. Vasiliev shrugged. The waiter explained it was a yoghurt drink. When he returned to the kitchen, he whispered to the cook.

"Russians! You think they have come to liberate us?"

She scoffed as she wound the dough in spirals around the cooking pan. "You, Branko, are a dreamer."

Vasiliev unfolded his napkin displaying the ring From time to time, he glanced around to see who had come into the *aščinica*. It had become a habit with him. Judging by the dress of the customers, they were locals. Nothing unusual caught his eye. The waiter hurriedly served him, distracted by a party of Muslim businessmen who entered the café. When Vasiliev had finished his meal, he pushed away his plate, and nervously twisted the ring. At that moment, the waiter reappeared to inquire about serving a sweet or fruit. He stopped dead and then whirled, hurrying back to the kitchen.

"So," he whispered to the cook in an excited voice. "A dreamer, am I! The officer wears the ring."

She stared hard at him. "Then you had best call Achmed Bey. You are acting like a child."

"First a dreamer and now a child," the waiter sneered. He left her with his head held high. He found the owner seated in his office wreathed in the aromatic odor of Turkish tobacco from the cigarettes that he smoked incessantly. A pot of Turkish coffee on a brass tray had just been brought to him. He was pouring the thick liquid into a porcelain cup when the waiter burst in.

"A Russian officer, *effendi*, he wears the ring and ordered *burek*," he gasped, failing to control his excitement, just as cook predicted.

Achmed Bey, born Nikola Vukich, had converted to Islam and changed his name when he feared that his life was in danger. He cursed the boy under his breath. How much did the officer know? Too risky to deny his membership, though he had turn away from the cause. He took a sheet of paper from a pile on his desk, scribbled a few words, and handed it to the young man. "Deliver this discreetly, say, under a plate of *baklava*, compliments of the house."

Vasiliev smiled as he read the words, "As a collector of rare jewelry, I see we share an interest."

****

Andrei Gregorevich had broken free of the crowd as they rushed pell-mell across the Latin Bridge into the old town. He made his way along the back streets to the Russian consulate. Ionin had not yet heard news of the shooting. Andrei Gregorevich was able to provide him with a concocted version of the incident at the gravesite. He explained that the mourners from two hostile Muslim sects had encountered one another on the grounds of the cemetery of Alifakovac.

"Some doctrinal squabble must have touched off an argument which led to violence. You know how these things happen, even in Russia."

Ionin was more worried about the disorders spreading and preventing their leaving for Cetinje.

"I will order the coach now and we will leave shortly."

"Splendid! I was able to take care of my business in the most satisfying way." Andrei Gregorevich held back as Ionin went to the stables. He accosted a secretary and handed him a note in a sealed envelope.

Achmed Bey

"The consul forgot to have this delivered by hand. He mentioned that it was quite important."

The secretary clicked his heels and slipped the message into the inner pocket of his tunic. The address surprised him, but there were more important matters to occupy his thoughts. The town was in an uproar.

At the hospital, Serov settled himself on a wooden bench outside the entrance to the ward. He studied the stretcher bearers who brought in more injured. The first time the doctor passed, he nodded but then ignored him. One of the nurses kept glancing at Serov. Finally, when the noise and excitement in the corridor diminished, she came up to him and asked him in perfect Russian whether she could bring him some tea.

He studied her face which reminded him of a girl in his village. She had to suppress a laugh when he imitated what he thought was the proper response of a Russian gentleman. "With the greatest pleasure, my pretty maid."

The tea was strong, prepared with aromatic leaves unfamiliar to him. He was tempted to ask her about her native province, but she was called away by the doctor. Strengthened by the tea, Serov assumed the position which had earned him in his youthful days in the village the sobriquet of *stolb*, the immovable pillar. In games with his comrades, he would defy efforts to find him by remaining immobile in hiding until they gave up, crying out, "you win *stolb*. Come out!"

Although now he was in plain sight, his rigid stance gave him the appearance of being almost invisible, especially as darkness crept over the garden outside the corridor windows. The ward grew quieter. Only an occasional moan could be heard coming from some poor wretch.

A male voice, thought Serov. Not Tamara, though he could imagine her in great pain. Still, he did not move a muscle. The Russian nurse entered the ward from time to time. When she left, the moaning stopped. She hardly took any notice of him.

It was very late when she made her last round. She had only taken a few steps down the corridor when two stretcher bearers came into sight, bearing a half-covered body. They moved quietly, almost stealthily. No one from the staff was with them. The nurse stopped in her tracks as they approached her.

"Not here," she spoke sharply. They brushed past her and she cried out. "The ward is full; you are not staff!"

The *stolb* came alive and moved quickly to the door of the ward. The nurse saw him and raised her arm in protest,

"Sergeant, these men do not belong here," she gasped. The two men maneuvered the stretcher like a ram to push her roughly aside.

Serov blocked their way.

"Careful, friends, you heard the nurse."

The men dropped the stretcher and a corpse rolled onto the floor.

The first man lunged at Serov, a mistake, while the other seized the nurse and clapped his hand over her mouth to stifle a scream. Serov was known not only as *stolb* in the village but as a seasoned street fighter. Now he moved quickly. With two rapid jabs he knocked the first man senseless. The second one released the nurse and whirled to run. Serov caught him from behind and hit him so hard that he bounced against the corridor wall, blood streaming from his mouth and nostrils.

Chapter
Forty-Nine

Sarajevo

Achmed Bey grunted as he unlocked and pulled open the draw in his desk, fumbling for the ring. He was dismayed then terrified when he tried to fit it onto the fourth finger of his left hand. His fingers like the rest of him had grown fat over the years since he had converted to Islam, and he put the ring aside. His frantic efforts failed to jam it back on.

"That stupid boy," he muttered. "I never should have told him those stories. And how in the name of the prophet, may his soul be blest, had that Russian officer discovered that he had been a member of the Cadmus organization. Few knew or remembered the heroic days; yes they were heroic, he recalled, but dangerous. Now he would have to invent some clever lie.

Vasiliev called out, "May I enter?" and without waiting for an answer, pushed aside the bead curtain and stepped into the smoke-filled room. Through the haze he saw a bulky figure, wrapped in a long white robe and a tunic.

"Welcome, friend," said Achmed Bey, twirling the ring in the fingers of his left hand, as if he had just removed it. "You seek help? Please be seated. May I offer you coffee?"

Here is a nervous man, thought Vasiliev

"Many thanks, no. I have enjoyed your splendid cooking and wish the taste to linger."

During the exchange of pleasantries, Vasiliev noted that the man made no effort to slip the ring back on, but continued to twist it in his fat fingers. He decided to avoid giving up much information.

"I come from Travnik where I met with our people. Have you heard from them recently?"

"No, no. Contacts have been infrequent."

"They told me that I could find a strong group of our friends here. What I need is a few good men or women to help me track down a dangerous man who employs renegades to carry out assassinations."

Achmed Bey composed his features into what he hoped would look like a thoughtful pose. He sipped his coffee.

"A dangerous man, you say." This was worse than he feared.

Vasiliev nodded.

Suddenly, a commotion broke out in the café. Loud voices could be heard, shouting, "Achmed Bey! Oh brother help us in the name of the prophet, his blessings be upon us!" Achmed Bey rose to his feet and hurriedly pushed aside the beaded curtain with greater alacrity than Vasiliev expected. He followed the portly figure into the café which was crowded by men carrying or supporting victims of the stampede. A few were bleeding, others were bruised with broken limbs from having fallen and been trampled. Vasiliev found himself being jostled and pushed against the wall. Achmed Bey shouted to him across the press.

"This is not time for idle chatter." He ordered the waiters to clear the floor of chairs and tables, lay down their burdens and bring pitchers of water. "Summon Talat Bey, the physician," he cried out.

The young waiter fought his way clear into the street. Vasiliev was right behind him. There were more people in the street, lamenting and crying for help. The waiter called out, "There is no more room here; seek comfort at The Heron Café."

"But the owner is a Christian. "

"No matter, he is a good man."

Vasiliev struggled to stay on his feet and keep up with the waiter until someone caught him by the arm and in a deep voice said, "You with the ring follow me." Bellowing curses in Bosniak, he forced his way through the crowd, managing to pull Vasiliev with him down a side street. Vasiliev saw the Cadmus ring on his fourth finger.

Still gripping Vasiliev's arm, the man stopped in front of a heavy wooden door. Pushing it open, he turned and said, breathing heavily, "here there are no loud voices or injured men."

They entered a dark room that smelled of incense and other fainter odors that Vasiliev could not identify. It was always this way, he thought, something elusive, suggestive in the sights and smells of interiors. The man released Vasiliev and clapped his hands. A young girl appeared. She bowed low and whispered a few words in response to what Vasiliev assumed was a command.

"Please be seated," said the man in Serbian.

"We will take coffee and then talk."

Within minutes the girl returned with a coffee urn and a plate of dry biscuits.

"Our humble refreshments are less tasty than those of Achmed Bey but the talk is more honest.

"I begin not with a question because we know who you are and what has brought you here from Travnik," said the man as he poured two coffees.

"Sad news travels faster than the good. So it has been with the tragedy in Travnik. There are those who place the blame for the death of our beloved brother Grigoriev on Albanians. But I am not one of them. No need to tell you why that is so. I know you seek the killer, a former Russian office named Andrei Gregorevich. No need to tell you how. So I have information for you. Then you will leave and never mention our meeting. Have I your word?"

"You have my solemn word as an officer and one who shares your purpose."

"This is well-put." The man paused after swallowing his coffee in quick sips, giving Vasiliev a chance to study him. His thick hair was grey and his face deeply lined but his body was that of younger man. Vasiliev could still feel the grip of his strong fingers.

"For many reasons we have placed the foreign consulates in Sarajevo under surveillance. Again, this does not concern you. But today a brother observed the arrival of the Russian consul from Cetinje. The man you seek, we have learned from a servant in the house, now travels with him. It seems they are returning back together to Montenegro."

Vasiliev nodded, having barely touched his coffee which was too hot and too strong.

"This is very valuable information, and I am very grateful to have it," he said.

"Good, then our duty is done. A pity you do not care for our coffee, but this is a weakness we can deal with."

Vasiliev thought he saw a gleam in the man's eye in the semi-darkness.

The man rose and extended his hand. Again a strong grip which Vasiliev returned. The man led him to the threshold and pointed the direction to take to the city center. The massive door closed quietly behind him.

Too many threads to trace, thought Vasiliev. Once again he wondered how he was going to weave them all into his report to Totleben.

He had no further need of Achmed Bey and made his way back to the hospital after several wrong turns. When he arrived he found the place in an uproar. Austrian police were everywhere, and contradictory orders resounded through the corridors. Vasiliev feared the worst. He managed to make himself understood to a uniformed officer who directed him to a room where Serov was being interrogated. He seemed to be calm and holding his own against some very aggressive questioning. Vasiliev introduced himself and requested a few minutes alone with his sergeant. Serov gave him a terse but full account of what happened.

Vasiliev felt a surge of anger. Why had he not been there? Serov told him the assailants had been arrested and carted away by the Austrian police.

"They wanted to haul me off too, but the nurse called me 'the savior'. Still they decided to hold me for questionin'."

Vasiliev knew instantly that the men were thugs hired to finish off Tamara. Andrei Gregorevich was behind it; it was another case of his having powerful patrons. Vasiliev felt sick at heart. Serov saw it in his face but in his way did not ask what they should now do.

"And why were they so aggressive in questioning you?"

"I think it's because I'm a Russian. No other reason. The nurse has backed me up in her story. The Austrians are embarrassed because their security broke down. They're takin' it out on me."

Vasiliev stared at the floor for a long time, thinking of the choice facing him. To stay in Sarajevo and try to protect Tamara from a further attack? But he had to admit that she was after all responsible in part for the killings in the Travnik Cemetery and the death of the noble Dmitry Alekseevich. The *bunjevici* would want to see her brought to trial and the Austrians would agree. A lost cause, then. To pursue Andrei Gregorevich, now under the protection of the Russian consul Ionin? To what end? He had no proof that would stand up in a court of law accused of his crimes. Also a lost cause. He had a duty to prepare his report for General Totleben. But what sense could he make of the floating loyalties, suspicions, hatreds and blood feuds in the region, going back decades if not longer that tore apart communities and families. Another lost cause? He had never felt so helpless.

Chapter Fifty

Sarajevo

Vasiliev had a few words with the captain in charge and Serov was released. The hubbub died down once the two fake stretcher bearers had been hustled off to Austrian police headquarters.

It took Vasiliev some time to find the doctor who had attended Tamara.

"She is very weak," he said. "An infection has set in. I have the feeling she has lost the will to fight it. She has been asking for you, if I understood her right."

He led Vasiliev to her room and persuaded the Austrian guard to let him in for a few minutes with the excuse that she wanted to give him important information. The doctor accompanied him and then stood by the window.

Tamara lay rigidly, her arms tightly pressed against her sides. She was hardly recognizable. Her head and face were heavily bandaged. Her eyes were closed. Vasiliev whispered her name.

She tried to move her lips, but they were too dry to utter more than a soft almost purring sound. Vasiliev bent over to hear. The doctor handed him a wet cloth to moisten her lips.

"Forgive me," were the first word he heard. A pause, a few unintelligible words and then, a whisper: "...my holy task."

A further sound, a few indistinct syllables. Her breathing became shallow and then ceased. The doctor was at her side.

"She's gone."

Vasiliev sat by her for a few minutes. When he got up he felt a strange mixture of pity, anger and something else, what was it?

As soon as Serov saw Vasiliev, he knew Tamara had died. He too felt strangely about this beautiful girl who liked his humor but ended up being an accessory to a massacre. He and Vasiliev never again spoke of her.

Vasiliev visited Austrian police headquarters. He was informed the fake stretcher bearers were Hungarians who turned out to be part of the renegade group from Travnik. They refused to say where they had found the dead body they carried into the hospital or who had sent them. But, as the Captain Tóth told Vasiliev, it was not clear they had committed a crime.

"But we shall hold them until we confirm the identity of the dead man and the cause of his death. So far, it looks as if he died a natural death several days before in the disturbance at the Alifakovac cemetery. He had no personal documents. But his body was claimed by a woman who said she was his wife. The two stretcher bearers claimed they were told a confused story that she wanted the hospital to perform a postmortem on him, which really made no sense. And they could not identify the woman. So a real muddle."

Vasiliev listened indifferently. He would never know what happened in Travnik now. And he was not sure that he cared. He felt very tired.

He and Serov walked back silently to a small hotel near the hospital that had been recommended by the doctor.

"We'll rest and then decide what to do," said Vasiliev.

He fell asleep quickly but then woke, startled by a nightmare which he could not remember. Tamara's last words were starting to haunt him. He puzzled over what she had whispered. He could not guess their hidden meaning; was she was asking him to fulfill her promise? Or did he only imagine that she was trying to say "promise me" when she died? Or perhaps she was just trying to justify herself, and lamented that she had failed in carrying out her holy task. He would never know for certain. Her death had done nothing to resolve the question of his duty or where his moral compass pointed. Was it all over, this quest for justice that no one now seemed to care about?

The faint light of dawn came through the latticed windows. He dressed quickly intent now on seeing Tamara buried side by side with her brothers and father. He roused Serov and they made their way to the hospital where they secured the release of Tamara's body. They hired a cab and conveyed her to the Alifakovac cemetery. It was there that the ceremony of washing and shrouding took place under the supervision of the imam. Vasiliev and Serov stood aside not to interfere with the ritual of interment. The imam chanted a few phrases when the coffin was gently lowered. As the workers filled in the grave, the imam cited verses from the Koran. Vasiliev gave the imam a purse with sufficient funds to erect a small granite stone marker. They left as silently as they had come.

When they returned to the hotel, Captain Tóth was waiting for them. He asked to speak to Vasiliev privately.

"As you know, Vienna has authorized me to assist you in whatever way you deem useful," he said once they had found an empty table in the lounge and ordered coffee.

"My instructions made it clear that we have the same interest in settling down the local population and putting an end to conspiracies and intrigues, no matter what their origins. As I understand it, the men who tried to gain entrance to the hospital ward may be members of the group of disaffected Hungarians you mentioned whose sole interest seems to be to sell their services to the highest bidder and to disrupt the normal life of the province. Do you believe they were responsible for the shootings at the Alifakovac cemetery?"

"Indirectly. The shooter could only have been the murderer of Grigoriev, the man I have been trying to track down. But the renegades were probably given orders to finish the job by killing the Circassian girl." Vasiliev had trouble pronouncing her name.

"So how can we help you?"

"Good of you to ask, captain. I do not wish to act at odds with your government. So, first, I need to question the two men you arrested at the hospital. Then, depending on what they say, I may need the assistance of a few of your men."

"Splendid. We should work together then, just as our governments did at Berlin."

Vasiliev avoided acknowledging the comparison. He was not certain that Berlin had really settled anything. He wondered whether he should press the point in his report to Totleben. But, what effect would the opinion of a lowly police inspector have on the Tsar and the heads of state of the great powers?

"So let us agree. We will arrange for you to conduct an interrogation of the two miscreants. In return, I would appreciate learning more about the motive of the killings at the cemetery and in general about the organization behind them."

"I will do my best," said Vasiliev with a mountain of unstated reservations. As they parted, he asked himself what kind of a tale he could spin to obscure the web of political and personal relations that brought him to this unhappy state.

Vasiliev would have preferred to conduct the examination of the two renegades alone, but Tóth insisted on sitting in.

At Austrian police headquarters, Vasiliev decided to take an aggressive tone that was unusual for him. He slammed down a thick file of miscellaneous documents having nothing to do with the case.

"Captain Tóth and I acting in full agreement, have collected overwhelming evidence," Vasiliev tapped the unopened file, "that you belong to an illegal underground organization aiming to subvert the peace and prosperity of the Civil Administration of Bosnia and Hercegovina created by the conference of great powers and enshrined in the solemn Treaty of Berlin. Do you understand that the seriousness of the crime? It could lead to a sentence that would deprive you of your liberty for the rest of your life. Or else, if the judge were so inclined to treat the crime as treason, given your citizenship in the Monarchy...well, I need not spell it out the consequences for you gentlemen."

His speech seemed to have no effect on the older of the two men, but the younger one appeared to shrink from what was in store for him.

Vasiliev turned to Tóth who also caught the difference in the reaction of the two miscreants.

"Captain, I believe these criminals should be given a few hours to reflect on their fate."

In the corridor, Vasiliev proposed that they interrogate the two men separately, beginning with the younger one who already seemed ready to crack. The captain agreed.

It did not take long to break down the feeble resistance of Viktor, as the young man called himself. Once he had been offered a lesser punishment, he seemed almost eager to talk.

"You have served Andrei Gregorevich for some time, is it not so?" Vasiliev opened the questioning while Tóth stood unobtrusively in a darkened corner of the room.

"For two years; he paid well."

"And what did he asked you to do?"

"Whatever he asked, we did."

"And what did he ask of you in Mostar."

Viktor hesitated and glanced into the corner.

"I was only the lookout."

"And what were the others doing that required a lookout."

"I did nothing wrong."

"Good. Then you can tell me who did and what it was that was wrong."

Viktor looked down at the floor and mumbled. "We...they were to seize a man, an evil man, we were told, but not to harm him."

"And this was to happen in the tower by the bridge. And you were all dressed like Albanians. If not to harm him, what then?"

"To bind and blindfold him and place him in a cart."

"The cart hired from Omar Pasha."

Viktor's head shot up, his mouth fell open. "You know everything. Why do you question me?"

"I want to make sure you are telling the truth about what I know so that I can trust you when you tell me what I do not know."

Viktor shrugged and lowered his eyes again as if he were seeking solace in the rough table surface.

"Not too bad then, just giving him a ride in a cart, eh? But something went wrong. Blood was spilled."

"He was strong and fought us like a tiger."

"But you subdued him; he was still alive when you lifted him into the cart. And then your friend, Bela, wasn't it who drove off, heading south."

Viktor merely nodded. Vasiliev, encouraged by his successful guess, pressed ahead.

"The idea was to dump him across the border." It was not a question, but Viktor said nothing.

"Now I must know the answer to the next question. So take your time and do not lie. Did Bela return soon?"

"Yes."

"How soon?"

"A couple of days."

"And without the cart, isn't that so? Did he tell you where he left it or where he was going?"

"No, he told me nothing."

"When you saw Andrei Gregorevich again, what did he say to you?"

"I never saw him again. It was Bela who told me later that we were ordered to go to Sarajevo and hold ourselves in readiness."

"For what?"

"I was not told."

"Were you at the cemetery?"

"No! No! I had nothing to do with the shooting." Viktor spread his hands on the table in supplication.

"So who was your contact in the city?"

A man who owned a café. I think his name was Achmed Bey."

Vasiliev froze his expression. How could he have missed that? The ring had misled him; but Achmed Bey had not been wearing it. The act of an apostate. Vasiliev cursed his lack of foresight. He turned to the dim figure in the corner and spoke in German.

"Captain, you will wish to interrogate Achmed Bey and probably arrest him. Now we need to question Bela." He rose and turned toward the door.

"What are you going to do with me?" Viktor's voice barely rose about a whisper.

"That is up to the Austrian authorities. I have no jurisdiction here."

"But you..." Viktor's voice broke.

Vasiliev left him quietly sobbing.

Chapter
Fifty-One

Sarajevo

Serov was waiting patiently for Vasiliev's return to the *khan*. He had already packed their few belongings and ordered horses to be ready.

Vasiliev gave him a brief report of his interrogation of the two thugs, Viktor and Bela.

"Thanks to you, my dear Sergeant, we now know that Grigoriev was probably still alive when Bela smuggled the cart across the border. At least that is what he insisted was the case when he turned over the cart to Andrei Gregorevich. Of course, we cannot be certain, but I doubt that these flunkies would have killed Grigoriev before Andrei Gregorevich had a chance to question him. They all wanted to avoid the responsibility of committing murder on the territory of Bosnia under Austrian occupation."

Vasiliev glanced at the packed baggage, and smiled.

"So you expected we would be on the move. My, my, Sergeant, you are getting to be far-sighted."

"Just doin' a bit o' guessin', beggin' your pardon."

Vasiliev couldn't help breaking out into laughter. It felt good. Something he had never expected he could do again.

"Captain Tóth will take over now. Perhaps with the arrest of Achmed Bey they will begin to round up the last of Andrei Gregorevich's gang of renegades in Sarajevo. Who knows where that will lead?

"The Austrians are determined to bring law and order into Bosnia. I wish them good luck, but it will be a formidable task. I'll have to put that into my report to General Totleben."

Vasiliev unfolded his military map and traced with his finger alternative routes to Cetinje.

"You see, we could retrace our steps and pass through Mostar. This is the route Tóth suggested. The way down the Drina to the east is more rugged and there is a greater danger of bandits. If we choose that way he even promised an escort. I politely declined. We would be less conspicuous travelling on our own. Anyhow, the Albanians love us. The trouble with the route through Mostar is that we do not know how many of Andrei Gregorevich's men are still at large in the town and surrounding hills. So, we'll take what he called the more dangerous route. The Albanians may not yet be disillusioned with Russia, but that will come. We have to be on our guard."

"And when haven't we been?"

"Ah my dear fellow. You always catch me out when I utter a cliché."

Serov was not sure he understood the meaning of the French word. But he took it as a compliment. He was pleased to see a familiar, determined expression on Vasiliev's face. Perhaps over time, the memory of Tamara would fade. But how long would that take? He didn't dare to guess.

Vasiliev's good mood was not to last. Just before they were to leave, a courier arrived and handed him a coded telegram from Ivan, the Iron Colonel, and his friend from St. Petersburg. Serov watched with dismay as he saw the frown that he recognized as the portent of bad news.

"Recalled immediately to Moscow," he ground out the words. "It seems that my further stay in the Balkans could only lead to international complications. Ivan does not spell out what is meant by that. The urgency of the message suggests we have no choice. So, now we have to act fast and adopt the one plan that I dread to execute."

He had rarely felt so depressed. It was as if he were still following a ritual as they mounted their horses and headed east to Vyshegrad and then turned south on the left bank of the Drina until the gorges became too steep. Then they struck out overland. For all Vasiliev's offhand comment on the Albanians, he thought it best to find shelter overnight in a Christian *zadruga*. They made their first stop when it was still light so that they would be recognized. At the entrance to a solidly built wooden house, they were greeted by an old man flanked by two of his sons holding rifles.

"You are welcome, men of *Rus'*. We are honored by your presence."

The old man ordered a sheep to be slaughtered. The men of the household gathered round the fire as women served them. Having eaten their fill, the men began to sing old songs that told of the days when ferocious beys ruled the land. One such related the story of a wedding party of Christians when a young girl displayed herself in gaudy clothes and her swain wore an equally colorful costume. A group of Muslims passing by took umbrage at the gaiety of their clothes and the boisterous celebration of the wedding party. They drew their daggers and fell upon the couple, hacking them to pieces on the grass while their friends shrank back in horror, fearing to intervene.

"But surely those days are over now, with the coming of the Europeans, "said Vasiliev licking his fingers to savor the last taste of mutton.

The men fell silent. Then the old man spoke. "We no longer fear impalement and other atrocities, but the hatred remains. It smolders like the embers of this dying fire. And who knows whether someone will fan it into a bright flame again." Vasiliev wondered whether he should insert that story into his report to Totleben.

The following day they saw no Christian *zadruga*. But the people seemed friendly enough on the road and in the Albanian Muslim villages where the houses were surrounded by spacious gardens, although the facades were in much need of repair. As they approached the frontier with Montenegro, a young boy ran out of a more substantial looking house with the walls of stone and a roof of solid looking timber.

"Men of *Rus'*, I come to invite you to pay honor to our house and share a modest repast," he said as if an adult had taught him these stock phrases which he memorized and now recited with pride.

A tall Albanian with iron grey hair and the face of an eagle met them at the door.

"Welcome, heroes of Plevna!"

"Will we ever shake off that greetin'?" muttered Serov.

The Albanian ushered them into a spacious room with walls covered by magnificent carpets and weapons of burnished steel. He led Vasiliev by the hand to the seat of honor on the divan. About a dozen armed warriors sat in a circle around him. No sooner was he settled, when a servant carried in a dressing gown of pale blue cloth lined with sable fur which was placed around his shoulders.

"You must understand," the Albanian spoke with pride in a beautiful tenor voice as the women quietly set down large pots of lamb stew on the ground in front of them, "I was one of the favored who met and formed the League of Prizen. There I met Ali Pasha who told me of the Russian officer who was on a quest. And so you come to my humble abode and I, like my brothers, wish to help you. At Prizen there were those who told us the story of a tall, bearded Russian, a former officer it would seem who was also on a mission, but an evil one. And in the place called Ierissos, outside the town of Thessalonika this evil man murdered three of our kinsmen who were cousins of mine. It would seem that we are joined together, you and my family, in seeking vengeance."

"Ah, my friend," said Vasiliev, "not vengeance but justice."

"But is not that the same thing?"

"Not in terms of the law."

"Ah, but that is your law, the Christian law. For us, the killing of a man is a private matter, to be settled in a private way."

Vasiliev was not predisposed to pursue the matter, but the sentiment struck a chord. He would long remember this conversation.

The next morning two young Albanians led them through a heavily wooded area where they could avoid the border control. They continued to ride with Vasiliev and Serov, crossing into Montenegro without incident. Serov was beginning to worry that Vasiliev had decided on a course of action that he might regret; or else his plan might be so risky that the chance of failure was greater than success. But true to his habit he asked no questions. As they came to the outskirts of Cetinje, the Albanians waved farewell and turned to go. But Vasiliev noticed they did not appear to be retracing their steps. He reigned in under the thick leaves of an ancient tree and leaned over the saddle.

"My good Serov, we cannot return home without serving justice, even if it will not be perfect. But I am still not sure that my thoughts are guided by reason. I will need your help."

"No need to ask!" Serov blurted out.

"Of course, not, except that I am not sure what we shall do is legal, you see."

"But it will be just."

"Yes that is the point. Now can you find your friend, the veteran who told you tales of the Crimean War when this adventure began?"

"He was tellin' me how he had a cottage just on the north side, not far from here."

"Good. I should have thought…Well, no mind. We can't afford to make a mistake now. Let's find him and hope he is still alive and willing to take us in for a few days."

Within the hour, Serov had located the place, a solidly built stone house. A few chickens were pecking the ground in front and the sounds of squealing pigs could be heard coming from a wooden enclosure to the rear. They stopped some distance away.

Serov went alone to rap on the door. It was opened slowly by a young boy in a soiled shift, holding a dead chicken in his hand.

"Grandpa!" he cried out in Russian, "a soldier in the imperial army." Better than callin' us the heroes of Plevna thought Serov.

The old man shuffled to the door from the inner room where a fire was burning. Squinting, he looked Serov up and down and then exclaimed:

"The Russians again. Have you come to win back what they took from us?"

"Ah, *batushka*, would that we could. But I have one last favor to ask in the name of our friendship and memories of Sevastopol."

"Yes, yes, of course. Everything I have is yours."

Serov explained that he and his commanding officer were on a secret mission and needed to conceal themselves for a day or two, all in the interests of Montenegro and its gallant people. He waved back to Vasiliev who had dismounted and held the reins of the two horses in the shadows.

"Quick, Mishka, put the chicken in the pot, with plenty of salt."

As Vasiliev came into view, the old man threw back his shoulders and saluted. "Greetings, Your Excellency."

Vasiliev wondered how long it could last, this mutual admiration of Russia by both Montenegrins and Albanians, rivals for the same lands and opponents in the recent war. They shared a hatred of Ottoman rule, but not for the same reasons. Was this enough to settle their differences? Another paragraph in the report to Totleben.

Vasiliev tried to lead the conversation into safe waters when the young Mishka who was serving them blurted out,

"And have you come to solve the mystery of the hidden cart?'

"What nonsense is this?" The old man said sternly. "Always making up stories, this one," and he tweaked the boy's ear.

"I would like to hear this story, though," said Vasiliev.

"Probably just another tale of cook's son at the consulate. Ever since the two boys found out they had the same name, my Mishka has been running errands for the other Mishka who fills his head with wild stories."

"But what is so wild about a cart?" Vasiliev asked innocently.

But Mishka had fallen silent.

"You know, Mishka," Vasiliev said in a quiet voice, "I am an army officer here, as you knew right way. But at home in Moscow, I am a detective. Do you know the difference?"

"Yes," said the boy, glancing sideways at his grandfather.

"Well, then tell me what you think it is, this difference?"

"Go ahead," said the old man reluctantly.

"An officer fights the Turks; a detective solves a mystery."

"Excellent. So now you have said there is a mystery about a cart. So, I have to put on my detective's cap to solve it, don't you agree?"

"If the cart exists!" exclaimed the old man.

Vasiliev waved aside the old man's skepticism. "Of course. It has to exist, Mishka! Does the cart really exist?"

Mishka shook his head up and down.

"Where did you see it?"

"In the ravine."

"I told you never to go there," the old man's voice became more agitated.

"And it smelled very badly, worse than our pig sty," the boy added almost defiantly.

"Phew! More of your friend Mishka's nonsense."

"He was there," said the boy. What he saw frightened him, so badly that he wouldn't tell me what he saw. He really was scared."

"What was he scared of, your friend?"

"Well, he told me once that there was this broken cart in the ravine and there was something bad about it. So I told him to show me, but he said he would never go there again. So I went by myself."

"This is not like you, Mishka, to disobey me," his grandfather said. "If your poor mother..." he seemed to draw into himself. Vasiliev placed his hand on the old man's shoulder.

"Listen to me. I believe young Mishka has discovered something very important. You must not punish him. He has also shown courage in going to the ravine by himself. You should be proud of him. Sometimes when we're young we disobey and it turns out to be a good thing. It is rare, but this is one of those times."

Mishka looked at him with wide open eyes. The old man's cheeks were wet.

Serov sat back and watched Vasiliev work his magic. He sensed that a plan was being formed.

"Now, I am asking this young warrior, your Mishka, to take me to the scene of this broken cart. We must observe strict secrecy." He turned to the boy. "Perhaps your exploit may become the theme of a new ballad."

The boy's face broke out into a broad smile, completely transforming his face. Vasiliev continued in a gentle voice.

"Can you also tell us what is happening at the consulate? There are rumors that the consul returned from the north with a stranger, a big man wearing an old army overcoat. Is this true?"

The boy nodded eagerly. "Mishka told me so. The stranger is staying at the consulate. But the consul is very upset."

"Why is that? Does he not get along with the stranger?"

"I know nothing about that. The consul is upset because one of his cats is missing. Mishka told me the cat is dead but was afraid to tell the consul."

"Too bad," said Vasiliev, but he dismissed the news as unimportant. He turned to the old man again. "Can we agree that Mishka will lead me to the ravine tomorrow?"

The old man smiled and placed his hand on Mishka's head.

"So a new ballad!" and the old man chuckled.

Serov happily observed that Vasiliev's mood had changed again.

They left before the first rays of light touched the mountain tops. Vasiliev held the boy on the saddle in front of him. Serov was sent off to the village once again in disguise to find out from his former contacts there what was known about the movements of the tall stranger outside the consulate compound.

Vasiliev tied his horse to a tree at the edge of the ravine and with Mishka leading plunged deep into the woods.

"They say the place is cursed and haunted by the ghost of unhappy lovers. But grandfather says these are just peasant tales. Still, he didn't want me to go here because there were other stories of bandits hiding here."

"Don't worry Mishka. Bandits usually can be found where there are people to rob."

After wandering for half an hour, a pungent odor reached them. Vasiliev immediately identified it as human remains, but mixed with another barely perceptible strain. He ordered Mishka to stay behind and pushed through dense underbrush on a downward slope until he caught sight of the broken cart. The headless corpse bore traces of having been further mutilated by animals, one arm was missing and the chest was torn open. Vasiliev picked his way around the cart until he spotted the mangled body of the black cat. Wheel tracks leading to the south had been partially covered by a new growth of wild grass. Judging by the shreds of clothing on the body, Vasiliev had not doubt this was all that remained of Grigoriev. The black cat must have been Ionin's Vulcan. Two mysteries solved, he thought grimly. So the murder must have been committed in Montenegro. Yet he knew from the evidence of the beheading that it had not been the work of Montenegrins. But why the hasty abandonment of the corpse? Perhaps the killer or, it would now seem killers, were in a hurry to flee, and had good reason to believe that no one would discover the wreckage deep in the ravine of this cursed place. Still, the haste betrayed carelessness. Did Andrei Gregorevich turn over the disposal of the body to his hired renegades with a simple instruction to get rid of it? This seemed most likely. Did he then order them to deliver the head to

Tamara? A sadistic act or a warning? Perhaps he would never know the answers to these questions but he now had enough evidence to devise a concrete plan. He would move against Andrei Gregorevich from two directions and catch him in a vise. As for the dead cat, Vulcan, wasn't it? He too would play a role.

Chapter
Fifty-Two

Cetinje

An interview with the Prince of Montenegro required no formal ceremony. There was no evidence of obsequious courtiers; just a single sentry was posted at the gate to the garden where Prince Nikola traditionally accepted petitions and received visitors. Vasiliev's uniform assured him of immediate access. The Prince wore the uniform of his army with only one decoration pinned to his blouse, the Russian Order of St. George, First Class. He had fought the Turks twice, in 1862 and then as an ally of Russia in 1876 when he conducted a brilliant campaign against them. Vasiliev remembered the state visit of Nikola to St. Petersburg a little more than ten years before. Would he remember his review of the Page Corps when as the top student Vasiliev had the honor of leading his class, sword held high in a formal salute? Surely not. He had been on the throne for almost twenty years. Befriended by the Tsar, Alexander II, he had seen many Russian officers in his time. But Nikola surprised him.

The Prince was seated on a high backed oaken chair elaborately carved which served him as an outdoor throne. He was bare headed and his closely cut hair and trimmed beard had turned grey since Vasiliev last saw him. But there were no other traces of advancing years.

Vasiliev saluted, bowed and spoke the traditional greeting in Serbian, identifying himself as Major Vasiliev, Vasili Vasilevich.

Nikola smiled broadly and answered in French which as Vasiliev knew was fluent, his having learned it while studying in Paris as a youth.

"I have had so little chance to converse in this most civilized of all tongues. If my memory has not failed me, I recognize you from some ceremony... let me think, in St. Petersburg was it not? So, you must have been a cadet in one of the elite schools and therefore your French must be very good."

Vasiliev bowed again. "A correct deduction, Your Majesty."

"But you do not wear the uniform of the Guards."

"I chose another way to serve my country."

"What? In a line regiment!"

"No, Your Majesty. I have been attached with the temporary rank of Major to the suite of the Grand Duke, Nikolai Nikolaevich, but my normal duties are as an Inspector of the Moscow Police.

"How extraordinary. And why does my old friend Nikolai need a policeman?"

"This is why I have come to request this audience with you."

"Even more interesting, but I will call you Vasili Vasilievich So, no need to stand. I think you have a lengthy story to tell me."

Vasiliev had given a good deal of thought to how he could explain briefly his two missions. Once he mentioned General Totleben, the Prince interrupted.

"*Cher ami*! You have somehow won the confidence of two of the three men I most trust among your countrymen, the grand duke, the general and of course your Emperor, Alexander Nikolaevich. So whatever you request I am ready to grant."

"I have no request, Your Majesty, only information of interest to you as the sovereign ruler of a gallant ally of my country."

Nikola frowned for a moment and then signaled Vasiliev to continue.

"You ask why a policeman. A man is now at large living not far from here who I believe on the basis of the evidence I have collected is responsible for having killed or directly ordered to be killed, a famous Russian volunteer with the Serbian forces in 1876. Perhaps his name is familiar to you, Boris Grigoriev."

The Prince started in his throne-chair.

"The murder was committed on Montenegrin soil and the headless corpse lies rotting at this moment in the notorious wooded ravine to the south of your capital." Vasiliev had calculated the risk of such a brutal revelation, but he had calculated correctly.

The Prince stood up abruptly and Vasiliev quickly jumped to his feet.

"But the evidence of the decapitation tells me, as it would you, that this was not the work of a Montenegrin. I understand the tradition is still alive here. But the blow is always delivered by a *hanzhar*, a short heavy instrument used to decapitate with a single stroke that produces a clean-cut wound. Such was not the case with Grigoriev. Also among your people head hunting is reserved for the enemy, a Turk or Albanian, but surely not a former Russian officer. My instructions were to find and arrest the killer, but these instructions were then cancelled, and there is a chance that he may escape justice."

"Cancelled? By whom? Surely if the Grand Duke..." But he did not finish his thought.

"Your Majesty, the explanation lies outside my competence."

"No matter, I will give the immediate order to have this killer arrested. In the vicinity of the palace, you say"

"As I mentioned, it is my duty to provide you with a full account of what I know. The killer for reasons I do not fully understand has been taken under the protection of the Russian Consul in Cetinje, Ionin, and therefore enjoys diplomatic immunity. The head has been quietly interred on the grounds of the consulate."

The Prince looked at Vasiliev with incredulity, his cheeks inflamed with a bright red color.

"This is intolerable, *mon ami*, intolerable. Surely Ionin is not aware..." but again he stopped short.

"Consul Ionin told me in Travnik less than a week ago that he had received orders from St. Petersburg to protect this man until he can be sent out of the country and that I was ordered off the case."

The Prince grasped Vasiliev by the shoulders. "I am grateful to you, yes a policeman with a sense of justice betrayed. Now the first step is to recover the body together with the head, and honor a heroic figure with a proper funeral. So I will assign several trusted men to accompany you to the scene of this outrage. I will immediately summon Ionin and demand an explanation and assure him of my intention to send a dispatch to St. Petersburg, yes even if necessary a personal message to Alexander Nikolaevich who will quickly lift this absurd immunity."

"Your Majesty, may I make one suggestion."

"Of course."

"I believe it is possible to win over the consul to your way of thinking, or at least to arrange a compromise that will lead to a just resolution of this question without turning it into a diplomatic incident. It would be unfortunate at this point in the cordial relations between Russia and Montenegro to initiate a dispute."

Vasiliev could hardly believe he was addressing the Prince of Montenegro like a high-ranking diplomat. But he saw no indication that Nikola was offended.

"So I do have a request after all. I would appreciate your delaying by one day the recovery of the body and the head. I believe that if we can show the consul the scene of the crime, we can gain his sympathy. A short delay will not violate your determination to serve justice. But I believe it will facilitate your aims."

"If you wish. You have earned my respect and I see no reason to refuse your request. So, one day's delay. I will also wait then to summon the consul until he has seen the horror with his own eyes. God go with you, Vasili Vasilievich."

Vasiliev hurried back to the cottage of the old man. Serov was waiting, having change back into his uniform. He told Vasiliev that all the witnesses he had spoken to agreed that Andrei Gregorevich never left the compound. The cook, who remembered him fondly, had overheard a conversation that the stranger would be leaving in a few days. But she did not know where he was going.

"Now the tricky part," said Vasiliev

"And what has it been up to now?" Serov asked blandly.

"Ah, Serov, always keeping things in perspective."

Is that what he was doing, thought Serov. Better now just to listen.

Vasiliev went over his plan. Well, Serov decided, it really was tricky.

Vasiliev scrawled a note with instructions to Serov to deliver it to the consul's secretary. In it he requested an urgent meeting with Ionin outside the consulate, in a small coffee house in Cetinje called the Bear's Paw with the explanation that he wanted to avoid any contact with Andrei Gregorevich.

Vasiliev also instructed Serov to mention to the secretary that he had been summoned home.

"Tell him we intend to ride to Kotor where we will hire a boat to take us back to Ragusa. There we will catch an Austrian steamer bound for Thessalonika and thence to Istanbul. We will wait until a Russian ship arrives to take us to Odessa.

"You must ask the secretary to send a telegram *en clair* to St. Petersburg announcing that we have made arrangements to leave Cetinje within twenty-four hours. Make certain the secretary remembers the details. Do you think you can find your old friend there, the Greek captain who served in the War of 1813? Let's hope he is still alive. We shall meet at the wharf. Go quickly now."

Vasiliev met Ionin outside the coffee house. "There is no time for a coffee right now," he said. He assured the consul that he was about to have two mysteries cleared up. But he added the solutions would not please him. "*Du courage, mon ami.* I am going to lead you into the haunted wood."

Ionin was in a nervous state. He was irritated by the disappearance of Vulkan, and then deeply worried as Venus seemed to act like a mourner, avoiding his caresses and slinking around in search of her companion. Andrei Gregorevich was not slinking around, but he might as well have, in Ionin's view. He was forever pacing up and down in his room and at every meal he pressed Ionin to arrange his departure from Cetinje and "this cursed land." But Ionin was waiting for instructions from St. Petersburg. The tension in the consulate had nearly reached the breaking point. The staff all suffered from Ionin's nervousness and the stranger's impatience, not to speak of the need to repress the secret, now shared by the secretary, the cook and the boy Mishka of what was concealed in the wooded ravine.

Ionin cried out when he saw the mutilated body of Grigoriev and then sobbed when Vasiliev pointed out the shattered remains of Vulkan. He appeared on the verge of collapse when Vasiliev seized him by the shoulders and turned him away from the dreadful sight. Vasiliev spoke quickly with all the urgency he could summon up.

"What has happened here is clear. Grigoriev was murdered on Montenegrin soil by Andrei Gregorevich. Vulkan the sole witness was killed too so that he would not lead you back here." Vasiliev had hesitated to lie even about the death of the cat, but no higher power would condemn him for that.

"The fact that the murderer is now under your protection and the head of the body buried on the grounds of the consulate could turn into an ugly diplomatic incident. Prince Nikola, once informed as he must now be, would demand that the criminal be punished by him for having violated the laws of the land. Remember too that Grigoriev was a hero in the eyes of the Montenegrin people. The Prince could not allow such a criminal to escape justice."

Ionin was still weeping, probably more for Vulcan than Grigoriev, Vasiliev coldly observed. He began to march Ionin back through the tangled undergrowth.

"But you, representing Imperial Russia, have taken this criminal under your protection and given him diplomatic immunity. You see what this means. A clash between two allies that neither can win. Both sides will have to endure the contempt of the Austrians and perhaps the English as well, with their exalted concept of fairness. I fear that you, Alexander Semeonovich, will not be able to escape the results of the scandal; you know better than I who will be caught in the middle and will be destroyed whatever happens. Unless…" Vasiliev paused at they emerged from the woods.

"Unless… yes, we have to discuss this. Now is the time for that coffee, perhaps laced with a little brandy. Come let me help you, for, you know, it is in my interest too to avoid a scandal. We are in this together, Alexander Semeonovich."

Chapter
Fifty-Three

Cetinje

Vasiliev allowed Ionin some time to recover enough from his shock before outlining his plan, or at least those aspects of it which directly concerned the consul.

"Alexander Semeonovich, you and I are caught in the midst of a struggle between forces much greater than us. We have both received messages from St. Petersburg that contradict one another and order us to carry out policies we do not believe in. Isn't that so?"

Ionin nodded dumbly, staring at the woods.

"And we should not forget the international dimensions. A false step could ruin us both." Vasiliev let that sink in before looking around in a conspiratorial manner as if to make certain that no one was listening. But the café was almost empty.

"So the immediate question is how we avoid the intrigues which involve highly placed persons in St. Petersburg competing for the ear of the emperor. You already know that some of those powerful figures sent me on my mission. Since then I have received support, and here I must confide in you, from men of great influence not only in St. Petersburg. I mention only Count Peter Shuvalov, but also others in Vienna and representatives of England here in the Balkans. Now we will face the wrath of Prince Nikola, once he learns of the crime on Montenegrin soil."

"My God, what should we do?"

Vasiliev had been hoping for this exact response.

"First you must recover the body of your beloved cat, Vulcan, wasn't it?"

Ionin quickly brush away a trickle of tears which had started again.

"Yes, yes," he mumbled.

"There must be no evidence of the consulate being involved. This should be done by a trusted servant in great secrecy." Vasiliev was determined to pull Ionin deeper into his net.

For the first time, Ionin looked up with an expression which Vasiliev interpreted as a mixture of appreciation and complicity.

"But then the problem remains of placating the Prince. How should we proceed?"

Ionin covered his face with his hands. "How is this possible?"

Vasiliev wondered how a seasoned diplomat could be reduced to a state of helplessness by the death of his pet. But he could not solve that mystery. He preferred to give the impression that he hadn't given the problem a thought before this.

"You are right, Alexander Semeonovich. How is this possible?" Then he snapped his fingers as if struck suddenly by an inspired idea.

"You are holding the key to solving the question, don't you see?"

Ionin was hooked now. "Of course," he stuttered.

"With your great diplomatic skills, you can convince the Prince that you intend to respect the sovereignty of Montenegro. How can you do this? Simple enough. You could inform him immediately, that you have discovered the body of Grigoriev and that you wish to turn it over to him together with the head for a decent burial in respect of his services to the Slavic cause."

"But he will ask about the murderer, and how can I justify this to St. Petersburg?

"Yes, Alexander Semenovich once again you have hit upon the difficulties. Now let's see...I can only think of one possible way out of this dilemma that you understand so clearly. It will require great skill, but I have confidence you have the will and experience to carry out."

Vasiliev wondered whether he was laying it on too thickly. But he saw that Ionin was listening attentively, desperate to save his reputation and his position.

"Let's see now whether you agree with me. The main thing is

to inform the Prince. Perhaps the best way to do this is to assure him that the discovery of the body obliges you to remove Andrei Gregorevich from your protection. Yes, that's it! Then you prevent a diplomatic crisis and save to yourself from the wrath of Petersburg. Isn't this your principal concern?"

Ionin nodded eagerly with dry eyes. But suddenly it occurred to him that this would not solve all his problems.

"But Vasili Vasilievich, wait! I must wait for instructions from St. Petersburg. Without it I might incur the wrath of the powerful protector of this man."

"But this eventuality can also be avoided." Vasiliev saw the fear return to distort the features of the consul. This was the critical moment.

"You must persuade Andrei Gregorevich that you are eager to help him flee the country. Isn't that what he wants?" Vasiliev realized that this was the most important guess of this entire adventure. He worried that he better be right.

"Isn't that why he put himself under your protection on the trip down from Sarajevo? Here in Cetinje he could plan to escape abroad by sea, the safest exit route, right? You will be praised for taking this initiative. It's just a matter of timing now. It is crucial to have him leave right way; tell him it is in his own interest. Explain that if Prince Nikola brings great pressure to bear on St. Petersburg to turn you over even a powerful protector might not be able to save you. How many times have statesmen sacrificed one man in order to avoid a major diplomatic crisis?"

"I see. Yes, that might work."

Vasiliev paused to give a final twist to his vice.

"You can then ensure your success. In the telegram to St. Petersburg explaining your reason for organizing the departure of Andrei Gregorevich, you have only to add that you have not only ordered me off the case but sent me out of the country. In other words, you have taken all precautions to guarantee the safety of this man who you must admit has been a heavy burden on your conscience."

"But will they believe me, I mean about your leaving?"

"I have just sent my Sergeant to Kotor to hire a boat. It will take us out of the country by tomorrow morning."

"So then Andrei Gregorevich will have no reason to hesitate."

"In fact, he will have every reason to leave quickly. He will not take the risk of being turned over to the Prince, especially if you make it clear to him that this is possibility. And you will avoid precipitating the crisis you are most anxious to avoid."

"This is brilliant, Vasili Vasilievich. Congratulations on an elegant solution, or should we say the end game of a chess master?"

Vasiliev reflected that he had one more move from check to mate.

Chapter
Fifty-Four

Cetinje to Kotor

Vasiliev left Ionin in a somber mood, possibly still despondent but not despairing. He rode back to the household of Suleiman Pasha, the Albanian with the face of an eagle. He was greeted as an old friend and over his objections was obliged to share a meal.

When the goat cheese and fruit was served, Vasiliev announced that he had come to say farewell and drew the small antique dagger which Serov had purchased in Travnik. He handed it to Suleiman as a remembrance of their friendship. He then spoke of his mission and how he carried back with him good memories of the Albanians but his disappointments too.

"So my Sergeant and I leave early tomorrow. So we will ride to Kotor tonight."

"This is not wise my friend. These are unsettled times. It would be best if you passed the night with us."

"How good of you! But please understand that I do wish to refuse your hospitality. But I have been ordered to leave the country before the man known as Andrei Gregorevich will be released from the protection of the Russian consul."

Vasiliev intercepted Suleiman's sharp glance to his right where his eldest son was seated. A signal? Vasiliev thought so.

"If you insist, then we must be certain you arrive safely. My eldest son, Mahmud, will accompany you with a few of my best men. God, who alone is great, has provided us with a full moon and cloudless sky tonight. You will enjoy your ride in good company."

Vasiliev bowed low. "Your hospitality knows no bounds,

Suleiman Pasha. And you will be certain to take my greetings to Ali Pasha when you next encounter him."

In a few hours Vasiliev and his escort arrived at the outskirts of Kotor where Mahmud bade him farewell. Serov was waiting at the Hotel Rialto. He reported that he had found the old Greek ship-owner and had made the arrangements to hire a ship to leave at dawn for Ragusa. He notified the harbor master of the hour of the sailing and made certain that he or his assistant would be on duty to record their departure. He informed the manager of the hotel that they would be leaving at the break of day and reached an agreement with him on the sale of their two horses. A cab would take them to the wharf. Vasiliev clapped him on the shoulder.

"Well done, Serov. You have done everything to make sure our exit from the scene is well-documented."

"And will there be a scene?" asked Serov.

"As our good friend Ali Pasha would say, *Inshallah!*"

"I'm guessin', begin your pardon, that this means yes."

"Ah, Serov you are incorrigible. Yes, I believe that would be a good free translation."

Ionin could have sworn that Venus had taken a dislike to Andrei Gregorevich. Now as he was giving his last-minute instructions, she curled up next to him and stared with a baleful eye at the tall figure in the military coat. There was no other way of letting her master know that she found his odor unpleasant.

"I have sent ahead to Kotor my secretary, a most reliable man, to arrange a boat to take you to Corfu. After that you are on your own. But there are still older people living there who remember stories about the last visit of the Russian fleet to the island in the early years of this century. They will help you find a berth on a ship to Istanbul. I regret I cannot provide you with an escort to Kotor."

"And I would not have one, not now. I only need to thank you for your hospitality. It will be appreciated also in Petersburg."

Ionin made an effort to smile, but the effect was not convincing. He felt as one with Venus, but the man's odor had nothing to do with it.

Andrei Gregorevich could not have cared less what the consul thought and was blissfully ignorant of Venus' opinion.

"All I ask for is a good horse."

Andrei Gregorevich left at dawn, riding hard but also occasionally turning off the trail and checking that no one was following him.

He arrived at outskirts of Kotor as the sun was high over Mt. Lorćen. The consul's secretary had been waiting some time for the familiar figure of Andrei Gregorevich to appear at the wharf where he had engaged a *trehantiria*. He looked at his watch and began to worry.

The secretary had no way of knowing that beyond bend of the Bay of Kotor in the shadow of a high cliff, the boat hired by Serov had come to a stop. The wind had died down but there was still a pleasant breeze. Vasiliev had requested the captain, a young Greek who spoke a few words of Russian, to lower the sail so that he could take a long look at the beautiful sweep of the bay and the town with its medieval Venetian fortifications. His thoughts carried him back to their first time in Kotor Bay, the three of them then. He felt a tug at his heart. Serov observed him closely, understanding only too well the expression on Vasiliev's face. He struggled to keep his own look fixed, expressionless, the image of *stolb*.

Serov knew he could never confess his feelings about Tamara to Inspector Vasiliev. Too many years had passed since they were boys, he and Vasya, tumbling in the dusty street of the village on Count Vorontsov's estate.

The boat drifted back into the bay but still under the shadow of the overhanging cliff. Soon Mt. Lorćen would gather snow around its summit and the lines from Lermontov came back to Vasiliev with a new meaning:

"On a bare hill's top, in the North, wild and cold,
A lone pine-tree somewhere stands;
She dozes, swaying, all covered by snow
With a mantel from feet to head."

His reverie was suddenly interrupted by a rapid succession of rifle shots. The young captain looked panic stricken. "They're shooting at us," he exclaimed. "Raise the sails!"

Vasiliev and Serov looked up, their eyes searching the cliffs above the bay.

"I think not, captain," Vasiliev said calmly. "I think not."

The rising wind had caught the sails.

"Quick, Serov, the binoculars!"

He handed them back to Serov after scanning the cliff tops. "You see them?"

Three of Suleiman's men, judging by their silhouettes, stood poised at the edge of a jagged cliff, two of them brandishing rifles. The third man held high a large round object by a thick shock of hair, waving it like a banner.'

"Vengeance?" asked Serov.

"Justice," said Vasiliev.

THE END

Epilogue

St. Petersburg and Berlin

The fate of Vasiliev's extended memo to General Totleben is not known. His best guess is that it was read by the general, then filed away and lost over time. It may also be guessed that it was buried and never resurrected because it contained too many prescient observations.

In any case, history records that Ekaterina Dolgorukova lost interest in the Balkans at the same time her dreams of imperial glory crashed to the ground with the assassination of her husband, Alexander II in 1881. Baron Kállay became Austro-Hungarian minister of finance from 1882 to 1903; as chief administrator of the Condominium of Bosnia and Hercegovina he introduced many of the modernizing innovations he had planned, including the first tram in the Empire. Count Shuvalov never recovered his prestige at home for helping to negotiate the Treaty of Berlin. He remained a staunch advocate of an alliance with Germany and a peaceful settlement of disputes over the Balkans. Prince Bismarck remained true to his view that "the whole of the Balkans was not worth the bones of a single Prussian Musketeer," and that it was imperative for Berlin "to keep the lines open to St. Petersburg." The failure to adhere to these principles led to Germany's fatal decision to back the Dual Monarchy in the Bosnian crisis of 1914 leading to World War I.

History and Fiction

In the spring of 1877, the armies of Imperial Russia crossed the Danube into the Balkans initiating a war against the Ottoman Empire. In the beginning, it was a popular war. The country had been swept by a ground swell of enthusiasm for the liberation of the Slavic peoples who had risen in rebellion against their Ottoman overlords. Even a reluctant Tsar, Alexander II, had been carried away, joined by his more ardently Panslav wife, Maria Alexandrovna, a converted German princess. Two years earlier, Russian volunteers under General Chernaiev had already begun to support the Serbs and Montenegrins who were the first to take up arms. The Russian campaign in 1877, was initially stalled until General Totleben, a hero of the defense of Sevastopol in the Crimean War, broke through the Turkish lines at Plevna in the Bulgarian lands. The Russian forces marched triumphantly to the gates of Constantinople (Istanbul) within sight of the strategic Turkish Straits, setting off a diplomatic crisis and threatening war with England and Austria-Hungary possibly with French and Italian support. By imposing the Treaty of San Stefano on the Ottoman Sultan in 1878 which created a Bulgaria twice its present size, the Russians had violated a previous agreement with the Austro-Hungarian Monarchy promising not to create a large Slavic state. The strong European reaction forced the Russians to back down and accept a compromise negotiated at Berlin under the benevolent eye of Prince Bismarck. In the meantime, the Russian victory had aroused nationalist sentiments among the many ethnic and religious groups tangled together throughout the Balkan Peninsula, including not only the Serbs and Montenegrins, but also Albanians, Macedonians, Bulgarians and Greeks whose territorial aspirations clashed with one another. Allegiances changed rapidly over the drawing of frontiers. Fighting at a low level continued as did blood feuds. Muslim Circassian tribesmen, who had fled Russian conquest of the North Caucasus twenty years before, were also involved. In this novel, the fictional characters of Vasili Vasilievich Vasiliev, a Moscow city detective on a special mission, and his assistant, Sergeant Serov are plunged into this cauldron of violence. Their imaginary adventures bring them into contact with historical characters and expose them to actual political and diplomatic situations. The descriptions of the geography and the life of the peoples have been drawn from contemporary sources in order to give as vivid and accurate a portrayal as possible of the period.

Historical Personages in Order of Appearance

Alexander Semeonovich Ionin, Russian consul in Montenegro

Count Luigi Corti, Italian diplomat and Italy's representative at the Congress of Berlin

Grand Duke Nikolai Nikolaevich, younger brother of Tsar Alexander Nikolaevich and commander of the Army of the Danube

General Eduard Ivanovich Totleben, hero of the siege of Sevastopol in the Crimean War who engineered the breakthrough of the Turkish lines at Plevna

Ekaterina Countess Dolgorukova, the mistress of Tsar Alexander and mother of his three illegitimate children including "Gogo"

Alexander Nikolaevich, Tsar (Emperor) of All Russia

Maria Alexandrovna, Empress, his wife

Alexander von Moritz, Russian consul in Thessalonika

Baron Heinrich von Haymerle, Hungarian diplomat and Habsburg representative at the Congress of Berlin

Baron Benjamin Kállay, Hungarian diplomat and Habsburg chief administer of the Condominium of Bosnia and Hercegovina

Count Peter Andreevich Shuvalov, Russian diplomat and Russia's representative at the Congress of Berlin

Arthur J. Evans, English journalist, traveler and archeologist

Anna Tiucheva, lady-in-waiting to Empress Maria Alexanderovna and wife of Ivan Aksakov

Edward Freeman, English consul in Sarajevo

Stojan Kovaćevic, Serbian rebel and bandit

Prince Nikola, ruler of Montenegro

In addition many historical personages are mentioned in their proper roles during and after the Russo-Turkish War.

Acknowledgements

I continue to be grateful to Anna Lawton, the editor of New Academia Press for her continued interest in the exploits of Vasili Vasilievich and support of his appearance in public. My gratitude to George O. Linabury, my dear cousin, to whose memory this novel is dedicated, goes back to our happy childhood and continued all our lives until he sent his last illustrations for these novels. Marsha Siefert, my wife, contributed in so many ways as usual to my work, both fiction and non-fiction. For Vasiliev's adventures in four novels, she has been an inspiration, given invaluable advice and provided enormous editorial and technical assistance. I always await her final verdict on everything I write.

www.ingramcontent.com/pod-product-compliance
Lightning Source LLC
Chambersburg PA
CBHW050150030726
47505CB00005B/1308